THE MORALS OF

Produced by:

FriesenPress
Suite 300 – 852 Fort Street
Victoria, BC, Canada V8W 1H8

www.friesenpress.com

Distributed to the trade by The Ingram Book Company

ACKNOWLEDGEMENTS

For my grandchildren; Stephanie, Jenita, Randy, Samantha, Joshua, Denyka, Danielle, Chelsea, Jordan, Nickolas, and Sheldon. Without you, this novel would never have been.

A special thank you to my sons: Wesley, Eric, Kevin, and Adam, also daughters in-laws; Rita, Carla, Crystal and Rayleen for encouraging me to follow my dream. To Samantha Van Damme who took the time to help me brush up on my computer skills and who became my sounding board throughout the whole process, a very special thank you. Also to my two American sisters, Shirley Lenoir and Elaine La Rocque for encouraging me to believe in myself, while I natter-ed their ears off, thank you, it meant a lot that you took the time to listen. To the rest of my family and friends for supporting me, thank you.

To my publisher, Kathie Allen for making the publishing process seem effortless, a huge Thank You.

To Joy Jackson for her art work, your work is truly amazing.

And, last, but not least, my undying gratitude to my husband Raymond for being so understanding, while I secluded myself in my office, pecking away at my computer.

THE MORALS OF

by Rita Van Damme

I slowly crumpled to the ground, my hands covering my face. Hot tears now flowed freely down my cheeks to drip soundlessly into the carpet of green grass beneath me. The horror leading up to this day made me shake uncontrollably, while memory after horrific memory flooded my mind. Finally spent, I laid back on the lush, green grass letting its coolness sooth my hot, wet cheeks. Time meant nothing to me now as I let my mind wander back to when it all started. I slowly turned over, looking up at the fluffy clouds drifting lazily overhead. It was at this very spot on a day much like today, I remembered with a shudder. If, I had known then, what I know now, would I have walked away? I would like to believe that I would have, but in my heart I wasn't so sure. I was once told that we are masters of our own destiny and that fact has come true, to be driven home to me in more ways than one. But for now all I can do is wait and watch while the chain of horror continues.

CHAPTER 1

I needed to think, to clear my head of all the mundane, tedious, day-to-day tasks. I also felt I needed to cleanse my soul and this was as close to God as I could get. I slowly climbed to the top of the hill to survey the scene below. God, but I loved it up here. Everything was green and glorious after the long, cold winter, which had smothered the country side like a heavy cloak. Sliding down onto the lush, green grass, I carefully folded my right leg under me. Not caring about the way my face twisted from the sudden jolt of familiar pain that started out as a sharp jab in my hip and then slowly crept down my leg to my toes where it became a dull ache. Lyle said it would get better with time and I believed him. Lyle Porter had been our doctor for ever, it seemed. He had nursed Charlie and me through some difficult times: Charlie's bout with a mad cow and my four miscarriages, to name a few.

It had been almost five years since the accident and the medical bills had slowly drained our finances to the point of almost nonexistent. Farming was a tough life and I wasn't much help to Charlie anymore. If only I had watched where I was going, none of this would have happened. If only I had closed the trap door to the loft after climbing through it. If only I hadn't stepped backwards into the open trap door after being startled by the pigeon. 'If only' didn't help when I fell the twenty-some feet to the cement below, driving my leg up into my pelvis and snapping my bones as if they were mere twigs. 'If only' wasn't going to change things now. Charlie had a favorite saying: "Don't worry; tomorrow will take care of its self." Over the years since I became Mrs. Beth Sanders I had come to believe in Charlie's saying.

His philosophy seemed to work for him, so I had found myself adopting the same attitude.

The pain was almost gone now, as I shifted a little to become more comfortable. Shading my eyes from the glare of the setting sun, I gazed down at the postcard scene below. I could see the house, a pristine white two and a half story with widow's peaks glistening in the spring sunshine. The red hip-roofed barn was situated a little to the right of it, along with the smaller sheds and various buildings scattered throughout the area, like small children clustered beside their parents. The clouds overhead, scattered softly throughout the clear blue sky like fluffy cotton balls gradually changing shape in the gentle breeze, completed the picture of serenity.

My vision straying further, I could even make out the fence that crisscrossed below showing each pasture. Along that fence, working hard to repair a broken wire the heavy winter snow managed to snap, was Charlie, his blond hair blowing in the gentle breeze. If I closed my eyes, I could even picture those twinkling blue eyes and that infectious lopsided grin. Charlie looked good for a man of forty-four, still slender without the paunch most men his age adopted. Charlie had become my life ever since he captured my eye at the summer fair in 1940. He said the first time he laid eyes on me, a petite five foot two with long blond hair and big blue eyes, he was hooked. Twenty-two years later, Charlie said I still looked like the girl he married. I knew different. I was still slender, but that long blond hair had changed to the color of dull straw. I hadn't been able to look after it since the accident, so had it cut just below my ears. The pixie cut just added to my delicate features, making me look frailer then I really was. The constant pain had given my face a pinched look, but Charlie could still make my heart flutter with that same grin. "You don't look a day different than the day we met, sugar," he would say.

The accident had changed our lives drastically, in more ways than one. Our savings had dwindled to nothing from the mountain of medical bills we encountered. The bill collectors reminded me of wolves, waiting around every corner to pounce. Where did those care free days go, I wondered, straightening my leg while another twitch started to settle in?

Resting gently on my arms, I surveyed the pond below. Where the stream widened swam two geese, mated for life, much like Charlie and I. The only difference was the large brood of goslings following in their wake, whereas our nest was empty and always would be. A deep sigh escaped me as I watched the goslings following behind their parents. I mentally shook my head to dislodge the cobwebs of the past, which seemed to creep up on me when I was least aware. I was suddenly reminded of the age-old saying, what will be will be. This saying had become a pattern which my life now seemed to follow.

A stiff breeze suddenly sprung up, whipping my hair into my eyes. Brushing it away, I surveyed the scene below one last time, my eyes coming to rest on the graveyard to the left of the house. No, I thought, shrugging my shoulders. It would do no good to dream about what could have been.

I carefully rose using the cane I now carried with me at all times. The breeze seemed cooler now that the sun was starting to set. Clutching my thin jacket together with my one free hand, I shifted my cane to get a better grip before starting the long climb down. I knew I would be tired when I got home, but the cleansing had been good for my soul.

It was just as I had anticipated. The long climb had taken its toll and I was noticeable weary from it as I set the table. Charlie never said anything while he washed up for supper, but I knew he noticed my weary movements.

"How was your day?" he asked, searching my face.

"It was fine," I lied, not quite meeting his eye.

"Are you sure?" he asked, taking another sip from his cup.

"Did you get the fence fixed?" I asked, quickly changing the subject.

"Yes, I'm really glad I had enough of that old wire for splicing. The new stuff is sure expensive now," he replied, plopping a huge spoonful of mashed potatoes onto his plate.

Somehow I managed to get through the whole meal before I finally broached the subject that had been weighing heavily on my mind all day.

"Charlie, what are we going to do? How are we going to plant a crop without any help? I can't help you. Remember the trouble we had getting a loan from the bank last year? I don't think we're the bank's favourite customers right now."

Charlie looked down at his large calloused hands before replying. "We have been over this before. Don't worry; I'm going to town tomorrow to see the bank about an operating loan and I still have some grain to sell. I'm sure they will see it our way for a change," he said, buttering his bread. "After I'm done there, I'll stop at the unemployment office. Maybe we'll get lucky and find some help there. Try not to worry so much, Beth. We'll get by. We always have, haven't we?"

"I don't know," I said, shaking my head. "What if we can't find any help?"

"We managed last year and I'm sure we'll manage this year. You worry too much! Tomorrow will take care_of itself." He flashed me a knowing grin.

I slowly smiled. "I guess you're right," I said, as I picked up our empty plates. Over the years Charlie had always proven to be right. Tomorrow would be just another day.

Charlie had always been an early riser and as usual was gone before I crawled from my bed. Wearily, I grabbed a cup of coffee and sat down at the old kitchen table that had seen better days. My mind slowly, drifted back to last night's conversation. I wondered if Charlie would be able to find someone to help with the planting this year. What kind of help would he find? The riff-raff he found last year was useless. What was his name again? George. That was it. That man had been as lazy as a pet raccoon. I'm glad he's moved on. Good help was getting so hard to find these days.

Charlie said he would be back before supper, so I decided to check our meagre supplies, noting that it would have to be stew again. Oh well, I might as well make extra, I decided, thinking about the new help Charlie anticipated bringing home. Working on the stew, I found my thoughts recalling some of the family history I had heard over the years. Glancing out the kitchen window, my gaze was captured by the old, fenced-in grave yard slightly to one side of the house. The white picket fence in stark contrast to the old, rusty gate with barbed wire which held it shut. Charlie's father Max was buried there, along with his grandparents and great grandparents and our tiny babies, which were not meant to be. Charlie's younger sister, Sheena, was also buried there. It was really sad how she had died. She was five when someone had told her that if she chewed wheat kernels they would turn into gum. She had taken treated seed from a bin to try it. The seed had been deadly poison. I knew Charlie blamed himself for her death, even though he never admitted it. Charlie never liked to talk about Sheena. In fact, Charlie didn't like to talk about his family at all. The only thing he told me was that the scars on his back were from the beatings his father gave him after his sister died. He was seven; two years older than her. He should have stopped her, his father had told Charlie over and over again while he brought the belt down on his back. His mother had disappeared shortly after that. If Charlie asked about her, he got a beating. He soon learned not to ask anymore.

Charlie was fanatical about the grave yard. Not a weed could be seen among the family gravestones. He insisted on weeding it himself and kept it immaculate. The other grave stones, which were not marked, were hidden by a tall hedge Charlie had planted. Since he didn't know who they were, he didn't see fit to bother attending to them.

Charlie had only managed to escape his father's clutches when the old man had died suddenly in his sleep. Charlie told me he just quit breathing. Some folks say he still roams the halls of this house, as he never realized he died. I often wondered if it might be true, for at times I would hear a door open or close when no one was around. Charlie used to laugh at me when I mentioned it. It's an old house, he would say. Things settle and the wind can do funny things in these old halls. Still, it always gave me the creeps whenever I had to go into the room at the end of the hall where Charlie's parent's bedroom used to be.

With the stew finished and simmering gently on the stove, I turned to the task of tidying each room in anticipation of the new help Charlie might be bringing home. Maybe this time things would be different, I thought, remembering last year's hired help with a shudder. He had been such a strange man.

I dreaded the thought of having to make the long climb upstairs to tidy the bedrooms. Although, I knew they would need a good airing after being closed up for the winter. A huge sigh escaped me as I slowly climbed the two long flights of stairs up to the rooms that were hardly ever used anymore. Since the accident I found it necessary to stop and rest on the landing. Today was no exception. I found my gaze drawn to the collage of family pictures gathered there on display. There in the centre, proudly surrounded by a group of smaller pictures, stood Charlie's parents' wedding picture. Charlie's mother, Grace, was beautiful, her long blond hair softly framing a cameo-shaped face. She looked young; her face so delicate and trusting was turned up to gaze with adoration at her new husband. Charlie's father's features were as dark as his wife's were fair. His piercing eyes seemed to focus intently on his new bride. I wasn't sure if it was my imagination, but I thought if one looked closely you could see the cruel mask glinting from behind those hooded eyes. I had tried to remove the pictures over the years, but Charlie insisted they remain where they were. Removing my gaze from the cluster of pictures, I turned away to finish my climb. As always, I felt a shudder build in my spine and shake me to the core from gazing into those evil eyes.

Upon opening the door to the far bedroom, I noted that faint, musty odor still wafting back to greet me. The room had been Charlie's parent's bedroom and I always felt slightly uncomfortable entering it. Over the years I had tried different ways to get rid of the smell, but even a new coat of paint and time could not mask it. I was still puzzled as to what it could be. I had just opened the window to freshen the room when I saw the headlights from Charlie's old station wagon turn into the lane leading into the yard. Dismissing the smell, I hurriedly left the room with its ghostly reminders. The uncomfortable feeling faded while I inched slowly down the stairs to meet Charlie and the anticipated help. I was surprised to see the small crowd of people fanned out behind Charlie when I reached the bottom of the stairs.

"Well, how was your day, Beth?" Charlie inquired, giving me his usual peck on the cheek.

"It was fine," I replied, craning my neck to get a good look at the four people standing quietly behind him at the door.

"This is our new help: Thomas, Rachel, Amy, and Vince."

I cautiously surveyed the four standing in front of me, unsure which one was which. The older couple I guessed to be around forty. The man called Thomas mumbled his name while slowly sticking out his hand to give mine a quick shake. I had the oddest feeling at the touch of his hand. It was as if I had just touched a snake by accident. Taking a step backwards, I tried to smother the involuntary shudder that ran down my backbone. Thomas was tall and willow thin with dark piercing eyes under a shock of dark brown hair, which needed a good trimming. But it was his eyes that captured my attention. They seemed cruel and unwavering. It was as if he was trying to peer into your soul. I made a mental note to stay out of his way.

The woman, Rachel, was as warm and friendly as Thomas was cold. She smiled pleasantly while coming forth to give me a quick hug and a cheery hello. She was slender, but with curves in all the right places. One couldn't help liking the sunny disposition, along with her twinkling green eyes and wavy auburn hair which framed her pixie face.

The two teens standing shyly together could have been twins. They were both about the same height and slender in build, with long drawn faces that looked too thin. Chocolate-brown eyes peered out from under thick, raven black hair. Vince's hair hung to his shoulders in an unruly shaggy mane that looked like it had been cut with a knife. Amy's hair, on the other hand, hung to her waist in a shimmer of dark silk- — it was her only truly beautiful quality.

The aroma of stew wafting from the kitchen reminded me we had not eaten. My god, what was Charlie thinking? Four more people to feed! They would eat us out of house and home. I would have to talk to him later. I mentally shrugged my shoulders. "I made stew for supper," I said to the newcomers. "You're welcome to join us." Four nods greeted me while I looked from one face to another.

"If you'll just follow me, I'll show you where the kitchen is. We're not very formal here. All our meals are eaten in there." I waved my hand pointing towards the kitchen.

Rachael chatted amiable and even offered to help set the extra place settings around the table. Waving my hand, I ushered them to the table where they all prepared to sit down at the position of their choosing. Rachael, preparing to sit down, pulled back the chair situated at the end of the table when Charlie's booming voice stopped her.

"You can't sit there!" he snapped emphatically.

"What? Why can't I?" she demanded with a frown.

I glanced at Charlie, who stared poker-faced at the lone chair gracing the end of the table, before deciding an explanation was in order.

"That was his father's chair. No one was allowed to sit there but him. After he died we just kind of kept up the tradition. Sorry— but you can sit here," I motioned to an empty spot to the right of it.

"Alright, thank you," she mumbled weakly, a frown still furrowing her brow while she sat down in the place I offered.

I sat glancing around at all the hungry faces. I was grateful I had made the extra stew. There would be no need to worry about leftovers. My assumption proved true. They ate as if it was their last meal, barely taking the time to answer my questions. When their appetite was finally satiated, they leaned back, clearly more relaxed.

"Rachel, where are you from?"

She leaned forward, a sly grin plying her mouth. "Here and there," she said.

"How far is here and there from here?" I asked.

"A ways," was the only reply I received. Clearly she didn't want to tell me anything.

I turned to Thomas. "What about you, Thomas? Where are you from?"

"Does it matter?" he replied sourly.

"No, not really," I replied, slightly affronted. I had never met such an unfriendly bunch as this. Oh well; they would be gone in a short time. In a few years I wouldn't even remember their names. I tried one more attempt at being friendly with Vince and Amy.

"Are you two from around here?" I asked with a smile.

"No," they replied in unison, glancing at each other. Nothing more was volunteered, so I decided to let it drop.

Charlie glanced up to quickly change the subject. "Beth, I might as well show them where they can sleep. I have a big day planned for everyone tomorrow and they will need their rest."

I motioned towards the living room. "If you will just follow Charlie, he'll show you the way. I have a hard time with the stairs now, so your rooms will be your own responsibility during your stay. Rachel, in the morning we rise early, so you will be expected to help prepare breakfast."

I received a quick salute and a cheery, "Yes, ma'am!"

One by one they disappeared up the stairs behind Charlie like a brood of goslings following a goose. I sat at the bottom of the steps waiting for his return. After a few minutes he came bounding down the stairs with a huge grin plastered across his face.

"I told you I would find help," he announced triumphantly.

"Yes, you did. But Charlie, why so many? We can't afford to pay that many. How are we going to feed them? Judging by the amount they ate for supper, they'll clean out my garden before winter!"

Charlie sat down in his favourite chair to patiently explain how he came by so much help.

"I met Thomas and Rachel scanning the help wanted ads on the bulletin board. They seemed very desperate for work. I told them I didn't really need that much help, but Rachael agreed to work for very little, including her room and board and the promise of a bonus after harvest. I thought you could use the help, along with the companionship, so I agreed to take her on."

"Well that takes care of those two, but what about the others?" I asked, motioning my head towards the stairs.

"Vince and Amy heard us talking. They literally begged me for a job. I told them no, but they said they would work for just room and board. They said they had no place to stay. I'm sorry, but I took pity on them. They looked like they could really use some extra help and I felt sorry for them. I'm sure they won't be here very long."

I could not argue with that. They did seem a little desperate. "Where did you put them all?" I inquired, motioning towards the stairs.

"Rachael is in the far bedroom at the end of the hall; Thomas is in the bedroom beside ours; and Vince and Amy wanted the attic space. Is that okay?"

"Sure, I don't care where they sleep; just as long as they clean up after themselves," I answered with a shrug.

Charlie grinned confidently. He seemed proud of himself at solving the dilemma of planting a crop. "It will all work out, you'll see."

"We will have to see about that," I said half-heartedly. A queer feeling of foreboding seemed to sneak in to warn me of things to come.

CHAPTER TWO

The next morning Rachel and Thomas were up at first light. Good, I thought. Maybe it would all work out. Now, if only they could show they weren't afraid of a little hard work. Vince and Amy had to be called repeatedly to get up. They wearily crawled down the stairs at a snail's pace. I surmised they were used to their own hours and resented being awakened from a deep sleep, judging by the sullen scowls on their sour faces. That would have to change if they wanted to stay.

Breakfast was a quiet affair broken only by Rachel's odd giggle, for no apparent reason. I soon learned she did this only when she was nervous. The twins ate with gusto though. They even managed a shy smile, along with their whispered thank you, upon cleaning their plates. Charlie was a good boss and knew how to get the most work from his employees, so I quietly sat back and listened to him dictate what was required from each of them.

Charlie's first order was for Rachael. "Rachael, I'm sure Beth can show you what needs to be done around here. So just do whatever she says."

The second order was for Amy. "Amy, the hen house needs to be cleaned and the eggs picked. That will be your job this morning."

I watched with amusement at the look of horror that flitted across her face. Her head suddenly swiveled to encounter Vince's eyes, focused thoughtfully on her. It was as if they could read each other's mind. Vince shrugged his shoulders slightly before giving her a weak smile and a quick nod. This slight conformation was all she needed from Vince. Turning towards Charlie, she nodded her head in agreement.

"Vince and Tom, you can come with me. The seeder has to be made ready and cultivator shovels will have to be changed before planting." Charlie stood and moved towards the door.

"The name's Thomas. Not Tom!" I heard Thomas snarl following behind Charlie out the door.

Charlie was going to have a confrontation with that one before the crop was in the ground. Oh well, I knew Charlie could look after himself and had proven it on more than one occasion.

Rachael and Amy, on the other hand, actually proved they could be quite useful. The morning passed pleasantly enough while I sat watching Rachael turn the earth ready for planting.

From my seat at the corner of the garden, I sat watching Amy endeavour to clean the chicken house. Her look of disgust was almost comical to watch as she attempted to balance the wheel barrow, only to have it tip over sideways, spilling its contents upon the ground. I thought she would give up. But no, she righted it again and with a look of fierce determination, reloaded it. It was like watching a small child learn to walk. To her credit she soon got the hang of balancing and walking at the same time. Maybe there was more to Amy than met the eye. Just maybe she was tougher than we all realized.

"It's time for lunch," I called out to Amy, motioning towards the house. She was more than willing to abandon her task to follow wearily behind me. Rachael, still full of pep, took up the lead as we climbed the steps leading onto the veranda.

Rachael was full of questions while we chatted amiably making the midday meal. The view of the cemetery from the kitchen window seemed to intrigue her the most. She kept drifting back to stare out at it, as if a magnet had her in its grasp. Question after question rolled off her tongue about Charlie and me. She seemed just a little too curious for my liking.

"You'll have to ask Charlie," I snapped, tired of her constant probing of our lives.

I felt chastised at the sudden look of discomfort flashing across her face, along with the nervous giggle erupting from her throat. Softening my voice, I hastily changed the subject to ease her discomfort. Her curiosity now seemed to focus only on Charlie. I watched her face for a clue as to where this fascination was coming from and was finally rewarded when she picked up a picture of Charlie. I watched as a dreamy quality suddenly transfixed her gaze. The picture was a favorite of mine which I had taken of Charlie surveying one of his crops in the fall. It was like a light bulb going off. She was infatuated with Charlie! I would have to watch her closely. Nobody was going to steal my man! Although, I felt the competition was a little in her favour physically, as I watched her waltz across the room to once again gaze out at the cemetery. I, on the other hand, had twenty-eight years of experience dealing with Charlie's likes and dislikes. It was on more than one occasion that I had to resort to a few of the tricks I had up my sleeve in order to deal with a few of the be-sot females around here. Rachael was no exception. I would have to be on my toes with this one, I wagered, watching her curvy form glide across the floor. She was just a little too cute for comfort.

The dinner atmosphere that evening was a repeat of the night before. The only conversation was from Rachael as she hung on every word Charlie uttered. I realized a talk with her would soon be eminent, noting the flirtatious banter that ensued between them. Amy's attitude had become sullen and withdrawn. She kept darting furtive little glances at Vince. I wasn't sure if she blamed him for her ordeal with the chicken house, or the world in general. I finally decided it was the latter, upon seeing her face reflecting the same sour expression to anyone whom dared ask her a question. I found myself slightly curious where this strange brood had come from. I tried once again, questioning them each in turn, only to be met with stolid silence. They all gave me the impression they had something to hide. No clues were forthcoming from any one's lips and probably wouldn't be soon, I surmised. The meal was hastily completed with only Rachael's chatter and nervous giggle filling the silence. I had been looking forward to the lazy days of summer, but if this kept up I would be only too glad to see it end.

The next morning Rachael decided that a tour of the cemetery was in order. Amy wanted nothing to do with it as she turned grudgingly to march towards the lesser of the two evils: the chicken house. I could see no harm in Rachael satisfying her curiosity and then just maybe we could get some work done. I patiently answered each of her questions as to who was buried in each of the graves. Finally she came to the unmarked graves at the back of the cemetery partitioned off from the front by the tall, neat hedge of trees.

"What about those?" she asked, pointing to the unmarked graves.

I had no answer for her.

"Not sure," I replied with a shrug.

With her curiosity now somewhat satisfied, Rachael agreed to finish planting the garden. The rest of the day passed pleasantly enough, with Rachael doing the majority of the work. Amy had finished her battle with the chicken house early, and now slowly drifted over to where I sat on an old pail watching Rachael tamping the earth over the last row of beans.

"What do I do now?" she asked wearily.

She looks tired, I thought, noticing her weary movements.

"Why don't you just sit down and rest for a while," I said cheerfully. She was only too happy to oblige, and sat down beside me. Sighing, she stretched out on a lush patch of green grass, letting the gentle afternoon sun settle on her slim form. I watched her face gradually relax while she stretched languorously like a contented cat. It was while in this stretched position that I noticed the slightly rounded curve of her abdomen, seemingly out of portion to her slim features. Aha, I thought. I had just caught a glimpse of what was behind her and Vince's arrival. Charlie would have to be told; she would be of no use in her condition.

"I'm finished. What do you want me to do now?" Rachael inquired, interrupting my quiet musings.

"C'mon girls, it's time to start dinner. There's no rest for the wicked," I teasingly told them. I would have to think about my discovery later, for a seed of an idea had been planted deep in my brain and was now starting to take root. Dinner was a quiet affair with only the idle chatter from the men discussing what was to be done the next day. Rachael seemed content to just sit back and listen. She seemed to hang on Charlie's every word with that dreamy expression still etched on her face. Amy was too tired to do anything but eat, her hand methodically going from plate to mouth. From the corner of my eye I caught the sympathetic glances Vince would shoot her from time to time. Their situation was becoming clearer and clearer, I noted, watching their silent exchange of communication.

Bed time could not come quick enough for me. I was fairly bursting to tell Charlie about my newly found discovery. I grabbed my night gown to slip it quickly over my head and then hurried to brush my teeth while waiting anxiously for Charlie's arrival. He was barely through our bedroom door before I blurted out my findings.

"Amy is pregnant!"

I was shocked when he answered, "I know."

"How did you find out?"

"Vince confided in me today. He wanted to make sure I wasn't too hard on Amy in her condition."

"Alright, what do we do now?" I asked, plopping down on the bed.

"Nothing, we don't do anything," Charlie said, balling his shirt up to throw it in the hamper. "Vince is too good of a worker to let go. He's three times the worker that Thomas is."

"But she can't do much in her condition, can she?"

"Just don't worry about it. It will all work out," Charlie said, closing his eyes.

Charlie was always right. He would know what he was doing, I thought, closing my eyes. I soon drifted off to sleep, dreaming of what it would be like to have a baby in the house.

CHAPTER THREE

"I'm all finished my work. I'm going outside to drink my coffee," Rachael informed me, grabbing her cup to leave.

"Alright, I might as well join you," I said, picking up my cup to follow her. I came outside to find Charlie, Thomas, and Vince standing in front of the shop talking with raised voices. "What's going on? What's the argument about?"

"I'm not sure. They were at it when I came out."

Charlie was a man that angered easily. That fact was now evident as his voice boomed out across the yard. I had learned over the years to tread softly when Charlie was in one of his moods. Apparently Thomas had not.

"Uh-oh," I said as Charles' voice rose in irritation. All hell was about to break loose.

"No! Vince will be on the seeder and you will be picking stones on the east quarter," Charlie declared, crossing his arms in front.

"No one needs to pick stones. Just leave the damn things where they are," Thomas sneered, pushing Charlie aside to climb up on the tractor.

No one pushes Charlie! Before you could say Jack Sprat, Thomas was lying face down on the ground with one arm pinned behind his back. Charlie sat astride him. "Things will be done my way or you won't be here. Is that clear?"

From Thomas's throat came a low mumble. "Alright, alright. I got it, man."

"I hope so. I don't want to have to repeat myself," Charlie ground out before relinquishing his hold.

Thomas slowly got to his feet, dusting himself off while he walked away without a backwards glance towards the stone picker. I could feel the tension radiating from the scene from where Rachael and I sat safely ensconced on the porch swing. Rachael seemed shocked by Charlie's sudden display of authority.

Leaning towards me, she whispered conspiratorially, "I sure wouldn't want to be on his wrong side." I nodded wisely.

"Would you like more coffee?" Rachael asked each person, coffee pot in hand, as she made her way around the living room that evening.

"Huh," Thomas answered with a shrug, dismissing her as easily as if she had been a bug before turning his face away, lost in thought.

★★★

Thomas' Story

I knew if I didn't get out of town the law would catch up to me sooner or later. That last job Billy botched was going to get us both thrown in the clink, and they'd throw away the key for good. I told him not to whack the old girl when she caught us going through her jewellery. But no, he's got to prove he's the big man and now I 'm stuck here with this ass-hole telling me what to do. I sure came close to letting him have it today when he decided to throw his weight around. I think I'm going to have a hard time controlling my temper from now on. On the other hand, this was as good as any place to hide out. Maybe, before I leave I'll have to teach Charlie a lesson or two with his old lady. She isn't too bad to look at, if you threw away her cane. If I play my cards right I might be able to make a few changes around here for my benefit. Come to think of it, Rachael is pretty easy on the eyes too. I saw the way she watches me. The next time I get her alone I'll have to show her who the real boss is. With a few adjustments this place could grow on a man. Maybe my ship has finally come in.

★★★

The next morning I decided to take advantage of the extra help Charlie had so conveniently provided for me by washing all the windows. Charlie was good to me. But being a man consumed with more important issues, he never noticed the dingy film that spread from window to window like a cancer until each one was consumed. Rachael had given up on doing things right and now had to be told over and over again until it was done to my satisfaction. The sunny disposition gradually faded, and now I could see the true Rachael emerging from her cocoon. I admit my patience was wearing thin and she wasn't any help with her infatuation with Charlie. She would follow him around with a moonstruck look on her face, asking silly questions. I tried to speak with Charlie about her obsession with him but he only laughed at my worries. There was bound to be to a clash between us sooner or later. Grabbing some supplies to wash the windows, I ushered Rachael and Amy outside to instruct them what needed to be done.

"Rachael here is the water. Be careful climbing that ladder until I get back with some clean rags. Amy, you go into the house and work on the windows from the inside. I don't think it's a very good idea for you to be up on the ladder," I instructed her before leaving to fetch the rags.

Upon returning I was surprized to find Amy on the ladder diligently scrubbing away at a window while Rachael stood inside pointing to the spots Amy missed.

"Amy, why aren't you inside like I told you? Come down off the ladder and go tell Rachael to come outside. I would like to speak with her."

"It's okay, I don't mind being on the ladder."

"I know you don't, but I do. Rachael needs to learn to follow orders."

Amy, bobbing her head, hurried inside following my request. Rachael's stride as she came towards me suggested she was not too happy about being rousted from her comfortable position. She strode to stand stiffly before me, arms firmly ensconced in front.

"What do you want now?" she demanded, her eyes narrowing into tiny slits while she surveyed me with a look of disgust.

"Rachael, I told you to do the outside windows."

"I do things my way. You can do it your way, when YOU'RE doing the work!" She haughtily turned her back as if the subject was closed.

I had noticed little things that seemed as if she was trying to slowly take control over my authority. Well no more, I had enough of her smart remarks.

"You will do what I tell you, when I tell you to do it, when you're working for me! I may me crippled, but I am the boss and when I say something, it better be carried out the way I want. Do I make myself clear?"

We stood eye to eye regarding each other with silent rage. Rachael finally conceded to my show of authority and slowly lowered her eyes. Glad her tantrum had ended, I turned away, only to have the ladder come crashing down, skimming my shoulder, before it careened to a stop beside me.

"Oops!" Rachael said with a sly grin on her face.

"That had better have been an accident or you'll be going back where you came from!" I snapped, holding my injured shoulder while I glared back at her. I knew Rachael had a mean streak in her, but never realized she would act upon it. I couldn't trust her anymore. From now on I would have to watch my back carefully.

Rachael calmly picked the ladder up to place it against the house, but not before I heard her whisper the words, "Stupid bitch," as I walked away.

★★★

RACHAEL'S STORY

I sure don't want to go back to living in that rat hole of a place on the east side. I had to live there for a week after I carved up my old man with a knife. I can still feel those cockroaches crawling on my skin. After that last beating he gave me, I swore if I ever got a chance I would make him pay. I had to wait patiently all evening for the alcohol to finally take effect, until he fell into a drunken stupor and passed out on the sofa. I'll never forget the way his eyes opened when I plunged the knife into his chest. "You bitch," he had screamed, thrashing wildly, before grabbing the knife to jerk it out of his chest. I didn't kill him, I thought fearfully while I ran from the apartment. I was afraid to even look back. I guess he didn't die. I never saw a notice in the paper. There's no way I'm going to take any chances he might find me. I was lucky when I found Charlie at the unemployment office. I was down to my last dollar and would soon be kicked out of that hell hole I was living in. I could get used to living here. Nice house, three meals a day, and the works not too hard. An added bonus would be that hunk of a man Charlie. The only thorn in this comfy picture is that mouse of a Beth. I wish that ladder had fallen on that self-righteous bitch's head. I should have pushed it more to the left. She doesn't deserve a man like Charlie and I'm aiming to prove it to him. I can see myself already as Mrs. Charlie Sanders. I deserve it after having to deal with that pig of a man I finally got away from.

★★★

That night, curled up beside Charlie in bed, I told him about the ladder incident. "You're too suspicious, it was likely an accident," he laughed.

"Humph, that was no accident!" I snapped, looking at Charlie with disgust.

Charlie gazed at me with a thoughtful expression before saying, "Rachael wouldn't do that! Why would she want to hurt you?"

Why do people do a lot of things to hurt others? I rolled over to turn my back to Charlie. This time I wasn't going to put up with any more Tom Foolery. I still smarted every time I thought about the incident with Margery. If Rachael thought I was going to turn a blind eye, she was sadly mistaken. The age old saying, Hell Has No Furry like a Woman Scorned, just might come true. I would watch them closely.

This became a pattern in the days to follow. I watched Charlie; Charlie watched Rachael; and Thomas watched us all. Vince and Amy watched no one. At the first opportunity they would scurry away to the sanctuary of the attic.

Chapter Four

The days seemed to meld together as the daylight hours became longer and longer. The grilling hours of farm work allowed no one time for leisure. There weren't any more confrontations between Rachael and myself, so I found myself wondering if Charlie had spoken to her about the ladder incidence. She was not overly friendly, but now managed to maintain a civil attitude towards me.

"How are things working out with Thomas and Vince?" I asked while brushing my teeth before bed.

"It's much better now. Vince doesn't seem too eager to leave and I know Thomas can be a pain at times, but things are finally getting done," Charlie replied, sitting down on the edge of the bed to remove his socks. "Even the bank hasn't been hounding us for money. The crops look really good. Now, all we need is some rain to have a good harvest."

The next morning Mother Nature decided to show us what she was capable of. The hammer of thunder and lightning rolled across the sky in a continuous light show, which gradually settled into a steady downpour. It enveloped us like a grey shroud for the next three days.

Vince and Amy took their meals and quietly retired to the sanctuary of the attic. Thomas would sit for hours in one spot, brooding about who knows what, while he silently watched the steady sheet of rain slide down the window panes. We all found ourselves listening to the steady drone of music that ensued from Mother Nature's symphony. Charlie and I had just settled down to our favourite pass – time of a long game of chess when Rachael bounded down the stairs.

"Can I get two strong men up here to help me?" she asked, batting those long lashes of hers and flashing a coy smile. "I'm rearranging my room and need help to move some furniture around."

Charlie slowly raised an apologetic face to mumble, "Sorry, Beth. This won't take too long."

I watched irritably as Charlie and Thomas rose to go to her aid. She sure didn't have to ask them twice, I thought pettily. Where Rachael was concerned, I was finding it very hard to be charitable these days. Slowly I rose to my feet, the curiosity getting the better of me, and followed quietly behind the trio making their way up the stairs.

Rachael flitted around the room like a sparrow while explaining to the men what she wanted done. This had to be moved to here and that to over there. All the while that constant giggle that annoyed me so much erupted from her throat making me feel like gagging. The men patiently tried to accommodate her every wish by pushing and pulling the furniture around to the exact location she preferred. Charlie was the main focus of her attention. She flirted with him shamelessly, constantly reaching out to touch him whenever she spoke.

"My goodness, I didn't realize you were so strong," she purred, running her hand down his arm, her face tilted up to gaze adoringly at him from below fluttering eye lashes.

How blatant, I thought, gagging silently to myself. Charlie caught my warning look to promptly move away from her. I nodded in approval before sitting down on the old family rocking chair situated in the corner. From this point I guardedly watched them attempt to move the last piece of furniture Rachael wanted transferred to the corner of the room. It was heavy as lead. The old antique armoire had sat in the same spot since Charlie was a child. With a lot of pushing and pulling, they finally succeeded in moving it to the spot Rachael preferred. The floor where the old armoire had sat was now discolored with age and the boards were sticking up slightly in places.

"Charlie, it looks like some of those boards are loose. Maybe you should fix them while you're here," I suggested. I was not going to give Rachael another excuse to get Charlie up here alone later.

"It looks like you're right," Charlie observed, kneeling down to inspect the boards. "There's quite a few not nailed down."

Rachael inquisitively knelt down beside Charlie to lift a few of the boards. It was when Rachael lifted the second board that we noticed the mouldy, sweet smell emitting from the hole in the floor. Charlie removed the rest of the boards. We all watched in horror to see the shape of a skeleton slowly emerge. No one seemed able to comprehend the atrocity of our discovery. We all remained speechless, looking from one to the other for an answer. Then all eyes swiveled downwards to stare in shock at the horror encased in its death shroud of the floor.

Thomas was the first to speak. "I'm out of here. This is just too weird for me."

Charlie, never taking his eyes off the skeleton, whispered to me, "Beth, go call Jim. Tell him he'd better get up here right away."

Jim Prince was our local sheriff and Charlie's first cousin from his mother's side. Jim and Charlie had only lived three miles from each other and had practically been raised together. Neither one had any siblings. They had gone to the same school, were in the same grade, and could easily be mistaken for brothers. You rarely saw one without the other and the family trait of blond hair and blue eyes ran deep on their mother's side of the family. Jim answered on the second ring stating that he would be here as fast as possible.

Upon entering the bedroom, I was shocked to find Charlie sitting on the floor holding his knees while he rocked back and forth, tears streaming down his face. Cupped in his right hand was a wedding band.

"It's got Mom's name in it," he moaned slightly, the anguish seeming more than he could bear. I gently put my arms around him, letting his full weight recline on me while he turned to sob into my neck over and over again. "She never left me. She was here all this time." Rachael silently slipped from the room, leaving us alone to face the horror of our gruesome discovery.

Charlie slowly regained his composure, standing to pull me up beside him. "Come on Beth, we'll wait for Jim on the porch," he whispered, leading me from the room.

Charlie's face was unreadable while we slowly wound our way down the stairs. Upon reaching the landing, Charlie stopped to linger. "Beth, do you think I'm like him?" He whispered, gazing up at the portrait, his eyes never wavering from his father's.

"You're nothing like him," I spat, looking with disgust into the dark, evil eyes that now seemed to mock me. Taking Charlie by the hand, I lead him down the stairs, slowly making our way to the veranda where we sat down upon the porch swing to wait for Jim. Thomas and Rachael, not wanting to be in the house were death resided, sat silently regarding each other from one end of the veranda. The rain still came down in a dull grey sheet, making the mood more oppressive than it already was. Charlie and I sat huddled together on the porch swing, drawing comfort from each other more for need than from the chilly dampness that crept over everything. Through the slate grey of the falling rain, the flashing red and blue of the police cruiser creeping closer and closer was evident, until finally it bathed us in its eerie glow. It quickly, ground to a halt before the house.

"God this weather is horrible," Jim muttered, striding quickly up the porch steps out of the rain.

Jim was tall like Charlie, with the same blond hair and twinkling blue eyes. Only now those eyes held the same sadness that was reflected in Charlie's. Charlie slowly held out his hand to let his mother's ring fall into Jim's hand.

"It was still on her hand," Charlie said, his voice cracking with the emotion he held in check.

"Bloody hell—," Jim declared upon examining the ring carefully. Slowly he looked into Charlie's eyes. The sympathy clearly etched on his face.

"I'm sorry, Charlie. I don't know what else to say right now, except I'm sorry," he whispered, placing his hand on Charlie's shoulder.

From the corner of my eye I spotted Thomas and Rachael silently slink out of sight around the corner. What did those two have to hide, I wondered? Apparently the law made them very nervous. After Charlie's mother's remains were removed from the house, Jim sat down to explain to us what would happen.

"I'm sorry Charlie. I know a crime has been committed here, but there's no one left to shoulder the blame. Your father passed away a long time ago and it looks like he is the only suspect, so you will just have to let it go and move on. I know it sucks, but that's the only piece of advice I can give you," Jim said with an apologetic shrug.

I knew Charlie would have a hard time accepting this answer. I would try to help, but from experience I found it better to leave him alone. He would have to work it out on his own. He would need time to put this all behind him. I looked at Charlie where he sat with his head bowed. What kind of monster murders his wife and buries her beneath the floor boards in their own bedroom? I could feel a shudder run down my back bone at the thought.

The rain that had been oppressing us for the last few days gradually subsided to a gentle mist, shrouding everything it touched to a silvery sheen. The weather seemed to fit all of our moods as we sat morosely around the kitchen table waiting for the funeral to start. It was a private affair with only Charlie, Jim and I in attendance. We had never had much to do with any of the neighbours before my accident, which only served to make us more reclusive than ever. Our closest neighbour lived four miles away and Charlie and he had never seen eye to eye. Thomas and Rachael declined to participate, stating that they felt out of place, while Vince and Amy watched with respect from the veranda.

Jim offered to show his respect by saying the eulogy for Charlie's mother. After a short but feeling service Jim clasped Charlie by the shoulder, his voice cracking with emotion. "I'm sorry, man," he mumbled. "This should never have happened. All you can do is try to move on from here now. I wish I could change things for you, but I can't. Just remember I'm always here for you whenever you need to talk to someone."

Charlie gazed down at his feet before slowly raising his eyes to take in the sombre expression on Jim's face. "I appreciate it. I know I couldn't have done anything. I just wish things could have been different," he mumbled, shaking his head.

I turned towards Jim. "Come up to the house, I have a fresh pot of coffee made and some of that apple crumb cake you love so much."

"That would be nice, Beth. I haven't had a slice of your apple crumb cake in a long time," he said with a smile, rubbing his hands together in anticipation of the treat to come.

Charlie shook his head at my offer. Turning away he said, "I just want to be alone for a while."

Jim and I walked slowly up the path towards the house. Peeking back over my shoulder I could see Charlie kneeling on the ground beside his mother's grave, his head bowed in prayer.

"Bugger. What a thing to find out about your father and mother," Jim muttered, rubbing his forehead before wearily sitting down at the old country table that had been Charlie's grandmother's.

I slowly poured him a cup of coffee, letting my hand rest lightly on his shoulder. "I want to thank you for everything you have done today and in the past. You're always there for us, Jim. We don't know what we would do without you."

His eyes darkened slightly and his gaze lingered on my face. "You know I would do anything for you, Beth."

The moment passed as quickly as it came. I turned away towards the window where Charlie was still visible kneeling by his mother's grave. Jim sat facing the window, his eyes narrowed, as he watched Thomas and Rachael by the pond deeply engrossed in conversation.

"I noticed you have some new help around here. Where did you find them?" He motioned with one finger towards the pond.

"Charlie found them at the unemployment office. They all seemed kind of desperate and God only knows we sure can use some help around here."

"They don't seem very friendly, do they?" Jim alleged, nodding his head towards the pond. "I hope you don't have the same amount of trouble getting rid of them when harvest is finished as you had last year. That leech you hired thought he was going to settle here permanently."

"Charlie knows how to handle their kind," I said, placing a large piece of cake in front of him. Changing the subject, we chatted aimlessly while Jim polished off the huge piece of apple crumb cake he liked so much.

Slowly rising to his feet, he stretched while patting his stomach. "You're a good cook, Beth. I'll try to visit a little more often."

"You can come anytime. You know you're always welcome."

"I know," he replied with a grin before giving my shoulder a brief squeeze.

"I'll say goodbye to Charlie on my way out. This won't be easy for him to come to terms with. I just want him to know that I'll always be there for him."

As I gave Jim a wave goodbye through the kitchen window, a queer feeling came over me. I had the unsettled feeling there would be more heartache to come before the summer was finished. Pushing the thought aside, I turned the tap, filling the sink with water where I placed Jim's dishes.

CHAPTER FIVE

The following day the rain that had been oppressing us subsided, leaving a shroud of mist over everything it touched and giving it a silvery sheen that sparkled and shone in the morning sunshine. The heavy mood surrounding us abated, taking flight like the small flocks of yellow canaries bathing in the puddles. Amy seemed the most affected by this change. She seemed to have accepted her situation with a calmness that became her. She would spend hour upon hour after dinner sitting beside the pond watching the geese show off their goslings to her. I could see her now, comfortably relaxing against a large rock. Picking my way down the path, I decided to join her in the hopes of finding out what her next move was concerning the baby. She never glanced up, choosing not to acknowledge my presence.

Her next words seemed out of context. "They know who their mommy is," she said, nodding towards the goslings swimming silently behind their mothers. I waited while she seemed to struggle with her next words.

"You know, don't you?"

"Yes. Do you know what you're going to do?"

"What do you mean?" she asked, looking up at me in surprise.

"Are you going to keep it?"

She turned towards me, her jaw dropping in astonishment at the idea. Her eyes never wavering, she regarded me steadily. A look of disgust became mapped on her face and she snapped, "Yes, of course. Why wouldn't I?"

"Hold it!" I cried, holding my hands up defensively. "I'm not the bad guy here. I'm only trying to help."

The fire seemed to go out of her while she considered this. "I'm sorry. I guess I'm a little edgy."

"Vince is the father, I'm presuming?"

"Yes, of course!" she replied frostily.

"What about your family?" I asked, raising my eyebrows slightly.

"They all died in a house fire. I've been raised in foster homes since I was four."

"I'm sorry," I mumbled, looking at her with sympathy.

"Don't be. It was a long time ago and I barely remember them. Anyways, I kind of like it here and would like to stay for a while. That is—if, it's alright with you and Charlie."

"Sure, that's fine with me. If that's what you want."

"What about Charlie? Do you think he will mind?" she asked, chewing her bottom lip.

"I know he won't mind. It's settled then. You'll stay until after the baby is born," I said, giving her my biggest smile.

"Yes, I'll stay," she said. She slowly, closed her eyes as if dismissing me from her thoughts.

★★★

Amy's Story

I like it here. It's so peaceful. I'm glad Vince stayed with me after I found out I was pregnant. He could have left, but he didn't. I knew if I stayed in that foster home they would have taken the baby away from me, being under age and all. Vince never should have asked his dad for help. It was bad enough that his dad told him, "I have enough mouths to feed. Now it's your turn. Get out and don't come back! I have enough troubles without you adding to it." He didn't have to break Vince's nose when he disagreed with him.

It wasn't too bad living in Vince's friend's basement. I thought things might work out until Vince got laid off his job. Not that it was much of a job; cleaning floors at the store. Then that stupid Luke had to come onto me. That really made Vince mad. We couldn't stay there after that. There was no way I was going back to that foster home, though. I heard they were still looking for me. Things sure seemed to get a lot worse after that. It was really cold sleeping in that abandoned building by the tracks. We just couldn't find a place to stay.

God, there wasn't anything on that bulletin board at the unemployment place either. We were so lucky we overheard Charlie talking to those other two about work. I'm really glad he agreed to give us a job in exchange for room and board. I wasn't looking forward to going back to that creepy building for another night. Vince told me that if he works really hard Charlie might keep him on steady. He's working so hard now, I hardly ever see him until bedtime. I'm glad Beth knows about the baby and told me it was fine and that we didn't have to leave, even though I won't be much help. She seems like such a nice lady. I wonder what they will say when they find out I'm more than six and a half months pregnant now. I'm lucky I don't really show that much, as we can't afford to buy maternity clothes for me. Not that I need them here. Oh well, at least we have a warm place to sleep and three meals a day. Maybe our luck is finally changing for the better.

★★★

That night Charlie and I chatted casually about each other's day while we readied for bed. "I sure hope we have a better crop than last year," Charlie said, tossing his shoe in a graceful arc to land beside where the other one lay.

"I'm sure we will. Everything looks good so far."

"I don't know. The cost of planting has really risen this year. It's going to make things a lot tighter than I thought."

"I have a feeling things are going to work out just fine. It looks more promising than last year," I said, giving him an encouraging smile.

Charlie sat studying his hands with a bleak look on his face before he whispered, "Beth, there's something I think you should know. I got a call from the bank today. They wanted to warn me that I was close to going over the limit on our operating loan. Last year was bad enough. This time they said they will foreclose on us if we're not careful."

"We just have to make sure we don't go over the limit. Everything worked out last year and this year we have more help. We just have to be extra careful until we get this crop off."

"I don't think you realize how bad it is, Beth. I can't lose this farm. I've put too much of my time into it already. I'm too old to start over doing something else. This was my grandparent's farm for God's sake. I will not lose it!" Charlie balled up his socks and tossed them into the corner of the room with a vengeance.

"We won't. I know you; I have faith in you," I cried, placing my hands on each of his cheeks to stare him in the eye confidently.

"Well, I hope I can live up to your expectations then," Charlie replied wistfully.

I tactfully changed the subject to inform Charlie about my conversation with Amy. "I think it's a good idea for her to stay until after the baby is born."

"Now Beth, don't you go getting any ideas about us raising that baby," Charlie said, shaking his head negatively.

"Why shouldn't I? I could look after it. Amy sure won't be able to," I fumed, crossing my arms in front of me.

"Give your head a shake. You have a hard enough time getting around as it is. What makes you think you can look after a baby on your own? What about Amy? I'm sure she's not going to just hand over her baby to you. Is she?"

"I'm not as frail as you think, Charlie Sanders! I could manage quite well. It's only the stairs that would give me a hard time and I think I found a solution to that problem. We could change the sun room into a bedroom for us. That way I could look after the baby on my own. What do you think? It would make it easier for me. I've always hated climbing all those steps anyways." I looked at Charlie eagerly waiting for his reply.

I could see his resolve melting while he watched me sitting on the edge of the bed, waiting with bated breath for his answer. Tilting his head to the side with that quizzical little smile I had come to know so well, he finally chuckled. "It looks like you have this all thought out," he said, his blue eyes crinkling with amusement as he patted the bed beside him.

"Not everything, but I'm working on it," I smiled before crossing the room to slide under the covers.

Charlie threw up his hands as if in surrender. "Alright, I'll think about making the sun room over, but don't get your hopes up too high about this baby thing. I don't think Amy will give up her baby very easily. I just don't want to see you get your hopes built up and then have everything come crashing down, sugar."

Charlie was right. I had pinned my hopes high on being a mother and now I was determined to have my dream become a reality. I wondered how much of a fight Amy would put up. Maybe none at all, I told myself with conviction. She could hardly look after herself, let alone a baby. I was sure she would be sensible enough to realize I was right. I finally conceded to sleep, a smile plastered on my face, as I saw a glimmer of my dream becoming a reality.

The next morning I sipped my morning cup of coffee as I carefully watched Vince and Amy. I was curious to see how close they really were, but found I could deduce nothing in my observation. I was not going to let my dream slip through my fingers that easily, so turning in my seat towards Charlie I asked, "Charlie, when can you start to work on changing the sun room over for me?"

Charlie, who had been staring absent mindedly at his plate, jerked his head up to give me a guarded look. Heeding his warning, I lowered my eyes. I wondered if maybe I was pushing things a little too fast.

I was relieved after a moment of silence when he answered, "You will have to wait until we have the calves all tagged and inoculated. I won't have time until then."

I would have to be content with that, I surmised. I should have known that just like his chess games, Charlie never made a move until it was all thought through first. I was just too impatient for my own good.

I watched Charlie spreading strawberry jam on his toast. He seemed to be in a thoughtful mood. Silently watching him, I wondered if it was my startling proposition that had him deep in thought. What was troubling him that left him in this semi-repressed mood? If I hadn't been watching so closely, I would have missed the secret smile he exchanged with Rachael. I felt sick with the realization that I had seen that smile before. I knew only too well what was behind it. I would need to get my head out of the clouds. Rachael was one enemy that would be a challenge to beat, but I was stronger than they all realized. There was more to me than anyone knew.

"What are your plans for the day, Charlie?" I asked for the second time.

"I told you before. I'm inoculating the cattle today," he snapped, avoiding my eyes.

"I know that! I just forgot for a moment. It won't take me long to get ready.

Hesitating slightly, he answered, "No, I think Rachael should be able to handle filling the syringes. You can take a break from it this year."

No way was I going to let that hussy spend the whole day with my husband! Giving Charlie my biggest smile, I offered a list of excuses of why that was not going to work.

"Charlie, the garden really needs to be weeded. You know how difficult it is for me to bend over. Rachael will be able to do it much easier than I can, so she will have to stay home to do it. I'm sure sitting upon a stool and filling syringes will be much easier for me," I said, smiling sweetly.

Charlie sat for a few moments contemplating what I said before finally nodding. "Alright, but we're leaving right after breakfast so make sure you're ready."

I glanced over at Rachael to be met back with such an icy glare that I thought I might be frozen to my chair. She was itching to say something, but I never gave her the chance. I promptly informed her when she was done in the garden, she could help Amy with the cooking.

Rachael's, "Yes, Boss!" was so sarcastic that even Charlie turned sharply to remind her in no uncertain terms, that yes, I was the boss; that things were to be done the way I instructed. Thomas sat silently watching this play of words with a sly grin on his face.

I quickly made sure I was ready and waiting so as not to give Charlie any reason to substitute Rachael for me. The morning air shimmered with a promise of heat to come that would soon turn all of us into limp noodles before the day was finished. For now I was content to watch

Charlie get things ready to go. Hoisting me up on to the seat of the pickup, he leaned down to whisper into my ear, "Well played, darling."

I smiled slightly. "Yes, maybe it was," I thought, settling back in my seat.

Chapter Six

"You should be out of the way here," Charlie said, patting the pail he had placed upside down for me.

I waited impatiently for my job to start while the men jogged back and forth in a variety of patterns, separating the cows from the calves. It made me weary just watching them.

"This is a waste of time. I can't see why you have to give them all a shot, anyways," Thomas whined, a disgusted look on his face.

"I told you before; they could end up with a disease if I don't inoculate them. It could wipe out the whole herd. Jeez! What part of that don't you understand?" Charlie shook his head in disgust.

I could see Charlie was becoming impatient with Thomas. All morning, Thomas had ignored Charlie's hand signals, allowing one or two animals to slip by him. He couldn't have cared less if they had to start all over again to re-pen them. This was a dangerous job, as each cow had the potential to inflict serious damage to anyone who separated them from their calves. They were now cranky and the din was deafening from their continuous bawling as they jogged back and forth inside the pens.

They finally had all the cattle corralled separately when all hell broke loose. Roscoe the bull was an ornery old cuss who needed to be watched carefully. He never gave much warning before he would charge. I had begged Charlie to get rid of him, for I knew he wasn't safe to have around, but Charlie insisted that he stay. He alleged that old Roscoe's blood line led the best calves he ever seen and the extra price per pound made up for his mean temperament. Charlie had warned Thomas and Vince about Roscoe on more than one occasion. The last thing you needed was two thousand pounds of ornery flesh grinding you into the ground with that massive head of his. We had learned to treat him with a healthy respect.

I never saw who opened the gate to let Roscoe loose. There was no way it could come open on its own, as it was double latched for safety. I turned suddenly at the sound of Roscoe's snort. His massive head was lowered to charge. His hoofs tore out great clods of earth while he pawed the ground to toss it over his shoulder.

"Charlie, Roscoe—," I screamed out in a warning. I could do nothing except watch in horror as Roscoe charged towards Charlie with a bellow. Charlie barely had time to roll under the fence. Roscoe, a few seconds behind him, slammed into that fence like a freight train against a cement wall. The fence groaned under the impact, but held fast. My warning had granted Charlie the few seconds he had needed to save his life. If Charlie had been any slower, old Roscoe would have ground him into mincemeat.

Vince was shaking so hard I thought he might faint. His face slowly turned a pasty white while he stared in horror at Charlie. Thomas, on the other hand, shrugged his shoulders nonchalantly and with a subtle grin continued to light his cigarette.

"Who the hell opened that gate?" Charlie demanded, turning to encompass Thomas and Vince in his vision. His face changed from a deathly white to red. Thomas and Vince turned away from Charlie's glare, neither one willing to admit to doing the foul deed. This only made Charlie angrier. His whole body shook with rage, his fists clenched tightly at his sides as he waited. "When I find out which of you unlatched that gate, you'll wish you hadn't been born," he spat, giving them each the evil eye. No one stepped forward to shoulder the blame, so Charlie knew he was beat. Cursing a blue streak, he spun on his heel to storm a short distance away. I could see him trying to master his anger. With a shake of his head he turned and stomped back towards the two candidates responsible for the wrong doing. Both simply stood with their eyes downcast. "Get back to work!" Charlie spat, glaring at them with disgust.

At least they were wise enough not to respond with a wise crack. Charlie trembled with the effort to keep his rage in check. Once Roscoe was re-penned the work progressed at a steady rate. Although, I noticed Charlie wasn't taking any more chances and he watched both Thomas and Vince more closely. From the corner of my eye I caught Thomas's face reflecting a smug grin that replaced his normal dour look. Thomas would have to be watched closely or someone could be seriously injured, I predicted.

That night Rachael was in a foul mood at being thwarted in her attempt to spend the whole day with Charlie. She declared open warfare where Charlie was concerned. She made no bones about showing her attraction to him.

"I missed you, Charlie," she said, laying her hand on his knee. "I'm sure that I could have been more help to you than Beth, in her condition and all," she said, smiling sweetly at me.

"What do you mean my condition?" I snapped, glaring at her hand on Charlie's knee. Before she had a chance to answer, I added, "And you can get your hand off my husband's knee."

There it was again, that silly giggle I was becoming to hate more and more.

"Aw, Beth, I was only teasing," she said, the tinkle of her laughter following behind her as she rose to go up the stairs.

Charlie took one look at my face before making a hasty exit, announcing over his shoulder that he had forgot something in the shop.

After that Rachael would follow Charlie shamelessly, that silly giggle never far from her lips. He seemed to regard her with indifference whenever I was around, but I sometimes caught his eyes following her with a silent scrutiny when he thought no one was watching.

What was there about his relationship with Rachael that made him suddenly divert his eyes at being caught in this indiscretion? If Rachael thought Charlie was the boss and she only had to answer to him, she was dead wrong! I didn't need to put up with the likes of her. She was easily replaced. She might find out quicker than she wanted too which way the land lay. There was no use mentioning anything to Charlie anymore, as he would only roll his eyes skyward and walk away. I was on my own where Rachael was concerned. She better wise up or she would have to go, I decided, watching her lay her hand on Charlie's shoulder as she passed him. Vince and Amy deemed it wiser to stay out of everyone's way these days and would retire to the attic at the first opportunity.

CHAPTER SEVEN

I waited patiently for the time to be just right before approaching Amy about the baby. Tonight was the time, I decided, watching out the window while Amy carefully wound her way down the worn path towards the edge of the pond. The pond seemed to have a calming effect on her and she would sit for hours watching the geese caring for their young. She soon settled down in her favourite spot to observe the young goslings chasing after their mother with reckless abandon. They took no notice of her anymore. Sometimes they would venture to the edge of the pond, craning their skinny little necks to gaze at Amy with small, black eyes filled with curiosity. The mother geese would then tentatively venture close enough to herd their stray brood back a safe distance from the human form sprawled along the pond's edge. There Amy sat, reclining against a huge rock, jutting its way out of the earth to provide a perfect back rest. Her legs stretched out in front of her while her long, black hair swayed in the gentle breeze. I slowly wound my way down the trail to the pond's edge. Amy never spoke a word to acknowledge my presence when I sat down beside her. Her gaze never wavered from the panoramic scene that was set before her. I couldn't blame her, as I watched the geese barely making a ripple, silently glide through the water. The sun was just starting to set and the red glow cast its reflection upon the water to be tossed back, creating a back drop of red and gold that was breath taking to view. I was reluctant to break the magical spell that Mother Nature, in all her glory, had seen fit to spread before us. I had seen this same scene many times over the years and yet I never failed to marvel at the beauty of it.

It was Amy who finally broke the silence. "It's so peaceful here," she said, without acknowledging my presence. "It will be hard for me to leave."

"Are you planning to leave?" I asked calmly, while my heart quickened at the thought.

"No! Not for a while," she said giving me a puzzled look, noticing the tone of my voice. "I would like to stay until after the baby is born. That is, if it's alright with you."

"Yes, of course," I answered, trying not to show on my face the instant relief that flooded through me at her words.

"How far along are you?"

"I'm not sure. I think I must be close to seven months now," she volunteered, giving me a sideward glance.

"Do you mean to tell me you haven't been to a doctor yet?" I choked out, starring at her swollen abdomen.

Amy's face flushed a deep rose. "No, I didn't think it was that important," she replied, twisting her fingers together in a gesture of embarrassment.

"I'm sorry. I didn't mean to sound like I was scolding you. It's just that I'm worried about you and the baby's health. It's extremely important that a doctor check you and the baby to make sure everything is alright. I don't want to scare you, but sometimes things don't work out the way we plan. I know only too well how things can go wrong when you least expect it. I always wanted children, you know. I made it to my sixth month with my first two pregnancies, five with the third, and seven with the last one." My voice cracked slightly with the last admission.

"Oh! I'm sorry. I just thought maybe you didn't want children," she said, scanning my face with sympathy, apparently seeing me in a different light.

"No, I always wanted children. I guess it wasn't meant to be for Charlie and me," I said, turning to watch the goslings in their play.

"Amy, I have a very good doctor. If you would like to see him, I can arrange it. Lyle Porter is the best doctor for miles around, and the kindest man I know. Would you like me to call him?"

Amy never answered me as she turned away anxiously at the sound of gravel being crushed underfoot. I turned also, aware of a man walking slowly down the path towards us. Shading my eyes from the setting sun, I was surprised to find Lyle shuffling down the path to greet us. It was as if I conjured him up just by asking Amy if she would like to see him. Amy gasped, her eyes darting frantically from side to side, searching for a place to hide. Realizing there wasn't any apparent avenue to escape, she turned to endure my hastily proffered introduction.

"Hi," she whispered shyly.

"Hello, Amy. It's a pleasure to meet you," Lyle responded, offering his hand for a quick shake. Then turning towards me, his eyes searched me from head to toe.

"It looks like you're improving more every time I see you. I haven't seen you for a while, so I thought I'd better come out and check on you. Besides, that offer of a piece of your famous apple crumb cake the next time I was in the area is pretty hard to resist," Lyle chuckled, giving me a huge grin.

I laughed. I reached out to take Lyle's arm while we retreated back up the path toward the house and the promise of apple crumb cake. Amy took up the rear, following along behind us while listening to Lyle and I exchange accounts of all that happened since we last spoke with one another.

Lyle never seemed to change. He was still that professional doctor wrapped up in a little boy suit. Over the years fate had thrown Lyle and me together on quite a few occasions. When I had lost my last baby, it was Lyle that sat beside me holding my hand while my heart broke. It was Lyle who gently wiped the tears from my face and encouraged me to continue with life. Lyle had become more than just a doctor to me. He had become a very dear friend. Now I sat fondly watching Lyle polish off his second piece of cake with such gusto it would have made any baker proud. He wasn't a big man, but one could see he had a fondness for sweets. It showed in his pudgy cheeks and rounded waist line. One look in those big brown eyes peering out from beneath the mass of chocolate curls, streaked with silver, and you knew you would be cared for to the best of his ability.

"Well, missy. I see we are to have a new arrival. When are you due?"

"I'm not sure," Amy replied, shaking her head.

"Did your doctor not give you a due date?" Lyle asked while his fingers tapped a faint tune on the table.

"I don't have a doctor yet. Beth mentioned you might take me on as a patient.

"I think I could arrange that," Lyle said, glancing curiously at me.

"I would like that, but I have to warn you: I haven't any money to pay you," Amy admitted, smiling shyly at Lyle.

"How about, we worry about you and the baby first. I'm sure that we can work out some form of payment later.

"Okay, if that's what you think is best," Amy replied, tipping her head to one side smiling.

"Beth, could you have Charlie bring her in to the clinic tomorrow?"

Amy quickly rose to face Lyle, her bottom lip captured firmly between her teeth. "No! I don't want to go to town. Can't you come here to see me?"

Lyle, clearly confused, glanced at me quickly while one eyebrow rose in an arc.

"Amy's shy," I whispered, not quite meeting Lyle's eyes. Amy's look of gratitude was worth the white lie. I guiltily looked away under Lyle's careful scrutiny, glad he had taken me at my word by not pressing the issue any farther.

"Alright, I'll be out tomorrow after clinic hours. We'll see you then, Amy."

"Thanks, Lyle. I knew I could count on you," I whispered, placing my hand on his arm to give it a tiny squeeze.

"No problem. We'll talk later," he said, giving my hand a gentle squeeze.

Well, that's one problem less I have to deal with, I thought while closing the door behind Lyle. Now all I had to do was convince Amy to hand over the baby to me voluntarily. That would be my next job.

CHAPTER EIGHT

The next morning we awoke to a grey dismal sky. The dark leaden clouds obscuring the sun, promised rain before the day was finished. Over breakfast I again approached the subject of changing the sun room into a bed room.

"Are you sure that's what you really want?" Charlie asked, his eyes lingering on my face.

"Yes, I haven't changed my mind," I said, raising my chin to look him in the eye.

His gaze softened at the determination displayed on my face. "Alright, you win. I hope you won't be sorry though," he declared, shaking his head in defeat.

I reached out to gently brush the shock of hair back that had fallen to partially cover his eyes. "Never," I whispered, giving his hand a gentle squeeze.

"Alright, then it's settled. I'll take a look at it this morning, but if it's too costly, you can forget it. You will have to make do with the upstairs bedroom."

Thomas, who had just entered the room, upon hearing there was going to be more work involved sneered, "I'm no carpenter. Don't expect me to help!"

Charlie swiveled in his chair to glare at Thomas before snapping, "I'm not either, but sometimes we have to do a thing that goes against the grain of who we are. And you will learn to do whatever that is needed to get by. Do I make myself clear?"

Thomas's eyes locked with Charlie's. He had a pained expression on his face but nodded his head in agreement, although his fists remained locked in a ball by his sides. Charlie's eyes remained glued on Thomas's face as he rose. Then he swiftly turned to stride from the room without a backwards glance, leaving Thomas staring after him. It wasn't too long before Charlie was back to inform me that it wouldn't take much for the changeover and they would start right away.

"I guess I'll go to town this morning for supplies. We can't do anything outside in this weather today. Do you need anything from town, Beth?"

"No, I guess not. Are you taking Vince or Thomas with you?"

"No, they can do some prep work before I get back," Charlie said, glancing up with a smile as Rachael waltzed into the room to pour herself a cup of coffee.

"I'll go with you, Charlie. I wouldn't mind going along to give you a hand. I'm sure I could be a big help to you," she purred sweetly before turning to flash me a smug grin.

"No, you are going to stay here and help me this morning," I declared, glaring at her.

"Charlie, you don't mind if I tag along with you for the ride, do you? I can help Beth later," Rachael stated, her lips forming a tiny pout while she batted her long lashes at him.

One look at my face was all Charlie needed to quickly turn down her offer and make a hasty escape. That done it! I would have that talk with Rachael; I had been putting off. I would not put up with her foolishness any longer! Fuming silently, I stormed towards the sun room where I found Charlie instructing Thomas and Vince as to what needed to be done in his absence.

"I'll be back as quick as I can," Charlie stated over his shoulder as he left.

Rachael, upon realizing that Charlie was not going to accept her offer, promptly turned to bustle from the room. Fine, I thought, watching her back retreating around the corner. I would deal with her later, I promised, watching Charlie drive out of the yard.

The clouds by this time had decided to release their burden and it had settled into a steady drizzle. Fuming silently, I realized that I needed to cool my temper. What better place than to calm my frazzled nerves than my favourite spot: the barn. Donning my old slicker, I stepped off the porch to brave the cold drizzle which slid down the collar of my rain coat and seeped down my neck to form a damp ring around my collar. Still, I never hurried. I had always loved walking in the rain. I opened the barn door to slide inside. Charlie had opened a fresh bale of hay, which beckoned to me with its heady aroma. I had always loved the sounds and smells associated with the barn. Even as a small child it seemed to have a calming effect on me. I lay back in the mound of softness with a sigh, its smell now enveloping me. The steady drone of the rain beating its frenzied tempo on the roof urged my body to slowly relax. I had drifted off to sleep on more than one occasion listening to the soothing sound of nature at its finest. A sigh escaping my lips; I curled up contentedly to let Mother Nature use her calming effect to sooth my ruffled feathers. Just as she promised, I soon found myself drifting off to sleep. This time my dreams were of holding a baby in my arms.

I awoke with a start. How long had I slept? I cursed silently, glancing at my empty wrist. I had no way of knowing. The rain pounding on the roof had increased its tempo to a steady drone. I made my way to the door to bravely push it open, only to encounter a sheet of icy, cold rain whipping me in the face. Peering through the grey curtain, I spied Charlie's truck parked at the front of the house. I had slept longer than planned. Buttoning my slicker, I stepped out into the sheet of rain to make my way through the rivets of water criss-crossing at my feet towards the house. I was glad I had chosen to squelch my temper in the solitude of the barn, for the nap had done me wonders. Scurrying up the veranda, I pushed open the door to be met with five pairs of accusing eyes. Charlie stood beside the sofa applying a cold cloth to Rachael's temple, who whimpered slightly as she clasped his hand.

"What the hell is going on here, Beth? Why did you hit her with your cane?" he demanded crossly.

"She could have killed me," Rachael sobbed, into the cold compress while her hand tightened its grip on Charlie's.

I stood there with my mouth hanging open, too stunned to acknowledge the accusations brought forth against me. "I don't know what you're talking about. I never touched her," I finally managed to stammer.

"It sure doesn't look like I," Charlie replied sarcastically, while giving Rachael a lingering look of sympathy. The fury depicted on my face was enough for Rachael to decide she should make herself scarce.

"I have a headache. I'm going to my room to lie down," she whined, sliding off the sofa to hurriedly leave the room.

Vince opened his mouth to speak, only to close it again. Clasping Amy's hand, they turned away to vanish into the kitchen. Apparently no one was going to stick up for me, I thought. Charlie still stood watching me with a pained expression on his face. That did it, I thought, storming to stand in front of him.

"Charlie Sanders, you know better than to believe this rubbish," I fairly screamed at him.

"Wait a minute. I never said you did it. I just want to get to the bottom of this, that's all," Charlie answered, not quite meeting my eyes.

"I can tell you what's at the bottom of this right now," I announced, tapping Charlie on the chest with one finger. "I have been trying to tell you for quite some time, but you just ignored me. Now we have this mess to contend with and I won't be blamed for something I never done! I want her gone from this house today," I instructed him, banging my cane on the floor.

"Alright, I'll go talk to her right now," he sighed, turning towards the stairs.

So much for my refreshing little nap, I thought before turning to storm into the kitchen. Amy and Vince were seated at the table, heads bent together whispering quietly. One look at my face was enough to make them both scurry from the room for safer quarters.

"Hey, I'm not mad at you guys. You don't have to leave," I called after their retreating forms.

The silence that ensued attested to how much they believed me. I sat sipping my tea, waiting for Charlie to return. Tea was supposed have a calming effect I had heard once. So far it wasn't working, I decided, as my temper blossomed anew. What was Rachael trying to prove with her dramatic acting? How did she get the wound on her head? I sure couldn't remember doing it. I wouldn't put it past her to hit her own self, I thought uncharitably. I was shocked that she would resort to such drastic measures to win Charlie's affections. Apparently I had been wrong. She would stop at nothing to achieve her goal. What she didn't realize was— it would take a lot more than her dramatic acting to turn Charlie against me. Charlie and I had been through a lot together. This was just another bump in the road for us to get over. Although, I found a tiny bit of niggling doubt gradually creep back into my mind. Charlie had jumped to her defence too quickly. Was I missing something? What was going on? Had I placed too much trust in Charlie? No, Rachael was the problem here. The sooner she was gone, the better!

It seemed like an eternity before Charlie finally rounded the corner into the kitchen. "Where is everyone?" he asked, sweeping the kitchen with one look.

"I'm not sure. They won't be too far away," I replied with a shrug. My feelings still smarted at not being believed.

"Well, did you talk to her?" I demanded sharply.

"Yes, but I'm sure you're not going to like what I have to say," Charlie said, before turning to look out the kitchen window.

"Rachael maintains that you hit her with your cane when you put your slicker on to leave the house. She realizes now it must have been an accident. She said, she is really sorry that she caused so much trouble," Charlie explained, not quite meeting my eyes.

I couldn't believe what I had just heard. "You don't believe that garbage, do you?" I exploded, shaking my head in disbelief.

Charlie tilted his head to study my face before replying with a shrug, "Now Beth, it could have happened like she explained. She says you're not treating her very nice since you found out about Amy's baby and she was only trying to get your attention. She really likes you and misses your chats."

"She sure has you fooled, if you would buy that load of crap," I snapped, glaring at him with a look of disgust. Charlie, knowing fully well what I would think of his next remark, avoided meeting my eyes while he shuffled nervously from one foot to the other.

Staring self-consciously at his feet, he hesitantly informed me of the outcome of their little talk. "I told her she could stay. Now hold on. Let me finish," he stated upon hearing my sudden intake of breath.

"I also told her that she will have to toe the line from now on."

"You have to be kidding! Not on your life!" I declared sourly, sloshing the tea from my cup while I pushed it aside in haste.

"Now Beth, be reasonable and think this through. I understand how you feel right now, but think about it. Rachael will come in handy when Amy has the baby. It will give you more time to spend taking care of it while Rachael does the work around here," Charlie claimed, watching my face eagerly for my answer.

I sat thinking about all the reasons I should keep Rachael on and all the reasons she should go. I grudgingly realized Charlie might be right. I would just have to watch her more carefully from now on. But when harvest was finished, she was gone.

Reluctantly I agreed. "Alright, she can stay, but she better not attempt any more tricks. And, for future reference Charlie, remember I'm your wife. You should believe me first. Not that harlot that drips lies from her tongue like honey.

Charlie hung his head. He at least had the good grace to look ashamed before whispering, "I'm sorry. It won't happen again."

Somewhere in the back of my mind the thought haunted me: there was more to this than met the eye. No, I would not entertain the thought that Charlie could betray me, again. He had promised, hadn't he? He wouldn't go back on his word, would he? The thread of doubt slowly began to wind its way into a huge ball as I continued to watch his back hurrying away from me.

Chapter Nine

Hearing a sound, I turned to see Rachael winding her way down the stairs. Upon seeing me watching her, she did an about face and scurried back up the stairs. "I still have a headache. I'm going to lie down," she said.

Good, I thought watching her disappear from sight. The more she kept out of my sight, the better. The men worked steadily all day making the changes to the sunroom while I busied myself by making Charlie's favorite dessert, rhubarb crisp. I was just taking it from the oven when Lyle sauntered into the kitchen.

"Hello," he said cheerfully. "I knocked, but I guess you never heard me," he said, sniffing the air. "Mm—something sure smells good in here. It looks like I timed it just right," he chuckled, pulling out a chair to straddle it backwards.

"You certainly did," I said, setting a huge bowl of pudding in front of him.

"Where is Amy?" Lyle asked, smiling at the bowl.

"I'm not sure. She can't be too far. I'll go and find her for you."

"Where's Charlie?" I asked Thomas and Vince, who were busy tacking on new trim around the door. They shrugged their shoulders in unison while their eyes remained fixed on their task. Glancing out the window, I was just in time to see Rachael emerge from the barn, scurrying through the rain towards the house, her rain coat flying open in the wind. I thought she had gone upstairs! What was she doing in the barn? A moment later, Charlie emerged from the barn with a slight smile on his face. I would get to the bottom of this tonight, I resolved, my temper started to fume anew. Charlie would have some explaining do.

"Amy, Lyle would like to see you in the kitchen," I said, motioning for her to follow me. "Here she is," I said to Lyle, upon entering the kitchen with Amy in tow.

Lyle looked up with a smile to greet us. "There you are Amy. I'm glad you weren't here when I arrived. It gave me time to sample Beth's cooking," he chuckled, looking down at his empty bowl.

"Beth, you are a fantastic cook. Charlie must be one happy man. He's lucky he found you first or I would have snapped you up in a second," he said, snapping his fingers. "No wonder I never found the right girl, she was already taken," Lyle said with a slight chuckle.

"I don't think Charlie would agree with you right now," I whispered, sadly looking out the window towards the barn.

Amy and Lyle both turned to stare at me. Their eyebrows arched while they waited for me to explain. I remained silent, still staring towards the barn.

"Beth, care to talk about it?" Lyle asked, patting my hand.

"No, I don't think so, but thanks for the offer," I said with a slight shake of my head.

"Alright, but anytime you need a friendly ear, just call," he said with a slight grin.

"I'm just feeling a little down right now," I admitted, squeezing his hand. "It's Amy that needs your help," I said, changing the subject tactfully. Lyle's thoughtful gaze followed me across the room where I had gone to stare out the window.

"Yes, you're right. Do you mind if I use your room to examine her?"

"No, go right ahead. I'll be up in a minute," I said, picking up Lyle's empty bowl to deposit it into the sink. A huge sigh escaped me. I turned quickly to find Rachael waltzing into the kitchen with a Cheshire grin plastered on her face. The question popped out of my mouth before I had time to think about it.

"What were you doing in the barn? I demanded sharply, noting her dishevelled appearance.

"I was just thanking Charlie for keeping me on," Rachael said, while a grin twisted the corners of her mouth.

I'll just bet, I thought, eyeing her with disgust. "I think you better thank me instead for allowing you to stay. Your headache must have disappeared quickly," I snapped waspishly, before turning to leave the room. I'll keep you so busy you won't have time to think, let alone thank Charlie for anything. I vowed silently to myself.

I met Lyle coming down the stairs with Amy wearing a huge grin, hot on his heels.

"Lyle says I'm healthy as an ox and the baby is fine and I'm going to have it sooner than I thought," she gushed, grabbing my hand in her excitement.

I couldn't help smiling at her exuberant mood. "Well, when is sooner?"

"Three weeks to a month," she announced, turning to Lyle for conformation.

"Is that right, Doc?" I asked, raising one eyebrow in surprise.

"Yes, I would be surprised if she makes a month," Lyle said, eying Amy's swollen abdomen.

"That brings me to the next thing I wanted to talk to you about, Amy. Where do you want to deliver the baby? We have a very good hospital about eighty miles from here. If you want I can set up a tour of the facility right away."

Amy's face reflected a look of panic at Lyle's suggestion.

"No, why can't I have it here? I heard more women are having their baby's at home than ever before. I want to have my baby here," she stated determinedly.

"You could, but this is your first pregnancy and you won't have the same options as in a hospital," Lyle said, a slight frown replacing his usual smile.

"I know, but I still want to have my baby at home. You said I was healthy and the baby was fine," Amy pointed out, tapping the table as if to prove her point.

Lyle could not argue with his own diagnosis. He had no option other than to give in to Amy's demand.

"Alright, I'll make sure you get some information on home deliveries, but I really want you to think about this. It's not a decision to make lightly.

"Alright, but you won't change my mind," she said with a tiny grin.

"I'll see you in a week, Amy. Beth, I want you to remember, I'm always here for you. Anytime you want to get a load off your shoulders, just whistle," Lyle said, giving my shoulder an affectionate squeeze.

"Lyle, you've been my rock on more than one occasion, but this is something I have to handle on my own," I whispered, patting his cheek with affection.

"Alright, but remember the offer still stands, any time you're ready," Lyle said with a smile before closing the door after himself.

The meal that night was a quiet affair. Everyone seemed lost in their own thoughts. I would catch Vince and Amy darting furtive little glances towards Rachael, Charlie, and myself. They were probably wondering what was going to happen between Rachael and I. Rachael remained silent throughout the meal, eating with her eyes downcast. After the meal, everyone scattered to their own prospective hideaways. Charlie and I were left to sort out exactly what was to be done with Rachael.

"I know you think Rachael should be allowed to stay, but I don't. I want her gone from here immediately. She's nothing but trouble!" I spat, looking him straight in the eye.

"She's really got to you. Hasn't she? You should know by now that you're my favourite girl. Nobody can take your place," he said with a slight grin.

"What were you and Rachael doing in the barn today?" I snapped. Charlie turned away hastily to fill his water glass, not responding to my question. "Well?" I demanded, my voice rising in agitation.

"She just wanted to thank me for letting her stay," he said calmly before taking another sip of water. Turning towards me he declared, "Rachael means nothing to me."

I watched Charlie's eyes for some glimmer of the truth behind this declaration, only to find no proof, one way or another. I would have to give him the benefit of the doubt. Although, no one was going to play me for a fool, I silently vowed. I would grant her the privilege of staying for a while longer. Although, I also vowed to keep her so busy she would not have any spare time on her hands to make further trouble. Charlie had made a good argument for her case. Harvest would be here soon. We would need all the help we could muster to get the grain in the bins before freeze up. He assured me when harvest was complete, Rachael would be gone. Until then, I would just have to keep the green-eyed monster corralled.

Charlie was shocked to find Amy was in the last stages of her pregnancy. My bedroom was finished, Charlie announced that evening. I was delighted at the results they had accomplished in such a short period of time, even to the painting of it: a lovely shade of sunshine yellow. I could hardly wait to relocate our old bedroom furnishings to this bright and airy space. The sooner the better, I thought, picturing a bassinet occupying one corner.

The next morning we awoke to a beautiful sunny day. It was one of those rare mornings you wish would never end; the air crisp and clean after the previous day's rain. The sky was a brilliant blue with fluffy wisps of snow white clouds scattered throughout. The previous day's rain had cleansed our surroundings to a brighter shade of color. This cleansing had spilled over to include the inhabitants of the house. All seemed to be in an amiable mood and treated each other accordingly. Amy chattered happily away, to the point of no one being able to get a word in edge wise. A mood so new to her we all sat in awe. Her infectious mood even had Thomas smile at one of her childish remarks. Vince, on the other hand, remained his usual quiet self.

"Beth, it's too wet this morning to cut hay, so we will be moving your bedroom furniture down here this morning," Charlie announced with a smile.

Good, I thought, everything was starting to come together. Soon, I would have everything I had always wanted. After breakfast everyone scurried to do Charlie's bidding. The men filled the sun room with piece after piece of furniture, positioning it to my exact specifications. I was content with my new room. The sunlight streaming across the patchwork quilt where I sat perched upon the bed added a homey touch to the room. The long panes of glass in the French doors leading out to the veranda gave me a perfect view of the world outside at a direct level. One corner of the room had been purposely left empty, waiting for the bassinet from the attic to fill that void.

Box after box was brought down for my inspection and supervision. I had forgotten about all the maternity clothes I had sadly packed away after my last miscarriage. Amy was in heaven when I informed her they were of no use to me, so she could have them. The boxes of baby clothes I had so lovingly packed away each time brought back fresh tears along with the forgotten memories I had sealed away. Shaking my head to clear away the cobwebs of the past, I resolved to have no more tears. It was a time to be happy, I thought, regarding Amy's swollen abdomen. Now all I had to do was sit back and wait. Soon my dream would become a reality.

Chapter Ten

The morning's work went well, with the bedroom being finished for my approval before lunch. After a hasty meal everyone scattered, busily doing their routine chores while I sat on the porch swing, lazily taking in the glorious day. From my perch, I observed Charlie explaining to Thomas and Vince how the haying equipment worked. His voice rose higher and higher in frustration as he tried to get them to understand. Haying was a demanding job and one that Charlie despised with a passion. His temper at this time of the year was like a pepper pot waiting to explode. It never took much to set him off. I had wisely learned to stay out of his way and could see this year was no exception as I watched Charlie's face turning redder and redder.

Thomas had not learned to keep his opinion to himself and dared to utter the words, "It's not rocket science. Any dummy could do it, right Vince?"

Vince silently backed away, one foot shuffling in the dirt. He didn't want to get involved in another confrontation between Charlie and Thomas. I felt sorry for him, apparently he could not endure violence in any form. Charlie's eyes narrowed in anger, his hands balled into fists at his side while he stood rigidly glaring into Thomas's face.

"That is how accidents happen! Some smart-mouthed ass doesn't listen, and then someone else has to pay for their stupidity!" he snarled.

"Vince, come here," I called, motioning with one hand.

"What do you want?" he asked, climbing up the porch steps, clearly relieved to be away from the argument that was still gaining in momentum.

"Nothing, I just thought you might like to put some distance from those two," I said, pointing towards Charlie and Thomas. "I gather you don't care for violence, verbal or otherwise."

"Thanks, you're right. I had enough of it from my old man to last a life time. I can still remember his reaction when I told him about Amy and the baby." He had a faraway look in his eyes as he sat silent, remembering.

★★★

VINCE'S STORY

I'm glad I found a place for Amy and I to live after we left Luke's basement. There was no way we could stay there after I caught Luke pawing Amy like that. I never realized he was such a pig. Charlie seems okay, although he really has a quick temper. I can't stand the way him and Thomas go after each other over the least little thing. I had enough of that from my old man to last a lifetime. Thomas is just plain mean! I saw him unlatch that gate to let the bull out. It's a wonder Charlie wasn't killed by the beast. Beth sure thinks something is going on between Rachael and Charlie and I can't blame her, the way Rachael acts whenever Charlie's around. It's as if she would like to take Beth's place. Although, the way she acts around Charlie sure makes me wonder why I caught Thomas sneaking out of her room late the other night. I don't trust either one of those two! Amy's really excited about this baby. I tried to talk to her about giving it up for adoption, but she wouldn't hear of it. Where does she think the money is going to come from? Charlie told me I could stay here, that he would give me some money after harvest is done. He said if I work really hard, he might be able to make the arrangement permanent. At first I thought it was a great idea, but now I realize I need a real job, not just a promise of a bit of money once a year. Amy's pushing me pretty hard to stay here, but I know there's no future here for me, and I don't like the way Charlie's temper can flare up so easily. I don't know what to do! Sometimes I wish I'd never met Amy. I'm not ready to become a father. I feel so trapped. I promised Amy I'd stick around until she has the baby. Then I might take off. I told her we can't look after a baby right now. If she wants to keep it, then that's her problem.

★★★

"Rachael, you might as well earn your keep," I said, motioning for her to follow me down the steps. Vince got up to leave also, as all was quiet again between Charlie and Thomas.

"What now?" Rachael asked, trudging behind me.

"Now we do some yard work," I said, turning at the sound of a vehicle approaching in the distance. Rachael and I shaded our eyes, watching as it rounded the bend into the yard.

"Oh my God, no," Rachael screamed, her face turning a chalk white. In a flash, she turned to sprint towards the house as if the hounds from hell were on her heels. My mouth hanging open, I stared dumbfounded after her fleeing form.

The truck screeched to a halt before me while the door flung open, allowing a large, burly man to jump from the vehicle screaming, "Come back here you bitch!" Sprinting after her, he stopped short as Rachael deftly slammed the door shut in his face. Being bereft of his prey, his howl of rage echoed against the closed door. Slamming his huge fists against it in vexation, he continued to pummel the door.

Charlie, Thomas and Vince rounded the corner of the barn at a run upon hearing the commotion. The stranger continued pounding his fists against the door, still uttering profanity. Charlie lengthened his stride, covering the distance with ease.

"What the hell is going on here?" he demanded, staring menacingly at the stranger.

The stranger abruptly stopped his attack on the door, now aware of Charlie's presence. Warily he stepped back, uttering an oath that would make a sailor blush.

"Who the hell are you, and why are you pounding on my door?" Charlie snapped, taking a step forward.

"I'm the husband of that bitch that's hiding out in your house! She tried to kill me! Now she's going to pay. And no farmer… is going to stop me!" he spat.

"We'll soon see about that! Get the hell off my land and don't come back!" Charlie bellowed into the strangers face, stepping forward with fists clenched at his sides. The stranger's eyes narrowed, assessing the trio standing in front of him. He was out numbered and knew it.

Turning abruptly, he strode to ward his truck, tossing back over his shoulder the threat, "I'll be back!" Slamming the door, he gunned the engine, the tires spraying us with a shower of gravel. Leaning out his window, he raised his lone middle finger, bellowing, "Tell the bitch she can't hide from me."

We all stood there staring after the departed vehicle, looking at each other in utter confusion. The vehicle now out of sight, all eyes swiveled to view the door where Rachael had disappeared so hastily.

Apparently sensing it was safe, she emerged from the house to throw her arms around Charlie's neck, sobbing, "Oh thank you, Charlie. I'm so glad you were here."

Charlie entwined her arms from around his neck before giving me a quick glance.

Stepping back, he eyed her warily, "Was that really your husband? Did you really try to kill him?" he demanded, firing each question at her in rapid succession.

Rachael hung her head, the tears rapidly welling in her eyes, before sobbing, "Yes he's my husband. He used to beat me over the least little thing. I had to leave—but I never tried to kill him!" Tears streaking down her face, her arms reached out towards Charlie for comfort.

"It will be all right. He can't hurt you here," Charlie said soothingly, his hand clasped tightly over hers.

God she was bold, I thought, watching her face. She was good, I'll give her that. I watched Charlie tut-tuting as he assured her that he would do his best to make sure she was protected while under his roof.

Motioning to Charlie when no one else was watching, I proceeded to stick my finger down my throat making a gagging sound. Charlie quickly glanced around, checking to see if anyone had noticed my indiscretion. Giving me a menacing look, he shook his head before stalking back to the barn to resume his work.

The next few days passed in an uneasy restfulness. I had never seen Rachael so quiet before. She would eat her meals, do what was asked of her without complaining, and then retire to the safety of her bedroom. It was like waiting for a time bomb to explode. We all knew Rachael's husband was going to be back sooner or later. Charlie tried repeatedly to coax her to contact Jim, but she flatly refused, stating she could handle it. Towards the end of the week she did a complete turn around and was now her old, chatty self. We all relaxed as there weren't any more threats from her husband.

During the week we worked hard. Sundays were different and allowed us the luxury of catching up on personal chores. It was a glorious day, so feeling lazy I curled up on the porch swing to read the local paper in peace. Thumbing through each section, I was startled to see the picture of Rachael's husband staring back at me. Under the picture the capitation read *local man found dead in apartment.* I continued to read, wondering what he had died from.

"Harry Lauder, age 46, was found dead in his Hill Street apartment by his next door neighbour, Choy Hong, late Thursday evening. Mr. Hong became suspicious when Mr. Lauder did not respond to the constant ringing of his door bell.

According to Mr. Hong, the victim's cat had been roaming the hallways of the building searching for food. Mr. Hong contacted the superintendent and they found the deceased in his bedroom, where he had been stabbed numerous times. The police are asking the public's assistance for any information involving this crime. Mr. Lauder's wife has yet to be contacted. As to her whereabouts, it is not known at this date."

Rachael sat on the far end of the porch, absorbed in putting a second coat of nail polish on her long nails.

"Oh my god! Rachael, look what I just found," I said, spreading the paper to point at the article written there.

Pushing the paper a side, her only reply was, "So?" and then, "This polish is really slow drying." She rose to vanish quickly into the house, leaving me to stare at her retreating form in astonishment. Why not even the least bit of surprise, I wondered? She was married to the man for

God's sake. Yet she showed not one ounce of empathy for him. Was she really that hard hearted, I wondered, folding the paper as I went inside.

Chapter Eleven

That night I snuggled against Charlie's back, informing him of Rachael's nonchalant attitude when I showed her the article outlining her husband's death. "You should have seen her reaction when I showed her the paper. She didn't show one ounce of sympathy for him. Really Charlie, I was shocked. She was married to the man, and not even one tear," I claimed, tapping Charlie's back.

Charlie tensed slightly at my touch. "Everyone reacts differently to bad news. Get some sleep, Beth. It's been a long day," he said in a gruff voice.

Rachel's reaction and Charlie's seemingly complete lack of interest in my discovery had me puzzled. I couldn't get over the feeling that something was amiss. Was I missing something? I drifted off to sleep, listening to the sounds a house makes at night.

The sound of a door being closed overhead aroused me from my self-induced stupor. I glanced at Charlie's inert form snoring gently while he slept. Charlie was a sleep walker. On more than one occasion I had found him carrying on a conversation with an imaginary presence. It wasn't Charlie this time. Who could be up at this ungodly hour? The wisps of sounds from two people deep in an agitated conversation drifted down the stairs to slice the quiet of the night. I carefully stole from my bed, making my way to the bottom of the stairs to start climbing. The voices were easily distinguishable from the top of the stairs.

Obscured from view by the safety of the hall corner, I heard Rachael vehemently announce, "I know what I'm doing. You can't tell me what to do!"

Thomas's infuriated reply of, "Apparently not, you stupid slut! That's the last favour I do for you," was punctuated by the slamming of his door.

"I paid you well for that!" she screamed, slamming her own door in a fit of fury. Rachael's door closing was my clue to leave for the safety of my own room. I crawled back into my bed, only to be met by a tumult of thoughts regarding the conversation I had just over heard. What was Thomas doing in Rachael's room? I was led to believe she was afraid of him. What was Rachael doing that Thomas was so against? What was Thomas trying to tell her to do? Apparently she was not going to listen to him and it made him very angry. What favour did he do for her and how did she repay him? She had no money, which I knew of. The questions kept rolling over and over in my mind. I found myself twisting and turning throughout the night, trying to make some sense of it all.

The next morning found me tired and wary of everyone. The previous night's conversations rolled back in my mind, returning to haunt me while I watched for any exchange between Thomas and Rachael. Charlie, catching me glancing from one face to another cocked his head to one side before giving me a quizzical look and a shake of his head. I knew that look! It was the look that told me to mind my own business. I quickly averted my eyes, staring at my uneaten breakfast.

Sunday, being a day of rest, found us all taking advantage of it in one form or another. Charlie left, stating he was going to check the cattle in the pasture. Thomas mumbled he was going for a walk, while Amy and Vince headed towards the pond. Off they went, scattering like a bunch of tumble weeds released from bondage. The previous night's lack of sleep had taken its toll on me. So, taking advantage of the quiet, I crawled up onto my bed in need of the rest my body so desperately craved. I soon drifted off, only to be awakened from a sound sleep by a queer feeling of being watched. Glancing towards the window, I noticed that darkness was just starting to settle in, judging by the first smackling of stars that studded the night sky. In the gathering gloom I could just make out a dark form sitting in a chair, watching me while I slept.

"Who's there?" I cried out in alarm.

"I didn't mean to awaken you," Charlie said quietly, rising from the chair to come and stand beside the bed.

It was only Charlie! "That's alright," I said with relief. "I had to get up anyways. Where is everyone?"

"I'm not sure. I just got back from checking the cattle," he said, sitting down on the edge of the bed.

"Why are you so late? Did you have trouble?"

"Yes, there was a broken fence wire and some of the calves were out. It took me longer than I thought to round them up and put them back into the pasture. Then, I still had to mend the damn fence," Charlie said sourly.

"Did you eat yet?" I asked. I could hear my stomach rumble at the thought of food.

"No, I never got a chance. I'm not really hungry anyways."

"Well I am! Come and keep me company while I fix a sandwich for us," I said, grabbing his hand, coaxing him to follow me towards the kitchen.

"Well what do we have here?" I said with a smile, upon seeing Amy and Vince seated at the kitchen table with a large plate of sandwiches set before them, along with a huge chocolate cake that smelt delicious.

"I hope you don't mind. I made sandwiches for dinner and a chocolate cake," Amy said, looking up from her half-eaten sandwich.

"Not at all, thank you. That cake smells wonderful. I didn't know you were such an accomplished baker."

Amy flushed with pleasure at the complement. "I hope you like it," she declared with a smile.

"I'm sure I will," I smiled. "By the way, where are Thomas and Rachael?" I asked, glancing around curiously.

"I heard Thomas go upstairs a little while ago. I'm not sure where Rachael is," Vince said, popping the last of his sandwich into his mouth.

"I saw her going into the barn while I was making the cake," Amy said, wiping her mouth daintily.

Charlie volunteered to call Thomas for dinner and check if Rachael was in her room. I was munching contentedly on my second sandwich when Charlie entered the room, followed by Thomas.

"Rachael isn't in her room. When was the last time anyone saw her?" Charlie asked, looking at us each in turn.

"She's a big girl. She'll come for food when she gets hungry enough," I snapped, slightly miffed at Charlie's concern.

"Maybe she's still in the barn. I'm finished eating. I'll go and see where she is," Amy volunteered, rising from her chair.

Thomas and Charlie were just finishing their second sandwich when Amy's blood curtailing scream could be heard echoing from the vicinity of the barn. Abandoning our half-finished meal, we all sprinted towards the sound of Amy's anguished wailing.

"Amy, what's wrong?" Vince demanded, hurrying towards her. Amy stood behind one of the stales, one hand over her mouth, staring downwards. All stared in horror as our eyes followed hers to view the partially clad body. There on the cement lay Rachael, her arms spread before her, fingers shaped like claws as if she had been trying to crawl away from her attacker. Her neck was twisted at an awkward angle while one eye gazed toward the ceiling in a vacant stare.

"Go call Jim, Beth. Tell him to get out here right away," Charlie said as he reached out with shaking hands to pull her yellow sundress down, covering her exposed buttocks.

Turning quickly away from the macabre scene, I caught sight of Thomas trying to light his cigarette. His hands shaking uncontrollably, he turned his face away from Rachael's still form, which lay sprawled on the cold cement before him. Amy, wrenching her gaze away, turned to hide her face in the comfort of Vince's arms. I saw all of this before turning to flee from the barn.

I hurried towards the house, my mind still visualizing the image of Rachael lying like a discarded doll on the cold cement; her life snuffed out like a candle. I immediately placed the call to the station, asking personally for Jim. He would know how to handle this situation better than anyone. I trusted Jim. Over the years he had always been there for us and I was confident he wouldn't fail us now.

"I'll be right there," Jim said when I told him the details. He must have been close, judging by the amount of time it took for him to arrive.

"That was quick. I didn't expect you for a quite a while yet," I told him as he climbed out of the cruiser.

"You were lucky. I was in the area when your call came through," he said before turning to stride off towards the barn. A few seconds later another police car careened to a stop beside him. Jim, never losing stride, motioned for his deputy Sam to follow him.

"She's in the barn, Sam," Jim said, hurrying in the direction of the barn.

Sam, a tall gangly youth, was new to the force and Jim's right hand man. He now hurried to follow in Jim's footsteps. Sam was always anxious to please him, ever since Jim had taken him in- – a confused foster child at the age of ten. Jim opened the barn door, calmly surveying the scene before him.

"Who found her?" he demanded in a gruff voice, looking at the group of people clustered together on one side.

"I did," Amy said with a sniffle, still firmly ensconced in Vince's arms.

"How long ago was that?" Jim asked, turning to look at her.

"We called you as soon as we found her, Jim," I answered, glancing at Amy.

"Did anyone move her?" he asked, glancing from one face to another.

Charlie strode forward, his hands jammed in his back pockets. "I never moved her. I only pulled her dress down to cover her."

"Alright then," Jim said, with a curt nod at all of us. "We will need statements from all of you. I would like you to go up to the house and wait for me. I'll be there when we're done here," he said, searching each face before his gaze finally came to rest on Thomas.

Thomas's face, an uncommonly pale shade, now flushed a deep scarlet. Nodding his head, he turned with a jerk, hands tightly balled into fists at his sides, to follow Amy and Vince from the barn.

"Beth, I would appreciate it if you would wait for me at the house also. I won't be too long."

"Alright, let's go Charlie," I coaxed, grabbing his hand.

"Charlie, I would like you to stay for a few more minutes. Sam, you might as well call the C. S. I. crew. Tell them to bring a rape kit, and while you're at it, you better call Lyle," Jim commanded, motioning with one hand towards the police car that stood bathed in the yard's eerie light. Sam hurried towards his car, eager to relay the messages to dispatch, while I slowly walked towards the house.

Going by his car I overheard him say, "No, we won't need an ambulance. Yes, send the coroner instead."

Thomas's face looked as if it had been carved from stone. He stared out the kitchen window, watching the proceedings beyond, while Vince sat at the table with Amy leaning against him, quietly sobbing into her hands.

"Do they know who done it?" Vince quietly asked, looking at Thomas.

"Why are you looking at me? I didn't do it, and that lousy sheriff had better not try to pin it on me," Thomas snarled, banging his fist on the table, which made Amy jump in alarm.

"Nobody's blaming anyone for anything. And, for the record, Jim is the best sheriff around. There's nobody fairer," I said, starring him straight in the eye.

Thomas hastily lowered his eyes. "I hope you're right," he mumbled, shame faced.

I found myself being drawn to the kitchen window like a moth to a flame as I stared at the scene beyond. The scene unfolding before my eyes reminded me of one of those murder mysteries played out on television. The kind where you have to figure out who done it. Vehicle after vehicle rolled into the yard until the barn was fairly surrounded with them. Each one only concerned with doing their job.

I never had time to think about how I really felt concerning Rachael's death and now, sipping my coffee at the old kitchen table, I realized I felt nothing. It wasn't a secret that Rachael and I didn't care for each other. Rachael had made her own rules and now she had been caught in her own game. I could feel no empathy for her, only a curious detachment.

I slowly got to my feet, completely forgetting about using my cane. Hobbling outside onto the veranda, I sat down before spying two men wheeling a gurney out of the barn bearing Rachael's body to a waiting hearse. Soon the lights of each vehicle left, winking out of sight until there was only Jim, Lyle and Sam left. I sat motionless on the porch swing watching them slowly make their way to the house.

"I made some coffee. Would you like a cup?" I asked of no one in particular.

"That would be nice. I'll have one after we get our business concluded," Jim said, opening the screen door to slide inside.

Slowly, we all shuffled into the kitchen to sit down around the table, waiting for Jim's next command. Sam efficiently produced a pad and pen, waiting with pen poised for each person to give their testimony.

"Beth, we'll start with you. The rest of you can wait in the living room until I call you," Jim said, nodding his head in the direction of the living room.

"Now," Jim said, watching the last one leave the kitchen. "Where were you this afternoon?"

"I was in my room having a nap."

"What time was that?"

"I'm not sure, sometime after lunch," I said, folding my hands on my lap.

"Did you see or hear anything unusual?"

"No, I never slept very well last night, so I was dead to the world when I hit the pillow. I only awoke when Charlie came in," I said, tensing at each scratch of Sam's pen.

"And then?" Jim asked, raising his eyebrows.

"We found her right after that," I concluded, glad that I was finished.

Sam quickly pushed the paper towards me. "Read this and sign it, if it's correct."

Complying with his request, I hastily scribbled my name before shoving the paper back to him.

Charlie gave his statement in the barn, so would you please tell Amy to come in? That is her name, isn't it?" Jim asked, motioning his head towards the living room.

"Amy it's your turn," I said, choosing the seat farthest from Thomas. Amy awkwardly rose from the chesterfield, a tiny grunt escaping her lips as she held her distended abdomen. Slowly she waddled towards the kitchen, glancing back once to give Vince a tiny smile. Vince nodded his head for her to continue while he nervously made a tent from his fingers. The clock seemed to fascinate him as he studied the pendulum in its repetitive tick tock, tick tock, waiting for Amy to return.

Amy was back in no time, lumbering to stand before Vince. "Your turn, Vince," she said motioning towards the kitchen.

"Amy, is everything alright?" Vince asked, watching her face closely.

"Yes, they only wanted to find out what happened to Rachael. That's all they're concerned with," she said, giving him a trace of a smile.

"Okay, wait for me here. I'll be right back," he said, jamming his hands into his pockets.

Amy's accompanying nod was all Vince needed to see before heading towards the kitchen.

"Poor Rachael, what kind of maniac would do something like that to her?" Amy asked, before plopping down on the sofa beside me.

"Someone who was tired of playing her games, I guess," I replied, shrugging slightly.

"I know you didn't like Rachael, but for her to die like that! It's just so horrible," she cried, giving a tiny shudder of revulsion at the thought.

"She was bound to rub someone the wrong way sooner or later. You can't go through life treating people the way she did without having to pay one way or another. This time I guess she must have really pissed somebody off, big time, to end up paying for it with her life," I said, noticing Amy's wide eyed look.

Amy sat eyeing me thoughtfully, chewing on her lower lip, before she replied, "I know she had a mean streak in her, but she always treated me okay."

"C'mon Amy, let's go upstairs. I need to get out of here," Vince said, briskly striding through the door way.

"What's wrong, Vince?" she asked, looking up with a frown.

"Nothing, I just need some space, that's all. Are you coming or not?" Amy meekly rose, shuffling slowly behind Vince towards the stairs.

"The sheriff wants to see you now, Thomas," Charlie declared, poking his head around the corner, motioning for Thomas to follow.

"Yeh, yeh, I'm coming," Thomas reluctantly answered, following behind Charlie into the kitchen.

Curious, I moved closer, changing positions to see and hear all that was being said. Thomas sat across from Jim and Sam, his long fingers tapping the table in sequential rhythm, while one foot jiggled up and down to some imaginary tune. He could only be described as a spring, wound so tightly it was ready to explode.

"Thomas Lyman. Is that your name?" Jim asked with his hands spread flat on the table, surveying Thomas's face.

"I'm not saying anything without a lawyer," Thomas declared, tapping the table with one long finger before resuming his drumming.

Jim sighed wearily, "Well, that is your right if you want, but were not booking you with anything. We just want to ask you a few questions. We're not interested in anything other than what happened to the victim. We only want to know if you heard or saw anything out of the norm this afternoon.

Thomas stopped his constant drumming to relax slightly, only to start again at Jim's next question. His spring was winding tighter and tighter, it seemed. "Where were you this afternoon?" Jim demanded, starring at Thomas's hands.

"I thought you said I didn't need a lawyer!"

Jim leaned forward, smacking his hands on the table, roaring, "I'm tired of your pussy footing around! It's in your best interest to comply. A woman is dead and we need your co-operation to find out what happened to her. Do I make myself clear?"

Thomas's eyes smoldered as he glared across the table at Jim, before immediately dropping his eyes and slumping dejectedly in his seat. Then, finding a spark of spirit, he spat out, "Yeh, perfectly."

"Again, where were you this afternoon?" Jim asked, tapping the table with one finger.

"I WENT FOR A WALK," he answered, enunciating each word carefully.

"Where did you go for this walk?" Jim asked, paying no attention to his manner.

"Around the lake," he said in a more subdued voice.

"Did any one see you? Did you talk to anyone that can confirm you're whereabouts?" Jim asked, firing each question in rapid succession.

"I don't know! I never paid any attention. Someone could have seen me. I just don't know."

"Do you know if Rachael had any enemies?"

"Why don't you ask Beth that question? She can answer that better than I can," Thomas said, glancing sideways in my direction.

Jim seemed at loss of words. Turning swiftly, he cast his eyes in my direction before clipping out, "That will be all. Sign this and you can go." Thomas quickly scribbled his name and, without a backward glance, stormed from the room. The questioning finished, I strode into the room, standing close to Charlie.

"How's my girl?" Charlie asked, his arm snaking out to encircle my waist.

"I'm fine," I lied, starring into Jim's eyes.

"That ole boy's just a little bit antsy. I think I'll run a check on him. Find out what he's been up to lately," Jim said, watching Thomas wind his way down the path towards the pond.

My eyes following Jim's, I glanced out the window. There stood Thomas, silhouetted by the moon beside the pond, his shoulders slumped. The picture of a solitary figure against the world, it seemed.

Lyle came over to stand beside me. "Beth, remember me telling you that cane was becoming more of a crutch than a cane? I'm glad you finally took my advice," he murmured, putting a hand on my shoulder to give it a slight squeeze.

Puzzled at his words, I glanced down to find my hand devoid of the cane which I had carried for so long. I hadn't even thought about using it, my mind being so preoccupied with the confusion surrounding us. I was wobbly and my leg ached, but it was bearable. My face beaming, I realized with a start that I could do without it.

"Way to go, sugar," Charlie whispered into my ear before giving me a tight squeeze.

I slowly poured coffee for everyone, ecstatic at my new-found freedom. Rachael's death could not even dim the ecstasy.

Jim's voice reluctantly brought me back to the business at hand. "Off the record, Beth, when you called, I was out on another call. The Steins called in to report a man trying to grab their daughter as she walked home from the school bus stop. She said the man was large, with a tattoo of a dagger on his arm and a teardrop tattooed at the corner of his eye. She said he seemed to have trouble speaking, kept mumbling some garble–gook. It could be he stumbled onto Rachael in the barn and one thing led to another. It shouldn't be too hard to find someone fitting that description.

"Yup," Sam piped up. "I put out an alert for all cars to watch for anyone fitting that description. It shouldn't be too long before someone spots him and turns him in."

"Beth, what was Thomas talking about? Do you have anything that you'd like to tell me, anything that I should be aware of?" Jim asked, staring into my eyes.

I looked into those bright blue eyes that were so much like Charlie's. My head held high, I stated, "I didn't like Rachael. We had a few falling outs. She had a thing for Charlie and I called her on it. She didn't take it too well, I'm afraid, but I never killed her."

"I never said you did. I just wanted to cover all the bases," Jim said, raising his eyebrows. "That's the one I'm mostly concerned about," he said, motioning his head towards the pond.

I turned to look out the window. Yes, he was still there, head bowed and shoulders slumped, still the picture of despair. How close were he and Rachael, I silently wondered? Was it grief he was depicting or guilt? Only time would tell, I decided, turning away.

"I'll let you know what we find out in the next few days. The autopsy report should be back by then," Jim said wearily, turning towards Charlie. "Oh, by the way, did she ever mention having any family, other than her husband that just died recently? Any kids or what have you?"

"Not that she ever mentioned to me" I replied, while Charlie shrugged his shoulders in unison.

"Alright, night all, I'll be in touch," he said, closing the door behind him.

I could see the strain on Charlie's face and knew it was mirrored on my own.

"Well pretty girl, time for bed. It's been a rough day and we both need our sleep," Charlie whispered, taking the dishes from my hands.

Yes, it had been a long day, I thought, hobbling along beside Charlie. It was ironic. Rachael had done more for me in death than she ever had in life. A smile graced my lips at the thought of the crutch I had left behind.

Chapter Twelve

"Charlie, will you please pass the jam," Amy asked, pointing towards the jar.

Charlie absentmindedly pushed the jar towards her. Breakfast was a solemn occasion that morning, devoid of Rachael's chatter. The conversation was limited to only the courtesies of please and thank you, which accompany each meal.

"We might as well work on getting the swather ready this morning. It needs a new knife," Charlie said, buttering his toast.

"Is that all you can think about, your damn work? For Christ's sake, she's not even in the ground yet," Thomas spat furiously, eyeing Charlie with a look of disgust.

Charlie swivelled his head to glare furiously at Thomas before snarling, "It won't bring her back just sitting on your arse crying about it. Life goes on! Deal with it, or do you just want another day off? The work is why you're here, or did you forget that?"

The silence was overwhelming. Each man sat glaring at the other across the table until Thomas, trembling with anger, slowly lowered his eyes.

Charlie, thinking better of it, softened his tone somewhat to reply, "Sorry man, I guess were all a little edgy this morning. Doing something will take your mind off things. It's easier than sitting here gnawing on the same old bone over and over again."

Thomas cleared his throat before answering bitterly, "Right."

The meal over, everyone scattered, making a half-hearted attempt at some semblance of normalcy. I, on the other hand, found myself humming in my new found pleasure of being able to walk unassisted.

Now I had a new reason to do without my cane, I thought, watching Amy waddle down to her favourite resting spot beside the pond.

Towards the end of the week, a heat wave settled in to simmer over the land. There was no escaping it. The only relief was on the porch, where a slight breeze would occasionally drift in. This was where Amy and I spent the afternoons trying to keep cool. I sat on the old wicker porch swing, my bare feet swinging back and forth, while I attempted to create some semblance of a breeze to cool myself. The last few days had been unbearable with the mercury soaring to read in the mid-nineties. The heat had taken its toll on Amy the most. She lay stretched out on one of the loungers. Her long black hair coiled in a bun atop of her head, she waved a book back and forth to create a breeze. In the distance I could just discern a rise of dust as a vehicle slowly wound its way around the hair pin turns leading down into the valley. The constant squeak of the swing, complete with the steady drone of insects gathering their pollen from the flowers surrounding the porch, soon had me dozing off.

"It looks like we have company," Amy announced, jarring me awake.

Rousing from my stupor, I watched Jim's cruiser pull to a stop in the driveway. Jim uncoiled his long legs from the cruiser before stretching slowly. Out of habit, he reached inside to pluck his hat from the front seat, deftly clapping it onto his head before climbing up the steps.

"God this heat is a bugger. Trying to keep cool, ladies? If this heat keeps up, I'll only have crab grass for a lawn." He yawned slowly before flopping down onto the seat beside me.

"And, a good day to you too, Jim. What brings you out our way today?" I asked, giving him a cheeky grin.

Jim sat watching Amy fan herself as if he had never heard me.

"Earth to Jim," I said, waving my hand in front of his face.

"I heard you. I don't need a reason, do I?" he said, tweaking my nose gently.

"No, I just thought—oh never mind," I said, deciding to dismiss his aloof attitude. "I made some lemonade earlier. It should be cold by now. Can I get you a glass?" I asked, watching a bead of sweat trickle down his face.

"That sounds great. I'll come back for it in a few minutes. I see Charlie in front of the shop working on the swather. I'll just mo-ssie on over there. There are a few things I need to discuss with him," Jim declared, stepping down from the porch to walk slowly across the yard.

Jim's exaggerated, "Good day, Charlie," was not lost on me as he glanced back with a slight grin on his face. I stuck out of my tongue, but it only made him chuckle while he and Charlie walked towards the pond. Jim could always make me smile. No matter how bad things got, he had a way of making you believe it would all work out for the best.

"Amy, here's a glass of lemonade for you. It might help cool you off," I offered, passing the glass to her.

"Thanks, but I don't think I'll ever be cool again," she said, holding the glass to the nap of her neck.

Jim and Charlie had walked down to the pond and now stood deep in conversation, judging by the hand signals that accompanied their movements. Finally, Jim turned, making his way slowly back to the porch. Wiping his brow, he sat down on the creaking porch swing beside me before taking a healthy swig of his lemonade.

"Boy, that sure hits the spot," he sighed, wiping his mouth with the back of his hand. "Thanks, I really needed that," he claimed, leaning back against the swing.

"You're very welcome," I said, taking another sip from my glass.

Jim sat silently sipping his drink while slowly surveying the yard, a worried frown replacing the smile he usually wore. "You've made quite a few changes. I like the way you put those flower beds in over there. It adds some colour to that spot," he said, motioning with one hand towards the end of the lawn.

I knew Jim only too well. Something was bothering him that he was reluctant to talk about.

I silently stared at him, a perplexed look on my face, before blurting out, "Alright Jim. Out with it! You didn't come here just to discuss my flowers."

"You know me too well. I could never get anything past you," he said, the corners of his eyes crinkling with amusement. The smile he previously displayed vanished, replaced by a thoughtful look as he absent mindedly turned his hat over and over in his huge hands.

"The autopsy report came back. I thought you might like to know what it revealed."

"Alright, go ahead. I'm listening."

"The cause of death was a cervical fracture of the vertebrae. In other words, her neck was physically broken."

I glanced up quickly upon hearing Amy's sudden gasp. "Was she raped?" I asked sharply.

"No, but do you remember the stranger I mentioned the other day? Well, we arrested him yesterday. The Stein girl has confirmed he was the one that she saw the day Rachael was killed. We can't get anything out of him though. He doesn't seem too bright and has a speech problem. I'll bet you a dime to a dozen the DNA matches when we get it back." Jim cleared his throat nervously before continuing. "Beth, I did some checking and I can't find any of Rachael's family. It looks as if she never had any. I know you and Rachael weren't very friendly. Hell, I might as well come right out with it. I was wondering if you would consider burying her here. I mentioned it to Charlie, but he said it was your call.

"NO DEFINETLY NOT, I don't want her anywhere near here," I spat, jumping to my feet in a fit of fury.

"Hold it girl, I was only asking. You don't have to if you don't want to," he stuttered, holding out his hands in front of him as if to ward off my attack of words.

Softening my voice, I timidly reached out to touch his arm. "I'm sorry, Jim. It's just that you surprised me, asking me something like that. What will happen to her if you don't bring her out here?"

"The state will cremate the body and she will be buried in the pauper's cemetery north of town."

"Humph! I think that would be for the best," I said, glancing at the cemetery situated beside the house.

"Alright, if that's the way you want it, that's the way it will be. I guess I'd better go. Don't worry about things. I'm sorry I asked. I should have known better," Jim said quietly before clapping his hat back on his head.

"It's not your fault, Jim. I'm just surprised that Charlie would think I would even consider it. No harm done. Okay," I said, smiling in an attempt to right things between us again.

"No harm done," he said, draping his arm over my shoulders to give me a gentle squeeze.

We sat watching Jim's police car dwindle out of sight before Amy finally spoke, "I guess it's for the best. Not bringing her here, I mean. I'm surprised you let her stay for as long as you did. The way she acted around Charlie and all."

I nodded silently in agreement, waiting for her to continue.

"She did treat you pretty horribly. I wouldn't want her brought out here either, if I was in your shoes," Amy uttered, shaking her head.

Would they ever find out who had murdered Rachael? Oh well, what would be would be, I decided as I shrugged my shoulders and picked up the empty glasses to go into the house.

CHAPTER THIRTEEN

Lyle came later that afternoon to check on Amy and true to his word, supplied her with a stack of information on home deliveries. He said she was in excellent health and to expect the baby any time soon. Amy was ecstatic to know it would be soon, stating she was really becoming quite uncomfortable. I envied her un-comfortableness. I had never got to that stage in any of my pregnancies. Reclining on the sofa with her feet up, she hungrily devoured all the information Lyle had supplied.

"Vince, it says here a coach is very important," she said, tapping the page with one finger. "It even has pictures to show how you can make me more comfortable. Come and see."

Vince gave her a withering look before silently getting up to leave the room. Amy looked crestfallen at his lack of interest.

"I don't think he wants the baby," she stammered, her lip trembling as tears formed in the corners of her eyes, threatening to spill over.

"I think you're right. He's very young to accept that kind of responsibility. You both are. It costs a lot to raise a child," I said matter-of-factly.

Amy, reclining quietly on the couch, let me continue to speak without interrupting me. "You don't even have a home to raise a child in! I don't think you realize just how much is involved."

"I'm not stupid," she finally said, her eyes sparking with anger.

"I didn't mean to give you that impression. I know you're not. I just don't think you're thinking rationally," I said, calmly setting my book aside. Taking her silence as a good sign, I gathered up my courage to bring up the thought that was never far from my mind.

"I could take the baby. I would raise it like my own and it would never want for anything."

Amy jerkily rose from the couch, anger showing in her movements, her face flushed with rage. "It's my baby and I'm not abandoning it, for you or anyone else!" she snapped frostily.

Startled by her reaction, I could see it was going to take more persuasion than I had anticipated. I would have to tread very carefully so as not to make an enemy of her, I thought, staring at her angry face.

"All right, I was just giving you an out. I missed out on raising a child of my own and would give anything to be given another chance. I just want you to think about it. You don't have to give me your answer right away. Just promise me you'll think about it."

"No! I don't have to, end of discussion!" she claimed, giving me a look of pity before turning to leave the room.

Well, that didn't go over very well. Maybe Charlie was right. It might take a lot more persuasion on my part to make her see reason. I would have to move very carefully if I didn't want to spook Amy into leaving. Maybe Vince was the right one to have this discussion with. He might be the one able to point out to her just how wrong she was. I silently vowed I would have a talk with Vince at the first opportunity. Although, time was running out very quickly, I thought, remembering Amy's swollen abdomen.

The opportunity arose sooner than I expected. Amy had declined to come down for dinner, so Vince, at my urging, offered to take her a sandwich.

"She can be so pig-headed sometimes," he muttered, placing the untouched sandwich on the table.

"Vince, may I see you outside please?" I asked, motioning towards the door. Vince raised his eyebrows at my request before getting up to follow me out the door.

"What's up?" he questioned, following close behind me.

"Vince, I don't know if Amy has told you anything about our earlier discussion. If she hasn't, here's the gist of it." I said, sitting down on the swing.

"I asked her if she would consider turning the baby over to Charlie and myself. We would raise it as our own. We have a lot to offer a child and I would make sure it never lacked for anything." Vince nodded his head, waiting patiently for me to continue. "We lost four babies prematurely and the chance of having one of our own was very slim. We applied to an adoption agency. They said we were good candidates, but then this accident happened to me. Out of the blue, I received a letter in the mail telling us our application had been denied. The reason they gave was that we were unable to cope due to unforeseen circumstances. That was four and a half years ago." I couldn't help keeping the bitterness from my voice, recalling the memory of rejection I had felt for something that wasn't my fault.

The moon was full and I could make out the look of sympathy etched on Vince's face. He sat for some time not saying a word while I waited with baited breath for his reaction. Looking down at his hands, he slowly raised his head and with a huge sigh, disclosed how he was really feeling.

"Beth, I don't think I'm ready to be a father yet. I know that in my heart," he said, placing his hand to his chest. I feel so guilty sometimes. I thought I could handle it at the start, but I realize now that I was only fooling myself. Amy is so wrapped up in being a mother; she never once asked me how I feel. She hasn't stopped to consider what it will really be like. She can't understand why I'm not excited about it."

I watched his face while he poured out all the feelings he had kept bottled up inside for months and could only sympathize with him in making the hardest decision he would ever make in his life. The feeling of relief that washed over me at his next words overshadowed my feelings of sympathy.

"I know you would make a great mother. You and Charlie have so much more to offer a child than Amy and I have right now. I think the baby would be better off here where it will be raised properly. I'll try to make Amy see it would be the best solution for all of us. I want you to understand though, Amy has the final say. I'll do my best to convince her for all of our sakes, but she can be very stubborn," Vince sighed, rubbing his hand over his face.

"Thank you, Vince. That means a lot to me," I whispered, placing my hand lightly on his arm.

"I'll try to do what I can," he shrugged, rising to let me know our discussion had ended.

That night I lay in bed listening to Charlie's gentle snoring, while I recalled the conversation I had with Vince. I had given him a way out of the predicament he was in and he had jumped at the chance to push the ball into someone else's court. Now all I had to do was convince Amy to make the same move and my dream would become a reality. I drifted off to sleep, dreaming of finally becoming a mother. I silently vowed I would not let this chance slip through my fingers. The opportunity would never present itself again.

Charlie was in such a foul mood the next day that I pitied Vince and Thomas having to work with him. The heat that had been oppressing us for the last week continued taking its toll on everyone. Amy looked so uncomfortable, I truly felt sorry for her. I could see Vince had spoken with her about our conversation for she was aloof with everyone, but more so with me.

Vince volunteered to brave the heat by picking all the peas for me that morning. After lunch I had placed a fan on the deck for Amy while she shelled peas. The breeze gently blowing on her face seemed to help alleviate some of the tension between us.

"It won't help talking to Vince, you know. The decision is mine. No one can make me give up my baby," Amy said, staring at me until I squirmed uncomfortably.

"Alright, I understand how you feel," I said, nodding at her. I decided to let the subject drop.

I would find a way to change her mind. No matter what it took, that baby would be mine, I vowed, starring at her swollen belly.

Charlie's foul mood had spilled over from the morning. When Amy politely asked him if he would please move so she could put her feet up, he had snapped, "There's other places to sit you know!"

That was it! I had enough of his negativity for the day. Standing unassisted, I hobbled over to stand in front of him, hands on my hips. "All right Charlie Sanders, who crapped in your cornflakes this morning?" You could have heard a pin drop in the room. I had never challenged Charlie's authority before. Charlie opened his mouth, only to snap it shut and glare at me. We continued glaring at each other while our crowd of onlookers waited with baited breath to see who was going to back down first. Charlie stared intently into my eyes, daring me to make the first move. Not wavering, I was rewarded with the corners of his eyes, slowly beginning to crinkle, his eyes twinkling in amusement.

"Pretty feisty since you lost the cane," he said with a sheepish grin.

"Come on, Charlie Sanders, it's time for bed." I grinned, taking him by the hand. Our small crowd of onlookers, being cheated out of the chance to see a showdown, soon drifted away one by one from the room.

"Alright, what gives?" I demanded, sitting down on the edge of the bed.

"Nothing, it's just this damn heat," he said, rubbing the back of his neck.

I continued to sit patiently; waiting for what I knew would soon follow.

"Are you sure you want this baby, Beth? It will change a lot of things around here. It won't be just you and me anymore," he said, running his fingers through his hair.

"Yes, I want it more than anything in the world," I whispered, staring into his eyes.

"Amy's not ready to give it up, you know."

"I know, but give it time. I'm sure she will see it my way eventually."

"I don't know. I just don't know. I think you're asking more than a person can give," he said, shaking his head.

"I just want to be a mother, Charlie. Is that too much to ask?" I sobbed, pressing my face to his chest.

Charlie took my face between his hands to give me a gentle kiss.

"I'll do everything in my power to make your dream come true, sweetheart," he whispered, enfolding me in his arms, gently rocking me back and forth. My tears of frustration slowly slid down my cheeks to be wiped away by Charlie's calloused hand.

Chapter Fourteen

In the morning a storm was visible cresting the rim of the valley. The thunder head's ominous boom could be heard in the distance, creeping closer and closer. I sat on the porch, watching the lightning streak from ground to sky in abrupt shafts of light that crackled and danced in the air. The air weighed heavily upon the earth in anticipation of the rain that would soon follow. I had been taught while a small child that there was nothing to fear from a storm. The fury of what Mother Nature could bestow kept me enthralled. I counted the seconds between each boom of thunder, gauging how close the storm was advancing.

Amy ventured out onto the porch, only to cover her ears each time an ear splitting crack cleaved the air. The storm, edging closer and closer with each snap of lightning, had her shuffling her feet nervously.

"How can you stand it out here? Aren't you afraid?" she asked, covering her ears at a particularly loud boom.

"No, I love it when a storm is brewing. It somehow makes me feel more alive than ever. I love listening to the sound of rain falling. It's very soothing."

"You're weird," she said, turning to look at a bolt of lightning streaking across the sky. "I think you're the only person I know that feels that way about a storm," she chuckled, shaking her head in bewilderment.

I laughed in agreement. I guess I could seem a little weird at times.

The storm was relentless for the rest of the day. By late afternoon it had turned into a steady drizzle that promised to continue for days. The heat was suddenly stripped away along with the layers of dust that covered everything in its path as the storm continued its relentless journey across the valley.

"Beth, I'm going out to check on everything. This storm is pretty wicked," Charlie said, donning his old slicker. Yes, it was a wicked storm I thought as I placed the dishes into the sink. From the window, I watched as the storm swallowed up Charlie's hunched form, bravely making his way across the yard towards the chicken house, his coat flapping in the wind.

The dishes finally finished, I sat alone at the old oak table, which had seen so many generations of use, listening to the endless drumming of rain cascading down the window pane in tiny rivets. The dry dust in the yard had changed into a muddy bog, the streams of water criss-crossing in their endless journey towards the lake beyond.

Unannounced, the kitchen door burst open, the wind laced with icy rain swept through the room making me shudder with its fierce onslaught. There stood Charlie framed by the doorway while a puddle slowly formed around his feet.

"Thomas, Vince, I need some help out here, right away," he bellowed, wiping the rain from his face with his sleeve.

"What's wrong? Can't it wait? It's the final period," said Thomas, the disgust clearly visible on his face.

Charlie shook his head. "No, the roof to the hen house had some shingles ripped of yesterday from the wind. We either have to fix it now or move all the chickens to the barn. So let's go."

"Aw! The game was just getting good," Vince cried, donning his raincoat to follow in Charlie's wake.

The couch now empty, I curled up on one end, listening to the steady drumming of rain beating its relentless tune against the window pane. Only now there was another noise, this one not associated with the rain. The sound of footsteps overhead, paced back and forth in a continuous pattern. I still found climbing stairs a chore, so grabbing my cane I slowly climbed the two flights to the top. What on Earth was Amy doing? Turning the hall corner, I was met with the image of Amy doubled over gasping as she leaned against the wall.

Oh, oh, it's time, I realized, watching her face contort with pain.

"The pain— it's awful," she cried out between clenched teeth.

"How long have you been like this?" I asked, placing my arm around her shoulders.

"I'm not sure. I woke up this morning with my back hurting. The pain wasn't this bad then, so I never said anything," she said while a slight shudder shook her body.

"Have you timed your contractions?"

"I don't know how to do that," she explained. Clutching her abdomen, she prepared herself for the next wave of pain to engulf her.

I glanced quickly at my watch, starting the count down. Amy doubled over as the pain ripped through her body. Leaning against the wall for support, her teeth gritted, she waited for the wave of pain to subside. Her face visibly relaxed upon finding herself free from that contraction.

"Maybe I should lie down before the next one comes," she whispered, shuffling down the hallway.

"I think that might be a good idea," I said, my arm around her shoulders as I escorted her to her room.

Waddling towards the bed, her slight whisper of, "Thanks Beth, I'm glad you're here," could barely be heard above the rain drumming on the window pane.

Amy had found an article on a list of supplies to have on hand for a home delivery and had done her best to have everything ready when the time came. The bassinet I had bought and stored in the attic stood to one side of the room waiting for the new arrival. She had not had to buy a thing. Everything in the room was there because of my loss. The thought brought back a fresh flood of devastating memories, which washed over me again and again. I blinked away the sudden tears that formed at the corners of my eyes at the unfairness of it all. Easing Amy down against the pillow, I gave my head a shake to clear away the cobwebs of the past. I would not dwell on bitter memories anymore. It was time for happy thoughts and Amy needed my help to make sure this little one was safe. Amy's contractions were ten minutes apart, by my calculations.

"I'll go and phone Lyle. Just try to relax until I return," I said, pulling the covers over her bulging abdomen.

"Don't leave me! Please don't go!" she begged, clutching at my hand, panic showing clearly in her chocolate brown eyes.

"Amy, you need Lyle. The sooner I call him, the quicker he will get here," I said, patting her hand soothingly, all the while trying to free myself from her tenacious grasp.

"I'll send Vince up," I suggested in an attempt to calm her.

"No! I don't want him to see me like this!"

"Alright, I won't. Don't worry, I'll be right back. Try to relax. It will make it a lot easier," I advised her before slipping out the door.

I picked up the phone to hear nothing, zippo, no dial tone. God, what a time for the phone to be dead! Lightning must have struck one of the poles. I would have to ask Charlie to go for Lyle. Donning my rain coat I sloshed through the pouring rain in search of Charlie. I soon spotted him entering the barn carrying a chicken in each hand. Vince and Thomas trudged along behind in the same manner. It was no use trying to call them. My voice would never be heard above the pounding rain. Sloshing through the puddles I made my way through the drenching downpour towards the barn. Upon opening the door, I was greeted by three looks of surprise as all eyes turned to focus in my direction.

"Good God, Beth. What are you doing out in this weather?" Charlie demanded, surveying my drenched appearance.

"I need you to go for Lyle. Amy's in labour and the phone is dead," I panted, out of breath.

Vince's face registered a look of shock at my words. "She said that she had a sore back this morning. Are you sure she's in labour?" he asked, eyes wide, waiting for my answer.

"Yes, I'm sure. You better go now, Charlie. I hate to send you, but there's no other way to reach Lyle."

"Alright, I'll leave right away. I'll be back in no time flat. Thomas, you and Vince finish bringing the rest of the hens over to the barn. Feed and water them and then you can call it a day."

"Maybe I should go and see Amy first," Vince wondered out loud.

"Amy doesn't want to see anyone right now," I said, shaking my head.

"Not even me?" he asked, frowning.

"I'm sorry, Vince, but that includes you." I couldn't help notice the look of rejection that washed over his face at my words. The hurt reflected in his eyes, he turned away without uttering another word, making his way back to the chicken house. He was so young to be saddled with a problem of this magnitude. Sloshing through the accumulating mud, slipping and sliding with each step, I made my way through the pouring rain towards the house. The rumbling sound, of Charlie's old, pickup truck could be heard clearly, over the sound of the rain, as it made its way out of the yard.

Upon returning to the house I was greeted by the sound of Amy frantically screaming my name, over and over again. Hurrying, I climbed the stairs to where Amy lay clutching her abdomen, curled into a fetal position upon the bed.

"Amy, listen to me. You have to calm down. You're not helping yourself by becoming hysterical. I'm here now and Lyle will be here soon. Everything will be alright," I promised her with my fingers crossed.

"I think something's wrong. Why is there so much pain?" she cried, the panic reflecting from her eyes as she clutched my hand.

"Amy, that's natural. Try to focus on your breathing. When you feel a contraction, try to relax. It will help," I urged, stroking her forehead in an attempt to calm her.

"I can't!" she screamed in anguish, curling into a ball at the next contraction.

"Yes, you can. You have to," I urged, lifting her chin to look me in the eye.

"I'll try, I'll really try," she whispered while the wave of pain gradually subsided.

"Good girl, that's all we can ask of you. I know it hurts like hell, but try to focus on the baby. You have to do whatever it takes to make sure this little one arrives safely," I said, patting her hand.

Nodding her head, she lay back against the pillow, cradling her body, spent from the physical and emotional exertion.

"Why don't you want to see Vince?" I asked calmly.

"He said he doesn't want the baby, so why should I let him see me?" she said, turning her face away.

"All right, I was just wondering. We will do whatever you want, okay," I said in an attempt to soothe her. I was surprised at the hostility dripping from her tongue aimed towards Vince.

"What did Lyle say when you called him?"

"Don't worry, he will be here soon," I calmly told her. I didn't mention that I had never spoken to him. Amy's face twisted into a grimace. She was too busy with her next contraction to notice my slight hesitation at her question. What do I do now? I wondered, thinking back to my own memories that had ended in tragedy. All I could do was to keep her comfortable. I had to insure this baby entered the world in safety. I would not let Mother Nature snatch this one from me also.

"Can I do anything to help?" Vince asked, peeking around the corner.

Amy looked up, only to glare at him as an unspoken message passed between them like an invisible thread stretched so tight it was ready to snap. Words were not needed by the look on her face.

Glancing from one to the other, I hesitatingly broke the silence to ask, "Would you please get some ice chips, Vince?"

Vince turned with a nod, quickly striding down the stairs in an attempt to escape Amy's wrath.

"He just wants to help. Give him a chance," I championed for him, only to be met with Amy's icy glare.

"I think he's done enough already," she vehemently declared, turning her back to me.

Point taken, I thought, searching out the window for a glimpse of Charlie's headlights. I knew it would take Charlie longer than normal in this weather to make it to Lyle's and back. Amy was becoming more and more uncomfortable by the minute. Glancing at the clock, I timed her next contraction. I was relieved to find there wasn't much change.

"Here Beth, I hope this helps," Vince said, edging into the room to hand me the glass of ice chips I had requested.

I nodded towards Amy, her back turned to us, as she lay curled into a fetal position. Lifting one hand, I motioned for him to give her the ice chips.

Vince cautiously walked around the bed to face Amy. Holding out the glass of ice chips to her, he declared, "Amy, I said I would help you get through this. So, here I am." Amy reluctantly studied his face before slowly nodding her acceptance. Gingerly, she reached out to take the ice chips he offered. I decided to take advantage of their new found truce to quietly slip from the room.

Slowly I descended the stairs, stopping upon coming face to face with the portrait of Charlie's father. Staring into those evil eyes, I taunted him.

The words bitterly slipping off my tongue, "This time you can't take away my happiness, I won't let you." Holding my head high, I continued on my way down the stairs. The memory, even after all these years, still stabbed deeply into my heart. I had been a mere bride, pregnant with our first child at the time. My last vision had been of those eyes as I fell, tumbling down the stairs. Now, reaching the bottom, I crossed the room to stare nervously out the window, relieved to find the gleam of advancing headlights evident through the dull, grey sheet of rain. Slowly the lights continued in their downward journey to the bottom of the valley. Charlie had made good time. The gleam now turned into a dim shine as it became brighter and brighter advancing through the gloom. Impatiently I hobbled to the front door, pulling it open for Charlie and Lyle, only to step back as the wind whipped the rain into my face. The force driving me back with its icy onslaught. Charlie and Lyle dashed through the open doorway, slamming it shut behind them. I shivered at the sound of the rain, now continuing its ferocious attack against the closed door.

"God, what a night," Charlie and Lyle echoed in unison, wiping the water from their faces with soggy sleeves.

"How is she doing?" Lyle asked, seeing my agitated state.

"She's pretty nervous and seems to be in a lot of pain."

"Well that can be expected. It's not going to get any better for a while. Although I guess I don't have to tell you that," Lyle claimed, giving me a soggy hug.

"Which room?" he asked, pointing towards the stairs.

"She's in the one at the far end of the hall." I said, motioning towards the stairs.

Lyle, one foot on the steps, promptly turned with an apologetic look, "Beth, I'm afraid you will have to be my assistant on this one. I couldn't get a hold of Peggy. The dam phones are dead and I didn't want to drive all the way out there in case she wasn't home. It would have taken too much time. So it looks like it's just you and me. Do you think you're up to it?"

I had no choice but to agree. "I'll do my best," I declared, faithfully following Lyle slowly up the stairs.

Upon entering the room, we found Vince sitting beside Amy, gently wiping her brow with a damp cloth.

"I'm glad you're here. Can you give her something for the pain?" he asked, jumping up to face us.

"How are you doing, Amy?" Lyle calmly asked, taking her hand in his.

"Not very well, I'm afraid. I don't think I can stand much more of this," she whispered, clutching his hand tightly.

"You'll be just fine. Let's just take a look to see when this little one want's to meet its momma," he said, patting her arm reassuringly.

"Vince, would you like to wait here or in the hall while I examine her?" Lyle asked, picking up his bag.

Vince, with a sheepish grin, looked apologetically towards Amy before replying, "In the hall."

I couldn't help smiling at how fast Vince had chosen to make his escape. Lyle examined Amy, asking her question after question, which she answered to the best of her ability. Finally satisfied, he motioned for me to follow him towards the hall.

"What's wrong?" I asked, feeling a wave of panic seize me in its grip.

"We have a bit of a problem. The baby is breech and she looks pretty tired already."

"Breech, what does that mean?" Vince asked, a slight wobble in his voice betraying his true feelings.

Lyle looked up at Vince soberly before replying, "It means the baby is backwards. It can be very touchy, but I'm sure everything will be fine. Amy is pretty tough."

The sound of Amy's sudden scream spurred us all into action. Each one bound to the duty they had been committed to. It promised to be a long night. I watched helplessly, holding Amy's hand while I encouraged her not to give up. Amy was visibly weakening after each contraction. I had never seen Lyle look so worried. Vince sat on a chair on the opposite side of the room with his head in his hands, one foot tapping nervously.

"I hope this works," Lyle said, meeting my eyes with a worried look. I silently said a prayer for the little one so desperately trying to make its way into this world safely.

Lyle's satisfied grunt echoed throughout the room, "It's a boy!" he said, holding the baby up.

I watched in awe while Lyle cleared the baby's airway to help him breath. Finally we were rewarded with a loud wail as he took his first breath of air. I never realized I had been holding my breath in anticipation. Now letting it out in a final swoop of relief, I sank slowly onto the nearest chair. The baby's wail was like music to my ears. I had waited so long to hear that sound. I couldn't help the goofy smile that spread from ear to ear where I'm sure it would remain plastered for some time to come.

Lyle wrapped the baby in a warm blanket before holding him up for Amy to see. "You have a son, Amy," he told her with a smile.

"Take it away. I don't want to see it!" she cried, turning her face away. We all stood there in shock, not quite sure what to think.

Vince spoke first, "What do you mean, you don't want him? He's your baby!"

"I don't want it!" she ground out between clenched teeth.

Lyle looked down at the new life he was holding to shake his head sadly. Placing the baby into my arms, he whispered to Vince, "It will be all right, son. She just needs some time. She's been through a lot."

My arms had ached for this moment for so long. I looked down at the tiny new life I held and whispered a prayer of thanks while holding him close to my heart. Lyle reached out to take the baby from my arms and placing him onto a table, carefully examined him.

"He looks like a healthy baby, Beth. I can't find a thing wrong with him," he said, placing the baby back into my out stretched arms.

Vince's face, a mask of puzzlement, starred at Amy before allowing his vision to stray towards his new son for a second. Turning abruptly, he strode from the room without a backwards glance.

"Fine, now can you take it out of here. I'm tired!" Amy snapped, her arm thrown across her eyes in an attempt to block her vision. Glancing down at the tiny face, I hurriedly left the room. The baby protectively nestled in my arms.

I sat in my room, not wanting to leave. A feeling of tranquillity washed over me at the sight of the bassinet filling the corner of the room. Alone at last, I took the baby and placed him onto the bed. Opening the blanket, I gently examined the perfectly formed fingers and toes, the tiny delicate ears and the soft, downy thatch of dark hair encircling the perfectly formed head. I watched in wonder, his tiny rosebud lips pucker into a perfect O, as he yawned and stretched. Studying the delicate features, I vowed to protect him as long as there was breath in my body.

Amy had drifted off to sleep when I later checked on her, completely spent from her ordeal. I hated to awaken her, but the baby needed milk and she would have to provide it.

I approached the bed to give her a quick shake before demanding, "Wake up Amy. I need to talk to you."

"What do you want?" she mumbled, pulling the covers tighter.

"The baby's hungry. He needs to be fed."

"So feed him," she replied, callously.

"I can't, you're the only one with milk."

"Give him some out of the fridge."

"Amy, he can't drink cow's milk yet and I don't have formula here so, it's up to you to provide it."

Her hand on her forehead, she sat in silence, digesting my words. "I don't want him anywhere near me," she finally uttered.

"You don't have to. You can use the breast pump," I said with a slight smile.

"Fine, bring it here and let's get this over with," she finally spat out, a pained expression crossing her face at the thought.

As I left the room, I turned back towards her, the question hesitantly escaping my lips, "Amy, what name did you have picked for him?"

Without thinking, she started to reply "Jarr....," then, turning her back to me, whispered softly, "Call him whatever you want."

I sat in the old rocker that had been Charlie's mother's, smiling as I watched the baby suck greedily on the nipple between his lips. I never heard Charlie slip into the room until he spoke.

"I've haven't seen you this happy for a long time, sugar," he said, leaning against the door frame, a grin plastered on his face.

The goofy smile returning, I said, "I've haven't been this happy for a long time. Look: he's perfect. What shall we call him?"

"Beth, he's not your baby. That's up to Vince and Amy."

I raised my chin in defiance to quickly inform him, "I asked Amy and she said I could name him whatever I wanted. She didn't care."

"You know she had a hard delivery. Lyle said she will come around after a while and want her baby back. Remember, she wanted him before he was born. I can't see her changing her mind that completely now. She will want him back," he cautioned, gazing down at me with a look of pity.

Bristling, I hissed, "NO, she can't have him back! She didn't want him when he was born. He's mine now and I'm going to name him Joey."

Charlie laid his hand gently on my arm and then, leaning over, planted a kiss neatly on my brow. "You know I'll do whatever I can to help you. I would never let you down, if I could help it. But I'm afraid you will have one hell of a fight on your hands. I hate to see you hurt."

"I know," I whispered, holding the precious bundle even closer.

"I would do anything for you. You do know that, don't you? You're my life, Beth," he whispered, gently lifting my chin with his calloused hand to gaze into my eyes.

"Yes," I whispered, drawing Charlie closer to be included in the protection of my arms while we gazed down at Joey in wonder.

CHAPTER FIFTEEN

Amy never asked about the baby. I thought it would be a fight every time a new supply of milk was needed, but Amy never had to be asked again. She continued to leave a fresh supply in the fridge on a daily basis. She also continued to avoid the baby with a passion. If I walked into the room carrying him, she would find some excuse to walk out. I wondered what was behind her sudden metamorphosing and also how long it would last. Secretly I was glad I didn't have to share Joey with anyone and would spend hours just watching him sleep. I revelled in my new role as a mother; each step a challenge to be conquered and enjoyed.

The weeks slipped by uneventfully. Joey consumed all of my time, by choice. Amy, recovering from her ordeal, now spent more and more time at the pond watching the goslings show off their newly feathered grandeur. Deep in my heart I knew it wouldn't last. Amy would want her baby back soon. I also knew I would do whatever it took to stop her.

Joey was now three weeks old and changing every day. Amy seemed to be spending more time in the house lately. I would catch her staying close to my bedroom door listening for Joey's cry as his next feeding drew near. This particular night she seemed more attentive than usual. Joey's cry echoing from the vicinity of my bedroom had me slowly rise to go to him, when Amy swiftly jumped to her feet.

"I'll get him," she said, bounding from the room. She came back, carrying him gently cradled in her arms and talking baby talk to him.

"I think he knows me," she whispered, cuddling him closer. I quickly reached for him, only to have her turn away and utter, "I'll feed him this time."

"No!" I cried, the words popping out of my mouth spontaneously while I frantically searched for a reason to reject her offer.

"He's used to me, I'll do it," I said, reaching out to take him from her arms.

Amy's shoulders slumped with dejection. Defeated, she slowly left the room. I fought back against the icy cold feeling of dread that settled like a huge ball of dough in the pit of my stomach. Amy would try to destroy my happiness. I couldn't let that happen, I thought, looking down at Joey sucking contentedly on his bottle. I would never let her take him from me, I vowed fiercely. Amy would have one hell of a fight on her hands if she tried. He was mine now.

I was getting along so much better without my cane. At first doing without it had made my body ache, but now I could carry Joey in his chair with ease. I would take him everywhere I went. Sometimes I would catch Amy gazing down at him with longing, her arms aching to hold him. I was terrified she would become attached to him if I allowed her any grace whatsoever. I was determined to never allow her the opportunity to pick him up again.

Joey lay in my arms breathing softly. His tiny hands relaxed, his arms cradling his head while he slept contentedly after his afternoon feeding. The motion of the rocking chair had lulled him to sleep and had also made me drowsy. I carefully eased him back into his bassinet and leaned back in the old rocking chair watching him sleep. I soon closed my eyes and drifted off to sleep as the sunlight streamed in the window, spreading me with its warmth.

I awoke instantaneously, jerking myself upright as a feeling of foreboding flooded my body. With a sinking feeling of dread, I starred in horror at the empty bassinet. Who had taken him? The lump in the pit of my stomach turned to lead after I searched the house from top to bottom, only to find it empty of all inhabitants. Fighting back the tears which threatened to fall, I leaned against the wall in frustration.

Oh my god, what do I do now? I wandered outside to sink helplessly onto the lawn swing. I looked vacantly around with despair, not sure where to search next. My heart soared in relief upon spotting Amy sitting by the pond, leaning against her favourite rock. The object of my despair held closely against her bosom. My mind screamed in rage at the nerve of her taking my baby. Sliding off the swing, I stormed down the trail towards Amy with the sole intention of getting my baby back. Amy, spotting the look of rage written across my face, deftly pulled Joey closer to her.

"What do you think you're doing?" I demanded, reaching for him, only to have her clutch him even closer.

"He needed to be baptized. God wants all his children baptized, so I baptized him," she said, with a slight smile.

It was only then that I noticed the soggy blanket surrounding him. I looked into her eyes shaking with fear while she sat rocking the baby, softly singing a lullaby.

"Hush little baby don't you cry
Mommy's love will never die
Daddy will love you, this you'll see
Because your soul has been set free."

I gently reached down to take him, only to have her scream, "You can't have him. He's mine. I never gave him to you and his name's Jarred, not Joey!"

My mind racing, fear squeezing my heart, I tried again. "Please Amy; I just want to see if he's alright."

"Why wouldn't he be?" she snapped, clutching him closer.

"His blanket's wet. I just want to make sure he's not cold. Can I just check him? Please?" I felt the tears of frustration making their way to the corners of my eyes.

"No, I'm his mother. From now on I'll be the one looking after him," she stated firmly. Her look dared me to say otherwise.

As if in answer to my prayers, one tiny fist thrust its self from the blanket while he let out a hearty wail. I slowly sank to the ground in relief. My knees threatening not to support me as a sob tore from my throat.

"You thought I hurt him. Didn't you?" she asked, searching my face.

She needed no reply from me. My answer was there, written on my face like an open book for the entire world to see.

A huge sigh escaping from her, she calmly stated, "Look Beth, I know I wasn't a very good mother at the start, but he's part of me. I can't give him up. Please try to understand. I would never hurt him. While we're here I'll let you help look after him."

I nodded my head in frustration, silently vowing that I would get him back. She had given up all rights to him at his birth. Charlie, upon entering the kitchen, took one look at my face and knew instantly that something was wrong.

"What's wrong?" he asked, taking me by the shoulders to look into my eyes. I couldn't help the sob that tore from my throat along with the tears sliding down my face.

"Amy says she wants Joey back," I told him between sobs.

Charlie sighed wearily, running his hands through his hair before taking my chin in his hand to stare lovingly into my eyes. "I warned you this was going to happen."

"What do we do now? I can't give him up, Charlie. I just can't," I cried, rubbing at the tears that escaped to run down my cheeks.

Charlie sank onto the closest chair. Head bowed, one hand covering a huge sigh, he sat not saying a word. I could feel him searching for an answer to my question before he finally looked up to render a verdict, which I didn't want to hear. "You'll have to play it by her rules for a while. I'll have to figure out how we can deal with this."

"I don't know if I can do that," I said as a tear slid down my cheek to plop onto my hand.

"You have to. Once she starts looking after him full time and sees how hard it is, I bet it won't take her too long to realize she made a mistake and will be quick to give him back."

"I hope you're right," I sobbed. I had no other choice but to grasp at the slim chance that Charlie was right.

True to her word, Amy started to spend more and more time with Joey. She insisted on calling him Jarred and would correct me if I slipped up. Also true to her word, she allowed me to spend time with the baby alone. She didn't seem to want to get up for his night feedings. So she regaled that chore to me and allowed the bassinet to remain in my room. I never complained. I would absorb whatever time I was allowed with gratitude. For now.

Amy still tried to get Vince to pay more attention to the baby, but he would have no part in involving himself with Joey's care. Sometimes I would catch him secretly watching me rock Joey to sleep or while I gave him his bottle. Amy, when not involved with Joey, would sit sullen, lost in her own thoughts, the depression threatening to envelop her.

The nights were still warm so I decided to take advantage of it before the cold that would inevitably set in. Throwing back my head, I sat on the porch swing gazing in wonder at the multitude of stars. The sound of the swing creaking back and forth blended with the sound of the crickets in their mating call.

"Can I join you?" A voice sounded from the far corner of the veranda, giving me a start.

"God, you startled me," I uttered, looking up to find Vince standing in the shadows. "Sure, I don't bite."

With a slight chuckle he sat down beside me. We sat in silence, the swing continuing its duet with the crickets, while I waited for Vince to say what was on his mind.

"Beth, I know you're not happy with Amy right now." I nodded, waiting patiently for him to continue. "I've tried to talk to her, but she won't listen to a word I say. She refuses to budge an ounce on this. I told her I was leaving as soon as harvest was done. We've had quite a few heated arguments over it. She can be so pig headed sometimes! I give up. She can do what she wants. I'm finished," he said, sighing in exasperation as he ran his hand through his hair.

I sat there quietly absorbing all Vince had told me. My heart slowly breaking, I felt my last chance of ever having a family slip through my fingers with each word he spoke.

"Mind if I join you?" Amy asked, pushing open the screen door. "Jarred finally fell asleep. It's such a beautiful night. I thought I would join you." I tensed slightly at hearing her use the name Jarred instead of Joey. Sensing something was amiss, she turned from Vince to me and then back to Vince with a forced smile to ask, "Vince, come for a walk with me, please?"

With a shrug he slowly got to his feet, following behind her onto the trail leading down to the pond. I watched them slowly make their way to the water's edge. The sound of their voices became louder and louder as the discussion heated up. I felt uncomfortable eves dropping on such a private conversation, so I climbed off the creaky swing and rose to go into the house to check on Joey.

"Where did everyone go? What's going on? " Charlie asked, looking towards the pond as he pushed open the door.

I motioned in the direction of the pond, "I think we better go inside."

Vince and Amy continued their agitated conversation at the ponds edge for quite some time. Charlie and I sat at the old kitchen table trying not to pay any attention to the voices rising and falling, which could be heard quite clearly through the open kitchen window.

Finally, we heard Vince scream, "Were finished! Do what you want! I can't pretend to feel something I don't."

Amy's answering remark could be heard quite clearly through the calm of the night. "Fine, I'll raise him myself. I'm not deserting my son. Do what you want! Run like your momma done at the first sign of responsibility."

Vince never stopped walking as he abruptly answered back over his shoulder, "Fine, I will. You're on your own, little girl!"

Amy's heartbreaking sobs could be heard drifting through the calm night air quite clearly. Her sorrow made my heart ache as each sob tore from her body. Finally, not being able to stand Amy's anguish any longer, I rose to go to her.

Charlie reached out to place his hand on my shoulder. "No, sugar. Don't interfere. Let them handle it on their own," he said, motioning for me to remain where I was. Placing his arm around my shoulders, he ushered me towards our bedroom where Joey slept, innocently unaware of the controversy he was creating.

Chapter Sixteen

The next morning we awoke to a dull, gloomy day. Dark clouds gathered over head, hanging low in the sky. Their accumulating shapes blotted out the sun while they waited to release their burden upon the earth. Standing at the kitchen sink, I surveyed the gathering gloom from the window, only to spy Vince standing at the edge of the pond.

His scream of, "No Amy. Oh my God! Please no," echoed off the water, bouncing back to be repeated over and over again as he slowly crumpled to the ground.

Joey held tightly in my arms, I hurried outside, following the path to the edge of the pond. There in the pond, eyes closed, long dark hair fanning out around her like a halo, arms and legs spread out as if she was making a snow angel in the water, lay Amy. She reminded me of a picture I had once seen of an angel, and now she had become one.

Vince sat in shock at the water's edge sobbing. "Oh my god! Why Amy? Why?" I silently turned away, fighting down the lump threatening to form in my throat to make my way back towards the house.

Upon opening the door, Charlie saw the look of horror etched on my face and hurried to take Joey. "Beth, what's wrong? You look like you've just seen a ghost."

I motioned to the window overlooking the pond. "It's Amy. She's dead in the pond." I finally chocked out the words and sank onto the nearest chair.

Thomas, who had been standing at the kitchen door, stammered, "The hell you say, I don't believe you." His voice trailed to a whisper as he made his way to the window to observe Vince by the edge of the pond.

Vince, on his knees, continued his repetitious wailing. Charlie handed Joey back to me. Grabbing the phone, he dialed Jim's number. Wasting no time on pleasantry, he said, "Jim, you need to come out here right away. No, nothing happened to Beth, she's fine. It's Amy. She's in the pond. The silence was overwhelming while he listened to Jim's voice on the other end before Charlie said, "Yes, I'm sure."

Charlie hung up the phone with a huge sigh, grabbed his hat, and called Thomas to follow him. Thomas appeared to be rooted to the spot, staring with horror at the scene framed by the kitchen window. Charlie appeared again in the door way.

"Come on, Thomas. Now, damn it, let's go," he snapped, motioning for him to follow.

Thomas finally lowered his eyes before turning to follow Charlie, while mumbling, "Alright I'm coming."

I sat holding Joey clutched close to my heart, watching the tiny chest rise and fall with each breath. He would never know his biological mother now. God and fate had chosen me to become his mother. I felt the tears threatening to seep down my cheeks at the thought of all Amy had given up. The feeling of guilt soon brushed aside, realizing I was secretly glad, for now I would now not have to fight to keep my son. Smoothing back the soft downy thatch of dark hair and brushing my lips softly over the tiny forehead, I vowed to watch over my son. He would come to no harm as long as I had breath in my body.

I stood slowly, drawn to the window where the flashing red and blue of the police cruiser, reflected off the water as it approached where Amy lay in her watery grave. Vince now sat to one side of Amy's favourite resting spot, his eyes never leaving Amy's body, his shoulders shaking with the sobs he tried in vain to suppress. The goslings, now fully grown, swam in a circle around Amy's body, honking softly as if to say good bye.

From the security of the kitchen window, I watched the coroner load Amy's body into the awaiting hearse. The guilt I felt over Amy's early demise crept back to the edge of my mind, only to be pushed away over and over again to no avail. Finally the tears that had threatened to envelop me slid gradually down my cheeks to drip off my chin. I found myself picturing the happy, smiling face of Amy, floating down the stairs, so excited about her pending mother hood. Wiping my eyes on my sleeve, I slowly rose to my feet, telling myself life goes on. I had a baby now to think about.

The shuffling of feet on the veranda brought me out of my stupor. Charlie, Sam, and Jim entered the kitchen, followed by Thomas and Vince. Vince, white as a ghost, eyes red and swollen, sank slowly onto a chair, as if in a trance. The emotion he had shown before was gone and his eyes stared vacantly into space.

Jim, surveying the cluster of people seated around the old dining room table, cleared his throat before speaking. "Can anyone tell me what happened here?"

We all sat in silence, eyes downcast, no one volunteering to offer any information. Jim's sigh echoed throughout the room while he surveyed each face in turn.

"I'll try again. Does anyone have anything to tell me that can shed some light on what just happened here?" The silence continued, each one glancing from one to the other. No one seemed inclined to speak.

"C'mon people, surely someone has something to tell me!" Jim coaxed, his voice rising in agitation, his patience stretched to the limit. He still received no response while we all sat huddled on our chairs, not daring to voice our opinion. It just seemed too horrific to contemplate, let alone voice it.

Jim silently surveyed each impassive face. Then, with a huge sigh, he slapped his hands down on the table, before declaring, "Look, I've known Charlie and Beth all my life. Pointing his finger at Thomas and Vince in turn he said, "You and you, I did not."

"Hold it, no one can pin this on me. Talk to Vince and Beth! They're the ones who made it so tough for Amy lately." Thomas sputtered, his face turning a deep shade of red.

"What do you mean? Care to explain that a little more for me?" Jim asked, turning to stare at Vince and me.

Vince lowered his eyes, intently studying his hands, before stammering, "This is my fault and now she's gone." Jumping to his feet, his anguish seemed to resurface again. Holding his hands over his face, he cried out, "Oh my God, what have I done?" The pain, clearly etched on his face, seemed more than he could bear.

"Hold it son. What exactly did you do?" Jim demanded, studying his face apprehensively.

"I drove her to this. Now she's gone," Vince whispered, slowly sinking onto his chair, his hands over his face while a sob wrenched from his body.

Jim stood studying Vince's bowed head before quietly asking, "Son, did you drown her?"

Thomas, sensing he would be off the hook, piped up, "They had a terrible argument last night down by the pond. We could hear them from up here."

"When I want to hear something from you, I'll ask. You got it?" Jim said, giving him a dirty look.

"I got it!" Thomas snapped back with sarcasm.

Vince looked horrified, finally comprehending just what Jim had asked. His face blanching even whiter, he shook his head from side to side, replying in a low monotone voice, "No. I would never hurt Amy like that."

"What was the argument about, son?"

"The baby," Vince declared, looking up at Jim while the tears rolled down his cheeks to drip off his chin. The thought of the baby brought a fresh wave of anguish and he moaned as if in pain.

"What about the baby?"

"I can answer that," I said, attempting to take some of the burden from Vince's shoulders. Jim nodded his head, encouraging me to continue. "We wanted Amy to let us take the baby and raise it as our own. After the delivery, she didn't want anything to do with the baby. She said we could keep him. I've been caring for him since he was born. The last while she was starting to have second thoughts and wanted him back. Vince was on our side. He knew they couldn't raise him themselves, so he was trying to talk some sense into her. That's what the argument we all heard was about. She had been awfully depressed lately and spent a lot of time brooding down by the pond."

Charlie, nodding his head in agreement, added, "Yes, she had been moping around for quite a while now."

"I'd be depressed too if someone was trying to take my baby away from me," Thomas said, glancing from Charlie to me.

"Were you trying to take her baby away from her, Beth?"

"No, it wasn't like that. Beth only offered to raise the baby. I realized we had nothing to offer him, so thought it was the best solution for all of us. Amy never agreed. She thought we could look after him ourselves. Even though, we don't have two dimes to rub together. That's why we were arguing so much lately. I never thought she would do this though. If only I hadn't left her by the pond last night, she might be alive yet," Vince cried, glancing down at his shaking hands.

Jim cleared his throat. Surveying us all in turn, he asked the question no one dared to utter. "Are you all telling me you think she committed suicide?"

Thomas sat as if made from stone, not answering, while Charlie, Vince, and I nodded our heads in response.

"Have you got that, Sam?" Jim asked, turning to his deputy scribbling furiously.

"Yes, one minute," he replied, raising a finger in response.

"What happens now?" I asked, turning towards Jim.

Jim slowly ran his hands through his hair before replying, "Well it doesn't look good from our point of view. Two women dead within such a short time; there will have to be an autopsy done, of course, considering the way she died. If it was suicide, it will show it. If it was something else, well then I'll be back demanding more answers. In the meantime, make sure those two stay put," he said, nodding his head in the direction of Thomas and Vince. As for the baby, since Vince is the father, I'll leave that for you two to work out. I'd keep an eye on that boy though. He seems pretty broken up over this. Wouldn't want him to do something stupid, if you know what I mean.

Charlie nodded. "Don't worry, we won't leave him alone. I'll keep a close watch on him for a while. Thanks Jim, for coming out. I really appreciate it."

Jim put his arm around my shoulders to give me a hug before saying softly, "You're family. I'll always be here for you. Don't worry. I'm sure things will turn out alright."

I nodded my head. "I hope so, Jim. I really hope so." From the bedroom, came a wail to inform me Joey was awake from his nap, ready for his next feeding. Giving Jim's hand a squeeze of thanks, I hurried towards the bedroom where my son waited for me.

True to his word, Charlie kept a close eye on Vince. I'm sure Vince never even noticed. One could only empathize with him in his sorrow. From the large overstuffed chair we could still hear Vince sobbing softly from time to time. The sobbing was replaced by huge sighs while he tried to come to terms with Amy's death.

That evening Thomas sat perched upon a chair, staring into space, which was his habit at the best of times, while I sat on the sofa sewing a button on one of Charlie's shirts. Without warning, an uneasy feeling crept over me, making me shudder slightly. I looked up to find Thomas watching me. His eyes were narrowed like a snake before it strikes.

"Makes it a lot easier for you now, don't it?" he claimed upon seeing me glance up.

"I don't know what you're talking about."

"Oh, I think you know alright," he said, rising to leave the room.

"Care to explain that remark to me?" Charlie asked, his arms crossed, leaning against the kitchen door frame.

Thomas turned on his heel to leave the room, mumbling under his breath, "I don't have to explain anything to you." Charlie's face was a mask of fury as he started to follow him, but stopped at my raised hand, motioning for him to stay.

"Let it go. It won't do anyone any good fighting right now," I claimed, patting the sofa beside me for him to sit down. Nodding his head, he came to sit down beside me. A huge sigh escaping from between his lips, he gently placed his arm around my shoulders, drawing me close. His eyes trained on Joey's face, he gently reached down to scoop him up. Holding him close, he looked into the tiny face before softly whispering, "Poor little bugger, I'm glad you won't remember any of this. I hope you have a better childhood than I had."

"He will. I'll make sure of that," I whispered, caressing Joey's cheek.

Whenever I held Joey, the guilt seemed more than I could bear. I was torn between two emotions; elation at finally having a child of my own and grief over Amy's death. The nights were the worst. I would lie awake, hour upon hour, rehashing the events leading up to Amy's death. When sleep finally claimed me, it was to dream of a dark haired angel lying beneath the surface of the water, the waves gently rocking her back and forth while the geese swam protectively around her, honking softly.

Three days had passed since Amy's death. Slowly we continued onwards with life. Vince was silent and morose. He would eat his meal and then retire to his room, avoiding human contact whenever possible. Sleep avoiding me; I lay awake listening to the sounds of Vince pacing back and forth in his room. Apparently I wasn't the only one unable to sleep.

Charlie had taken to walking and talking in his sleep again. One night I found him in his parents' old bedroom, staring vacantly at the floor where his mother's body had been found. I quietly took him by the hand and led him back to bed. The next morning he had no recollection of the previous night's wanderings. My only ray of sunshine through all of this was Joey. I held him close, strengthening the bond between us even more. I didn't have to worry about sharing him with anyone now. I would catch Thomas watching me, the chill in his eyes warning me to tread softly. He never spoke to me in front of Charlie again, but when Charlie's back was turned he would sneer at me with disgust. His cryptic remarks tried to goad me into acknowledging I was to blame for Amy's death. I finally had enough and that night told Charlie that Thomas would have to go.

"I can't take much more of Thomas's attitude. He blames me for Amy's death. I want him gone from here. Nothing is worth than being treated like a criminal in your own home," I said, arms crossed, waiting for his response. I was shocked by how tired he looked. The long hours of swathing were taking their toll, along with all the sleep walking he was doing.

"Harvest will be done soon enough. You'll have to put up with things for a while yet. I need Thomas right now, even though he's the worst worker we've ever had."

"Can't you do without him? He gives me the creeps. I'm afraid of him."

"No, I told you, he has to stay until we finish harvest. He'll be the first one out the door, I can promise you that," he said, nodding his head.

"Alright," I finally agreed, slowly nodding my head in acceptance.

Placing his hand under my chin, forcing me to look into his eyes, he said, "You have your baby now, just like you wanted. Just focus on that and everything else will fall into place."

"Yes," I whispered. I have Joey now. I have a son, I thought, smiling.

The next morning I was pouring my morning coffee when a knock sounded on the door. "It's about time you got up to make that coffee," Jim stated, poking his head around the screen door with a grin.

"Oh! You startled me," I exclaimed, taking a step backwards. "How long have you been waiting out there?" I asked, motioning for him to come inside.

"Not too long. It gave me a chance to catch a few winks while I enjoyed the morning sunrise," he said cheerfully.

"I never heard you drive in. You must have a ghost car," I said with a slight chuckle at my own joke.

"Good one! You're pretty sharp for first thing in the morning."

"Yes, I know, and I haven't even had my razor blades yet," I replied soberly.

Jim's booming laughter echoed throughout the kitchen. Straddling a chair backwards, he accepted the steaming cup of coffee I offered him while staring at me with a thoughtful expression on his face.

"Well, how are things going?" he asked, sipping his coffee.

"They could be better," I said, sinking onto the nearest chair, coffee cup in hand.

"I thought that might be the case. You look kind of frazzled."

"Do I?" I asked, a frown creasing my previously smiling face.

"Care to tell me about it? I have broad shoulders, remember."

I looked at Jim, taking in the worried blue eyes that were so much like Charlie's that now surveyed my face with concern. "All right, Thomas is giving me a hard time about Amy's death."

Jim, sucking in his breath, replied, "Is that so? Looks like I might need to have a talk with that old boy."

I shouldn't have said anything, I thought, mentally kicking myself for doing so. "Never mind Jim, I can handle it. Charlie needs him until after harvest and that won't be much longer. I guess I can put up with him until then."

"I wouldn't mind setting him straight for you. It would be my pleasure," he said, smiling deviously.

I sat considering Jim's generous offer, but with a shake of my head decided to decline. "It might make things worse. Don't worry, I can take care of myself," I told him, pouring another cup of coffee for him.

"Heh, you two, what's going on in here?" Charlie asked, sidling into the kitchen carrying a wiggly little bundle in his arms.

"Joey's awake? I never heard him cry," I exclaimed in astonishment, reaching out my arms to take him from Charlie.

Charlie waved my hand aside before replying, "He's okay. He was just lying there awake talking to himself in baby garble gook. I couldn't resist picking him up. He's such a good baby, even though Beth spoils him rotten every time he squeaks," he said with a cheeky grin.

"I do n–o–t," I stuttered to Jim and Charlie's laugh of amusement.

Jim looked up quickly, his grasp tightening on his cup, upon seeing Thomas and Vince enter the kitchen. "I just came down to tell you the results of the autopsy," he said, frostily starring at Thomas as he put his cup down on the table. "There was no foul play involved, so you're off the hook, Vince. It looks like a clear case of postpartum depression. No one is to blame," he stated, emphatically eyeballing Thomas until he slowly lowered his eyes to squirm uncomfortably in his seat.

Vince slowly nodded his head, reluctantly accepting the fact that he was not to blame. "What happens now?"

"I don't know what you mean. With what are you referring to?" Jim asked, patiently waiting for his answer.

"The baby. What will happen to him now?" Vince asked, frowning.

"You're his father. You get to make that decision now," Jim said with a nod in Joey's direction.

Vince's face, now an uncommon shade of red, shifted his gaze to stare silently at the table before finally muttering, "Oh!"

"Vince, I'm sorry for your loss. I realize this has been very difficult for you, but there's one thing more we have to discuss."

"What?" Vince asked a perplexed look on his face.

"What do you want done with Amy's body? We couldn't find any next of kin and as her common law husband, the responsibility falls on your shoulders."

Vince slumped in his chair like a balloon pointedly deflated by the prick of a pin, his face turning beet red.

"I don't know," he said, a look of bewilderment and despair crossing his features in turn.

"Vince, she can be brought here. Charlie and I will help you through this," I said, placing my hand over his in sympathy. "All right Charlie?" I asked, swivelling my head to encompass his surprised look.

"Sure, we'll help any way we can," Charlie said with a displeased look in my direction.

"Thanks. That means a lot to me," Vince said, nodding his head at each of us in acknowledgement.

Jim, clearing his throat, rose from the chair to put his cup into the sink before saying, "I guess I'll be going then." Turning towards Vince, he withdrew a piece of paper from his pocket, which he pushed into his limp hand, stating, "There's a number on there for you to call. They will help to arrange everything."

To Vince's credit, he rose from his chair, squaring his shoulders, his chin up, to offer his hand to Jim in friendship for a quick shake.

Tipping his hat as he went out the door, Jim called back over his shoulder, "Thanks for the coffee, Beth."

CHAPTER SEVENTEEN

Everyone remained quiet throughout the hastily prepared breakfast, lost in their own thoughts while I busied myself feeding Joey his formula.

"How is he handling the formula? It's not making him sick is it?" Vince asked with a slight frown.

It was the first time since Joey's birth that Vince had uttered a word concerning Joey's well-being. "No, he's fine," I stammered, looking up with surprise.

Charlie, looking at me then Vince, rose abruptly, pushing back his chair to turn towards Thomas, demanding, "C'mon, time to go to work, Thomas."

"Yeh, Yeh! I hear you," Thomas muttered, slowly getting to his feet.

Vince started to rise, only to stop as Charlie waved his hand, motioning for him to sit back down. "Don't you need my help?" Vince asked, looking slightly bewildered.

"No, I won't need you this morning. You can stay here to call that number Jim gave you. Beth will help you. Won't you, Beth?" he asked, one eyebrow rising slightly.

"Sure," I muttered, looking into Vince's sorrowful face. Charlie had left me no choice, just as I had left him no choice when I had volunteered to help Vince.

Vince opened his hands, palms up, while giving me a quizzical look. "Well, what should I do first?"

"What religion was Amy?" I asked, thinking about the way she had baptized Joey.

"I don't know. She was raised in an orphanage until she was seven, then she was put in one foster home after another, that's all I know."

"Alright then, I'll call our minister to see if he will do a service for her."

"Thanks. I 'm kind of lost with this. I don't know what she would have wanted."

I studied his face while he made this declaration, realizing just how young he really was.

While I spoke to the minister Vince sat beside me, head bowed, hands in his lap, twining his fingers together nervously.

Pushing the phone to him, I got up from the table. "Call the number Jim gave you. Tell them the funeral will be tomorrow morning." Finished with my part, I left the room, allowing Vince to make the arrangements to have Amy's body brought home. I went to my bedroom to gaze with wonder upon Joey, sleeping contentedly while he sucked periodically on the soother hanging slack in his mouth. Standing watch over him, I raised my eyes heavenward, my hands clasped together in prayer.

"Thank you, Amy," I whispered. Gently, I brushed the thatch of dark hair from the tiny, sleeping face. Then, I made him a promise I vowed to keep with my life. "I'll always protect you. I'll make sure no one ever hurts you."

I jumped, startled, as Vince leaned over my shoulder to say, "He's kind of cute, you know." Then, turning on his heel without waiting for my answer, he left the room.

The funeral was a very quiet affair with only Vince, Thomas, Charlie, and I holding Joey in attendance. The weather seemed appropriate for the occasion, I thought, glancing up at the dull, grey canopy overhead. The breeze blowing from the east carried a chill to remind us the warm weather would not last much longer. I shivered as a cold breeze crept under my skirt, making me wish I was a thousand miles away from this spot at the moment. The minister's words droned on and on while in the background I could hear Vince's huge sighs. His eyes downcast, he stared at the plain coffin. I felt detached from the scene spread before me, as if I was watching a play. The people involved did their best to act out their part to the best of their ability. It was only Joey's wiggling that brought me back to reality. The minister concluded his sermon by picking up a handful of dirt and trickling it onto the coffin, repeating the age old verse used for generations, "Ashes to ashes. Dust to dust. Lord bless her and keep her. May she find everlasting peace."

Vince, raising his chin at the minister's final words, stepped forward holding out his hands to take Joey. I shrank back, clutching him closer, not accepting what he was asking of me.

Charlie leaned down to whisper in my ear, "Give him to Vince."

The fear etched on my face was only echoed by the fear in my chest, my heart squeezing in dread. Taking Joey in his arms, Vince wandered down the familiar path where he sat down at Amy's favourite spot overlooking the pond. The geese that Amy had watched from small goslings to now fully grown birds glided silently throughout the weeds warily watching from a distance the stranger that had come to inhabit their world. Pressing his forehead against the small bundle held in his arms, Vince wept freely the sobs tearing through his body to shake him uncontrollably.

Thomas stood watching me, not speaking. Then, turning abruptly, he walked back to the house, where he disappeared inside. Charlie's eyes bored into mine before he also turned to stride towards the barn only to disappear inside. I was left standing alone in the centre of the yard with the feeling that this was somehow my fault. It infiltrated my brain to creep silently around until it filled every inch of my being. No! I would not accept the blame for this! How dare they make me feel this was my fault? Amy had made her own choices, I reasoned, turning slowly towards the house.

The rain that threatened to fall finally edged into our corner of the world. A cold rain! Not one of those warm summer rains in which a person loves to walk, not minding getting wet. This rain chilled you to the bone. The grey shroud was in no hurry to depart, leaving us with little else to do other than keep each other company in the sanctuary of the house.

The funeral atmosphere we had just left spilled over to enfold us all as we sat at the kitchen table watching the rain obliterate our view of the yard. Slowly we sipped our steaming coffee. No one chose to speak. The space we inhabited was ours alone; no one dared venture into it, even though we sat shoulder to shoulder. Two empty chairs now graced one side of the old table. I was relieved to finally hear Joey stirring from his nap. Leaving my coffee barely touched, I hurried away to comfort him. I was only too glad to be away from the oppressive atmosphere surrounding the inhabitants seated around the table.

That night everyone retired early. The strain of the day had taken its toll on all. Charlie sat rocking in his mother's old rocker in the far corner of our bedroom, staring vacantly across the room.

Reaching down deep inside me, I finally gathered up the courage I needed to blurt out, "You blame me for all of this. Don't you?"

Charlie swiveled his head to stare at me, his eyes continuing to hold a vacant stare while he tried vainly to pull his conscious mind back to the present.

"Well do you?" I demanded. My body shook slightly at the icy chill that crept up my spine without warning.

The vacant look finally left Charlie's eyes. He said, "No, I don't blame you! Why would I?"

Starring down at the quilt I was seated on, I picked at the loose thread I had been worrying on to reply in a whisper, "Because I have Joey now."

"You didn't kill her! Let it go. What's done is done. We can't change things now. You don't have to feel guilty about anything. Just let it go."

I slowly nodded my head, the tears trickling down my face to drip silently off my chin. Charlie was right; it was time to let Amy go and move on.

"Come to bed. I need you to hold me."

Burying my face in his shoulder, we lay stretched out, holding each other while I continued to sob until a restless sleep finally claimed me.

Jerking myself awake, I sat up blinking, trying to adjust my vision to the darkness that completely surrounded me. What had awakened me? Joey was my first thought. I stumbled to his crib, only to be reassured by the sound of a slight sigh as he snuggled under his blanket. Feeling around in the darkness, I realized Charlie was gone. My ears straining to hear what had awakened me from a sound sleep, I was finally rewarded with the sound of voices deep in agitated conversation. What was going on? Who was Charlie arguing with at this time of night? Using the wall to guide me, I inched closer towards the sound, straining to hear the conversation taking place. Peering into the darkness, I turned the corner, entering the kitchen to find Charlie seated at the table. The room bathed in an eerie glow from the full moon, casting long fingers of shadows over the lone inhabitant who sat with his hands clenched into fists. I stood there listening as he vehemently declared between clenched teeth, "No, I tell you. No! Don't make me!"

Not again! Wearily I reached out for Charlie's hand, not wanting to wake him. Lyle had cautioned me it was not wise to awaken a sleep walker abruptly.

"Charlie, come back to bed," I whispered, reaching for his hand, encouraging him to follow me.

Not answering, he followed me docilely, fingers tightly clenched around mine, stumbling through the darkness towards our bedroom. Three times through the night I awoke to search for Charlie and led him quietly back to bed. This was the worst I had ever seen him. Charlie had always walked in his sleep, but lately it was getting worse. I would have to talk to Lyle about this new episode.

The next morning to my surprise I found another person had been walking the house throughout the night. There, sprawled out on the sofa lay Vince, one arm across his eyes, all gangly legs and arms that had not muscled out to a full man yet. His dark hair spread across his forehead, mouth slightly ajar, snoring softly. I could envision Joey at his age in the future. He would look just like Vince, I thought, turning away from the still form to silently tip toe away so as not to awaken him.

Chapter Eighteen

The rain from the previous day continued, enveloping the house like a shroud while drumming its relentless beat against the window panes. Charlie, his hair tousled, his eyes bleary and red rimmed from lack of sleep, shuffled his way into the kitchen.

Flopping onto the nearest chair with a sigh, he ran his hands over his unshaven jaw to mumble, "Morning, Beth."

I clicked my tongue in exasperation while I pushed a steaming cup of coffee into his shaky hand. "Charlie, Charlie, what are we going to do with you?"

"Huh! What do you mean?"

"I spent half the night leading you back to bed, that's what!"

"I don't remember a thing about that," he said, shrugging his shoulders.

"Maybe you should talk to Lyle."

"I don't have to talk to anyone! Leave me alone!" he snapped, turning his back to me.

"Sorry, I just wanted to help. I didn't mean anything by it."

"Well, you're not helping," he snapped, reaching out to grab the telephone in mid ring. I sat listening, struggling in vain to piece the half conversation together without success.

"Three days isn't very much time," he told the caller, his face twisted into a grimace. "I know," he said. "No! Don't do that, I'll get you the money by then. If I say I will, I will," he ground out between clenched teeth. "Damn bankers, they think they own you when you borrow a little money from them," he said, slamming the phone down.

"Who was that Charlie and what did they want," I asked, going to stand in front of him.

"We have three days to come up with some money or they will foreclose on the farm," he sighed wearily before going to stand silently, starring out the window.

"They can't do that. Can they?" I asked, watching Charlie's chalk-white face.

"They can do anything they want," he said, wearily running his hand over his unshaven jaw.

"I thought they would wait until after harvest. What do we do now?"

Charlie continued to stare out the window, not speaking. Turning towards me he said, "I'll have to haul in that barley we were keeping for feed this winter. It's not much, but maybe it will hold them off until we get harvest finished. Damn! Why can't they wait for harvest to be finished? The new crop will bring us in some cash, but this rain better quit soon. All the wheat we have cut lying in the swath will have dropped a grade already. Every time it drops a grade, it's that much less money in our pocket."

On that note he turned, taking his coffee cup with him to go and sit on the porch swing where he could be alone in his misery. A feeling of dread once again crept up my spine, threatening to suffocate me in its wrath. This was my fault. Would it never end, this feeling of helplessness that wrapped its invisible arms around me, sucking me down into its unfathomable depths. Would it ever be finished? Dumping my half-finished coffee into the sink, I hurried back to my bedroom where Joey lay sleeping. There, oblivious to the turmoil surrounding him lay the only anchor that made sense in my world lately.

That afternoon the rains ended, leaving everything fresh and clean once more. The day that had started so dismal now seemed a little brighter. I smiled, watching the sun peek out from behind a cloud to bath everything in a warm golden glow. Joey tucked into the crook of my arm, I watched Charlie from the porch swing slowly back the truck up to the grain bin to auger on a load of feed barley. The guilt I continued to feel hovered near the edge of my mind. The last three years had been rough. The bank had threatened to foreclose on our farm each year until we came up with enough money to make our payments. Each year we had scrapped by only by the skin of our teeth. Charlie had higher hopes for the crop this year. He had them sowed earlier and even Mother Nature had cooperated, along with our extended help. Things had looked so much brighter for us until the bank had phoned with their threats. The farm had been in Charlie's family for generations. The view of the family cemetery attested to this fact. It would kill Charlie having to hand it over to the bank after all the work he had put into it over the years. Farming for Charlie was not just a job, just as it wasn't for any man who had chosen this profession. It became a way of life that ran deep down through their veins. The sleepless nights spent watching cows birthing their calves. The times, you depended on Mother Nature to cooperate, only to have her lash out, ravaging a field of wheat ready for harvest with hail. For every catastrophe that happened, the scale would tip back in your favour. How can you explain the feeling of joy one feels when you save a life, whether it be man or beast, or when you sit watching over a clean field of golden wheat waving in the gentle breeze under a setting sun? Charlie felt all of these defeats and accomplishments, but now the threat of failure hovering over his head was becoming more then he could bear.

Charlie's cantankerous mood was still evident while they loaded the grain into the truck. He snapped at Vince and Thomas for the slightest miscalculation on their part. Once the truck was loaded, Charlie climbed inside to rev the engine. Deftly shifting gears, he left Thomas and Vince standing in the centre of the yard, watching as he drove off in a huff. Spying me on the porch swing, a sleepy Joey in my arms, Vince wandered over to sit down beside me. The creaking of the swing while it swung back and forth made the only sound while Vince and I sat in a comfortable silence, enjoying the warm sun shining down on our faces.

Breaking the silence, I offered apologetically, "Charlie doesn't mean to be such an ass. He just has a lot on his mind right now."

"Humph! Well, if you say so."

"How are you handling things? I asked, turning my head in his direction.

"I don't know what you mean. Handling what things?"

"I noticed you've taken to sleeping on the sofa lately. Is there any particular reason for that?"

"I didn't think anyone would notice." Vince lowered his eyes, a tinge of red hastily creeping up his neck to fuse his cheeks into a rosy glow.

"Of course I noticed. It's pretty hard to miss a hundred and sixty pound guy sprawled across my sofa snoring," I said with a chuckle, pushing the swing with one toe to get it moving again.

"I guess you're right," he said, a wan smile crossing his face while we swung back and forth.

"Alright, Vince. What gives, why the sofa?"

"If I tell you, you'll think I'm crazy," he said with a shudder.

"No, I won't. C'mon, spill it."

"You promise?" he asked, looking down at his hands.

I realized Vince was serious. His hands were actually shaking. This was not something funny. Something was seriously wrong here.

"I won't laugh. I promise," I said, placing my hand on his shoulder in encouragement.

Taking a deep breath, Vince shuddered while lowering his eyes nervously before replying, "I think this house is haunted."

"What? Why would you say a thing like that?" I asked, blinking in surprise.

Now started, the story spilled forth from his lips in a cascade of words that were hard to understand. "I see things—things that don't make any sense—talking all the time—it never quits—I think it actually follows me," he said, his hands shaking as he rubbed them over his face.

"Whoa, slow down. There has to be a good reason for what you're saying," I said, trying to piece the information together to have it make sense.

"What did you see?

Vince looked up to meet my eyes while a shudder rippled through his body, making him shiver with apprehension. "I woke up in the middle of the night to find someone sitting on the edge of my bed watching me."

"What did you do?"

"I asked who was there and they wouldn't answer me. Then the thing just stands up, takes a step backwards, and disappears. Poof, then nothing! It's gone just like that," he said, snapping his fingers.

"It was probably Thomas jerking your chain. He has a mean streak in him. I wouldn't put it past him to try to scare you just for kicks."

"No, it wasn't Thomas. I went straight to his room, thinking it might have been him. I was going to confront him, but he was sound asleep— not faking it, either!"

"Maybe, it was Charlie. He walks in his sleep."

"No. It looked like it had black hair and I just know it wasn't him, I can't explain it, but this thing seemed pure evil. It felt like it wanted to eat me up and spit me out, just for the fun of it. I don't know, but it sure gave me the creeps," he said with a shiver, suddenly checking my face for my reaction.

"It was dark, wasn't it?"

"Yeh, but I still know what I saw and this thing was pure evil."

"You've had a hard time with things lately. It was probably your mind playing tricks on you. You've been under a lot of stress since Amy died. I'll bet it was Charlie walking in his sleep."

"I know what I saw. I tell you, this place is haunted and no one could make me sleep up there again, not for any money," he said, lifting his chin to look me squarely in the eye.

"Wait a minute. I never said you had to. I have no problem with you sleeping on the sofa. That's up to you. You're the one that won't be very comfortable. You said something about talking. What was that all about?"

Letting out a huge sigh, Vince divulged what he had heard.

"Even when Amy was here we would hear people talking at all hours of the night. Sometimes it sounded like they were right in our room. It sounded weird, kind of muffled, as if they had something over their mouth. We got up a few times to see who it was, but the talking would stop whenever we put the light on. After that we slept with the light on."

"That was probably the wind creeping in one of the cracks in this old house. God only knows there are enough of them. This house has a lot of vents. You probably heard someone talking close beside one and the sound followed it up. That's probably your ghost," I chuckled, punching Vince's arm playfully.

"I knew you wouldn't believe me. I know what I saw and I know what I heard and it wasn't normal," he mumbled, shaking his head before looking me squarely in the eye.

"I'm only trying to give you a logical explanation for what you think you saw and heard."

"Yeh, well I'll be sleeping down stairs from now on," he said, jumping off the swing to turn his back and enter the house, clearly disgusted with my lack of belief.

I watched his retreating form, remembering over the years all the times I had heard voices whispering in the night, only to have Charlie laugh my fears away. A small part of my brain wanted to scream out, you're right, Vince! I know you're right! But my tongue remained silent, as if an evil force was at work, preventing me from uttering a sound.

CHAPTER NINETEEN

That afternoon Charlie returned whistling happily, his foul mood dissipating like the rain. "Where are Thomas and Vince?" he asked, sitting down beside me at the table with a cup of coffee.

"I'm not sure," I mumbled, giving him a fleeting look, preoccupied with folding one of Joey's diapers.

"That sure turned out to be a beautiful day out there," he said with a huge grin plastered across his face.

"I'm glad to see you're in a better mood."

"Heh, what makes you think I was in a bad mood?" he asked, rolling his eyes heavenward at the thought of such a possibility.

"Oh never mind. What happened at the bank? Are they still going to foreclose on the farm?" I asked, grabbing another diaper.

"No. They promised they would wait until harvest was done before making any hasty decisions. We can breathe a little easier now."

Picking up Joey and placing him in the crook of his arm, he whispered into the tiny ear, "Now I have more reason than ever to keep this farm."

That night after supper Vince hovered close to Joey and me. He seemed to be more and more enthralled with Joey all the time. Watching Joey making little slurping noises on his bottle he asked, "How do you know when he's had enough?"

"Watch and see. When he's had enough, he'll push the nipple away with his tongue."

"Really, he's that smart already? He must take after his father," he replied proudly. Joey's tiny hand reached out to close around his finger.

My breath caught in my throat as I looked up to see a dark shadow cross Charlie's face before he stood up and hurriedly left the room.

"Can I hold him for a while?" Vince asked, unaware of what he had just implied.

"No. He needs to be burped now."

"I can do that," Vince insisted, reaching for Joey.

Holding Joey even tighter, I ignored Vince's outstretched arms, searching for a reason to prohibit him from holding his son, "He might throw up and I don't have a towel handy. You don't want to get covered in baby puke, do you?"

"I really wouldn't mind," he murmured, his hands falling to his sides, a dejected look on his face.

I continued to burp Joey, ignoring Vince's offer to help. Dismissing the hurt emitting from Vince's eyes, I offered the excuse. "I have to change him." Rising quickly, I hurriedly left the room for the safety of my bedroom. Upon opening my bedroom door, I was surprised to find Charlie stretched out on the bed, hands propped behind his head, staring at the ceiling in concentration.

"You better have a talk with him or I will. Joey's not his son anymore. He's ours now," he declared with a vengeance that shocked me.

"I know Charlie, it's just that he's been through so much already and he's so young," I said, giving him a feeble smile.

"He's not that young. He was old enough to make a baby and be on his own."

"Aw—Charlie, you know what I mean!"

"No, I don't. Talk to him, Beth. Soon—or I will!" Charlie snapped, sliding off the bed.

"I will. The first chance I get." Charlie always knew what was best, I decided.

That night Joey seemed fussy, refusing to drink his milk when offered. I worried over his lack of attentiveness. Noting how listless he seemed, I decided to call Lyle. He would know what was wrong. Lyle answered on the second ring.

"Hi Lyle, I hope you don't mind me calling you this late."

"No not at all! Do you have a problem?"

"Yes. I don't know if I should be very concerned, but Joey won't drink his milk and he seems very fussy," I said, the magnitude of my problem sounding feeble even to my own ears.

"Is there anything else?"

"Yes, he doesn't seem very attentive. I know it doesn't sound like very much, but my instinct tells me something is wrong. I'm probably just being a worry wart, but I would really like you to take a look at him, just to be on the safe side."

"I planned on coming out there in the next few days anyways. We'll just make it tomorrow instead. Don't worry, it's probably nothing. Babies can get upset tummies just as well as grown-ups. If you notice anything different, don't hesitate to call me."

"Thanks Lyle, I'll do that," I said gratefully into the phone.

"No problem. We'll see you tomorrow, then. Bye Beth."

"Bye Lyle."

Upon entering the living room, I found Vince had been listening to my conversation with Lyle.

"What's wrong with Joey?"

"Lyle thinks it's nothing, just an upset tummy. He'll be out tomorrow to check on him."

His arms crossed over his chest while giving me a fixed stare, Vince stated, "I want to be here when he comes."

"No, you don't have to be. Charlie and I will make sure he's looked after. We are his parents now," I said, turning to leave.

"Not yet you're not. I don't remember signing any papers."

Reeling backwards, as if I had just received a physical blow to the stomach taking my breath away, I stammered, "But—you said he would be better with Charlie and me. You even tried to convince Amy of that."

Vince flinched at the mention of Amy's name. Raising his chin with a steely look in his eye he informed me, "That was before Amy died. Whenever I think back over Amy's death, something just doesn't seem right. Even yet, I can't get her final words out of my head. She said she would never desert her son. Then she suddenly walks out into the pond to drown herself. Why would she do that?" Vince asked, frowning while he stared fixedly into my eyes, waiting for my answer.

"I don't know. You said it yourself, she was awful depressed."

"I realize now she was right all along. He's all I have left of Amy. I won't lose him too," Vince said, his words piercing my heart like an ice cold knife.

"Vince, you can come and see him any time you want, I won't take that away from you."

"No. We will be leaving tomorrow, right after Lyle checks him over," Vince said, staring straight ahead.

Appalled, I tried desperately to change his mind. "Where will you go? You don't have a home to take him to," I pointed out.

"I thought about that. My grandma will take us in until I get back on my feet. I know she's old, but I'm sure she won't turn us away."

"He's just a tiny baby. I'm all he knows." I said, the tears forming in my eyes threatening to block my vision.

"I know, but he is just a baby. He won't remember any of this," Vince said, shaking his head.

"Vince, you can't take him away from us! I've been his mother since he was born. Don't do this! Please?" I begged with a sob, feeling my heart shatter into a million tiny pieces.

"No! He's my son! I've made my decision. We'll be leaving tomorrow," he spat, turning his back to inform me the conversation was over.

I stumbled back to my bedroom, the tears blinding me while I sobbed quietly into my hands. I shut the door, leaning against it, only to slide to the floor while sobs racked my body in spasms. Charlie was at my side in an instant, gathering me into his arms. Gently smoothing the hair back from my face, he peered into my eyes.

Catching his breath at the despair etched across my face, a single word spilled from his lips, asking the silent question, "Joey?"

I nodded my head, the lump in my throat choking off any sound from escaping. Sitting down on the floor with me, Charlie gently lifted me onto his lap, wrapping his arms around me while gently rubbing my back, willing me to calm down.

"He wants to take Joey from us. He says he's leaving tomorrow," I repeated with a moan, looking towards Joey's crib.

Charlie stiffened upon hearing this news. "We'll soon see about that!" he ground out between clenched teeth.

Standing abruptly, he pulled me up after him. Turning to open the door, our movements were temporarily frozen at the high-pitched scream emitting from the crib where Joey lay. Turning, I ran to the crib, all thoughts of Vince fleeing my mind upon finding Joey screaming in pain. His tiny legs were pulled up tightly to his abdomen, his skin a bluish tinge, while sweat formed a sheen on his tiny face. Reaching down, I pulled him into my arms, trying in vain to comfort him.

"I'm going to call Lyle," Charlie said over his shoulder, running towards the kitchen.

"Sshh, Joey, I'm right here," I whispered into the tiny ear, while gently rubbing his back.

"He'll be right here," Charlie announced, coming back into the room to give my shoulder a squeeze.

Vince appeared into the room as if by magic, "What's wrong with him?" he cried out in alarm.

"I don't know!" I said, holding Joey to my shoulder, continuing to gently rub his small back.

"Can't you do anything?" he asked, pacing back and forth in agitation.

"I'm trying, can't you see that?" I snapped at him.

Slowly Joey's screams turned to a weak whimper, his breathing shallow. He now lay limp in my arms. Rocking him gently, I sat waiting for Lyle, praying that whatever was wrong with Joey was minor and Lyle would tell me I was just being over protective, but in my heart I knew different. The sound of Charlie talking to Lyle in the hall flooded me with relief.

"In here, Doc," Charlie said, ushering him into our bedroom.

My relief at seeing Lyle soon turned to dread upon him taking the baby from me.

Placing his stethoscope on Joey's tiny chest, he looked up frowning before demanding, "Call an ambulance. Tell them it's a baby in distress and to hurry!"

Listening to everyone talking all at once I felt myself becoming unbearably hot, their voices slowly drifting away. It was like I was in a bubble, hearing and seeing everything in slow motion, but not being able to participate.

Lyle, sensing something was wrong, looked up at me, to usher the command, "Charlie, sit her down."

Before Charlie could react, I slowly crumpled to the floor in a heap, the thought of losing Joey more than I could bear.

I slowly opened my eyes to find Charlie's worried face hovering over me while he applied a cold cloth to my forehead. His voice repeating over and over, "It's going to be all right, Beth. You just fainted."

"Joey," I muttered, trying to rise while searching Lyle's face for a clue.

Lyle, seeing the panic registered in my eyes, tried to assure me. "I'll do everything in my power, Beth."

Placing all my faith in him, I nodded numbly. I knew he would do everything he could to help Joey. The ambulance's arrival goaded us all into action. Following behind Lyle, we made our way outside to the waiting vehicle. Lyle, clasping my hand tightly in his, pulled me through the open ambulance doors while he said to Charlie, "You'll have to follow behind."

Vince started to climb into the waiting ambulance, only to be stopped by the ambulance driver's hand, restraining him from entering the vehicle. "I'm sorry, but only one of you can go. I think it would be best if it was his mother," he said, nodding towards me.

I flinched as if I had been stung with a whip at Vince's next words. "She's not his mother. His mother is dead. I'm his father and I'm going with him."

Lyle, seeing the look of shock registered on my face, quickly said, "She's a patient too. Take them both."

The ambulance driver nodded slowly, observing Lyle's stern look. Pressing his lips together, he climbed into the waiting ambulance, allowing Vince to climb in beside me. The scream of the ambulance echoing throughout the valley, along with the flashing lights bouncing off the canyons walls as we sped by in a blur, made me nauseous. I listened to Lyle ushering commands while he worked feverishly to keep Joey breathing. The words pulmonary hypertension, cyanosis, and congestive heart failure floated from Lyle to his assistant. I looked at Vince to see the same horror mirrored back from my face onto his. Vince, apparently forgetting his animosity, reached out to clutch my hand in a ferocious grip. His face chalk white, he starred at Joey.

Chapter Twenty

I felt as if the ride would never end, but actually we arrived at the hospital quite quickly. Pulling up in front of the hospital doors, we were met by two orderlies pushing a gurney. Joey was placed onto it and then whisked away down the halls to disappear between two large doors. I pushed open the doors to follow, only to be stopped by a nurse, putting her arm around my shoulders.

"I'm sorry, but you can't go in there," she whispered, leading me to a chair. "Let the doctors do their magic. You'll only get in the way. They'll let you know what is happening soon enough."

Nodding my head, I sank slowly onto the chair. The nurse disappeared down the hall, only to return a few moments later with a glass of water, which she pushed into my shaking hand.

Sipping at the water, I glanced around. Taking stock of my surroundings, I found Vince slumped in a large arm chair, one hand on his forehead while the other encircled his body as if he was trying to comfort himself.

All at once, Charlie was in the room reaching for my hand, "Do you know anything yet?"

"No. They wouldn't let me stay with him," I cried, shaking my head while tears slid down my cheeks to drip off my chin.

"It will be alright. Lyle knows what he's doing," Charlie said, sinking slowly onto the chair beside me.

We all sat staring vacantly at the clock before us, the pendulum swinging back and forth in a continual motion while we waited for news of Joey's condition.

Finally the two large double doors swung open. Lyle and his colleague slipped through them to come and stand before us.

"This is Dr. Carlton," Lyle said. We quietly acknowledged him with a nod before we turned back to Lyle, waiting for him to finish speaking. Glancing at us each in turn, he sighed before revealing the answer we all waited anxiously to hear. "Well, we have him stabilized," Lyle said.

"Can I see him?" I asked, starting to rise from my chair.

"No, not yet. I need to talk to you first," Lyle said, motioning for me to sit back down.

"What's wrong with him?" I demanded, glancing from one face to the other, the fear showing plainly on my face.

Pulling up a chair in front of me, Lyle took both of my hands in his, staring intently into my eyes, before asking, "Have you ever heard of the term Ventricular Septal Defect?"

Shaking our heads in unison, we replied as if one. "No."

"Well maybe you've heard of the more common term, a hole in the heart," he said, glancing at each of us before continuing. "It's a condition you're born with. You didn't do anything wrong," he promptly assured us. "The hole in Joey's heart is fairly large. It's causing pressure to build in his lungs. Un-oxygenated blood is being pumped backwards into his body. That's why his skin has a bluish tinge to it. It doesn't always show up right away. If Amy had taken prenatal care, we might have had a better chance of spotting it sooner. As it is, we can only move on from here," he said, spreading his palms face upward.

"How bad is it?" I asked, knowing only too well it wasn't good.

"I won't lie to you, Beth. It's pretty bad, but it is fixable. He will need an operation."

"How risky is it? I want to know the truth," I demanded, raising my eyes to stare into Lyle's, which at the moment were filled with sympathy.

"Any surgery is risky and in an infant, even more so. I can tell you one thing though. Without it he will die."

Charlie sucked in his breath sharply before asking, "When would you do the surgery?"

"Dr. Carlton has a team ready to go right now. It would be within the hour. We have a problem though. Joey's blood is rare, type AB negative. There isn't any blood of that type available here. We can check the donor list to see if we could possibly get someone to come in that would match his, but that takes time."

"There is another possibility," spoke up Dr. Carlton, nodding towards me. "Being his mother, you are the best chance of having the same blood type."

"His biological mother is dead," I mumbled, starring at the floor.

"He has no family here?" he enquired, a surprised look on his face while looking at each of us in turn.

"I'm his father. I have the same blood type," Vince said, with a nod of his head.

"Alright, I'll have a nurse come out to explain everything to you. She'll bring a form for you to sign allowing us to do the surgery." Smiling, he gave Vince's hand a quick shake before turning to exit through the two large doors where Joey now laid waiting for his surgery.

"I want to see him," I demanded, plucking on Lyle's coat sleeve to get his attention.

"Alright, I'll take you to him," Lyle said, taking my hand in his. Turning my hand over and giving it a gentle squeeze, he looked into my eyes. "He has a lot of tubes hooked up to him, don't let that alarm you."

I nodded my head, my heart squeezing with fear. I followed behind Lyle towards the two large doors. Joey lay on a covered table. The whir of machines linking long tubes to his tiny being were the only sounds present in the alien atmosphere. I felt Lyle's arm slide around me in anticipation of my first sight of Joey hooked up to the monstrous machines, which enabled him to breathe easier. Reaching out, I gently traced the outline of the small face turned towards me with his eyes held tightly shut. I felt my breath catch in my throat upon Joey opening his eyes to give me a shadow of a smile. I felt like scooping him up into my arms and running with him as fast as I could away from all the hurt and pain he had to endure. But, for now, all I could do was stand there helplessly. Blindly trusting in strangers to do what was best for my son. Holding the tiny little hand, we waited for the doctors to come and whisk him away from us. I couldn't stop the silent tears that ran from the corners of my eyes, to be absorbed by the mask covering half my face.

Reaching down and taking Joey's tiny hand in his, Vince whispered, "Heh, little buddy. Daddy's here. You're going to be fine. I'm going to make sure of that."

Charlie flinched as if physically hit at hearing Vince make this declaration to his son. I could see the pain reflecting from his eyes before he turned his back, trying to gain control of his emotions. Taking a final look at his son, Vince turned away at the touch of a tall nurse with flaming red hair, dressed in frog green operating attire. Placing her hand on his shoulder, she motioned for him to follow her.

Charlie suddenly stepped forward, taking the place Vince had just vacated. Gently smoothing the hair back from the small forehead, he said softly, "I'm here pal. I won't leave you. I'll make sure you're going to be alright."

I turned my face away from the small eyes that silently watched us. Wrapping my arms around myself, I felt the gut wrenching sobs tear through my body. Turning back to watch Charlie with Joey, I silently prayed the promises Charlie and Vince had made would become a reality, knowing it was up to God and strangers now to determine if the promises they pledged would be kept or broken.

All too soon an orderly entered the room to whisk Joey away from us. Kissing the tiny hand, I whispered to him, "You'll be right back Joey and I'll be right here waiting for you."

Sitting in the blue waiting room, the cloying smell of disinfectant wafting up to cling to the insides of my nose, another time flashed back, flooding my memory with horror. I was six at the time. Terrified, I had clung to my father's hand, my face pressed into the coarse blue fabric of his overalls, faintly smelling of oil and hay, to watch the double doors swallow up my mother. The look in my father's eyes terrified me even more then the large double doors, which had swung shut to make her invisible to us. I could still feel my father's hand gripping mine, squishing my fingers unknowingly. I had drifted off to sleep when the doors finally opened. The thudding sound awakening me with a jerk, I sat up rubbing my eyes to see the doctor in frog green, splattered with huge stains of blood, silhouetted in the open doors. He walked slowly towards where my father and I sat waiting and then placing his hand on my father's shoulder. He shook his head. A look of sympathy etched into the fine lines on his face, he announced, "I'm sorry. We did our best, but there was just too much damage. There was nothing more that we could do. I'm afraid she's gone." My father, the man who had chased monsters from under my bed so ferociously, who was afraid of nothing, now sank slowly onto his chair in a heap, screaming over and over, the same words, "No! Oh My God! No!" while tears streamed down his face. I was too young to really understand the significance of all that was said that dark night. All I knew was I wanted my mother and she wasn't there.

Later, when I was older, I learned that the drunk driver who had hit my mother's car head on had walked away without a scratch. He had lost his licence for a year. I had lost my mother for life. Now, all these years later, I sat here again, waiting for news of another person I had given my heart to. "Please God! Don't take him from us," I prayed.

The hours ticked by, minute by minute, so slowly I thought I would eventually scream or go mad if I didn't hear something soon. The pendulum in the large clock swung back and forth. It seemed to mock me, as if repeating the same words over and over again, *just wait—just wait—just wait.* Charlie lay sprawled on a chair, his head twisted back at a crazy angle, dozing. Vince, after donating his blood, lay sprawled across two chairs, using his hands for a pillow, snoring lightly. He had done all he could, I acknowledged gratefully. The two large doors finally swung open. Lyle, followed by Doctor Carlton, still dressed in frog green, came to stand before us.

"Well, it's over. He came through like a little trooper. He'll be out of post-op soon. You'll be able to see him after a bit," Lyle said, a grin lifting the corners of his mouth.

I slumped in my seat, the relief overwhelming me. Raising a trembling hand to my lips, I said, "Oh My God, thank you, thank you," as tears of relief misted my vision.

Doctor Carlton pulled out one of the chairs to sit facing us. "The operation went well, but he's not out of the woods yet. He's going to have a long recovery time and will need a lot of TLC for quite a while, I'm afraid. I don't anticipate any lasting effects, but only time will tell."

"You'll just have to take it one day at a time. He's one sick little boy yet," Lyle added soberly.

"He'll be here for a while before he gets the green light to go home," Doctor Carlton said, encompassing us all with a sober expression. "He will need one parent to stay with him. It's up to you which one. Just ask at the front desk for a cot to be put in his room," he said, rising to his feet in preparation to leave. Then, taking Vince's hand and giving it a quick shake, he nodded his head before swiveling on his heel to exit the room.

"In my opinion, I believe it would be wiser if Beth stays with him," Lyle said, looking Vince fully in the face.

Vince slowly nodded his head in acceptance. "Yes, I think you're right," he conceded, his eyes searching mine for confirmation.

"Yes! Of course, I'll stay. I wouldn't want to be anywhere else. Joey needs me," I declared, nodding at Vince.

Charlie turned towards Lyle, his voice cracking with emotion as he gave Lyle's shoulder an affectionate squeeze. "Thanks Lyle, I don't know what we would have done without you."

"Enough. I was just doing my job. The rest is up to you now," Lyle said with a slight grin.

A slightly mousey looking nurse stuck her head around the corner of the door to say, "He's awake. You may see him now, but only for a few minutes." Dressed in our gowns and masks, single file, we passed through the doors. We were all eager to gaze once more upon the face of the tiny little boy that had captured our hearts so completely.

Staring down at Joey still hooked to a horde of machines, I realized how truly lucky we were to have him still here with us. Saying a silent prayer of thanks, I caressed the tiny cheek, now devoid of the bluish tinge, while Joey's eyes tried desperately to focus on me. It would take a long time for him to recover, but I knew in my heart he would. He was a fighter, my little Joey.

Vince, without announcing he was staying, returned with Charlie to the farm to continue with harvest preparations. Joey stayed in the hospital for two weeks before we were allowed to finally take him home. The hospital bill, I acknowledged gratefully, was covered by the state since Vince was underage and Joey's mother was deceased.

★★★

CHARLIE GOES HOME
CHAPTER TWENTY ONE

I knew Beth would never leave that kid with anyone else. She's like a wild cat with new young. You couldn't have pried her out of that hospital for any money. God, I wish I could have stayed to help her, but I have to get back to the farm or else I'll have that dam bank breathing down my neck again.

Come on, Vince! What's taking him so damn long? Looking around I searched for any sign of him between the parked cars lining the hospital parking lot. The first time I laid eyes on him and Amy I had felt sorry for them. Not so much now. Vince had a way of annoying a person without realizing he was doing it. I wish Beth wouldn't feel so damn sorry for him all the time. Christ, when I was his age I had more responsibilities than you could shake a stick at! My old man would have tanned my hide if I acted like him. Those beatings with that piece of harness he kept hanging by the fireplace—No, I didn't want to think about that anymore. That part of my life was in the past, over with, dead just like him. I smiled to myself, remembering the freedom I had found the night he died. My smile slowly disappeared at the thought of my mother. He told me she had left, that she didn't want to have anything to do with a snotty-nosed brat clinging to her skirt all the time. For years I thought I was the reason she left. I blamed myself for everything. Then I find out the old bastard did her in. Jim says I should let it go; move on. I guess he's right, but it's so damn hard. I can tell Beth's worried about my sleep walking. I'm glad she doesn't know everything. My little sister, Sheena, would be alive today if it wasn't for me. Someday I'll tell her the whole story, but she has enough to deal with right now.

"Finally found you," Vince said, poking his head in the window to interrupt my musings of the past.

"What took you so damn long?"

"I got lost. This place is huge," he replied sheepishly.

"You should have followed me out like I told you. God, you'd get lost in a back yard," I said, shaking my head.

"Yeh, right! Look, I'm here now. It's no big deal," he said, shifting his butt around on the seat to get comfortable.

God, I thought, gritting my teeth, it's going to be a long ride home. Vince gratefully remained silent as I manoeuvred the truck from lane to lane heading towards the outskirts of the city. The long drive home gave me time to think about everything that had just happened. Beth had nearly come unglued when Joey got sick. I had never seen her that bad, even when we lost our own babies. There's no way in hell I'll let Vince just walk away with our son. I'll take it to the highest court in the country if I have to. Poor little bugger! He sure had me scared when he turned blue like that. I hope he's not going to be sickly from now on. Doc said it would take time, but he'll be just like any other kid. I sure hope he's right. I know Beth will make sure that kid gets whatever he needs to turn out alright.

I could feel the need for sleep edging into my body after driving for so long with only myself for company. Man that kid sure can sleep! He was asleep before we got outside the city limits. Speak of the devil I thought, watching Vince sit up to blink his eyes like an owl.

"Where are we?" Vince asked, running his hand over his face.

"We're nearly home, just heading down into the valley now," I replied, my voice sounding weary, even to me.

"Would you like me to drive now?" he asked, looking out the side window.

"No. You don't know these turns and they can be very tricky if you're not used to them."

"Whatever," he replied, turning back to look out the window, just as the first rays of morning sunshine filtered over the rim of the valley.

Home had never looked as good as I pulled up in front of the house to kill the engine. We weren't going to get much done this morning, I realized, weaving my way down the hall towards my bedroom. Just a few hours of sleep, I told myself, flopping down on to the bed.

I awoke to the tantalizing smell of bacon frying. I hadn't eaten anything since Joey had become sick and now my stomach growled at the mouth-watering scent. Making short work of changing into my work clothes, I followed the enticing smell wafting from the kitchen.

Thomas was cracking eggs into a large frying pan with his back turned to me. He asked, "How many eggs do you want?"

"Smells good, two is fine."

"How's the kid doing?"

"He sure gave us a scare, but he'll be okay. He's a tough little guy."

Thomas slid a plate of scrambled eggs and bacon across the table to me before motioning towards the living room, "What's with the kid sleeping on the couch now?"

"He's afraid of ghosts," I chuckled.

"Little big for that, isn't he?"

"Have you seen any ghosts in your bedroom?" I asked, raising my eyebrows.

"Sure, the ghost of my old lady's backside when I kicked her out the door. Does that count?"

I wearily shook my head, "Depends on your definition of ghosts, I guess."

The sound of Vince's shuffling footsteps could be heard approaching the kitchen. "Anything left for me?" he asked, rubbing his eyes.

"I'm not working for you. Make your own," Thomas replied sourly before forking another mouthful of eggs into his mouth.

"Nice." Vince said, rolling his eyes. Then, ambling over to the counter he proceeded to make his own breakfast.

"Vince, you can clean up here while Thomas and I thresh a sample of wheat to see if it's dry enough. When you're done, come out to the west field behind the barn. You do know we're that is, don't you?"

"I know where it is! Whatever you say, boss," Vince said, cracking another egg into the frying pan.

Gritting my teeth, I left the house. Jeez, that kid really knows how to push my buttons. He was starting to get more annoying than Thomas, if that was possible. Making my way towards the combine, I turned sharply to glance back at the old house. From the corner of my eye I had thought I saw a shadow flit across the attic window. I must be seeing ghosts, I thought with a chuckle. The smile died on my lips as that niggling reminder crept back into my brain. The past was now bound to the future and my only chance for escape lay in death. Shaking my head to clear the morbid thoughts away, I climbed into the combine, telling myself that there's work to be done and to forget it. With that thought in mind, I slowly inched my way out of the yard, manoeuvring the huge machine towards the edge of the field.

Sitting up high in the monstrous machine I had a clear view of the scene spread out before me. This was my life; this is what I was born to do. My heart lifted as I gazed out over the golden field below. The sun shone gloriously down upon row after row of golden wheat, snaking around the field in a continuous chain, while in the distance the majestic mountains rose, their snow-capped peaks glistening under a clear blue sky. At the base of the mountains, sparkling like a jewel, one could just discern the vivid blue of the lake peeking out between the huge pines. As a child I had often sought solace in the comfort of the huge old maple tree behind the barn, which offered me the same view I was witnessing now. Forty years later that view could still make my heart lift.

A sudden banging on the combine snapped me out of my lackadaisical mood. Glancing down I found Thomas's face peering up at me from the ladder, motioning he was ready to start. Thomas was useless when it came to driving the combine. He seemed to have difficulty with even the simplest task involved in operating it, so I deemed it wiser to have him haul the grain to the bins. With Vince's help he shouldn't have any problem backing the truck up to the bin to empty it. The only problem being, while waiting for me to fill the combine's tank, he would doze off to sleep, leaving me sitting at one end of the field waiting for him, the combine's tank too full of grain to continue threshing. After having to trek twice from one end of the field to the other on foot to wake him up, my patience had stretched to the limit.

"What the hell do you think you're doing?" I yelled, opening the door to find him sound asleep once again.

Thomas jerked himself awake mumbling, "What—I didn't see you motion for me to come."

"That's because, you're stretched out dead to the world. I'm not paying you to sleep," I claimed frostily.

"What does it matter if I take a little nap? What's the big rush all about? We'll still get it done."

Gritting my teeth, I fairly screamed at him, "I'll tell you what the matter is. If I don't get this grain threshed while it's dry, if it gets a rain on it again, I can kiss it good bye. It will only be good enough for feed. That is, if I can get it threshed at all. That means no money for the bank and no money for you. Do I make myself clear?"

"Perfectly," Thomas snapped, turning away while mumbling, "You'd think I had murdered someone."

"What the hell does that mean?" I demanded, grabbing him by the front of the shirt to jerk him forward.

"Nothing, nothing, I didn't mean anything by it," he said, trying to jerk free from my grasp.

"You had better not!" I said, withdrawing my grasp from the front of his shirt as I shoved him backwards.

Thomas nodded, eyes downcast, before starting the truck. Then, putting it into gear, he slowly drove across the field towards the waiting combine, leaving me to follow on foot. Fool, I thought, following behind.

The rest of the afternoon passed in relative ease. Thomas made sure he was on time to collect the grain each time the grain tank was full from then on. Vince never showed up until well into the late afternoon.

"Where the hell have you been?" I demanded, looking down from the combine.

Not looking up, he said. "It takes longer than you think to clean up after you guys."

"I wouldn't think washing a few dishes should take that long."

"There was more to do than washing a few dishes," he said, clearly insulted.

"Never mind, come over here to the bin. I'll show you what your job is," I said, striding over towards the steel bins. "All you have to do is guide the truck back towards the auger when Thomas backs up. Do you see these steel panels? They go in these slides on each side of the door opening. As the grain goes up the auger into the bin, you have to drop the panels into the slides on each side of the door until the hole is closed completely. Do you think you can manage that?"

"It doesn't look too difficult. Sure I can manage that," Vince said, looking up at the row of shiny grain bins that resembled huge steel bottles stretching towards the sky. They each had a round red cap on top, one jauntily sitting open with a long auger that appeared to be peeking inside. "No, I won't have any problem," he said again.

"Alright, then I'll get going. The sooner we're done this field, the better. It doesn't look like we're going to get any rain for a while, but I'm not taking any chances."

"Charlie, do you think Joey's going to be alright?" Vince asked, eyes downcast, pushing the toe of his boot in a circle on the ground.

I looked at this big overgrown kid, shyly asking if the child he had fathered was going to be alright and realized there was no way in which he would be able to provide for that child. "He'll be fine," I said, climbing onto the combine. As I slowly pulled away, I glanced back to see Vince still standing there, hands in his pockets, a frown on his face while the dust and chaff swirled around him in a cloud.

The confrontation with Thomas had helped. When the combine's tank was full of grain, he would make his way over towards me in the truck, waiting patiently while I unloaded the grain from the combine. Then off he would go, making his way to where Vince waited at the bins, ready to assist him with the unloading.

It was almost a relief when the combine started to groan, protesting that the swaths were too wet with dew to continue. The house cloaked in darkness, not a light to beckon us, was a reminder: Beth would not be there to greet us when we pulled up in front of the house. The meal that evening was hastily prepared, being a bachelor's staple of beans and wieners. It proved filling, if not appealing. Placing the dishes into the sink, we all wearily made our way to our beds, too tired for small talk. Vince crawled under his blanket on the sofa, sighing in contentment as I walked by.

A muffled, "Good night, Charlie," came from under the blanket, leaving me shaking my head at the sight of a fully grown man afraid of ghosts. While from the attic came a low moan, as wind crept under the crack of a window. The eerie sound caused the mound of blankets to shake ever so slightly. "What's that noise?" Vince whispered, poking his head out from under the blankets.

"That's the ghosts in the attic moaning," I said, with a chuckle.

"That's not even funny," Vince said, turning his back to me, which only made me break into a full chortle as I made my way to my bed room.

The next morning proved to be a repeat of the previous day. The weather seemed to be cooperating nicely. There wasn't any sign of rain in the forecast in the near future. Thomas and Vince had settled into a convenient routine, which helped me relax. Thomas, I found, had meta-morphosed overnight, somehow developing a warped sense of humour to ease his boredom. He was constantly trying to think up new ways to scare Vince. This particular night being more bored than usual, he decided that I would become a recipient of one of his pranks.

The night was black as pitch. Not even a star could be seen overhead while the combine inched slowly around the field, devouring the swaths of wheat that lay in its path. The only source of light shining down on the swaths was that of the combine's headlights, bathing everything in an eerie glow. The slow tedious pace and the steady hum of the engine from the huge machine winding its way around the field had become hypnotising. All of a sudden, illuminated in the beam of the headlights, Thomas, like a jack in the box, jumped out from where he had been hiding under the swath. Stunned, I slammed on the brakes, stalling the huge engine dead in its tracks. Thomas quickly disappeared into the darkness like some kind of nymph while his gleeful laughter echoed throughout the quiet of the night. He had succeeded in his quest to scare the living bejesus out of me. After my heart quit racing, I had to smile to myself at the creativity involved in his pranks. One thing about it, you would not be bored with Thomas around. Although so far his pranks had proved harmless, I wasn't sure if they would remain that way. All the way home that night Thomas sat quietly watching me, a smug grin plastered on his face when he thought I wasn't looking.

The next morning we found a light rain had fallen throughout the night, coating everything in a veil of mist. It would delay our harvesting until late afternoon. Vince had become quite a hand at the domestic services involved in running a home. He rose early and would have breakfast made for us without being told what to do. He was still annoying, but anyone who could make such delicious pancakes was much more tolerable, I reasoned.

"Vince, I see you can handle things here, so Thomas and I will check the equipment over for any breaks and change the oil in the trucks this morning. The swaths won't be dry until after lunch." Pouring a huge stream of syrup over my pancakes, I added, "Oh yeah and you may as well do some work in Beth's garden. You can pull out all the dead plants for her and till it up. I don't think there's much left out there except the potatoes. You can leave those for a while yet."

"All right, I can handle that. I don't think it should take too long," Vince said, spearing his fourth pancake.

We all resumed our eating in silence until the sudden jangling of the telephone echoed throughout the kitchen, causing Thomas to jump.

"Jeez, that thing is loud," he said, his hand held over his heart.

"It's just payback time," I chuckled, giving him a smug grin before picking up the phone to answer it. The call was from Beth.

"Charlie, it's me. I'm glad I finally caught you in. I only have a few minutes, but wanted to hear your voice. I can't tell you how boring it is around here. How are things going there?

"Fine, but how is Joey doing?"

"He is doing wonderful, although the doctors haven't given us any indication when we will be allowed to go home. I'm just feeling a little homesick. It's nothing to worry about, really. I have to go. The nurse is here with Joey's medication. I'll call later, bye."

I hung up the phone to find Vince leaning forward in anticipation, "How is Jarr— Joey doing?"

"He's coming along fine." I said with a frown, hearing Vince's slip of the tongue.

"That's good. I knew my boy was a fighter," Vince said, letting out a slow sigh.

"He's not your boy!" I ground out between clenched teeth, glaring furiously at him.

"He is my boy!" Vince snapped back.

"You gave up all rights before he was born. If I remember correctly, I seem to recall someone saying they weren't ready to become a father and we could have him," I snapped, daring him to say otherwise.

Vince flinched at my words, before he abruptly stood to say, "I changed my mind!" Then, turning on his heel and pushing open the screen door, he paused to say, "I have that right, you know," punctuated by the slam of the screen door.

So, I thought, the gloves are off. If it's a fight you want, it's a fight you will get. Vince would soon find out just how much of an adversary I could be.

Thomas, deciding it was better to have his bread buttered on both sides, so to speak, piped up to say, "I heard him say that he didn't want the kid. I'll tell that in court."

Glaring at Thomas, I decided to ignore his ill-placed remark.

"Let's go, there's work to be done," I snapped, pushing open the screen door to follow in Vince's footsteps.

CHAPTER TWENTY TWO

Farming involved being a jack of all trades. Regular mechanical maintenance was one job that required time and patience. Of the two, I could not say patience was my best forte. Thomas' complete lack of knowledge in this area left a lot to be desired; he didn't have a clue what was required. The scene with Vince had left me in a foul temper, leaving Thomas to become the recipient of my ill-fated mood. I watched Vince from the corner of the shop, feebly attempting to pull the dead plants from the garden. He sat between the rows, gazing out at the pond, absent mindedly plucking a few dry plants from the row to toss them onto a slight pile.

I finally had enough of his pitiful display of workmanship, so striding to where he sat, I yelled, "Get up and put some effort into the job! You're not getting paid to sit on your ass."

"Why, should I? I haven't seen any money for my work yet," he declared sourly.

"The deal was that you would get paid after harvest, only by my good grace, I might add. I seem to remember you saying you would work for just room and board. I am right, or am I not? You can leave today if you want," I stated, glowering at him.

Vince slowly lowered his eyes, carefully examining his shoes to mumble, "Yeah, you're right."

Having vented my anger, I turned back towards the shop, remarking over my shoulder, "Now, get back to work and put some effort into it!"

The next time I looked, Vince was vigorously pulling dry plants out and tossing them on to a huge growing pile.

Lunch was a quiet affair. No one seemed to be in a mood for small talk. Thomas, becoming bored, decided to stir the pot, so to speak. With a Cheshire grin lighting his face he asked, "When will Beth be home with your son, Charlie?"

Glancing at Thomas, I took a sip from my coffee and seeing the smile plastered across his face, I replied icily, "Give it a break, why don't you."

"What? Did I say something wrong?"

"Don't play the innocent with me. You're far from it," I informed him, draining my coffee cup in one gulp.

"Can't a guy ask an innocent question around here without getting the third degree?" Thomas muttered, leaving the table.

"When is Beth coming home with Joey?" Vince asked.

"How the hell should I know? It's time to get some work done," I said, pivoting on my heel to leave the room.

Harvest seemed to be going at a steady pace. Thomas and Vince had found their place and neither one had to be told how to do their job twice. Thomas was the one I was worried about the most, having been on the receiving end of a few of his ill-placed antics.

"Thomas, this is the last load of barley for this field. You can take it over to the bin and unload it while I bring the combine."

"No problem boss," he said, his voice lacking any kind of emotion, while putting the truck in gear to leave.

I followed along behind at a snail's pace, the dust from the truck obscuring my vision. I arrived at the bin to find Thomas backing the truck up to the auger. Vince stood behind the truck, motioning Thomas with hand signals to guide the truck into position. Thomas, completely missing his target, continued to back up the truck all the while, ignoring Vince's screams of stop, whoa, stop, at the top of his lungs. I watched with fear as he was being sandwiched between the truck and the bin. Thomas, looking in his rear view mirror, grinned deviously while he continued to aim for his target—Vince. Then, abruptly slamming on his brakes, he brought the huge truck to grinding halt only inches from where Vince stood.

"I bet you'll have to check your shorts now, ghost boy," he chuckled, looking back out the window with a snort of laughter at his own joke.

Vince ran around to the side of the truck to jerk the door open. Reaching in, he grabbed Thomas by the front of the shirt, dragging him forward. "You could have killed me," he said, bringing his fist back to slam it into Thomas's face with a satisfying crunch. "You bloody ass hole. That's not even a joke you dumb son of a b—. Oh, what the hell is the use? He doesn't have a bloody brain in his head anyways," Vince said, shoving a surprised looking Thomas backwards before turning to walk away.

"You little twit, no one punches me and gets away with it!" Thomas said, jumping from the truck, blood streaming freely from his nose. Grabbing Vince by the hair, he swung him around to face him, ready to deliver a reciprocating blow to Vince's face.

"That will be enough!" I yelled, grabbing Thomas's arm before he could deliver the blow.

"Let me go. He's not going to get away with this!" Thomas screamed, spittle oozing from the corner of his mouth.

"You started it. Now I say it's finished!" I yelled into his face while slowly twisting his arm behind his back, bringing him to his knees.

"Aw—k, you're breaking my arm!"

"No, but I will if you don't calm down. Right now," I added.

Thomas rapidly jerked his head up and down like a marionette while whining, "Alright, man. Let me go."

"Promise to behave," I asked, twisting his arm a little further in encouragement.

"Yeh, Yeh, I promise," he stuttered, nodding his head again.

"Good, that's all I wanted to hear. Now go play nicely," I said, patting his cheek while I released him.

Thomas stood there, blood dripping from his nose, glaring from me to Vince, undecided what his next move should be.

"You're both a pair of bloody assholes!" he ground out from between clenched teeth while he turned towards the truck. Reaching behind the seat, he grabbed a grease rag and, holding it to his nose, strode from of our view to hide with embarrassment behind the bins.

"Don't push your luck, Thomas, or I'll finish what Vince started."

From behind the bins came an indistinct mumble, which sounded like 'up yours'. Let him lick his wounds in private, I decided, ignoring his ill-chosen remark.

Climbing into the truck to back it up properly, I couldn't help the twitch of my lips, which turned into a silly grin as I pictured the surprised look on Thomas's face when Vince ploughed him in the nose with his fist. I guess even Vince had his limits. I would have to be more cautious around him from now on.

The next morning Vince was up early to make breakfast. "What's up for today?" Vince asked, pushing a plate of bacon and scrambled eggs complete with hot buttered toast towards me.

Shoving a fork full of eggs into my mouth, I said, "The same as yesterday. Man, what did you do to these eggs to make them taste so good? Where did you learn to cook like that?"

"I grew up without a mother, so my brothers and I had to take turns doing the cooking. Breakfast was my specialty," he said smugly.

"Is that supposed to make us feel sorry for you?" Thomas asked, entering the kitchen.

I nearly choked on my eggs when I looked up at Thomas' face; his bulbous nose, a bright red glow, followed by two black eyes. "Wow, can you see over that thing, Rudolph?" I chuckled.

"This is not over yet," Thomas solemnly promised, giving Vince a sour look.

"Aw, come on Thomas, you know you got what you deserved. You've been pushing Vince's buttons all week. What did you expect? Let it go. It's over with."

Vince, setting a steaming plate of bacon and eggs in front of Thomas, replied calmly, "Yeh. I'd say we're about even. Have some breakfast, I just made it."

Glaring at Vince, his eyes narrowed into tiny slits, Thomas swiftly pushed the plate away saying, "I just lost my appetite. You eat it ghost boy." Knocking his chair over in his haste, he jumped up to storm towards the door, slamming it shut upon his exit.

"I will," Vince said smugly, pulling the plate forward.

"You had better watch your back from now on. He's not going to let this rest," I cautioned, nodding my head in Thomas' direction.

"I'm not afraid of him," Vince claimed, his hand shaking slightly as he brought a forkful of eggs to his mouth.

"Maybe not, but I just thought you might heed a warning, anyways. It's going to take him a while to forget by the look of things."

It wasn't just Vince Thomas was angry with. He had seemed fit to place me in the same category. Vince completely avoided him, where as I could not. Gone was the metamorphosed Thomas; the real Thomas emerged in his place. The threshing was going well until I heard the grinding sound every farmer hates to hear. Groaning at the thought of what a mechanical break could entail, I brought the huge combine to a halt. Cursing under my breath, I climbed down to inspect the damage. The break was bad, but not atrocious enough to halt harvest. Signalling for Thomas to come and pick me up, I stood waiting for him to respond. Nothing! Zippo! God, the idiot must have fallen asleep again. Glancing up at the blazing sun, I trudged across the field towards the silent truck. Wiping the sweat from my brow, I found myself getting hotter and hotter by the minute. That lazy piece of crap! Just wait until I get my hands on him, I thought, wrenching open the cab door to find Thomas curled up in a ball moaning, his eyes glazed over with pain. My anger instantly dissipated at the sight of him when I realized he had not even acknowledged my presence.

"Thomas, what's wrong?" I asked, giving his shoulder a quick shake.

Thomas slowly raised his head, his eyes trying to focus on my face while he forcibly whispered, "Sick man, really sick."

Jumping into the truck, I hurried towards the bins, honking the horn for Vince to come.

Vince, upon opening the truck door, looked down at Thomas, his eyes huge with shock while he mumbled, "Did I do that to him?"

"I doubt it, but I'd better get him to a hospital."

Thomas continued his moaning all the way to the hospital. Vince turned slightly in his seat to stare at Thomas, who lay curled up on the back seat in obvious pain.

Motioning his head towards Thomas, Vince whispered, "I hope I'm not responsible for that. I never meant to hurt him that bad."

"I'm sure you're not to blame. I have never seen a punch in the nose do anything like this," I assured him, glancing in the mirror to see Thomas still moaning.

Thomas was placed on a gurney and wheeled quickly away upon our arrival at the local hospital. A tall, skinny nurse studiously appeared bearing a clip board, urging us to fill out Thomas's medical history. "I can't tell you anything about him," I said, shoving the clipboard back to her.

"You can't give me any information at all?" She asked, raising her eyebrows in doubt, her foot tapping in agitation.

"No, I can't tell you anything about him," I assured her emphatically, shaking my head in response. Clicking her tongue, she finally moved away, a sigh escaping from between her lips in exasperation.

The hours seemed to drag by while we waited for word of Thomas' condition. Approaching the desk for the fourth time, a kindly nurse, whom had just came on duty, checking her charts, asked, "May I help you?"

I patiently explained what I wanted to know.

"Thomas, Thomas Lyman. Oh, here he is," she said, running her finger down a chart. "Are you related?"

"No. I just brought him in. He works for me. We've been waiting a long time now. I just want to know something one way or the other. I have to go home soon."

Searching my face, the nurse smiled apologetically, before saying, "Hold on, I'll see if I can get the doctor to talk to you for a few minutes. Just have a seat, I'll be right back."

Within minutes the doctor emerged from a room at the end of the hall, coming to stand before Vince and me. "Hi. I'm doctor Shibane. I understand you would like information about your friend?" he said, shaking my hand slightly. "Your friend will be fine," he nodded encouragingly. He developed a condition called Renal Colic. Do you know what that is?" he asked, seeing our puzzled expressions.

"Not a clue, Doc," I said, shaking my head.

"Have you ever heard of kidney stones?

"Sure," I said, while Vince nodded his head in acknowledgement beside me.

"Thomas had developed a rather large stone, which was lodged high up in his ureter. It can cause extreme pain. We inserted a cystoscopy viewing tube and could fortunately pull the stone out. We had to sedate him rather heavily for the procedure and would like him to rest for a few more hours until the anaesthetic wears off. He will have to take it easy for the next few days, but then he should be back to normal.

"He can come home today?" I asked incredulously.

"Sure. And one other thing, we straightened his broken nose. He seems reluctant to talk about it. Just out of curiosity, do you know how that happened?"

"Not a clue." I said, shaking my head.

The doctor glanced from me to Vince. Nodding his head he said, "Alright if there's nothing else, I have a patient waiting for me in pre-op."

"Thanks, Charlie," Vince whispered, watching the doctor stride away. "What do we do now?" he asked.

"We go and get our parts for the combine and then come back and pick him up. It looks like the rest of the day is wasted. We won't get any more work done."

Thomas dozed fitfully on the ride home. Walking unsteadily, he climbed the stairs, muttering "I'm going to bed."

I wasn't sure if it was the procedure he had to go through, or if he was still mad at Vince and me. I guess we'll find out soon enough, I reasoned, unconcerned either way.

Thomas stayed home for three days while Vince took over his job in the field driving the truck. On the fourth day I informed Thomas over breakfast that his services would be required to haul grain once again.

"I can't. I'm not feeling well enough yet," he whined, shrugging his shoulders while he lay back in his chair, a pitiful sigh escaping from between his lips.

"You can sit on your ass in the truck just as well as you can here," I reminded him frostily.

"What do you mean? I've been sick."

"Well, you're not sick anymore. I talked to your doctor, just in case you didn't know that. He assured me there is no reason for you not to do your job. So guess what? It's time to get back to work."

"Sure, sure, kick a man when he's down," he said, taking a huge swig of coffee.

"I'm sure we could arrange that, if you like," I said with a smirk.

The ringing of the telephone halted any other excuses Thomas could invent. It was such a relief to hear Beth's voice. I had been so busy I never realized just how much I had missed her until now.

"We can come home today. Doctor Carlton says Joey is doing wonderfully. He's even started sleeping through the night."

"What time do you want me to pick you up? I asked, smiling at the thought of Beth finally coming home.

"Oh, you don't have to pick me up. Lyle is bringing us home. He said he was going out that way anyways. We'll probably be there around two."

Vince, who was not attempting to hide the fact that he was eves dropping, quickly asked, "Is Joey coming home too?"

"Of course, my son will be coming home with her," I said, scowling.

Vince's eyes narrowed at my statement before he icily replied, "We'll see." Turning on his heel, he exited the room before I had a chance to retaliate.

The rest of the day seemed to drag by. I found myself checking the road from time to time in anticipation of Beth's arrival. Vince avoided me whenever possible, while Thomas, though quiet, watched Vince stealthily through narrowed eyes. I could see he was biding his time until the chance arose for him to get even with Vince for breaking his nose.

Looking towards the distance, I was rewarded with a blue dot followed by a spiral of dust. Lyle was making his way down the winding road to the bottom of the valley. Beth and Joey would be home soon.

★★★

Beth returns Home
Chapter Twenty Three

Grateful to be home, I walked from room to room inspecting my kingdom for any damage. Finding none, I lowered myself onto one of the high-backed chairs flanking the old scarred kitchen table, Joey still sound asleep in my arms.

"Happy to be home?" Lyle asked, watching me move from room to room.

"No truer words were ever spoken," I said, a grin splitting my face from ear to ear. "I wonder where everyone is," I mused, looking around at the lunch dishes stacked neatly beside the sink.

"You won't have to wonder for long," Lyle chuckled, upon hearing the sound of an approaching vehicle, followed by the slamming of a truck's doors.

"You finally made it home. I was kind of worried, you being with Lyle and all," Charlie said, giving me a huge hug.

"Well, you don't have any reason to worry, all though I did try to get her to dump you and take off to Vegas with me. But, as luck would have it, she shot me down. You're one lucky man, Charlie. She wouldn't even consider it," Lyle said with a twinkle in his eye.

"I know I am. You don't have to tell me twice," Charlie said, giving me a slight squeeze.

"How's he doing now?" Charlie asked Lyle, taking Joey from my arms.

"He's doing very well considering all he's been through. He still has a long way to go, but it looks good from here on in. I don't think he has any permanent damage, but only time will tell. He will have to be watched closely for quite a while. Beth has been briefed on that. She knows what to watch for," Lyle said with a nod towards Joey.

Vince stood to one side, listening carefully to what Lyle said, his eyes glinting with hostility while he watched Charlie with his son. Joey, now awake, lay listening, his small dark eyes trained on Charlie's face.

"How's my little man doing?" Charlie whispered, stroking his tiny cheek.

Vince stood to one side not saying a word, his hands clenched into fists at his side while Charlie gently cradled Joey, talking softly to him.

I turned slightly as Thomas entered the room. "Oh my God, what happened to you?" I demanded, looking at the tape bridging his swollen nose framed by two large black eyes with bags beneath them. He looked as if he had aged ten years since I last saw him.

"Vince punched me in the nose. For no reason, I might add," he said, eyes flashing as he glared at Vince.

"You did that?" I asked, turning to look at Vince incredulously.

Vince lowered his head, studying his shoes intently before looking up. "Wait a minute, it wasn't for nothing. He deserved it," he said, his chin jutting out in defiance.

I looked towards Charlie, my eyebrows arched in disbelieve, beseeching him to fill me in on what had really happened, "Really! It looks like a few things have happened in my absence," I said, glancing from Thomas to Vince.

"Things just got out of hand a wee bit. It was nothing really," Charlie maintained, while an impish grin lit up his face.

"That's too bad, Thomas. I hope you're feeling better soon," I said, glancing at Charlie's amused grin.

Vince angrily strode to stand in front of Charlie, a determined look on his face as he held out his hands, "Can I hold my son now?"

Charlie's eyes glinted dangerously as he barked, "No! He's not your son."

"Let him hold him, Charlie. It can't hurt anything," I said, motioning for him to give him to Vince.

Charlie opened his mouth, only to snap it shut at the warning look I gave him. Glaring furiously at Vince, he grudgingly handed Joey to him.

Vince turned away from the hostility shooting from Charlie's eyes to stand before me. Looking down at his son, he said, "I think he's lost some weight. Are you sure he's going to be alright?"

"Positive. I'll make sure of it." I assured him with a smile.

Vince, nodding his head, walked from the room to sit on the sofa, where he continued to stare thoughtfully at his son. Charlie stood glaring after him from the kitchen door way.

"Lyle, would you like a cup of coffee? I'll make a fresh pot," I announced, walking towards the sink to fill the pot with water.

"Sure, I guess I could handle a cup, even though I don't have a piece of that famous crumb cake of yours to go with it," he said with a slight grin. "Beth, I can't get over the improvement you've made these last couple of weeks," Lyle declared with a slight shake of his head.

Charlie snapped out of his oppressive mood long enough to turn away from where he had been studying Vince to ask, "What? What improvement? What are you talking about?"

"Beth! That's what. Can't you see the difference in her?" Lyle asked, waving his hand in my direction.

"No, but she always looks good to me," Charlie said, giving me a seductive wink.

Blushing, I stuttered, "I – I – I took physiotherapy on my leg while I was at the hospital for the last two weeks. It's made a huge difference. You can hardly notice that I limp now."

"I told you a few years ago you should have been taking it," Lyle said.

"I know, but we really couldn't afford it. I couldn't believe my luck when you said it was free as long as I was staying there."

"Yup, you sure were lucky there," Lyle said, with a secretive grin. "Well, I guess I should be going now," he said, placing his empty cup into the sink.

"Oh, already? Well, thanks for giving us a ride home. I really appreciated it. And thanks for everything else you've done," I said with a knowing grin.

"Not a problem. You can count on me for anything. You know that. Don't you?" he asked, giving me a hug.

"I do know that," I said, returning the hug.

"Ahem! I do believe you're trying to steal my favourite girl right out from under my nose," Charlie said, trying to look ferocious but failing miserably.

"If I could, I would, but I can't. That's just my luck," Lyle said with a tiny chuckle. "I'll be back at the end of the week to check on Joey. If you have any questions before that, just give me a call. Take care of my girl for me, Charlie," he said with a wink, before sauntering out the door.

"You can count on me," Charlie laughed, glancing in my direction.

"Well, break's over. It's time to go back to work. Come on guys," Charlie announced, the screen door snapping shut behind him.

Vince carefully placed Joey into my arms. "Thanks for looking after him so well, Beth," he whispered.

"You're welcome Vince, but he is my son. I would never turn my back on him, no matter what happens to him," I said soberly.

Nodding his head, Vince followed Charlie out the door.

I looked into the dark little eyes, surveying me intently, to whisper conspiratorially, "I think we have a big problem." To my amusement, Joey grinned and nodded his head as if agreeing with me. Laughing, I gathered him close. I would worry about Vince later. For now I was just happy to be home and grateful to be holding my son. Upstairs a door slammed shut, making me jump with its suddenness.

Leaning close, I whispered to Joey, "Bloody ghosts." Joey, staring at me with huge, round eyes, suddenly broke into his first laugh. I was ecstatic. "You laughed, you really laughed," I cried happily, dancing Joey around the room.

Joey giggled again and again as if he understood me, making my heart soar with laughter. I could hardly wait to tell Charlie.

That night Charlie looked gratefully at the meal I had prepared. "Beth is home. No more canned stuff," he said enthusiastically.

"I noticed there were a lot of beans missing," I chuckled, looking around at the eager faces.

"Heh, I always made a good breakfast for everyone while you were away," Vince piped up, feeling slightly under appreciated.

"That you did," Charlie admitted with a nod.

"And what did you contribute?" I asked Thomas.

Glancing up at my question, he swallowed a bite of meatloaf before declaring, "Nothing, apparently."

"Oh. Alright then, I see," I maintained, a ghost of a smile hovering on my lips.

"Charlie, you should have heard Joey laugh today. His first true laugh," I announced, bubbling with remembered pleasure.

"Really? That's great," he said, smiling at my enthusiasm.

"It looks like that little fellow, has you wrapped around his little finger," Charlie laughed.

"No. It's just that it's a first," I replied indignantly.

Vince sat quietly chewing his food, listening thoughtfully to Charlie and my easy banter. Thomas' eyes, down cast upon his plate, hurriedly shoveled bite after bite into his mouth, avoiding all conversation. Pushing his plate away, he belched before turning to wander into the living room where he slumped into a chair, staring morosely around him.

After dinner everyone seemed too tired for small talk as they scattered quickly towards their bedrooms in anticipation of an early retirement. Vince had not given up the sofa in favour of his true bed. Grabbing the bedding from where it sat neatly folded on a chair, he proceeded to make his bed.

"Okay, what's been going on here?" I asked, closing our bedroom door.

"Whatever do you mean?" Charlie chuckled, giving me an impish grin.

"Vince beat Thomas up," I cried incredulously.

Charlie chuckled in amusement. "Naw, not really," he just gave him one good punch in the nose. It was a good one though. Bloody well deserved it, he did. I know you'll find this hard to believe, but Thomas can be quite a trickster when he gets bored. He just pushed Vince's buttons once too often, that's all."

"Really, I never would have believed it in a million years. Thomas playing a joke on anyone, it's hard enough just getting him to smile."

"That kidney stone they took out of him, sure never made him smile. It must have been really painful. I sure hope I never have one of those," Charlie said with a shudder. "Well, there's one good thing that came from it all: his nose will be straight now. Doc fixed it for him at the same time."

"Whoa, back up. Thomas passed a kidney stone? You had to take him to the hospital. What else happened while I was gone?"

"He never really passed it. It was more like it was pulled out of him," he said, his face twisting into a grimace at the thought. "And what else happened was, I really missed you," he whispered, pulling me into his arms to kiss me. "I really, really missed you," he whispered, kissing my neck passionately. And then he proceeded to show me just how much he really had missed me, while all thoughts of Thomas and Vince fled our minds.

Chapter Twenty Four

The next morning the swaths were coated with heavy dew, halting combining until late after lunch. Charlie was anxious to get finished with harvest but once it started to rain in September. It seemed to continue for weeks at a time, making it difficult to get the last of the crop off the fields before snowfall. Winter had always come early this close to the mountains. Now we couldn't afford any delays, for the bank was pushing us hard for the money we had borrowed.

That morning, framed by the kitchen window, Charlie could be seen crawling on hands and knees, patiently clearing the weeds away from around each headstone. A new one had been added in my absence with the simple word 'Amy' in large block letters. Beneath her name, in smaller letters was the phrase, "May She Rest in Peace." When he was finished with the weeding, he took a few moments to go and sit beside his mother's grave, head bent, silently saying a prayer. Brushing his fingers slowly over the words inscribed into the granite stone, he got up, squaring his shoulders to slowly leave the cemetery without a backwards glance.

Thomas sat quietly in Charlie's old chair watching Vince from between hooded eyes when he thought no one was looking. He couldn't seem to let it go, knowing that Vince had bested him with one punch. I shuddered as he glared at Vince's back, his eyes narrowed into tiny slits, like a snake waiting to strike. Charlie was also the recipient of his evil looks. Thomas' narrowed gaze followed Charlie when he walked into the room. Charlie and Vince would have to watch their back, for Thomas was just waiting for the opportunity to strike back with a vengeance.

Charlie, spying Joey sitting in his chair, smiled happily before lifting him into his arms. He seemed to take such delight in being a father. I had never realized how much he had craved having a child until I watched him with Joey. Cradling Joey on his lap, he whispered to him all the things they were going to do when he got bigger.

"I'm going to teach you how to fish," he would say, smoothing Joey's cowlick down with his huge hands. "I never had a bike, but I'm going to make sure you have one," he told Joey, holding the small hand gently. Vince, watching Charlie from the doorway, hastily turned away to leave the room.

The next morning I decided to take Joey outside for some fresh air in his stroller. The cool, clean mountain air contained a hint of a chill, as if to warn us of the approaching winter. It seemed like overnight the trees had lost their lush green and were now decked in their fall coats in various stages of yellows, oranges, and reds. The grass, crisp and brown, now harmonized with the colors that Mother Nature had seen fit to dress her foliage in. The reeds around the pond still retained their crisp greenness, reluctant to let summer go, it seemed. Down by the pond, I was surprized to see the brood of geese that Amy had so diligently watched from goslings to fully feathered adults still gliding smoothly in circles around the center of the pond. This was my favourite time of the year and I was reluctant to leave it for the indoors. The honking of geese overhead had me scanning the clear blue sky in search of the v-shaped flock winging its way south. I leaned back against Amy's rock, a sigh escaping my lips at the simple pleasures. I had come to love this quiet way of life. As I took another look around, another thought popped into my head. This is what the bank was trying to take from us. I would hate to have to leave, I thought, gazing around at the beauty surrounding me. No! It would never happen. Charlie wouldn't let it. If push came to shove, he would die before giving it up. I shivered as a cloud passed over the sun. I had stayed long enough. The pleasure now dimmed, I slowly got to my feet, a sigh escaping me before I turned towards the house. As always that annoying feeling of being watched hovered over me as I looked up at the attic windows. I was sure I had seen a face pressed to the glass a moment earlier.

The days were shorter now and Charlie pushed the day's work to the limit, as rain had been forecasted for the following week. Thomas remained in his foul mood, sometimes even refusing to speak when spoken to. Whereas Vince would stay close by my side whenever Charlie was absent from the room, asking question after question as to why I did this or that while attending to Joey's needs. It was during one of these question periods that I had enough of his constant inquisition. Turning to face him, I summoned up my courage to gently remind him that Joey was ours now, so he didn't have any need for the information he sought. As Vince ran his fingers through his hair, I was reminded of Charlie whenever he was faced with a difficult decision.

"I still haven't made up my mind about that," he said, a hint of reproach creeping into his voice.

Expelling a huge sigh, I turned, studying his face, before warning him. "You don't stand a chance in court and I'm willing to take it that far."

Vince remained silent, digesting my words. Turning abruptly, he left the room, but not before I saw his eyes flood with unshed tears. I hung my head, my heart going out to Vince in his pain. It was Joey's welfare that I had to be concerned about, I reminded myself. Joey had been through a lot in his short life and would require more care now than most children. I prayed Vince would come to realize that it was in Joey's best interest for him to remain with us. I also knew the difficult decision Vince would have to make would haunt him for the rest of his life.

After dinner Charlie would take Joey out of his chair and settle on the sofa, talking to him softly, explaining how his day had gone, while Joey would appear to listen intently. "I think you're going to be a farmer like me," he whispered with a grin at the tiny upturned face listening to him attentively.

Vince, upon hearing these words, jumped up to stride from the room, slamming the door sharply on his way out. Charlie, noticing my frown, shrugged his shoulders nonchalantly. "Don't worry about him, Beth. He'll get over it sooner or later," he said, seemingly unconcerned.

"I don't know Charlie. He thinks he can still look after Joey himself. He wants his son and I don't think anything will stop him from trying to take him," I said, frowning at the thought. Returning to the kitchen, I leaned against the counter, watching Vince through the window storming determinedly down the path to the edge of the pond. Then, settling himself against the huge rock Amy had always chosen to sit against, he lifted his head to watch the geese gliding silently through the water.

Charlie's voice sounded from the living room, declaring forcefully, "He's not going to take my son away from me. There isn't a court in the country that would give a baby to someone that can't take care of himself, let alone a child that has the problems Joey has. Joey is our son now and he better not forget that."

"I hope you're right," I whispered to myself, watching Vince leaning against Amy's rock with his head down cast, held between his hands. Thomas, who had left the room when Charlie entered, now, sat on the porch swing, a devious smile playing at the corners of his mouth, watching Vince's discomfort through glinted eyes.

That night Charlie started wandering again in his sleep. I awoke to find him not curled up beside me anymore. He was not to be found on the first floor, so, climbing the steps to the second floor, I soon found him arguing with his imaginary adversary again. Taking him by the hand, I quietly lead him back down the stairs to our bedroom. The creepy feeling that we were being watched made me shudder in apprehension. The next time he was standing quietly, looking down upon a sleeping Vince, who lay sprawled upon the couch.

"Come on Charlie, back to bed," I whispered, taking him by the hand.

The next morning the testosterone was running high. Charlie, Thomas, and Vince would snap at each other over the most trifle remarks. I silently shook my head, only too glad I would not have to be around them working together in the field.

"I'll take the combine to the west field. Thomas, you bring the grain truck. Vince, you can hook the auger behind my half ton and follow behind us to the bins. Then you can set it up in the first bin, alright? Have you got that?" Charlie commanded, draining his remaining coffee with one gulp.

Thomas nodded as he rose to leave, not uttering a word in response, while Vince replied, "Yeh! Yeh! I got it."

I could see Charlie's back stiffen at Vince's tone while he walked out the door.

"Why do you try so hard to push his buttons the wrong way?" I snapped, glaring at Vince.

Vince's shoulders slumped at my remark. "I don't know. I don't really mean to. It just comes out that way," he said sheepishly.

"I did a lot of thinking last night and I realize you're right. I can't look after Joey like you can. I can see you really love him a lot, don't you?"

I nodded my head. "You know I do. There's nothing I wouldn't do for him," I said, squeezing my eyes shut in relief at Vince's words.

"I know that. I haven't any way to look after him right now. Can I come and see him sometimes?" Vince asked, tears forming in the corners of his eyes.

"Sure, that won't be a problem. Just one thing though, I want a lawyer to draw up the papers so everything will be done legally. I want him listed as Charlie's and my son."

Vince hung his head thinking. "I don't know. I never planned on that," he said. Slowly he raised his face. "Alright, get a lawyer to draw up the papers and I'll sign them. I'm trying to do what's best for him, Beth. It's not an easy decision to make. I hope I don't regret it for the rest of my life," he said, while tears trickled from the corners of his eyes.

I could see the pain that his decision had cost him as I watched his tears being wiped away in embarrassment by a shaky hand.

"Thank you, Vince. I know this hasn't been easy for you, but for what it's worth, I think Amy would approve of your choice," I said, giving him a hug in gratitude.

"I hope you're right. I'm going to come back and see him sometimes. I don't want him to think I abandoned him. No matter what, he's still my son," he said, chin held high before turning towards the door.

Charlie's blond head emerged fleetingly through the open door, demanding angrily, "What the hell is taking you so damn long?"

"He was just leaving, I'm afraid it was my fault, I held him up longer than I should have."

"Alright then, well let's go. I can't wait all day," Charlie growled.

Vince's look of gratitude made me smile as he hurried after Charlie towards the waiting truck.

"Wait, Charlie! I have something to tell you," I yelled after him, but Charlie had not heard me. Revving the engine, he drove away without looking back.

I would have to wait until tonight to tell Charlie of Vince's final decision. Joey would soon be ours legally, I thought happily, waltzing into my bedroom where I could hear Joey starting to stir from his night's sleep.

★★★

Chapter Twenty Five

Charlie in the Field

Beth is too easy on those two. She lets Vince walk all over her. For two cents I'd give him a good swift kick in the pants. I'm getting so damned tired of trying to get those two lazy jerks to do some work. I can hardly wait until harvest is done and out of the way. Then I get to go fishing for a week. No interruptions; just me and Jim out on the lake with a few cold beers and a fishing rod. Well, I guess it will have to wait for a while yet. There were a lot of things to finish first, I realized, climbing into the combine.

This was the last field to harvest and rain was forecasted for tonight. I'd better get my butt in gear or I won't get it finished. Lowering the combine's huge pickup teeth, the massive beast roared, grinding its way slowly around the field. This crop looked to be the best in years. All I needed to do was get it into the bin before the rain struck. Maybe next year I wouldn't have to depend on help from strangers.

Thomas had reverted back to his undependable self. My patience wearing thin with him, I finally snapped. "Can't you tell when the combine is full? I shouldn't have to wait on you for so long to get here!"

Thomas, not saying anything, proceeded to leave his lone middle finger inserted into the air when he thought I wasn't looking while he slowly crawled towards the bins. Jerk, I thought. I would be glad to see the last of him.

It was getting close to dark when I spotted the thunder heads looming on the horizon. Lightning crackled and danced in the distance. The wind abruptly picked up in velocity, teasing the edges of the swaths, as if to warn them how easily they could be picked up and tossed away at a moment's notice. I found myself pushing the heavy beast of a combine to move faster while I watched the sky darken, the storm edging closer and closer. It was going to be a race to the finish, I thought, eyeing the remaining swaths.

I silently cheered, watching the last of the remaining swath slide over the combine's hungry teeth, the last of the grain deposited into its huge tank. If we were lucky we would get it unloaded before the rain hit. What was taking Thomas so damn long to get back? I watched for a glimmer of the truck's headlights in the distance. Finally, feeling the first plop of rain hit my hand, I spied Thomas slowly inching his way back towards the field. A bloody snail could move faster, I thought.

The last of the grain deposited into the truck, I yelled at Thomas for him to follow me with the combine. Thomas' answer was drowned out by the roar of the combine as he pointed back towards the bin. Yes, I acknowledged, nodding my head and pointing at the bin. Jumping into the truck, I hurried across the field before the rain struck in earnest. I had just finished unloading the truck and was proceeding to close the top of the bin when the rain started to come down in a thin sheet. Thomas arrived with the combine, just as I crawled down the ladder from the top of the bin.

"We just made it," he said, in a more jovial mood than I had seen for a while. "Where's Vince?"

"I don't know. He wasn't here when I got here," I told him, suddenly noticing the pickup still sitting in the same place it was before.

"When was the last time you saw him?" I asked, searching behind the bin.

Thomas looked up sheepishly. "He was having a hard time getting the last panel to slide down to close the door, so I told him to climb inside. The slide came down and he couldn't get it back up, so I thought I'd teach him a lesson and left him there. Didn't you hear him yelling to be let out before you emptied the truck?" he asked with a look of horror on his face. "I told you in the field to let him out when you got here."

"You didn't! You left him in the bin?" I cried, starring at the bin through the veil of rain now sheeting its way to the ground.

Grabbing a flash light, I climbed to the top of the bin. The rain made the steel treacherous to walk on; it was so slippery. Inching my way across, I opened the lid, shinning the light down into the interior. Cursing, I looked inside to see nothing but grain illuminated by the dim beam of the flash light. No one could survive with that much weight dumped on top of them. Climbing carefully down from the top of the bin, I turned to find Thomas standing quiet, face white as chalk, waiting for my verdict.

"I can't see anything. If he's in there, he won't be alive," I said, staring at Thomas, who was shaking slightly. "I'd better go call Jim. Maybe with luck Vince will be sitting at home waiting for us to have the last laugh," I said without conviction. I dreaded the thought of telling Beth.

Soberly we drove home.

★★★

"Beth, is Vince here?" Charlie asked, looking quickly around the room.

"No. I haven't seen him. Why, was he supposed to be here?" I asked, slightly puzzled at the odd request.

Charlie appeared to be very upset with Vince. "What did he do now?" I asked. Feeling the need to protect Vince, I tried to smooth it over for him, "Don't be so hard on him, Charlie. He doesn't mean any harm."

"It's not that. He's missing!"

"What do you mean, he's missing?

Charlie chose not to answer me. Turning his back, he dialed police headquarters. As Charlie recounted to Jim what he suspected, I gasped in horror at the thought of Vince smothering under the grain. Charlie took one glance at my face and, placing his arm around me, he guided me to a chair with the order, "Sit down."

"Is he really in the bin?" I asked, as the horror of what I had just heard washed over me.

"I guess so. If I had to bet on it, I'd say there's a ninety-nine percent chance he's in there."

"I can't believe it. This morning we talked and he agreed to sign over all claim of Joey to us. He told me that he finally realized he couldn't take care of him but knew we could. He agreed to contact a lawyer and said to have the papers drawn up and he would sign them. "Now he's dead!" I cried, placing my hand over my mouth at uttering the thought out loud.

"What? When did he tell you this?"

"This morning after breakfast we had a discussion about it. That's why he was late getting outside."

"Why didn't you tell me sooner? I could have...thanked him before..." Charlie whispered, his voice dwindling to nothing as Thomas called from the door to announce that Jim had arrived.

Jim and Sam entered the kitchen together, nodding in my direction while the rain ran off their slickers making puddles on the floor.

"Which bin, Charlie?" Jim asked, hanging up his dripping raincoat.

"It's the bin by the west field. The one we made a tree house behind when we were kids, remember?"

"I know where it is," Jim confirmed with a nod. "It's going to be a lot of work getting him out of there. I called the fire crew to come and help. They're on their way here right now. I hate to wait until morning, but with this storm the way it is, we might have to," he said, shaking his head.

Walking to where Jim stood, I placed my hand on his arm, willing him to listen to me. "You can't leave him in there all night. It just wouldn't be right."

"I will do everything I can to get him out of there right away," he sighed, clasping my hand in his huge one.

"Thank you, Jim," I whispered, a huge tear escaping the corner of my eye to plop indiscreetly on his hand.

"It will be alright. Try to take it easy, alright?" he said, giving me a quick squeeze.

"I'll try," I said as another tear escaped to follow the previous one.

"Good girl. I know this isn't easy," he said, turning towards Charlie and Sam.

"Where is that stupid ass that locked him in the bin?" he demanded, searching for Thomas' face.

"I'm not to blame. I'm not the one who filled the bin!" Thomas cried indignantly upon entering the kitchen. Turning slightly, he looked pointedly at Charlie while making this declaration.

"Maybe you're not the one who filled it, but you're sure as hell responsible for him being in there in the first place," Jim snapped, jabbing his finger into Thomas' chest.

"It's not my fault!" he snapped again. His face red with rage, he pushed Jim's hand away in disgust.

Jim continued to stare at him, anger written plainly across his face. "Sam, while we wait for the fire crew, we might as well get a statement from each of them," he said, his eyes never wavering from Thomas.

"You're first," he pointed at Thomas, motioning for him to sit down. Thomas' face flushed a deep red. Stomping over to the chair, he flopped down onto it, his arms folded across his chest, glaring at Jim with hostility.

"Why did you lock Vince in the bin?" Jim demanded, smacking the table with his huge hand.

"I didn't. He went in there on his own," Thomas ground out between clenched teeth.

"But you knew he was in there and did nothing to help him get out. Is that correct?"

Thomas hung his head mumbling, "Yes."

"Why not? Surely you knew he couldn't get out on his own and yet you say you did nothing to help him."

"I was going to let him out when I got back. I was just getting even for him breaking my nose. I didn't mean for him to die," Thomas said, looking down at his hands, which seemed to flutter on their own accord.

"When you got back, why didn't you let him out?" Jim asked, calmer now.

"Charlie unloaded that load, I drove the combine. I yelled at him before he left. I told him to let Vince out of the bin. I thought he would. He was done unloading it when I got there," Thomas said, looking up, the strain evident on his face.

"Alright, have you got that all, Sam?" Jim asked, turning to face his deputy.

"Yes, you may continue," Sam said, pen poised, waiting for the next statement.

"Charlie, your turn now," Jim said, motioning for him to sit in the chair Thomas had just vacated.

"Alright, I'll tell you what I can," Charlie said, sitting down backwards on his chair, arms folded over the back to study Jim's face.

"Did you unload the last load of grain?"

"Yes, it was starting to rain and I was in a hurry to get it unloaded."

"When Thomas told you Vince was in the bin, why didn't you let him out when you got there?"

"I never heard Thomas say anything. I heard him yell something, but couldn't tell what he said over the noise of the combine. He just pointed towards the bins and I nodded yes for him to follow me there. He didn't seem too concerned about anything."

"When you backed up to the bin, didn't you hear Vince yelling to get out?"

"No, I started the auger right away. If he made any noise, I wouldn't have heard it over the auger's engine running," Charlie said, looking pointedly at Thomas. Thomas' Adam's apple bobbed up and down while he looked hastily away.

"After you emptied the load, what did you do?" Jim asked, hands folded across his one raised knee, the toe of his boot resting on the edge of the chair while he leaned forward balancing himself.

"That's when Thomas asked where Vince was. I looked behind the bins but couldn't find him. I thought it was strange that the pickup was still there but not Vince."

"When did you find out he might be in the bin? Jim asked, glancing at Thomas.

"That was when Thomas told me he left him there. I took a light and climbed to the top but couldn't see or hear anything. That's when we decided to come home and call you. That's all I can tell you."

"All right, that takes care of that, "Jim said, nodding at Sam.

The flashing red of the fire crew's vehicle bounced eerily off the kitchen walls, announcing their arrival. I opened the door for the fire crew, only to be met with a ferocious onslaught of icy cold rain.

The wind whipped it into frenzy as I closed the door behind the four members from the fire crew.

"Whew. What a horrible night out there," a tall, red-haired man with a thick, red moustache claimed, mopping the water off his face with his sleeve.

"I haven't seen a night like this in years." A mountain of a man with snow-white curly hair that hung past his shoulders piped up.

All four stood there, a sober look on all their faces, waiting for a command from Jim as to what their next move would be. The beeping of Jim's radio echoed throughout the room, announcing that headquarters was paging him.

"May I use your phone, Beth?"

"Sure, go right ahead," I motioned towards the phone.

Jim soon returned his next words strained at seeing the look on my face. "We won't be able to go out until this weather dies down a bit and I won't put any man's life in danger for someone who might not even be in that bin and if he is, well, I'm sorry but he won't be alive anyways."

I nodded my head, busy with the task of making coffee for the crew of men that had come out to help. It would be a long night.

Jim turned towards the small group of men clustered in the hallway, his voice rising slightly as he brusquely informed them, "Anyone that can't wait for this to die down can leave now, but it will be at their own risk. It's pretty bad out there."

No one moved, all deciding to wait it out until the storm subsided. I was kept busy for the next while supplying the crew with hot coffee and the cookies I had baked that afternoon.

Hearing Joey stirring, I excused myself to go and attend to him. The mound of blankets neatly folded and stacked on a chair halted me in my tracks. Vince would have no need for them tonight, or any other night from now on. Death was so final. There had been no need for Vince to die, his life cut short because of a stupid prank. I ran my hand over the blanket's surface, imagining Vince as I had last seen him this morning. A tearful young man who was trying to do the right thing for his son, his last words seemed to echo through my brain, "I'm going to come back to see him sometimes. No matter what, he's still my son." A hand on my shoulder brought me back to the present.

"Are you okay, Beth?" Charlie asked, turning me to face him.

"No, I don't think so," I sobbed, the tears cascading down my face. Charlie's sigh echoed in my ear while he gathered me close. Pressing my face to the front of his shirt, I continued to sob. "There was no need for this," I cried.

"I know," he whispered with a sigh against my hair. "If I could change it, I would, but I can't. We just have to be strong now, okay?" he said, holding me at arm's length to peer into my face. "For Joey," he said with a weak grin.

Wiping the tears from my face with a shaky hand, I nodded. Joey's wail sent me scurrying to my son's bedside to pick him up and hold him close. As I looked down into the small face, I could see Vince's eyes peering back at me through his son.

CHAPTER TWENTY SIX

The rain continued to fall throughout the night. The steady drone had a hypnotic effect on the people scattered throughout the house. Soon they nodded off, only to jerk awake as their heads nodded too far in one direction or another. I sat in the large overstuffed chair, which was Charlie's favourite, holding Joey. I too found myself dozing off while the hours drifted by.

The sound of the coo-coo clock announcing it was six o'clock brought me fully awake. Glancing out the window, I found the rain had stopped sometime throughout the night. It was as if Mother Nature sensed our mood and was trying to match it, for the day presented its self as being dull and dreary. Rising silently, Joey still clutched in my arms, I padded softly into the kitchen. Charlie stood silhouetted in the kitchen window by the morning light, staring out. Still as a statue, he surveyed the family graveyard.

"What do you see?" I whispered softly.

Charlie turned at the sound of my voice, his voice barely above a whisper to answer with a weak grin, "Nothing, I was just thinking: this grave yard seems to be getting full fast."

"It does seem like that," I said, brushing his hair back with my one free hand.

The sound of someone shuffling into the kitchen made us both turn to see a dishevelled Jim plopping down onto a chair. "It looks like the rain has stopped," he said, peering out the kitchen window. "God, you'd think I hadn't shaved in a week," he muttered, running his hand over his morning stubble. "Well, I guess we'd better get out there. By the look of those clouds, it looks like it could start up again at any minute," he announced, glancing out the kitchen window again.

"I'll go and get everyone," Charlie said, grabbing his jacket on the way into the living room.

"Charlie really feels bad about this, Jim. I think he blames himself. It was a stupid mistake," I said, clutching Joey close.

"I know. I don't blame him. There was no reason for Vince to be in that bin in the first place. That stupid jerk Thomas should have known better. That's where the blame lies," Jim sighed, running his hands through his hair, having adopted the same habit as Charlie.

Looking up, I was just in time to see Thomas silently slip out the door, his face twisted with rage.

I watched them all file silently out the door, shuddering as I envisioned the outcome of the mission they had set out upon. Vince had been just a kid. He never deserved to die the way he had. Jim was right, Thomas was to blame.

The tick tock of the clock seemed to mock me as I sat watching it, waiting for the nightmare to end. Joey, asleep in his chair beside me, would never know his father and now I prayed he would never find out how he had died. Finally I couldn't stand the waiting anymore. I had to do something or go mad. So, grabbing Joey, I went outside to search for a vehicle. Charlie had left the pickup in the yard. Hoisting Joey onto the seat, I placed the truck in gear, pointing it towards the bins where Vince was entombed. The scene enfolding before my eyes stopped me in my tracks. There before me were the men, all in a single line, passing a continuous chain of pails from one to the other. As fast as one pail was filled from the bin, it was passed to the next in line until it was dumped back into the waiting truck. Charlie glanced up at the sound of my truck approaching. Quickly he left the chain, hurrying towards me.

"What's wrong? Is something wrong with Joey?" he asked, looking at the baby still asleep in his chair.

"No, he's fine. I couldn't stand the waiting any longer, so I came out here."

"You shouldn't have come. You had better go home. I'll come and tell you when we find him," Charlie said, running his hand through his hair.

"No, I'm staying here," I claimed, crossing my arms across my chest. Charlie's stern look soon had me babbling. "Please Charlie, don't send me back home. I can't stand the waiting."

"Alright, stay, but it's against my better judgment. I want you to stay in the truck with Joey though," Charlie commanded, shaking his head before turning to resume his position in the chain.

Emptying a whole load of grain from a bin with just a pail was a tedious task, but it was the only way to get the grain down below the slides in the door. The roof opening was too small to allow a person access. They were doing the best they could, I thought, watching the huge fireman with the white hair dump another pail of grain into the truck.

Jim, at the start of the chain, finally announced, "I think there's enough gone to get the slide open."

Charlie cautiously climbed the ladder to the roof top. "I don't see anything yet," he said, looking down into the opening of the bin, as he shone his flashlight around inside. "I can't see a thing, it's too dark," he said, coming down the ladder.

The two firemen at the front of the bin soon pried the panel from the door, allowing the grain to slowly escape, trickling onto a pile below the door. The smallest of the firefighters, elected by his comrades, wiggled his way inside the bin through the opening they had supplied. From where we waited, we could hear the grunts of the firefighter wadding through the grain in search of Vince. The sound seemed to echo in the clear mountain air. Finally, the grunts stopped. The silence following was over whelming, while we all waited anxiously for conformation that he had found Vince.

Finally, a dark head poked out from the bin to announce, "He's not in here."

"What? What do you mean he's not in there?" Jim demanded, turning to look at Charlie and Thomas.

"You must have missed him, he has to be there," Charlie exclaimed, his brows knitted together in a frown.

"No, he's not in here. I covered every square inch and there is no one here."

I couldn't help the bubble of laughter that escaped me at the look on Thomas' face while he absorbed the shocking news. Charlie looked stunned also, as if he couldn't comprehend what the fire fighter had just announced. All eyes stared at the bin, until one by one they broke into a smile at the news there wouldn't be any body to recover here after all. Vince had got the last laugh anyways, I realized, tears of mirth running down my cheeks at the irony of the situation. Vince was still alive.

I looked down at Joey, my laughter freezing in my throat as comprehension dawned on me with full force. Vince had backed out of our agreement. He wasn't going to sign the papers that would make Joey ours legally. His final words now came back to haunt me, "No matter what, he's still my son." I knew deep in my heart that we had not seen the last of Vince Shepard. When he came back, it would be with the sole intention of reclaiming his son.

"Well, I guess that takes care of that. I guess he played us all for a bunch of fools," Jim said, shaking his head in disbelieve.

Thomas sat on the ground, a stunned look on his face. "When I find him, I'm going to kill him," he said. Breaking into a wry grin, he chuckled, "I guess the son of a bitch did get even."

The fire fighters wasted no time in leaving, stating they would have to report to the station and had to leave. Jim, seeing Charlie eyeing the partial load of grain on the truck, chuckled. "I guess you have another load of grain to empty again." His face sobering, he said, "We have to find him you know. Technically he's still reported as missing. He'll have to answer a few questions when we catch up with him."

Charlie looked up at Jim to say, "He'll have to answer a few questions for me, too."

Sensing something was wrong, Charlie hurried towards the truck. "What's wrong Beth? I thought you'd be happy to know he was alive."

"It's not that. I'm glad he's not at the bottom of the bin. It's just... he skipped out of signing those papers. He'll be back and when he does, he's going to want to take Joey away from us."

Charlie lifted my chin to stare into my eyes. "No! He'll never get Joey. When he comes back, I'm going to make sure he signs those papers or I'll shove them down his throat until he does."

Joey, now awake, sat watching us, a small frown creasing the tiny face as if he understood all that was being said. I slowly turned the truck around, heading towards home. The ball was in Vince's court now. What he does with it would now become a waiting game. The trouble being, I was not very good at waiting games.

Upon entering the house, I had the immediate impression someone had been there while I was gone. I cautiously glanced around the rooms, checking for any unwanted intruders. I was surprised to find the used plate sitting beside the sink next to the clean ones I had previously washed. Whomever had been here had decided to fix themselves a snack, I thought wryly. I walked through each room, realizing there were more things different. The most obvious being Vince's few meagre belongings were gone, along with the blankets that had been folded on the chair. Vince had come back in my absence to raid the refrigerator and pick up his belongings. Perhaps, I thought wryly, he had been here all along, listening to what was being said. At that thought, a form of intuition kicked in to tell me where I would find the answer to my question. I climbed the stairs, my destination being the room where Amy had delivered her baby. Yes, there on the bed, the covers haphazardly thrown back, was the outline still evident of where a body had been lying. Vince had been here the whole time!

CHAPTER TWENTY SEVEN

Oh my god, it would have been so easy for him to snatch Joey away when I wasn't watching, I thought with horror. Was Vince still in the house? This thought had me running towards the stairs, in a flash realizing Joey was alone right now. Pushing open the door of my bed room, I was aghast to see Vince standing over Joey's crib, looking down at his son.

"Don't touch him," I screamed, rushing at Vince, pushing him aside.

"Heh, I wasn't going to hurt him," Vince said, taking a step backwards, his hands held out in defense. Ignoring his remark, I grabbed Joey from the crib, shielding him close to my body. "He's my son. You're not going to take him!"

"He's not your son, he's mine and I can take him if I want," Vince screamed, his face red with anger, his hands clenched tightly into fists at his sides.

Backing towards the door, Joey clutched tightly in my arms, I turned to run, Vince in close pursuit behind me.

"Come back with my son!" Vince screamed, only spurring me to move faster as I sprinted for the door. Vince closed the gap easily. Grabbing me by the collar, he swung me around to face him. "He's my son, now give him to me!" he demanded, arms outstretched.

"No! You would have to kill me before I'd give him to you!" I screamed, shaking with rage.

Vince, breathing heavy, ground out between clenched teeth, "That might have to be arranged."

From outside the sound of doors being slammed could easily be heard. Thomas and Charlie were home. Vince froze, his eyes glinting dangerously. Glancing towards the outside door, he seemed to waver in his decision. His eyes watching me, he hastily turned to slip quietly through it, but not before he whispered back menacingly, "I'll be back." Shaking with fear, I screamed for Charlie while running for the safety of the kitchen.

"What the hell?" Charlie said, seeing my wide-eyed look of fear. "Beth, what's wrong?" he asked, pulling me into his arms as my body shook with fear.

"Vince—, he's here. He was—trying to take Joey," I managed to choke out, still shaking.

"What? Where is he?" he asked, turning to search the room in a glance.

"He went outside from our bedroom."

Charlie sprinted towards the bed room in pursuit of Vince, yelling back over his shoulder. "Thomas, stay with Beth.

Thomas ushered me towards the couch, where he sat down beside me, mumbling, "He was here all along, wasn't he?"

I nodded my head, my body continuing to shake at the thought of how easily Joey could have disappeared from my life forever.

"Son of a bitch. He was here, sitting right under our noses the whole time," Thomas said, shaking his head in disbelieve.

Charlie was soon back. No Vince in tow, to announce that he was nowhere to be found. Shuddering, I relayed all that had happened between Vince and me. If I closed my eyes, the memory of Vince's frantic eyes swam before me. The image seemed burnt into my brain. I had no doubt he would follow through with his threat. Vince would come back to claim his son.

Charlie worriedly ran his hands through his hair before motioning for Thomas to follow him. "Come on. Thomas. We'll search the buildings outside. Beth, lock all the doors and windows. If he's around here, we'll find him."

Following Charlie's advice, I hurried to lock everything, making the house as secure as possible. All the while I carried Joey with me. I would not let him out of my sight until Vince was dealt with. The task finished, I went to the phone to call Jim. He would know what to do about

Vince. Charlie and Thomas entered the kitchen to hear the tail end of my conversation with Jim.

"We didn't see anything. He seems to have vanished," Charlie said, shaking his head before grabbing a cup of coffee. Good idea to call Jim, Beth, he'll know how to handle this," Charlie declared, nodding soberly.

Calmer now, I sat sipping my coffee, feeling safer in the protection of the two men. Slowly, I glanced around my tidy looking kitchen, taking in the comfortable, homey look I had achieved with my decorating skills. Joey had drifted back to sleep and now lay snoring softly in his chair beside me on the table. I loved my life and Joey had just made it complete. No one was going to spoil it for me now, I vowed, while we waited for Jim to come. Vince would never again be given the opportunity to steal my son.

Jim arrived sooner than I thought was possible, a worried frown replacing his usual smiling face. "Beth, are you alright?" he asked, holding me at arm's length, searching my face.

"Yes, we're fine. Charlie got here just in time."

"I'm glad. Don't worry, we'll catch him," Jim said, expelling a huge sigh.

Jim and his deputy searched the out buildings from top to bottom without success. Searching the house proved to be more of a task. It was a large home, complete with all sorts of nooks and crannies; one could disappear without being found for a while. There was even a servant's quarters, complete with an outside entrance that remained locked at all times. Jim was familiar with the house, for he had played here with Charlie as a child.

Charlie had once let it slip that he had hidden in the house for three days before his father found him to administer one of his beatings. He said that was the last time he had done that. The outcome being that he was beaten so badly, he could hardly walk for two days. Jim had become his saviour, helping him with his chores so he wouldn't get another beating. It seemed when Charlie's father was angered, life became a living hell for Charlie. His rage would not abate for days on end. Charlie's life would not be allowed to continue in any sort of semblance of normal until his father found another outlet for his anger. Over the years, Charlie and Jim had bonded closer than most blood brothers. Jim confided in me that one time he had even offered himself to Charlie's father for a beating instead of Charlie. It was he who had broken the vase that had been sitting on a table, not Charlie. Charlie's father's only reply was to beat Charlie worse. He alleged Jim was lying to protect Charlie. Jim had been forced to witness that beating and said he would never forget it as long as he lived.

Vince had seemed to have vanished into thin air. Not a sign of him could be found. Searching the area appeared futile. True to his word, Jim posted a car in our yard around the clock and I faithfully kept the doors and windows locked day and night. The nights were the worst. I would lie awake in bed, hour upon hour, listening to the house for any sounds that were out of key with it. The slightest creak or groan would have me sitting up in bed, ready to spring into action. Charlie snored softly beside me, acting like a balm to soothe my frazzled nerves.

Sometime throughout the night I was awakened by a queer feeling. Something wasn't quite right. I reached for Charlie in the darkness, my hand finding only the warm imprint of where he had lain. Joey, sucking softly on his soother, was the only other sound permeating the still of the night. I waited, listening, my eyes trying to penetrate the darkness for some conformation of the sound that had awakened me. Finally I was rewarded with a snatch of conversation coming from above. Scooping up Joey so as not to awaken him, I tip-toed to the closet. There, I placed him into a large wicker basket, closing the lid softly. Then, closing the door quietly on the still sleeping babe I stole from the room in search of the voices I had heard. Slowly, I climbed up the stairs, the voices becoming more audible with each step. They were in the attic, I realized, straining my ears to listen. Carefully, I climbed the third row of stairs leading to the top floor of the old house. Peering through the gloom, I witnessed Charlie's silhouette by the full moon, cringing before a dark form that loomed threateningly over him.

"No please, I'll do whatever you say," Charlie begged, cowering before the dark shape.

I flicked on the light switch. Mystified, I stared at Charlie's lone form, still cringing on the floor. What had I seen? Was my mind playing tricks on me? I was sure that I had seen a dark form looming over him. It must have been a shadow, my mind reasoned, glancing around the empty room nervously. I reached out slowly to touch Charlie's hand so as not to awaken him, only to have him jerk his hand back, fear etched across his face while his eyes stared vacantly into space.

"Charlie, it's me, Beth," I said, taking his hand slowly. I was instantly rewarded with a lightning grip on my hand as if he had been drowning and had reached out his hand to a saviour.

"It's alright, Charlie. Everything will be fine," I whispered, coaxing him towards the stairs.

He visibly relaxed, following docilely beside me. Edging down the stairs, I had the niggling feeling that we were being watched and had just escaped something horrendous. I glanced nervously back over my shoulder to make sure we were not being followed. Charlie never uttered a word as I ushered him back to his bed. Only a slight sigh escaped his lips while he snuggled down under the covers, his eyes already closed. Opening the closet door, I was rewarded with the sight of Joey, still sound asleep in his basket. Sliding him into my arms, so as not to awaken him, I sat down in the old rocking chair, watching the tiny little face sleeping so innocently. As I glanced over at Charlie's still form in the bed, now gently snoring, I shuddered recalling the vision I had witnessed. The scene kept playing over and over in my mind while I tried to visualise exactly what I had seen. I could now fathom the depth of Vince's fear in sleeping alone in that room, for I had felt that fear also. I closed my eyes, remembering the dark shape looming out of the dark-ness over Charlie. The remainder of the night, sleep evaded me while I watched Joey sleep, his crib bathed in the moonlight.

Thomas had become very sullen since Vince's disappearance. Sometimes I would catch him watching me, his eyes surveying me from top to bottom with a curious light in them, fading only when he turned dejectedly away. He would sit for hours not saying a word while glanc-ing from one object to another.

Charlie had gone on a fishing trip with Jim every year after harvest. It was their passion. They had offered to take me with them on more than one occasion, but I had declined. I had soon learned it was wiser to stay put at home. The comforts of home outweighed the need to spend hours in a small boat spearing a helpless worm onto a hook. I felt no need to sit waiting patiently for my line to jiggle; alerting me a fish had finally taken the bait. This year though I could see the hesitation in Charlie at the thought of leaving me and Joey alone.

"When are you going fishing?" I asked, sipping my morning cup of coffee while waiting for his reply.

Charlie, who was buttering his toast, looked up surprised at the question. "I don't think I'm going this year," he said, shrugging his shoulders before returning to the task of spreading jam on his toast.

"Why not," I asked? "Joey and I will be fine, if that's what you're worried about."

"I wouldn't feel right, leaving you alone with Vince still on the loose."

"I was thinking about that. I really think you need to unwind. You've been so tense lately. I think the trip would do you good, so I asked Jim if Sam could come and stay with me while you're gone. He said it would be fine with him if it was okay with you. What do you think?"

"I don't know—," Charlie slowly replied, a glimmer of hope shinning from his eyes at the thought.

"Come on, it will be fine," I coaxed, placing my hand over his.

"Charlie grinned happily, before saying, "I'll think about it. We still have a lot of work to finish before winter sets in. I'll talk to Jim about it, okay?"

"Okay," I said, watching Charlie offer the first true smile I had seen in days.

We all visibly relaxed. Vince had not been seen or heard from, so it was assumed that he had left the area for good. Jim had decided his man was needed elsewhere, so the police car was now absent from the position it had taken for the past week. Although, Jim said he still felt uncomfortable, so would send a car out to check on us every other day.

CHAPTER TWENTY EIGHT

I felt more at ease now that Vince had not been seen, so I decided to take advantage of the glorious fall day. Leaning back leisurely, I settled onto the porch swing. Gently gliding back and forth, I watched Chipper the squirrel chattering ferociously from the top of a tree, warning me I had inhabited his space. I found myself smiling, contentedly as I watched the last dragonflies from summer still whirling about, like tiny helicopters gone mad while they searched for their food. In the distance a tiny ribbon of dust made its way around the curves down into the valley, forewarning me that I would soon have a visitor. I didn't have long to wait. The police cruiser slowly pulled into the yard, stopping in front of the house. Jerry, one of the local police officers from the area, languidly climbed out of the cruiser to come and sit down beside me. Jerry was a soft spoken man who had married his childhood sweetheart. They now had two children, with the third due any day now, I had heard.

"How's it going, Beth? Do you mind?" he asked, indicating a pack of cigarettes he had pulled from his shirt pocket.

"Everything is fine and by all means, go ahead," I said, motioning at his unopened pack. "I thought Jim said you had given up that bad habit," I said, grinning up at him.

"I did. Which time were you referring to?" he chuckled, lighting the tip.

"Have you seen anything out of the norm?" he asked before blowing a smoke ring into the air.

"No, it's been pretty quiet. I'm starting to think Vince is really gone," I said, looking around the yard. "Would you care for a cup of coffee and a piece of cake?" I asked, rising from the swing.

"Is it the famous crumb cake Jim's always raving about?"

"It's one and the same," I said with a grin.

"Sure, wait until Jim hears what he missed," he said, a huge grin splitting his face from ear to ear while he held the door open for me.

"Has Marilyn had the baby yet?" I asked, placing a huge piece of cake, in front of him.

"No, she's overdue. We're just playing the waiting game now. I carry a pager with me so I can keep in touch with her. We've had a few false alarms so far," he explained, before shoving another forkful of cake into his mouth.

"Mm, now I see why Jim's always raving about your cake," he said, smacking his lips in satisfaction.

We chit chatted a few more minutes before Jerry announced he had to leave. "I'd keep the doors locked for a while yet. I don't think he's around these parts anymore, but I'd feel better knowing you're safe. It won't hurt to be extra careful for a while," he said on his way out the door.

"Don't worry, I will," I said, locking the door behind him.

Joey's wail from the bed room sounded, informing me he was awake and would need a diaper change. "Are you happy now?" I asked Joey, patting his bottom as I returned to the kitchen. What's Jerry still doing here, I wondered? I glanced out the window to see his car still parked in the same spot, the door flung haphazardly open. Curious now, I edged closer to the window to get a better view of what he could be doing. There on the ground lay Jerry, his hat lying to one side while a pool of blood seeped from a gaping hole in his head.

"Oh my God," I screamed, running towards the front door only to stop abruptly, at the sight of a dark head visible through the glass. I looked down to see the knob rattling, as he tried to turn it. Oh my God, Vince is back! My heart pumping with fear, I backed away from the locked door towards the phone, only to realize there wasn't a dial tone. Vince must have cut the phone wire coming into the house. Hurriedly I grabbed Joey bounding towards the stairs, realizing that my only hope now lay in hiding. I quickly followed the hallways that crisscrossed, looking for a place to hide. I soon came to the locked door of the servant's quarters. Reaching above the door, I felt for the key, praying it was still there. I could hear Vince below searching for us. With shaking hands I inserted the key, praying the old rusty lock would turn on the first try. Hearing a faint click, I breathed a sigh of relief before slipping through the door, locking it behind me.

The room hadn't been used for years. Having a live-in servant had become a thing of the past. When Charlie and I had first gotten married, I had envisioned turning this room into a play room for our children. That dream had also become a thing of the past. The room was small, complete with an old bed pushed into the far corner of the room, a dusty, stained mattress covering its rusty springs. Lining the other wall stood an old wardrobe closet, the door gapping open, hanging from one hinge. The only other piece of furniture in the utilitarian room was an old wash stand, cracked and peeling from continuous use over the years. There wasn't anywhere to hide, I realized while a sickening feeling settled into the pit of my stomach. I placed Joey on the bed, searching desperately for a weapon; anything I could use to protect myself. Finding nothing, I searched for the key to the outside door, with no luck. Maybe I would be able to escape when Vince was in a different part of the house, I told myself. So, trying to be as quiet as a mouse, I sat on the bed, praying Joey would be quiet. I could hear Vince talking to himself while searching one room and then another, throwing things with reckless abandon in his search for us.

"You bitch, wait until I find you! Where the hell, did she go?" he screamed in frustration, firing another object against a wall.

I closed my eyes, picturing the Vince I had come to know so well; the Vince who had seemed so shy and was afraid of ghosts. Gone was the young man that had lain sprawled on the sofa snoring softly. The man I had so envisioned Joey to be like in the future. What had happened to Vince to turn him into this monster that was now searching for me? The thought of Jerry's lifeless body sprawled on the gravel in front of the house made me want to gag, while a low moan involuntarily escaped my lips. I could hear Vince coming closer now in his search for us. The sounds of doors being savagely kicked open, along with his angry snarls, echoed throughout the halls. Move, I told myself. Get out of here before he tries the door to this room. I moved cautiously to the door, placing my hand on the knob, only to jerk it back, startled, when the knob slowly started to turn on its own accord.

"Wait until I find you!" Vince screamed, banging his fists against the door.

Horrified, I leaned against the wall, my knuckle jammed against my mouth to keep from crying out. From the top floor, the sound of a door slamming could be heard. Abruptly the beating on the door stopped. Vince, upon hearing the noise overhead, turned instantly away from my door. The echo of his feet pounding down the hallway towards the attic stairs could be heard from where I stood, trembling. This was my only chance to escape. I still had the key in my hand. Just maybe it would also open the door to the outside and the rickety old stairs leading to the lawn below.

Tip-toeing across the room, I quietly slipped the key into the lock, willing it to turn. Breathing a sigh of relief at hearing the faint click, I picked up Joey, holding him close to my body while I opened the door before slipping cautiously outside. Safe or not, I scrambled down the steps, my feet slipping and sliding as I encountered the moss covering the old, rotten boards. Each step became more treacherous than the first as I continued my downward spiral to the lawn below. The old boards creaked and groaned from my weight as I slid over them. I silently said a prayer, hoping they would support me until I reached the bottom. Joey, clutched tightly in my arms, began to whimper weakly, as if sensing my urgency. Finally feeling solid ground under my feet, I breathed a sigh of relief. I sensed Vince's eyes upon me before I saw him. My eyes drawn upwards at a movement, I stared in horror to find Vince framed in the attic window starring down at me, his face twisted with rage. Move, I told myself again. Turning, I sprinted towards the front of the house, searching frantically for an avenue of escape. There before me sat Jerry's police cruiser, the door still hanging open while a voice over the radio continued in its attempt to reach him. I could hear Vince's feet pounding down the stairs inside the house, making his way towards the open door he had so savagely kicked in. Jumping inside the car, I scrambled to jab the locks down, effectively sealing us both inside. Vince howled with rage and tried to wrench the door open, only to find it locked from within.

Grabbing the microphone, I screamed into it. "Help, I need help. He killed Jerry and he's going to kill me too. The voice on the other end talked softly, willing me to calm down and explain who I was and what exactly had happened.

"I can't! He's trying to get in!" I screamed.

Jim's voice suddenly boomed over the radio, giving me hope, "Beth, I'll be there in a few minutes, just hang on. I'm only a few minutes away."

Vince continued beating on the windows, his eyes wild. He realized in vain they could not be smashed that easily. I watched helplessly, while he searched for something to smash the window. Seeing nothing adequate, he ran towards the barn. The keys… where were the keys? Searching frantically, I finally looked towards where Jerry lay. My heart sank with dread, upon spying the keys still clutched in his hand. Vince, as if by magic, abruptly appeared in front of the car, an axe clutched in his hands.

"Jim, oh my God, he's got an axe!" I screamed frantically into the microphone.

"Hang on, Beth. I'm only two minutes away," Jim claimed, as Vince brought the axe back, smashing the window with one blow.

I screamed, scrabbling backwards away from the splaying glass. Vince instantly reached through the smashed window, flipping the lock up on the door before thrusting his arm inside to grab for me. Batting his hands away with my one free hand, I fought in vain while he grabbed me by the hair to yank me roughly from the vehicle, kicking and screaming, Joey still clutched in my arms.

"Thought you'd get away from me, eh bitch?" he crooned in a voice that somehow I couldn't connect with being Vince's. "Now give me my son!" he screamed, his spit flecking my face.

"Never! You'll have to kill me first," I screamed, trying to escape from his grasp.

Jerking me to my knees, he continued to hold me by my hair while he brought back his fist, his voice strangely purring softly, "I told you before that could be arranged."

The wail of a police siren filled the air, the car coming to a screeching halt. Dropping his arm, Vince turned to run as a voice called out, "Police, freeze!" Vince continued to flee heedlessly until a shot rang out, toppling him to the ground in mid-stride.

"Hold it!" Jim yelled, twisting Vince's arms behind his back before snapping a pair of handcuffs on him. Vince now lay face down on the ground, a low moan escaping from between his lips while a police officer read him his rights. All of a sudden Jim was there, gathering me and Joey into his arms. I buried my face against his chest, allowing the scalding tears to cascade down my face, to be absorbed by Jim's uniform.

"Sshh, Beth. It's okay. You're safe now," he whispered into my ear. Rubbing my back, he continued to hold me against him.

Finally spent, the tears gradually subsided. Gulping huge drafts of air, I surveyed the scene before me, only to find myself gagging upon observing an officer in the act of placing a sheet over Jerry's body. Now there were more police cars surrounding us. One had been dispatched to pick up Charlie, thanks to Jim's instructions. He would be here soon, I gratefully acknowledged. A tourniquet had been placed on Vince's leg where he had been shot. As, the ambulance attendants lifted him onto the stretcher, Vince held out his hands, motioning for them to stop.

"Stop, wait!" he commanded in a gravelly voice. Swivelling his head, he stared straight at me before uttering the parting words, "I just wanted my son. I'll be back for him."

"Get him out of here!" Jim yelled, motioning for the attendants to continue.

I shook with fear at those words. While the gurney was pushed into the waiting ambulance, Vince's sudden wail of, "Oh my God, what have I done," resounded throughout the yard followed by his gut-wrenching sobs. Finally, the ambulance doors closed, silencing the sound while it sped away. Without warning, a beeping sound filled the air. All eyes quickly shifted to view Jerry's body. The sound of Jerry's pager emitted from below the sheet, announcing his wife was in labour with their third child.

"Come on, Beth, you don't need to hear this," Jim said, ushering me towards the house.

One of the officers took Joey from my arms, holding him close as we walked into the house.

It wasn't very long before Charlie rushed into the house. Holding out his arms, he beckoned me to come. Stepping forward, I found the comfort I craved while dry sobs shook my body anew.

"Where is the son of a bitch?" Charlie ground out between clenched teeth.

"We had to take him to the hospital, but after that he'll be on his way to jail. He won't be bothering you from now on. You've finally seen the last of him," Jim said, placing his hand on Charlie's shoulder.

"Thanks, Jim. I'm glad you were here."

"Not a problem man. I'm just glad we got here when we did," Jim claimed, nodding at Charlie while he patted my shoulder.

"So am I," Charlie said, tightening his grip on me.

"I'll make some coffee," I mumbled, searching for a grain of normalcy. The slight shake of my hands was the only thing to belie the fact that inside I was still a mess. The sight of Jerry's body covered with a sheet nearly had me scurrying back into the protection of Charlie's arms. I turned away, fighting down the lump of hysteria that formed in my throat. Closing my eyes to avoid the scene before me, I gripped the edge of the counter, swaying slightly until the feeling passed.

Charlie was beside me in an instant. "Beth, are you alright?"

"Yes, I'll be fine," I said, scooping coffee into the percolator.

Jim put his arm around my shoulders, gently pulling me forward. Motioning towards a chair, he encouraged me to sit.

"I hate to do this right now, but I have no choice. I have to ask you for a statement while everything is fresh in your mind. A good cop is dead and we don't take that lightly."

"What do you want to know?" I asked. Taking a deep breath, I sank slowly onto the chair facing him.

"Why don't you start at the beginning? And take your time."

"Okay, I'll try," I said, closing my eyes, remembering back to when the horror started.

"I was outside enjoying the nice weather when Jerry pulled into the yard. He asked if everything was alright. We talked for a bit and then I asked him if he wanted some coffee and cake. He said that Marilyn was overdue and he was waiting for a call any time. He ate his cake and then he said that he had to go. He told me to lock the door when he left and said you can't be too careful," I relayed, the tears sliding from the corners of my eyes.

"Then what happened?" He coaxed with a nod.

"I went to get Joey. He had just awakened and was crying. When I got back I saw Jerry's car was still here and Jerry was lying beside it. There was blood all around him," I cried, covering my face with my hands while a huge sob tore through my body. "Why did he do it? Jerry never did anything to him," I sobbed, turning my tear-stained face towards Jim.

Jim shook his head sadly, his eyes clouding with unshed tears while his Adam's apple bobbed uncontrollably. Leaning forward, he quietly said, "He was a good man and the best damn cop you ever saw. Beth, before you saw what happened to Jerry, did you hear anything? Voices, or a shot, anything at all?"

"No, Joey was crying, I didn't hear anything."

"Do you know if Jerry was dead at that point?" Jim asked, watching my face for the answer.

"Yes," I whispered. "I saw his head. No one could be alive after that."

Jim sat for a moment, his eyes focused on the floor before he asked, "Alright, and then what happened?"

"I realized it was Vince at the door and knew we had to hide, so I grabbed Joey and ran upstairs. I found the key above the old servants' quarter's door and went inside. There wasn't any place to hide. I just sat there waiting, trying to be quiet so he wouldn't find us."

"And where was Vince all this time?"

"I could hear him looking for us, kicking doors open and throwing things. He was talking to himself, calling me dirty names while he searched for me." I shuddered, replaying the scene over in my mind.

Jim nodded for me to continue. "I know this is hard, but try to remember everything. Don't leave anything out."

"Here, Beth," Charlie said, setting a glass of water down in front of me.

Nodding at the glass, he smiled, encouraging me to continue. Grateful, I sipped, using the time to compose myself before continuing.

"He was trying all the doors. When he came to my door, he tried turning the knob but I had locked it. I thought he was going to kick it in, but he didn't. I think he heard a noise in the attic. I guess he thought it was me, so he ran up there. I knew he'd find me sooner or later, so I tried using the key from the inside door to open the outside one."

"Is that how you got outside?"

"Yes, I went down the outside stairs. When I got to the bottom I looked up at the attic window and saw Vince looking down at me so I ran and got in Jerry's car and locked all the doors. Then I called on the radio for help."

"How did Vince get you out of the car?"

"He ran and got an axe from the barn. He used it to break the window."

"Why didn't he use the keys? They were in Jerry's hand. He just had to reach down and pick them up."

"I don't know. It was as if he was blinded with rage or something. I don't think he saw them."

Jim remained silent, waiting for me to continue. "He grabbed me by the hair and pulled us out of the car. He said he was going to kill me," I cried, remembering the strange voice that I had heard coming from Vince's mouth.

Charlie abruptly slammed his fist against the table, making us all jump. Seething with rage, he jumped to his feet pacing. He snapped, "The son of a bitch! I wish I could get my hands on him right now."

"I know how you feel, Charlie, but please sit down. Let Beth continue," Jim said, motioning for him to sit down.

"Beth, go on," Jim encouraged, tapping my hand.

"That's when you got here."

"That's it. There's nothing else you can remember that stands out in your mind."

"Well, there was one thing, but you're going to think I'm crazy."

"No one is going to think you're crazy. You never know, it might help."

Glancing at Charlie and Jim, I bowed my head before explaining. The next words that came out of my mouth were even hard for me to believe. "I don't think it was Vince. I mean, I know it was Vince's body— but he didn't act like Vince. It didn't sound like him either. His voice wasn't the same. It was kind of gravely, rough, if you know what I mean."

I glanced up quickly at Charlie's sudden, sharp intake of breath, a silent unspoken message passing between Charlie and Jim.

"What? What, did I say something wrong?" I frowned, glancing from one face to the other, waiting for their reply.

"No, you did fine," Jim said, all the while searching Charlie's face.

Charlie abruptly turned away, mumbling, "I'll be right back."

Jim's eyes remained focused on Charlie's back while he left the room, a thoughtful expression on his face. Without looking at his deputy, he asked, "Did you get that all, Sam?"

"Sure Jim, I got it all," Sam said, staring at Jim, a frown creasing his normally smiling face.

Jim's pager suddenly beeped. Pressing a button to silence it, Jim looked up to announce, "I have to leave. They're waiting for me down at the station. I'll call you soon, alright? Charlie will take care of you now."

"I don't know how to thank you, Jim. Words just don't seem enough," I said, throwing my arms around his neck.

"No thanks necessary. Just take care of yourself and that little one," he said, motioning towards Joey. "I'll call you in a few days," he said before slipping swiftly out the door.

Jim had assured me Vince would not be back. Gradually, I relaxed. Charlie on the other hand, hovered over us. I think he felt guilty for not being there when we needed him. He doted on Joey and me, refusing to let us out of his sight, to the point of even instructing Thomas to go back to work alone, unsupervised. Thomas looked at him bewildered before turning to climb into Charlie's pickup. Even though I found myself slowly returning to normal, I couldn't bear to look at the spot where Jerry had lain. Someone had attempted to wash all evidence away, but a dull rusty ring was still evident in the gravel where Jerry's blood had been spilled.

The time Charlie spent watching over Joey and I allowed him to bond closer than ever with Joey. I watched Joey holding on tightly to one of Charlie's huge fingers, his small dark eyes intently riveted on Charlie's face before breaking into a delightful chuckle. "Beth, did you hear that?" he laughed. "Look, he did it again," Charlie said, reveling in the sound of Joey's laughter. "I think he's the best baby in the whole wide world."

"I have a tendency to agree with you on that subject," I said, placing my arm around Charlie.

"Thanks for staying with me. I'm glad you're here," I said, leaning my head on his shoulder.

"I wouldn't want to be anywhere else," he said, squeezing my hand.

"I guess we better go upstairs and tackle the mess Vince made. I've put it off long enough," I said, sighing wearily.

"Don't worry about it right now. Thomas and I can tackle it later," he replied offhandedly.

"No, let's get it over with. The sooner it's done the better. I would like to see things get back to normal around here."

I found climbing the stairs easier now. Why I had clung to the dependency of my cane, I couldn't say. I now realized it had been a mistake. It had virtually kept me a cripple. I still ached, but it was a good ache, the kind one feels when they run that extra mile and feel proud of the achievement, even though their body cried out otherwise. Charlie held my hand while we slowly climbed the stairs. Stopping on the landing, he stared upwards at the collage of pictures displayed there. Then, between clenched teeth, he said the words I never thought he would utter, "I always hated you. I'll never treat my son the way you treated me." Turning away, he continued up the stairs. Glancing back at the picture, I felt as if the eyes were following me with a look of pure hatred. Shuddering, I turned away to follow Charlie up the stairs.

The upstairs bedrooms were a mess. It was as if a hurricane had struck each room, tossing things at will against the walls, toppling dressers and throwing bedding in heaps in its fury. Vince had done more damage than I had realized. Somehow the image of Vince doing this didn't seem to fit with the young man who had sat beside me on a swing, quietly talking to me about his future. What had happened to change him so completely? Was he always like that and I had been too blind to see it?

I looked down at the rubble surrounding my feet to spy a china doll that had been Charlie's mothers, its head savagely snapped off. My god, what if he had found us? I slowly crumpled to the floor, my tears seeping from between my fingers while, my hands shielded my eyes in attempt to block out what my mind didn't want me to see.

Charlie sat down beside me, carefully placing his arms around me. Rubbing my back, he tried to comfort me. "Sshh—Beth, it will be alright. It's all finished with. He can't hurt you anymore. I won't let him hurt you ever again."

Wiping my nose with the back of my hand, I looked up at Charlie to give him a weak smile. "I know. It just all seems so bloody pointless."

Charlie hung his head, not saying a word, only nodding in agreement.

"Never mind, Charlie. I'm just feeling sorry for myself. Let's get this mess cleaned up," I said, looking at the chaos surrounding us. The rest of the day was taken in righting the rooms Vince had trashed. Night time brought with it a weariness I had never felt so strongly before. I think my brain needed to shut down so it could recuperate from the trauma it had been put through. I slowly drifted off into oblivion with Charlie holding me tightly.

The next morning I opened my eyes to sunlight streaming across my bed. Charlie had slipped away earlier, allowing me the luxury of sleeping late. Wiggling my toes, I stretched contentedly, letting the sun shine warmly down on my face.

"Good morning, sleepy head. We were starting to think you might sleep all day," Charlie chuckled, leaning against the doorway, holding an attentive Joey in his arms.

"I had a terrible nightmare," I said before clasping my hand over my mouth, realizing it wasn't a dream at all.

"It was a nightmare and all nightmares come to an end when we wake up. You're awake now. The nightmare has ended," Charlie stated matter-of-factly.

Yes, it was over. We could finally move on.

CHAPTER TWENTY NINE

"What are you doing this morning?" I asked, before taking another sip of my coffee.

"I'm not sure yet. I sent Thomas out a little while ago to cultivate the east field. He's getting better at following instructions," Charlie said with a wry grin. "I guess this thing with Vince has shaken him up more than he lets on. He seems changed somehow. No more wise cracks, anyways."

"I don't get it. What do you think happened to change Vince so completely in such a short time?"

Charlie looked away, avoiding the question. "I'd better get to work if I want to go on that fishing trip," he said, hastily getting to his feet. Giving me a quick peck on the cheek, he quickly vanished out the door.

Well, I thought watching his retreating form. It was certainly obvious that he didn't want to have any discussion about Vince. Joey sat in his chair making little cooing sounds in agreement. Maybe Charlie had the right idea after all. I had enough of the past. I was more than ready to move on with my life. No more hiding away behind locked doors. I was alive and I was bloody well going to enjoy every last minute of it.

"Come on, Joey," I said, placing him into his stroller. "It's a beautiful day. We might as well take advantage of it," I said, pushing the stroller out the door. I loved the fall season: never too hot and never too cold, just the right mix. We leisurely strolled down the path towards the pond. Breathing deeply, I watched the leaves, now changed to deep reds and bright yellows. They scuttled across the path at my feet, as a sharp breeze teased them to dance in the sunlight. The honking of geese overhead slowly drew my eyes skyward. Shading my eyes from the sun, I watched as the perfect v-shaped silhouette winged its way across the sky heading south. I wasn't surprised to see the birds, which Amy had watched so diligently from gosling to full feathered geese, had finally left for warmer surroundings. Soon the pond would be covered over with ice, along with the first blanket of fluffy, white snow. But for now I intended to take advantage of the warmth. Settling down against Amy's rock, I found myself snuggling my back even closer as the heat from the rock gradually seeped through my thin jacket. Along the path, a small squirrel, his cheeks full of nuts, scurried to deposit his bounty in a hole, high in the old oak tree. Closing my eyes, I found myself nodding, the heat from the sun cloaking me with its warmth, mollifying my senses.

Snapping my eyes open, I turned my head upon hearing the sound of gravel being crunched under foot. Shielding my eyes from the glaring sun, I watched as Jim sauntered down the path towards me. Not saying a word, he slid down beside me, our shoulders touching. There we sat in an amicably silence, feeling the sun warm our faces. "Look," Jim said, pointing at a flock of small birds swirling high in the sky, only to spy them drop in a flash, scooping insects off the pond with a graceful swoop.

Leaning my head on his shoulder, a sigh of contentment escaped my lips. "I'm glad you're here," I whispered.

"You've had it kind of rough lately, haven't you?" Jim said, squeezing my fingers between his.

"I'll survive. I'm tougher than anyone thinks, but thanks for caring," I said, looking into the clear blue eyes, which always seemed to twinkle in amusement.

"I know you will and I know you are. But sometimes we just need a shoulder to lean on," he conveyed, the merriment evident in his voice.

I could feel the warmth of his body against mine. Turning to look at him, I dared to ask, "You're in uniform, care to tell me why you're here?"

"Can't I just want to see how you're doing? Do I have to have a reason?" he asked, raising one eyebrow.

Shaking my head, I looked at him quizzically, raising my eyebrows, the question still evident on my face.

"God, you know me too well," he chuckled.

Jim sat quietly thinking, a pregnant pause between us, before declaring, "I really did come out to see how you were. But I also have to speak with Charlie."

"Why?" I asked, staring him in the face.

"I need to ask him something," he said, squirming slightly, his face turning slightly red.

What is he hiding, I wondered upon noticing how uncomfortable he was becoming? "What?" I persisted.

He hesitated slightly before replying, "I don't really understand it myself, but for some reason Vince keeps insisting he wants to talk to Charlie. He says he won't give a statement until he talks to him first. He insists he wasn't alone in what he did."

I frowned. "That doesn't make any sense. There wasn't anyone else there," I said, a queer feeling creeping up my spine, but not quite reaching my brain.

"We both know that, but he still insists he wants to talk to Charlie."

"I don't know, Jim. Charlie has a bad temper. I don't think it's very a good idea."

"I know, but it's the only way to get him to talk. He just freezes up whenever someone tries to get anything out of him. He just kept saying that he has to talk to Charlie first."

"Where is he being held?"

"He's still in the hospital. Will be for a while yet, I guess. That shot smashed his leg up pretty bad. He'll walk with a limp from now on."

"It could have been worse. He could have ended up like Jerry," I said. The same feeling of horror creeping into my mind as I envisioned Jerry the last time I had seen him.

Nodding his head in agreement, Jim continued. "Marilyn had the girl they had been trying for. Most men want a son, but Jerry always wanted a daughter. Did you know he came from a family of only boys? He said he was tired of the rough housing and wanted a little girl he could treat like a princess."

"I wish with all my heart I could change things for them," I said, rubbing at the tears starting to form.

"Beth, there's no use beating yourself up. It won't change anything. Sometimes we just have to take the ball that is thrown to us and run with it," he declared grimly. "Anyways, they're having a private service; just the family. We've decided to set up a fund for them. I'm sure all donations would be accepted gratefully."

"Okay. I'll make sure I set something aside for them. When do you want Charlie to come in?"

"As soon as possible. I'd like to get this one wrapped up quickly. We all need to get on with our lives."

"I'll talk to Charlie when he comes in tonight," I said, nodding my head in agreement.

"Thanks, Beth," Jim said, lifting my chin to stare me in the eye. "And, remember, I do have a shoulder for you to lean on, any time you want."

"I know you do. I don't know what I would do without you," I said, giving his hand a slight squeeze.

"I would do anything for you. I hope you know that," he said, before rising slowly. Turning quickly, he walked back down the path in which he came, leaving me with a disquiet feeling settling into the pit of my stomach. I sat there for a while thinking, reliving some of the horror that had unfolded. The rock I was leaning against gradually lost its warmth, making me shiver slightly. The day that had seemed so glorious before now changed along with my mood. The sun abruptly disappeared behind a cloud leaving a chilly dampness in its wake, making the pond now look dark and ominous. A slight shudder rippling down my spine, I grasped the stroller, heading quickly down the path towards the house.

Charlie's pickup truck was easily distinguishable from a fair distance. Hearing the familiar rumble coming closer, I pulled the fresh biscuits from the oven. Wrapping them in a clean towel, I placed them in the center of the table. I could hear Charlie and Thomas talking in the porch as they washed up before dinner. Charlie was in an infectious mood, whistling the only tune he had ever learned while a child: 'Twinkle, Twinkle Little Star'. I smiled, listening while he diligently scrubbed his hands, the sounds drifting towards the kitchen.

"Don't you know any other songs? That's all you've been whistling all day. I'll probably have that tune stuck in my head all night," Thomas said, sounding annoyed.

"Well then at least you would have something stuck in there, right?" Charlie said with mirth evident in his voice.

I could barely make out Thomas's indistinct mumble of, "What an ass hole."

Charlie's mood seemed almost contagious while he chattered away happily about his upcoming fishing trip. Between bites he regaled us with humorous incidents from trips of the past. Thomas, on the other hand, looked completely bored with the whole conversation. Swiping the last bit of gravy up with his biscuit, he let out a healthy burp before pushing his chair back to leave. The tune of 'Twinkle, Twinkle Little Star' could be heard drifting down behind him while he slowly climbed the stairs to his room.

Charlie was so happy. I hated to bring his world crashing down by mentioning Vince's name, but I had promised Jim I would speak with him.

"I had a visitor today."

"Oh, who was that?" Charlie asked, spooning another mountain of pudding into his mouth.

"Jim. He came by to check how I was doing. He also wanted to talk to you."

"He probably wanted to talk about our trip. I'll call him later," Charlie said, scraping his bowl.

"No, that's not it. He told me Vince wants to talk to you. He said Vince won't give a statement until he talks to you first. He was wondering if you could go in tomorrow. He would like to get this whole thing wrapped up as quickly as possible."

Charlie placed his spoon into his bowl, pushing it slowly away. A frown now replaced the smile he had previously worn. "I don't know if I want to do that. I don't know what I might do if I come face to face with him right now," Charlie revealed, his hands held tightly into fists upon the table.

"I can't tell you what to do, but I have a feeling that something isn't quite right.

Something was wrong with Vince that I can't explain." Lowering my eyes, I whispered, "Charlie, I don't think it was really Vince that attacked me."

Cocking his head to one side, Charlie sighed faintly. "You know it was Vince. What makes you think there was someone else?"

"I don't think I'll ever be able to forget that voice, Charlie," I stuttered, remembering the strange, gravelly voice erupting from Vince's throat. "It wasn't Vince's voice. I know it came out of his mouth, but I tell you, it wasn't his voice," I said, shaking my head in confusion. Charlie sat staring into space, not responding at all to what I had said. "Did you hear me?" I asked, waving my hand in front of his face.

"I heard you," he said, an annoyed look replacing his vacant stare. "I guess I'll go tomorrow morning to find out what it's all about. I want this whole thing done and finished with so we can go on with our lives. And it sounds like we won't be able to do that unless Vince talks to Jim."

"I think I'll go with you. I'm kind of curious what Vince has to say that can change what he did."

"I don't think that's a very wise idea," Charlie declared, shaking his head.

"Charlie, I'm going. You can't talk me out of it. I need to put this thing behind me and I don't think I can unless I find out what the reason behind it all was."

Charlie sat quietly weighing what I had said in his mind. Finally he muttered, "All right, but it won't be easy to take."

That night Charlie tossed and turned all night, mumbling in his sleep. The next morning, his eyes red-rimmed, he instructed a confused looking Thomas what his work for the day involved. The ride to the hospital that morning was silent except for Joey's cooing while he blew tiny little bubbles from his mouth. Once at the hospital, we were ushered to a separate room by a tight-lipped aid who told us to just sit and wait for Jim. He would explain everything when he arrived.

Jim, poking his head around the corner, startled us, breaking the heavy silence with, "There you are. I was wondering if I had the right room. These hospital corridors all look the same to me."

Charlie stood hastily shifting his feet from one side to the other before declaring with a grimace, "Let's get this over with."

Clearing his throat before answering, Jim said, "Alright, but there are a few things you should know first before we go in there. First, you can't touch him, Charlie. No matter what comes out of his mouth. Do you understand?"

Charlie nodded, "Alright, but it might not be easy."

"There's more," Jim divulged, relaying the rest of the conditions he was imposing before we came face to face with Vince. "You have to sign a waiver saying you won't use what he says against him in a court of law. I'll be listening from the other room. You don't ask him anything. You just listen. Let him do the talking. Do you think you can do that?"

Charlie, growing impatient, glanced towards the door. Shifting his feet, he growled, "Alright, I hear you. Now let's get this damn thing over with!"

Jim in the lead quickly strode down the hallway towards the room Vince was being held in. Stopping before two uniformed guards that sat flanking each side of a door, he motioned for them to remain seated. "Cal, Bob, how are things going here?" Jim asked, glancing from one to the other.

"Everything is pretty quiet in there. We haven't heard a peep out of him since we brought him in," the officer named Cal declared with a shrug.

That's good. I would like you to keep an eye on this little man here for a while," Jim said, motioning towards Joey. Then, pushing the door open, he allowed us our first glimpse of Vince since the attack.

The figure in the bed looked nothing like the person who had so ferociously attacked me. From under the blanket, two dark brown eyes stared back at us, his face as white as the sheet on which he lay. His one leg, slightly elevated, was hooked to a pulley-like contraption while both hands were handcuffed to the sides of the bed.

Vince's eyes held mine for a few seconds before he quietly asked, "How's Joey doing?"

"He's fine," I managed to choke out.

Vince's face crumbled, two tears slowly sliding from the corners of his eyes to plop quietly onto the white sheet covering his slim form. Looking into my face, his voice cracking with emotion, he finally choked out, "I'm sorry, Beth. I never wanted to hurt you. I hope you believe that."

My throat, feeling like someone had slid sandpaper down it, refused to make a sound. Nodding, I silently turned to look away. He looked so small and innocent tied to that bed. Now it sounded like the Vince I had come to know so well. Turning his head so we couldn't see the tears slipping down his cheeks, he uttered in a small voice, barely above a whisper, "I want to talk to Charlie now."

A doorway connected the two adjoining rooms. Jim and I now stood in the adjoining room, watching Charlie standing despondently beside Vince's bed. Vince turned his head towards Charlie and with such a forlorn look it brought tears to my eyes, struggled valiantly with what he had to say.

"Why did he use me, Charlie? I didn't want to hurt anyone. You know that, don't you? It wasn't me who did those things. It was him. Now no one can help me except you. I'm going to rot in hell for what they think I did. You have to tell them, Charlie! Tell them the truth. Tell them it wasn't me. Maybe they'll listen if you tell them. They'd believe you, Charlie. Please! I don't want to go to hell. Breaking down completely, his hands shook violently, making the handcuffs tinkle in an offbeat tune against the bed frame. He sobbed over and over again "Tell them it wasn't me".

Charlie stood as still as a statue, his head hanging down. Then, hastily pivoting on his heel, he turned to stride hurriedly from the room while Vince's voice, full of anguish, could be heard screaming behind him. "You know it wasn't me! Tell them the truth, Charlie. You tell them, Charlie. Charlie—."

Searching the hallways we finally found Charlie staring morosely out a window. Turning his face away at the sound of my voice, he rubbed the tell-tale tears from his eyes in embarrassment before gruffly announcing, "I have to get out of here."

Jim put his hand on Charlie's shoulder. "Don't worry man. I'll take care of it from here on. The poor bugger needs a doctor, not a jail. I guess Amy's death pushed him over the deep end."

Charlie stared at Jim, studying his face with concentration before finally nodding his head to confirm, "Yes, that's it. He's gone over the edge."

Jim slowly nodded back while he stared Charlie in the eye, "I'll take care of it, alright."

Charlie silently nodded, his eyes trained thoughtfully upon Jim's face.

"Come on, Beth. Let's get the hell out of here," Charlie said gruffly, grabbing my hand to pull me along the hallway we had come. Pushing open the hospital door, he headed towards where our car sat. Slamming the door, he put the car into gear before pulling out of the parking lot in a fury.

Charlie didn't utter a word for miles. His thoughts elsewhere, he stared steadily out the window in front of him. Finally, curiosity getting the better of me, I dared ask, "Charlie, what did Vince mean when he said you were the only one who could help him. Why does he think that?

"How the hell should I know? You heard Jim, he's crazy! Just forget about it."

"But, Charlie I can't—."

"I said, forget about it! I'm finished talking about it," Charlie vehemently announced, turning his concentration back to his driving.

Charlie's face remained stolid, his hands gripped tightly on the steering wheel. Quietly I leaned back against the seat, watching the scenery whiz by until Charlie pulled into our yard.

I still had trouble viewing the spot where Jerry had lain and today was no exception. Turning my face away, I scurried briskly towards the house.

Charlie, feeling contrite about how he had treated me in the car, came over to put his arms around me. "I'm sorry. I had no right to snap at you like that," he whispered against my hair.

Nodding my head, I slipped into his arms to be held tightly against him. Dropping his arms, Charlie whispered, "I have to go to work." Giving me a kiss on the cheek, he slipped out the door, leaving me with a hollow, unsettled feeling.

CHAPTER THIRTY

They say time heals all wounds, and just maybe there is some truth to that, for life slowly returned to normal for us. Charlie and Thomas worked feverishly all week trying to get the fall work done. During dinner Charlie was focused on one thing and one thing only as he chattered happily away about his upcoming fishing trip.

"I have to get some new hooks," he stated out of the blue.

"You're really excited about this trip, aren't you? When are you planning to leave?"

"I'm not sure. Jim and I haven't picked a date yet. I'm going to call him tonight."

"What do you have left to do before you leave?"

"Not much; haul some grain in for the bank and cultivate the west quarter; just a few odds and ends. I can move the cattle home when I get back," Charlie said, slathering a healthy measure of butter onto his bread.

Thomas, who had been sitting quietly throughout the conversation, now piped up, "So, what do I do now?"

Charlie looked up at him in confusion. "What do you mean?

"Do you want me to leave or do I stay here?" Thomas asked, fidgeting with his knife.

Charlie had been so consumed with the thoughts of his fishing trip that he had not given a thought to Thomas.

"Can you stay until after I get back from my fishing trip, or are you in a hurry to leave?" Charlie asked, starring at Thomas intently.

"I'm in no hurry to leave. I have nowhere to go," Thomas replied, grinning at me.

"Surly you have some family to keep in touch with," I said, trying to come up with an excuse for him to leave.

"No, not really. I have a brother, but we haven't seen eye to eye since I caught him sleeping with my old lady," Thomas said, turning a passive face towards me.

"Oh," I replied, pretending to be absorbed in cutting my meat.

Charlie, chewing thoughtfully, said, "It's settled then. Thomas you can stay on until I get back from my fishing trip and then we will get things settled up, alright?"

"Sure, I think I can find something to occupy my time with," Thomas said, flashing me a sly grin.

I finished my meal in silence. There was no way that I was going to stay here alone with that leering jerk watching my every move. Upstairs, the sound of a door slamming shut seemed to confirm my thoughts while I glared at Thomas.

Charlie was so consumed with the thoughts of his fishing trip that he failed to notice the tension mounting at the table. Pushing back his chair, he grabbed the phone to announce he was going to call Jim.

"Jim said he would be over right away. We want to go over all our supplies and finalize our plans," Charlie announced with a huge grin upon returning to the table.

"Well, it looks like I have my plans all mapped out for a while," Thomas said, giving me a wink before he turned to leave the room.

Charlie was so happy, I hated to spoil his plans, but when Thomas left the room, I whirled on him, demanding, "What the hell are you thinking?"

Charlie took a step backwards, looking at me with confusion before asking, "What are you talking about?"

"Thomas, that's what I'm talking about!"

"What about Thomas?" he asked, looking totally confused now.

"Didn't you see that lewd wink he just gave me? Don't you see the way he watches me all the time? He gives me the creeps. I don't trust him!"

"No, I didn't. I'm sure you're just being paranoid, but if you're that concerned, I'll have a talk with him before I leave," he said, taking me by the shoulders, his nose touching mine.

"How is that going to help when you're miles away fishing and I'm on my own with him?" I snapped, jerking away from him.

"Because if he lays one finger on you, I'll break every bone in his body and I'll tell him so," he determinedly announced, before turning me to face him. "I won't be gone that long and I'll get Sam to look in on you well I'm away. At least we don't have to worry about Vince anymore," he said, tugging me closer.

"Don't worry pretty lady, Thomas is afraid of me. He won't touch you," he whispered, rubbing his nose against mine before he enveloped me in a huge bear hug.

"Are you sure he's afraid of you?"

"Yes, if I said boo, he'd turn and run. I guarantee he won't touch you."

"Do you promise me that you'll have a talk with him before you leave?" I asked, relenting slightly before giving him a hug back.

"I solemnly do promise thee," he said with an exaggerated bow.

Jim showed up within the hour, just as excited as Charlie. "This is going to be so much fun," he purred, rubbing his hands together with glee.

Charlie and Jim spent the next hour lugging out their fishing supplies. Soon their talk turned to the different hooks that were required to catch the big one. After an hour of fishing talk, I soon got bored. So, changing the subject, I asked, "What do you do if your boat gets swamped?"

Jim and Charlie both looked up at me, shocked that I would ask them such a thing. It was as if I had sprouted another head.

"It won't happen. It never has yet. In how many years has it been, Charlie?" Jim asked, turning to Charlie for conformation.

Charlie nodded his head in agreement, confirming Jim's assessment before saying, "I guess it must be close to twenty-five years now."

"Alright, I get it, you're both super fishermen and nothing bad ever happens," I said sarcastically, not willing to let the discussion drop.

"I guess you could say we're both super fishermen," Jim contended, puffing his chest out with pride.

"No modesty there," I chuckled, pointing at Jim.

"No really, we're very good at what we do. We've never came home without our limit of fish and we have never, I repeat never, had a boat go over yet," Jim said proudly.

"Well, I'm glad you're so proficient in the art of fishing," I declared with a chuckle. "How are you versed in the art of camping?" I quizzed, fixing Jim an impish grin.

"The best in the west," Jim declared, breaking into a wry grin at his own joke. "No seriously, we had to take a survival training course one year in school. They put us out in the woods with only a pocket knife while the teachers camped out in a tent observing us. That was the longest two days I ever spent without a hamburger or toilet paper, in either order," Jim chuckled.

"Jim sucked at it, but I passed that course with flying colors. The teacher told me I was a natural. That I could survive anywhere," Charlie stated, giving Jim a smug look.

"Yeh, well the only reason for that was, you were half wild anyways," Jim giggled, sounding somewhat like a girl.

Talk then switched to what if's from Jim. Charlie deftly answered each question confidently. Soon I became tired of their easy banter so, I switched the subject again.

"Jim, would you like a piece of apple pie?"

"Sure, I thought you'd never ask. I could smell it when I came in," he said, rubbing his hands together while strolling towards the kitchen. I sat quietly studding Jim's face while he ate his pie.

"Jim, what did Vince mean when he said he wasn't alone?"

Jim paused, a fork full of pie poised ready to go into his mouth. Putting the fork aside, he looked up to study my face carefully before he answered, "He's not right in the head anymore. We had a psychiatrist come in to examine him. He diagnosed him with acute schizophrenia. Vince believes someone was telling him what to do. There will be a hearing next week to see if he's fit to stand trial. More than likely he'll end up in a facility where he can get the help he needs."

"Really, you mean he might not have to go to jail?" I asked, shocked.

"That's right. Also, you might be called in to give some form of statement. That won't be a problem will it?" Jim asked, picking up his fork again.

"No, I can handle it," I maintained, looking Jim in the eye confidently.

"Good girl. The sooner this thing is over with, the better. Now pass me another piece of that pie, you know I can't stop at one piece." Jim chuckled, pushing his plate in the direction of the pie.

CHAPTER THIRTY ONE

Thomas and Charlie were gone from sun up to sun down doing fall work. Coming home at night, they would gobble their dinner down and retire to their bedrooms for the night. Joey became my only companion throughout the long evenings. I would sit and talk to him for hours. It amused me how he could sit there so quiet, his eyes intently watching my lips with each word I spoke. They say babies understand more than we think. Joey surely gave me that impression, for at times, he would seem to nod at just the right moment.

Jim was proven right. Four days later I got a call from an official sounding person saying my presence was required at Vince's hearing. I declined Charlie's offer to come with me, stating I needed someone to watch Joey in my absence.

I had never been in a courthouse before, so I was feeling quite antsy when I walked up the huge steps. Walking down the huge halls, I soon felt overwhelmed by the presence of dark wood paneling stretching from ceiling to glistening marble floor. Slowly I turned in a circle, inspecting my surroundings with awe. The sight of Jim seated at one of the long benches outside two massive wood doors with brass handles of lion's heads made me smile at how well he blended into the opulent surroundings.

"I'm over here," he motioned with a smile, patting the seat beside him. "I'm glad you made it," he said as I sat down beside him.

"Me too," I squeaked, looking around again.

Heh, this won't be as bad as it looks," he advised, seeing my wide-eyed look upon spying the two guards standing on either side of the huge doors. Nodding my head, I continued to stare at the two guards with their guns strapped to their sides.

"Let me explain what will happen. Maybe things will seem easier if you know what to expect," he said.

"Go ahead, I'm listening."

"Vince has already seen a psychiatrist. He has been catalogued as having Schizophrenia. He will be reviewed by a judge and a panel of doctors to determine what will be done with him. Your job will be to answer some questions truthfully on how dangerous Vince was the day he attacked you. Do you think you can handle that?"

I nodded my head while he propelled me towards the huge doors, ushering us inside to take our seat on the cool benches beyond.

"All rise. This hearing will now be in session. The honourable Judge David Krat preceding," A bailiff with impeccable posture barked out. The judge, dressed in a black robe, appeared to be in his early sixties. He was a tall, thin man with a thick head of silvery hair and a rather hawk-like nose. Soberly he climbed behind the huge desk facing the court room.

"You may be seated," the same bailiff announced.

The judge soberly surveyed the courtroom before speaking. "I would like to remind you all that even though this is not a formal hearing and you have not been sworn in, you will be expected to abide by the same rules as if you were. That is, that you must tell the truth, the whole truth, and nothing but the truth. Do I make myself clear?"

We all nodded like puppets on a string, agreeing to abide by the judge's warning.

Vince, seated at a table to my left, his hands over his face, moaned slightly. A pudgy, balding man in an old-fashioned pin-striped suit seated to Vince's right, turned towards him. Tapping him on the back, he leaned forward to whisper something in Vince's ear, which caused him remove his hands from his face and stare vacantly at the judge. Vince never once let his vision stray to where I sat observing him carefully, checking for any sign of the man I had known.

Seated to my right, carefully observing Vince, were the panel of three doctors. The three men reminded me of a set of triplets. All wore the same dark-rimmed glasses and all had the same black, wavy hair, parted to the same side. Even their dark suits seemed to be the same color and style. The first person called to give testimony was the psychiatrist who had diagnosed Vince with his affliction in the first place.

"Dr. Michaels, will you please explain Mr. Vince Shepard's presumed affliction to the rest of the panel?" the balding man who had been seated beside Vince instructed.

"Yes, of course," one of the triplets said, taking a seat to face the court. "I examined Mr. Shepard and found him showing classic symptoms of Schizophrenia. He was very delusional and kept claiming he had heard a voice telling him exactly what to do. He truly believes what he is saying and will follow the orders of the voice he is hearing."

"Do you not think he could possibly be faking hearing these voices to escape punishment?" the pudgy, balding man asked, sidling up close to hear the doctor's next words.

"No, we hooked him to a lie detector and it confirmed he truly believes he heard voices instructing him what to do."

"Doctor Michaels, in your opinion, is it safe to allow Mr. Shepard to be released to live amongst the public without hurting anyone else?"

"No. It is my opinion that Mr. Shepard, at the present time, is unfit to be released to live in society without doing further harm. He is a threat to anyone who comes in contact with him and he also poses a threat to himself."

"Thank you, Dr. Michaels. That will be all," the pudgy man claimed, nodding his head.

The other two triplets relayed the same opinion as the first of the triplets, confirming that Vince was a danger to himself and society.

Finally, the pudgy man turned to look directly at me. "I would like to call Mrs. Beth Sanders to the stand."

Jim urged me to rise, motioning with his head to go and sit in the chair the last triplet had vacated.

"Mrs. Sanders," the judge said, causing me to swivel in my chair to view him. "This hearing is not to pass judgment on Mr. Shepard. It is only to deem if he is fit to stand trial and to be held accountable for the wrong he committed. Do you understand the difference? If so, you may continue."

Nodding my head, my voice barely above a whisper, I confirmed the judge's question. "Yes, I understand."

"Mrs. Sanders, you and your son were attacked by Mr. Shepard. Is that correct?" the pudgy man asked, leaning in so close I could smell an odour of onions and garlic on his breath.

I confidently raised my eyes to stare at Vince, whose eyes remained fixed staring straight ahead as if he was trying to peer beyond the court room.

"Yes, that is correct," I stated.

"At the time that Mr. Shepard attacked you, in your opinion was this act out of context with his normal behaviour?"

"Yes. I could never see Vince doing what he did. It didn't even sound like Vince," I shuddered, remembering that gravelly voice coming out of Vince's mouth.

The pudgy man leaned in even closer to ask his next question. "What do you mean it didn't sound like him?"

All participants leaned forward, their gaze locked upon my face, waiting in anticipation for my answer.

"It—it wasn't his voice coming out of his mouth. His voice sounded different; gravely, deeper somehow. I don't think it was Vince in control of himself," I said, stuttering slightly.

I now had Vince's full attention. He stared directly at me, a slight smile curving his lips. Nodding his head, a silent whisper of thanks exited his lips.

"That will be all Mrs. Sanders. You may take your seat now," the pudgy man said, motioning towards were Jim sat.

"Thank you, Mrs. Sanders. The court will now take a short break while I confer with the rest of the panel," the judge said, looking around the court room.

"All rise," the bailiff announced again upon the judge rising to leave the room. I'm not sure how long we sat waiting for the judge to come back, but it seemed to take forever. Leaning my head on Jim's shoulder, I found myself dozing. The booming voice of the bailiff announcing," All rise," had me jumping to attention.

After we were seated again, the judge slowly surveyed the courtroom. His eyes finally came to rest on Vince. His glance not wavering, he cleared his throat before speaking. "Mr. Shepard, will you rise, please?"

Vince stood, the tinkle of his handcuffs echoing throughout the silent room. His head bowed, he waited silently for the judge's decision, which would seal his fate for the rest of his life.

"Mr. Shepard, section sixteen of the Criminal Code states, 'No person is criminally responsible for an act committed or an omission made while suffering from a mental disorder that rendered the person incapable of appreciating the nature and quality of the act or omission of knowing that it was wrong.' It is the findings of this panel that you fall into this category. Therefore, we find you unfit to stand trial for the wrong you committed. We also deem you would be unfit to function in society at the present time. Therefore, I am recommending that you be placed in a mental facility immediately following this hearing, where you can get the help that you require. Your release will be determined by how well you respond to treatment. That will be all," he stated, rising to leave the room.

Vince, his head down, hands and feet shackled, was lead out of the courtroom. It would be a long time before I would lay eyes on Vince Shepard's face again, I wagered.

"You did great, Beth. It's all over with. You can go home and enjoy that son of yours now, without worrying about anything else," Jim said, ushering me from the court room.

Smiling at the thought of Joey, I pushed open the door to make my way down the massive steps leading from the courthouse towards my car. The burden I had been carrying lifted, floating from my shoulders, making me feel lighter, the world brighter.

Hearing Jim's voice calling, I turned to glance back over my shoulder. "Tell Charlie to get ready. Those fish are waiting for us."

"Alright, I'll tell him," I promised, waving goodbye.

CHAPTER THIRTY TWO

Charlie met me at the door, a smelly Joey held out awkwardly in his hands to deposit him into my waiting arms. "Boy, I'm glad you're home."

"Well, I'm glad to see you too. I gather you didn't change your son's diaper," I laughed sarcastically, watching him holding his nose.

Charlie, shuddering at the thought, replied sheepishly, "No, I took one look and that was enough for me. Did you ever look in there after he does one of those jobs? It's pretty scary!"

"Charlie, he's a baby. How bad could it be?" I said, laughing at the look on Charlie's face,

"Take a whiff and then you tell me," Charlie said, holding his nose.

"Really? A little baby poo can turn you to mush like this," I said, raising one eyebrow.

Charlie, looking sheepish, shrugged his shoulders before asking, "Well how did it go?"

"I felt so sorry for him. He won't stand trial. They're sending him to a mental facility for treatment. It doesn't sound like he will be getting out for a long time.

"Well don't feel sorry for him. Just remember, you could have ended up like Jerry. Don't waste your sympathy on something like that," Charlie snapped, looking out the window at the graveyard beyond.

A sick feeling slowly invaded my body while I thought about what Charlie had implied. Once again, an image of Vince with his fist clenched, pulled back ready to hit me, wavered across my vision. Charlie was right. We would be better off if we never saw the likes of Vince Shepard again.

Thomas sat on the couch, listening to all that was said with a slight smile lifting the corners of his mouth. "What is it that you find so amusing, Thomas? Care to share?" I asked, staring at him with a look of disgust.

The smile swiftly disappeared from his lips. Getting to his feet, he muttered, "No, I don't know what you're talking about. I'm just sitting here minding my own business. Jeez, everyone is sure touchy around here lately," he said, shuffling from the room.

Charlie shrugged his shoulders, an apologetic grin creasing his face as he said, "What can I say, he's Thomas."

"Come here Charlie, let's cuddle," I said, patting the couch beside me. "I want to tell you about my day." I could tell Charlie was becoming bored with the conversation after his third yawn. The slamming of a door upstairs served as a reminder that I had not closed the windows.

"Will you please go upstairs and close all the windows? It looks like rain tonight. I'll rub your feet for you," I cajoled with a slight grin."

"Well, you better make it worth my while, not one of those two minute rubs. It has to be a full five minutes on each foot," he declared, crossing his arms, waiting for my answer with a devious grin plastered across his face.

Hanging my head as if in defeat, I agreed to Charlie's terms. He bounded towards the stairs, eager to get his task over with to obtain his reward. Smiling, I pulled my feet up, tucking them underneath me. Snuggling back into the couch, I waited for Charlie to return to claim his bounty. Charlie seemed to be taking a long time and I soon found myself dozing contentedly.

The sound of approaching footsteps coming down the stairs stirred me from my slight nap.

"Charlie, is that you?"

"Who the hell else do you think it is?"

Puzzled at his tone, I decided to ignore it. "Well, do you want your rubdown?" I asked cheerfully.

"Huh! Just like the one you gave Jim today?" Charlie snorted, looking at me with disgust.

Shocked at what he was implying, I jumped to my feet, stammering, "Charlie, what—what, are you saying? Jim's our friend and your cousin. He's always been there when we needed him."

"Jim, Jim, Jim. All I hear about is wonderful Jim," he sneered, coming to stand rigidly in front of me. His face turned red with anger, his hands clenched tightly into fists at his sides.

"Charlie, that's not fair, Jim's—." I tried to duck when Charlie raised his hand. Too late, the force of the slap lifted me off the floor, snapping my head backwards. I felt myself falling, the sharp edge of the coffee table splitting my lip as I slowly crumpled into a heap on the floor, the suddenness of the attack stunning me.

"You filthy slut, I'll teach you!" The words came pouring out of Charlie's mouth while he raised his hand again.

That voice! Oh my god! I recognized that voice! I closed my eyes, my mind swirling into oblivion, the darkness enfolding me as I collapsed like a rag onto the floor.

I could feel myself fighting to regain consciousness. Forcing open my eyes, I became aware of Charlie sitting on the floor, a few feet from me, rocking back and forth. Tears streaming down his face, he repeated the same words over and over again, "What have I done?"

Blinking to clear my vision, I continued to stare at Charlie, puzzled as to why I lay in a heap on the floor.

"Oh my god, Beth, I'm so sorry," he cried, upon seeing my eyes open. Crawling towards me, he held out his hand to touch me.

"No!" I screamed, scuttling backwards, remembering his raised hand coming towards me.

Tears streaming down his face, he held his hands palm up, beseeching me to come to him. "I won't hurt you. It's me, Charlie. I'm so sorry. I'll never hurt you again."

Not moving, I continued to stare at him. The slight metallic taste of my own blood oozed between my lips before trickling from the corner of my mouth to dribble down my chin. An icy cold feeling of dread settled into the pit of my stomach when I remembered the voice erupting from deep within his throat.

His hands slowly falling to his sides, Charlie continued to stare at me. The depths of his despair showing in his eyes, he softly whispered, "Beth, I'm so sorry." Then, putting his hands over his face, he sobbed like a child again, his shoulders shaking as each gigantic sob tore from his throat like his heart was breaking. I could feel his pain as if it was my own. Slowly, I crawled back to him. Enfolding him in my arms, I rocked him gently as if he was a small child.

"Sshh, it's alright. Sshh, it will be okay," I whispered while the tears streamed down my face.

Charlie's sobs gradually subsided, reduced to the odd sniffle. Standing quickly, he drew me to my feet in one swift motion. Placing his arms carefully around me as if I might break, we stood hip to hip, rocking gently.

"I promise I'll never hurt you again. I'll die before I ever lay a hand on you again," he uttered, looking into my eyes.

Taking me by the hand, he led me to our bed where we stretched out, locked in each other's arms, not saying a word, until we finally drifted off to sleep.

I awoke cold, Charlie's hand still draped over my hip, snoring softly. Lifting his hand gently, I slid from beneath his embrace to crawl from my bed. Standing beside my bed, I looked down at him sleeping peacefully. How could the man I love do what he had done to me? Would I ever be able to trust him again? Sickened, I turned away and walked over to Joey's crib. I gently placed my hand on the tiny chest, feeling the rhythm of his breathing while his tiny chest rose and fell. The love I felt for him oozed from every pore in my body. I gently reached out, smoothing the shock of dark hair from the tiny forehead. I had to protect him, and now felt that challenge doubled four-fold as my eyes strayed to the bed where Charlie slept. Grabbing the throw from the back of the chair, I pulled it tightly around myself, sitting down in the old rocker to gently rock back and forth. That icy cold feeling of dread crept back into the pit of my stomach, quickly spreading to encompass every fibre of my being. I found myself rocking faster and faster, the thoughts swirling through my brain in disbelief, remembering the voice.

Chapter Thirty Three

I awoke to the sound of Joey grumbling in his crib, his diaper soggy from the night. Glancing towards the bed, I found Charlie had left quietly without waking me. I had fallen asleep in the old rocker sometime throughout the night and now my muscles ached with the effort it took to rise. Slowly I hobbled over to Joey, scooping him up to rain tiny kisses on the sweet little face turned up to greet me with a smile. With Joey in a new dry diaper, he now lay watching me, a tiny frown furrowing the small brow.

"What, do I look that frightening?" I asked, touching my face. Stepping across the hall, I hurried towards the bathroom, only to step back in shock at the sight of the woman in the mirror staring back at me. Her face was swollen with one eye peeking out from between a slit, while the corner of her mouth, now trembling, was caked with dry blood. The most horrifying of all was the purple imprint of a hand clearly outlined across her cheek. I watched while the woman silently started to cry, tears sliding slowly down her face to drop off her chin and plop in the basin below. Dry heaves abruptly made her body shake, as if a cold wind had lashed out to encompass her in its grip. Her crying stopped as quickly as it had started while I continued to stare with hollow eyes at the vision represented there. Turning the tap, I splashed cold water on my face, drawing in my breath at the icy sharpness of it hitting the tender flesh there. The cold water seemed to revive my senses. Patting my face dry, I opened my makeup case, searching through it to find something to mask the damage. Stepping back, I surveyed the results. The purple hand print still stood out clearly, only now it looked softer around the edges. Giving up, I turned away from the mirror. I could do no more.

Charlie and Thomas were seated at the kitchen table drinking their morning coffee. They glanced up when I entered the kitchen carrying Joey. Charlie winced at the sight of me. His face changed from white to red in a flash before he turned his head away to gaze out the kitchen window.

Thomas, sucking in his breath sharply, uttered, "Whoa! What the hell happened to you?" Turning quickly, he looked straight at Charlie.

"I hit the door in the dark," I lied, looking down at my feet.

"It looks like the door hit back," he said with a smirk.

Charlie glared at Thomas, his face a red crimson, before he slunk from the room.

"Maybe someone should have a word with that door. It just might decide to do it again. You must have really pissed it off, heh," Thomas said, an annoying grin lighting up his face at the macabre thought.

"Mind your own damn business!" I snapped, grabbing Joey's bottle before turning to leave the kitchen.

I could see Charlie out in the yard tinkering with the tractor, getting it ready to go back to the field. I also saw that same Charlie leaning against the tractor wheel, slowly slide to the ground, his hands covering his face, his shoulders shaking with each sob. Charlie tried his best to make things right between us, but the trust was gone now. It would take time to recoup what we had lost.

That night after dinner, Charlie placed his hand over mine and whispered, "We have to talk. I have to tell you something."

"Alright, go ahead, I'm listening," I nodded, folding my arms protectively around myself.

"I don't want Thomas to hear us. Will you come down to the pond with me?"

"Charlie, it's dark out there. Why can't we talk here?" I asked, with a puzzled frown etched on my face.

"Please, Beth. Can't you just trust me on this?" he murmured, running his hands through his hair.

"I don't know. I'm finding it very hard to trust you right now," I said, moving back from the table, arms crossed in front of me.

"I guess I deserved that," Charlie said, rubbing his forehead with his hand.

"I'm sorry, but I can't do it right now. I won't go outside in the dark with you. Not yet, anyways," I said, turning to leave the kitchen.

"Beth, wait. I think I should cancel my trip with Jim for tomorrow. I can't leave you like this. I have to explain and I can't here in this house," he said, his lips pressed firmly together.

Whirling around, I declared, "No. Don't cancel your trip." Then, trying to soften my tone at the look of alarm on his face, I quietly told him, "I think we need the time apart to let things ease up a bit between us. I need time to try and make some sense out of this whole mess. Until I do, I won't be able to trust you."

The look on his face was enough to almost break my heart as he shook his head. "You don't understand. That's what I need to talk to you about, but I can't do it here," he whispered impatiently before glancing nervously around.

"Alright Charlie, you can explain it all to me tomorrow before you leave. That's the best I can do right now." With that I turned and left the kitchen.

Chapter Thirty Four

The next morning Charlie was up before the sun, sitting glumly in the kitchen, waiting for Jim to begin their fishing trip. He had everything packed ready to go, I noted upon observing the large stack of camping gear that rested by the door.

"I don't think I should go. There are things I have to tell you. I can't leave with things the way they are," Charlie cried, the sorrow reflecting from his eyes.

I knew he was suffering for what he had done. Walking to him, I placed my arms around him. "No, I want you to go. Just give it time. Things will get better, I promise."

"I would never hurt you. It wasn't me! You have to believe that. I would kill myself before I would ever hurt you," he cried, pulling me close to him.

"Sshh, don't ever say that," I said, placing my finger against his lips.

"I have to tell you something, but I can't in here," he whispered, removing my finger. "I'm going to tell Jim I can't go," he said his voice full of anguish.

"No, I don't want you to. We'll talk when you get back. I'll be fine. I want you to go. I need the time to myself," I said sternly.

The door suddenly opened and Jim's voice boomed out, "Heh, coffee on?"

"Yup, sure is," I replied, making an attempt to be cheerful. Turning away hastily, I went to fill Jim a cup of coffee, needing time to collect myself before he saw my face. I knew he would never believe the lie I had told Thomas. Pausing, I placed the cup in front of him, wanting to get it over with. I knew Jim would not take it lightly. I stood quietly waiting for his remark. It didn't take long. His sharp intake of breath echoed throughout the kitchen while he stared at me.

"What the hell happened?" He paused, noting the fading purple hand print on the side of my face. Seeing my downcast eyes he froze, his eyes swiveling to take in Charlie's look of guilt.

"Jim, it's alright. It's not as bad as it looks," I pleaded, placing my hand on his arm.

"If I had a dollar for every time I heard that," he ground out between clenched teeth.

"Really, it's alright. I promise," I said, giving him a weak smile.

"Charlie! Outside, now," Jim barked, motioning to Charlie.

Charlie's face blanched, his eyes downcast. He slowly rose to his feet. Opening the door, he did what Jim instructed, without saying a word. Jim walked behind Charlie, giving him a push every few feet until he guided him a safe distance from the house. I watched frantically from the veranda, wondering what was going to happen. Jim swiftly grabbed Charlie by the front of the shirt, jerking him around to face him. Charlie, his chin resting on his chest, held his hands out to each side, palms up, while he spoke to Jim. I don't know what was said, all I know is what I saw. Then Jim, shaking his head slowly, lowered his hands while he continued to listen to Charlie. They stood talking for some time before turning to retrace their footsteps back to the house. This time, Jim in the lead strode determinedly ahead while Charlie followed slowly behind at a snail's pace. Jim climbed the steps to sit down beside me. Clasping my hand in his, a huge sigh escaped his lips when he looked at my face.

"He'll never touch you again. I'll make sure of that," he claimed, touching the side of my face gently.

"I guess we had better get going," Charlie said, spotting Jim holding my hand.

It didn't take very long to pack Charlie's supplies in Jim's car before they were ready to go. Thomas, standing to one side, listened carefully, nodding his head occasionally, at Charlie's instructions.

Jim strode over to where I stood waiting to envelop me in a huge bear hug. "If you need anything don't be afraid to call Sam, he knows how to reach me," he whispered into my hair.

"Don't worry, I'll be fine," I said, wiggling out of his embrace.

Charlie slowly came forth to take me into his arms, "I wanted to explain something to you, but I can't right now. It will have to wait until I get back. Do me a favour though," he murmured in a hushed tone before taking me by the arms to stare seriously into my face.

"What?"

"Don't go upstairs. Promise me that at least," he said, taking in my wide eyed look of surprise at his request.

"What? Why shouldn't I?" I asked, with a puzzled look on my face.

"Just do me this one favour. I told Thomas he has to sleep on the couch until I get back too. He promised me he would.

"What? I don't understand?" I said a puzzled look on my face.

"It's the best I can do right now. Everything will be alright as long as you don't go upstairs. I'll explain when I get back," he said, his eyebrows knitted together in a frown.

Nodding my head, I reluctantly agreed to his strange request.

Motioning his head towards Thomas he said, "Don't worry about that one. I had a little talk with him. I told him if he laid one finger on you I'd break every damn bone in his body. He knows better than to try anything; he's afraid of me. If it wasn't for Jim I would cancel this trip, but he's counting on me. He cleared his throat. I'll give you the time you want.

I silently nodded, unable to answer. The feeling that I would dissolve into a thousand tears if I attempted to speak overcame me. I did the opposite. Hugging Charlie one more time, I smiled, giving him a push to get going while I waved goodbye to him.

Charlie looked back over his shoulder before getting into the vehicle to mouth the words, "I'll be home soon."

Jim gave me a final hug. Breathing softly into my ear he whispered, "No one will ever hurt you again."

I watched them drive out of sight. The same words, 'It wasn't me! You have to believe me,' suddenly came back to haunt me as I remembered Vince declaring this to Charlie from his hospital bed. A premonition of doom swiftly rose up inside me. Choking back the feeling, I turned to make my way back into the house.

Chapter Thirty Five

Charlie and Jim would be gone a week, of that I was sure. How I would get along with Thomas in Charlie's absence, I was not so sure. Thomas now sat at the table waiting for his breakfast, a sly smile on his face. I hated to turn my back to him because he watched my every move quite openly now that Charlie wasn't here. As I placed the bread in the toaster, he started to hum the children's nursery rhyme 'There Was an Old Lady.' I knew the words by heart and found myself repeating the words in my head along with the tune he hummed. I stopped instantly my hands froze in their task at the realization of why he had chosen that particular tune to hum.

He knew I would remember the words to the first chorus: there was an old lady that swallowed a fly. I don't know why she swallowed the fly. Perhaps she'll die. There was an old lady that swallowed a spider. She swallowed the spider to catch the fly.

I looked up at him with the sickening realisation of who was the spider and who was the fly. Thomas, nodding slightly to confirm my guess, just sat there enjoying my discomfort, grinning wickedly.

"Make your own damn breakfast!" I snapped, throwing the unbuttered toast in front of him.

Turning, I stomped from the room, his ensuing chuckle drifting behind me. The one good thing was I didn't have to deal with him all day. Charlie had given him enough work to keep him very busy while he was gone and he knew it better be finished on time or there would be hell to pay when Charlie got back. The nights were different. The evening meal was a time to sit and converse over the day's happenings.

Thomas sat on one side of the table and I choose the other side, as far away from him as I could possibly get.

Making an attempt at being civil to him, I asked, "How did the work go today? Did you have any problems?"

Thomas, steadily devouring his food, looked up in surprise. "No, everything went alright," he said, a slight frown on his face. The rest of the meal was completed in silence.

His hunger final sated, he belched before leaning back in his chair. Making a tent of his fingers, he looked at me curiously before uttering, "Your face looks like hell, you know. What did you do to piss your old man off so badly that he decided to slap you around a bit?"

"That's none of your business!"

"Come on sweetie, fess up," he urged, tapping his fingers together, waiting for my reply.

"First of all, I'm not your sweetie and second, it's none of your damn business what goes on between Charlie and me," I spat furiously, eyeing him with disgust.

"Aw, get off your high horse. You're no better than any other broad that likes to step out on her man and finally got caught. I see the way you act around Jim all the time, with that sweet little me look that says, 'come hither'," Thomas retorted, giving me a look of disgust.

"You were listening! You know what happened!" I said, looking at him in disbelief.

"So what if I was," he said, leaning back in his chair, a smug grin plastered across his face.

My palms itched to slap the smug look off that egotistical jerk's face. Instead, giving him a look of pure hatred, I ground out between clenched teeth, "You're a complete ass hole!" Slamming my chair back, I ran from the room with only silence following me. Hurrying to my bedroom, I closed the door, leaning against it while I trembled with rage. Turning hurriedly, I engaged the lock with a satisfying click.

The next day I found myself watching the clock, dreading the coming evening. That evening I hurried to complete my meal before Thomas came in. Pulling a chair out for himself, he sat down, waiting for his food, a smug grin plastered on his face. Silently I set his plate before him. Turning away, I crossed the room to leave.

"What, are you too good to eat with me now?"

"Count your blessings that you're getting any food at all. If it wasn't for Charlie, I'd have tossed you out long ago," I snapped, crossing my arms over my chest.

Thomas' dark, smoldering glare focused on my face. Without warning he snarled, "I'm getting tired of this haughtier then thou attitude you have lately. At first I thought it was kind of cute. Now I find it rather annoying. So snap out of it!" he yelled, slamming his fists down on the table while starting to rise from his chair.

Startled, I jumped back in alarm. Turning to flee, I was soon halted by his next words. "He just might not come back. A man could have a nasty accident in those woods out there," he said with a smirk.

Whirling to face him, I fired back, "Charlie is coming back and you're an idiot if you think otherwise. When he gets back, I'll be watching as you get your skinny ass kicked off this property. I can hardly wait to tell him how you've been acting."

Thomas's eyes narrowed, his face changing suddenly to a motley shade of red while he stood rigidly with his hands clenched tightly into fists at his sides. Then, calmly sitting down, he replied, just above a whisper, "We'll just have to see about that. I can always change your mind about me. But it might take some persuasion, if you know what I mean." He grinned wickedly as he gave me a sly wink.

Feeling nauseous at the thought of him touching me, I retaliated with, "I'd rather be dead first." Turning, I hurriedly left the kitchen.

Five more days, five more days until Charlie comes home, I kept telling myself. I only had to avoid him for five more days. The trouble being, five more days seemed forever. I had solved the problem of being around Thomas in the evening by leaving his meal in the warming oven before retiring to my bedroom. Securely locking my bedroom door, I sat playing with Joey on into the evening. I could hear him pacing back and forth in the hallway outside my bedroom door. Occasionally feeling brave, he would try turning the knob to see if it was locked. This became a continuous pattern for the next three days. I could hardly wait for Charlie to come home. In the evening I would bundle Joey and take him outside where we would climb onto the porch swing. From this vantage point I would always be alerted to Thomas' return. Upon seeing Charlie's old truck turn onto the road leading to the farm, I would hurry to my bedroom where I would lock the door. There I would stay until I heard Thomas go upstairs to bed.

CHAPTER THIRTY SIX

It was dusk when I saw the dim headlights of an approaching vehicle making its way around the twists and turns down to the valley floor, the lights changing from dim to bright. I watched curiously, knowing it wasn't Thomas, while the approaching vehicle drew closer and closer. It wasn't long before the vision of a police cruiser came into view. My first thought was maybe Charlie and Jim had gave up on their trip and returned home early. Disappointed, I watched Sam unfold his long legs from the car and climb the steps to sit down with a sigh beside me.

"What brings you all the way out here, Sam?" I asked, a knot of fear edging into my stomach at the look on his face.

Sam cleared his throat. Lifting his eyes to stare into my face, he said, "I don't know how to tell you this, Beth."

I closed my eyes, the fear shaking me to the core, waiting for him to continue.

"Charlie is missing. Jim called into dispatch about an hour ago. He said the boat they were in capsized and Charlie went under into the rapids. He never resurfaced. Jim searched the water and the shore line, but never found him. We're sending in a search and rescue first thing in the morning."

Putting his arms around my shaking shoulders, he tried his best to sooth me. Drawing me close, he whispered against my hair, "Don't worry, we'll find him."

Joey's small body squirming in my arms caused me to look down only to find two small shoe button eyes watching my face intently. A small frown was on his upturned face as if to tell me, look I'm still here.

"Oh Joey," I cried, lowering my face to touch his. Two small fists suddenly reached up to tangle themselves in my hair, pulling me closer.

My tears falling on Joey's tiny face, I sat rocking back and forth in anguish, "Oh Joey, what are we going to do?"

Sam cleared his throat, awkwardly patting my shoulder. In vain he tried to comfort me. His hand falling on my shoulder, he gave it a final squeeze before he rose from the swing. "We'll find him. Jim won't stop searching until he brings him home."

Brushing the tears from my face, I stared at him. Nodding slowly, I sniffled, "I know you'll do your best."

I watched as Sam wearily climbed into the cruiser. Giving a slight wave, he called back to me, "I'll call you as soon as I hear something."

I had never felt so alone in my life, watching the cruisers tail lights wink out of sight. Gulping back a fresh sob that tore from my body, I leaned against the wall, a continuous tide of memories flooding my mind in rapid succession. Charlie had promised me he would be home soon. Now I looked to the heavens, whispering, "Charlie, you promised me you would be home soon, so you better keep your promise." But there was only the whisper of the night breeze to answer me while I searched the heavens above. I had been so lost in thought I had not seen the headlights from Charlie's old truck approach. Startled, I turned to run, only to realize with a sickening dread I was too late as Thomas nimbly jumped from the truck to charge up the walk way.

"Why was Sam here?" he demanded, a slight smile curling his lip.

Shrugging my shoulders, I stared silently at my feet, trying to think of a way to avoid answering his questions.

"What, is your old man missing?" he asked, a smirk lifting the corners of his lips.

Momentarily blinded by rage, I lashed out with my one free hand, slapping him across the face. The resounding smack that ensued filled me with such intense pleasure that I was appalled at myself for receiving so much enjoyment at another person's pain. My hand stinging from the impact, I quickly stepped backwards, out of his reach, my hand falling limply to my side. Thomas' eyes widened with surprise at the ferociousness of the sudden attack. He appeared stunned, holding his offended cheek.

"That was for Charlie. You better pray they find him," I spat, inching slowly backwards away from him."

"Whoa! You mean he's really missing?" he asked, forgetting about his offended cheek.

Turning, I fled with Joey into the house, only to be followed by Thomas, demanding, "What happened? Did he have an accident or what?"

Stopping in an instant, I whirled to face him. The words Thomas had taunted me with earlier came back to haunt me, 'He just might not come back. A man could have a nasty accident in those woods out there.'

Stabbing him in the chest with my finger, I screamed, "If, you had anything to do with this… if you harmed one hair on Charlie's head, I'll see you rot in hell."

Thomas grabbed my finger, bending it slightly backwards, his lips curling back in a sneer. "Don't ever point your finger at me again. In case you've forgotten, I've been right here all the time," he ground out, starring coldly into my eyes.

Snatching my hand back, I turned and fled for the safety of my bedroom. Slamming the door in his face when he tried to follow me, I quickly locked the door. The satisfying click of the lock told him he was not welcome in my domain. The words 'stupid bitch' echoed down the hallway as he made his way back to the kitchen.

Joey's small face remained trained on mine. He seemed to study my every expression. Smoothing the thatch of dark hair from his tiny face, I sat rocking him gently. Outwardly I appeared calm, while inside my emotions churned with despair at the thought of Charlie alone and hurt in the wilderness. I would not entertain the thought that Charlie would not be coming home. Jim would find him, I told myself confidently. Joey's lazy little smile agreed with me, it seemed. I sat rocking Joey long into the night, reluctant to let him go, and then it was only to take him and lay him on my bed where I stretched out beside him, watching the tiny chest rise and fall while he slept.

I kept envisioning Charlie's face before he left. In my mind I heard his last request. The promise I had made not to go upstairs. What was it that he feared so much up there that he felt it necessary to delegate me to keep such a promise? We had lived in this house for so many years and not once had Charlie ever made such a strange request. Now he was not here to answer that question for me and might never be. The thought of never seeing Charlie again brought a fresh wave of tears. The pain seemed more than I could bear. Curling into a ball beside my son I let the sobs rack my body.

Sometime throughout the night I drifted off to sleep, only to awaken with a start, recalling the nightmare that had awakened me. In it I had watched Charlie sink beneath the cold, deep water, where I searched frantically in vain to find him. When I surfaced from the water, it was to spy Thomas standing along the shore laughing, pointing his finger at me, and saying the words, "I told you so." For the rest of the night sleep evaded me while I lay shivering beneath the covers.

The next morning was as dim and grey as my mood. Padding softly in my bare feet into the kitchen, I watched through the window while Thomas drove away in Charlie's old pickup truck. Grabbing my coffee cup, I settled down at the old table to stare dismally out the window that afforded me a clear view of the yard beyond. I watched despondently while Chipper the squirrel scurried across the yard, oblivious of the tumbleweed crossing his path. His cheeks full of nuts from the old oak tree, he climbed the corner of the shed to disappear into a hole under the eve of the roof. Fall was almost over; the trees had shed their glorious dress and now stood naked, silhouetted against the grey sky. I watched dismally as a small whirlwind circled the yard before disappearing as spontaneously as it had appeared. Dark clouds scuttled across the sky, blotting out the sun, the wind whipping the tree tops into frenzy. A storm was brewing, coming in from the north, I noted, watching the tree tops bow to the south. I prayed they would find Charlie before the full force of it hit. Where was he? Was he cold and hungry? Was he hurt? My head was spinning with unanswered questions. All I could do was wait and trust in Jim, for I knew he would be diligently searching for Charlie. The jangling of the telephone had me nearly jumping out of my skin, the noise piercing the calm of the kitchen. I hastily grabbed it, anxious for any news of Charlie, only to be disappointed at Lyle's voice drifting from the receiver.

"Hello, Beth. I just phoned to see how you were doing."

"Not so good right now. Charlie is missing. I was hoping you were Jim telling me they found him."

"I know. I was talking to Jim earlier this morning. He wanted me to check on you. He's pretty worried about you. He said to tell you they're searching for Charlie and will call the minute they had any news."

"I know. Sam told me the same thing yesterday."

"I'm going to send Peggy out to stay with you for a while. I know she's a bit of a chatter box, but she means well and will be good company. It will help take your mind off of things for a while. I know you're going to say you're alright, but humour me, okay? I'd feel better knowing you're with someone I can trust. "

The hell that Thomas was inflicting on me wiggled its way into my mind. I surprised Lyle with my enthusiasm, readily agreeing to his request. "I would love to have Peggy stay until Charlie comes home," I said.

"Alright then it's settled. She will be out there this afternoon," Lyle said the relief clearly visible in his voice.

Peggy was a buxom lady in her late sixties with the disposition of an angel and the energy of two people. She had also been Lyle's right hand for more than thirty years now. She lived alone with just her cat for company, so whenever she had a chance for a conversation where the recipient could talk back, she made the most of it. It was rumoured her husband had slipped away in the night to avoid her constant chatter and she had never heard from him again. Lyle adored her though and had kept her on well past retirement age as her expertise and youthful air could not be found easily elsewhere.

I found myself hovering near the phone all morning, willing it to ring with some news of Charlie, only to have it remain silent. Finally I couldn't wait another second so, calling into police headquarters, I was rewarded with a sleepy sounding secretary telling me Jim was away and I could leave a message. Exasperated, I wearily headed to the living room where I flopped down on the sofa, closing my eyes, saying a silent prayer to keep Charlie safe.

The thump, thump of something banging overhead drew my attention to the top of the stairs. One of the shutters must have come unlatched from the wind. I dreaded the thought of climbing that long flight of stairs, but knew I would have to shut it before the wind ripped it off. When I placed my foot on the first step I could hear Charlie's voice so plainly in my mind. I instantly stopped, looking cautiously around to see if maybe he had come into the house unaware. I had made a promise to Charlie not to go upstairs. Now I stood here wondering why. What would it hurt if I went upstairs? There was no reason not to, I told myself. I slept up there for years. Why had Charlie made me make such a foolish promise? Even Thomas had declined Charlie's instructions, stating there was no reason why he shouldn't be comfortable in his own bed.

The banging continued overhead more urgently now than before. Casting all my doubts aside, I continued on my way up the long staircase to the first landing. There I stopped as always to gaze at the pictures displayed there. There seemed to be some tangible difference in the picture of Charlie's parents, which I couldn't quite put my finger on. What was different, I mussed cocking my head from side to side, studying the picture closely?

The ferocious banging continued from overhead, seeming more urgent now than before. Giving the picture a last unsettling glance, I continued slowly up the stairs. Had the halls always seemed so dull and dreary before, I wondered, moving from room to room checking the windows? I made a mental note to give them a fresh coat of paint in the spring. The windows were all fine here. My curiosity whetted, I continued to search for what was making the banging noise, only to realize that the noise was now directly overhead. God, it is chilly in here, I thought, rubbing at the goose pumps that popped up on my arms. Working my way up the third flight of stairs, I was seized with a premonition so clear it made me draw up short. In it I saw myself standing at the top of a stairs while a dark shadow enfolded itself over my body before I hastily disappeared. The premonition of doom seemed so real that I turned hastily around, making my way back down the stairs. A feeling of being watched made the hair on the back of my neck stand up.

From the bottom of the stairs came a faint, "Hello, any one here?"

My relief at seeing Peggy peering over her glasses, gazing up at me with a huge smile, was so immense that I rushed down the stairs to give her an amiable hug. From the corner of my eye, I glanced back with a slight start upon spying a flash of a shadow drift back into the darkness at the top of the stairs.

"Peggy, I'm so glad to see you," I gushed, leading her down the hall way toward the first stair case.

Reaching the landing, Peggy abruptly stopped to stare up at the pictures displayed there. "I never saw their wedding picture before," she said, her eyes never leaving the picture.

"Oh, I didn't realize that you knew her," I said, genuinely surprised.

"Yes, but not very well I'm afraid. She used to bring the children in when they were sick to see Dr. Roberts. That was before he retired and Lyle took over the practise. I was young then, fresh out of school. Dr. Roberts hired me on the spot. He taught me everything I know. I never had to look for another job again."

"What was she like?" I asked, trying tactfully to change the subject.

"She was a pretty little thing, all blond sunshine. She really worshipped her kids. You could see it in the way she treated them. You know, I kind of felt sorry for her. I always felt her husband had a mean streak in him, a real control freak to boot, if you know what I mean. I thought she got smart and left, but then I heard what happened to her. Poor thing, she didn't deserve that," she said, shaking her head. "Look, even in the picture she wouldn't look him in the eye. She always walked with her eyes downcast like a whipped dog following along behind its master."

That was it! That was what was different. How could a picture change? She had always been looking up before. I peered closer, studying the image carefully. What kind of trickery was this? Had I only imagined the look of adoration she had, gazing up at her new husband? A picture couldn't change, could it? Shaking my head puzzled, I continued down the stairs. From the bedroom came a distinct wail to inform me that Joey was awake from his nap.

Upon entering the kitchen, I found Peggy had made herself at home. Her soft grey curls bobbed around her cherub face as she made a pot of tea. Her big blue eyes twinkling, she said, "I hope you don't mind. I made tea."

"Not at all," I said motioning for her to sit.

She sat with her ample backside firmly ensconced on a chair with her feet propped up on another. "So this is the little man I've heard so much about. My goodness, you are a cute one, aren't you," she said as she chucked him under the chin.

"I would have to agree with you on that," I said, brushing the shock of dark hair away from his tiny face.

Turning slightly she looked out the window. "It looks like we're in for a bad storm by the look of those clouds rolling in," she said. Looking up, I watched the trees twisting and turning as a ferocious onslaught of wind held them in its grip. Without warning, the tears I had been keeping in check quietly ran down my cheeks to drip silently off my chin. Peggy, spying the tears, wrapped her arms around me in a motherly hug. Clucking her tongue, she pushed a towel into my hands while softly saying, "My goodness, this will never do. I know you're worried, but try to have a little faith in Jim. I just know that he'll find Charlie. I don't want you to give up hope."

"You're right. I'm just feeling sorry for myself," I managed with a weak smile, dabbing my face with the towel.

By dinner time the storm had hit full force. A true northerner, as the old timers used to say. The wind howling from the north encircled the house making it shudder and groan. The rain lashing against the window panes had my stomach in knots imagining Charlie out battling the elements, maybe even hurt.

Sam called to inform me they had not found Charlie yet. They were combing the shore-line for any sign of him, but the storm was hampering the search so they were calling it off for the night and would resume at first light. Jim was still out searching and would call me in the morning, Sam assured me.

Peggy, being a dear, tried her best to take my mind off Charlie's plight. She seemed oblivious to the annoyed looks Thomas would shoot her from time to time at her constant chattering.

"Where are you from, Thomas?"

Thomas pointedly refused to answer her. A disgusted look etched on his face while he turned his back to her.

"I've never seen you around and I know most folks from the area. You must be from the city, right?" she guessed, smiling sweetly.

"It's none of your damn business where I'm from!" he snarled pushing back his chair. He dared her to say anything else as he gave her a withering look before turning to leave the table.

"My goodness, I sure ruffled his feathers. I didn't mean any harm. I was just trying to be friendly," she said, her cheeks turning red with embarrassment.

"Don't worry about Thomas. He's as sour as a pickle," I informed her, patting her hand gently.

"I dare say he's more than a little sour, I think he's just plain mean. I'm sorry dear, but I just don't trust him. There's something about his eyes that frightens me."

"I know what you mean. He gives me the creeps too."

"What was Charlie thinking, leaving you alone with a man like that? Tsk, tsk, I think I just might have to have a word with him when he gets back," she said, shaking her head.

"I'm glad you said when, not if," I choked out, giving her hand a squeeze.

"Of course I said when. I just know he'll come back," she whispered, giving me an encouraging smile. Joey, watching from his chair, nodded his head as if in agreement while he kicked his feet. "He's such a happy baby. Why, he's no work at all," she declared, giving Joey's foot a tiny squeeze.

Peggy's chatter helped take my mind off Charlie. She soon had me caught up on the latest gossip while we worked amiably together tidying the kitchen.

"Which room do you want me to take?" she asked, motioning her head towards the stairs.

A feeling of foreboding seemed to rise from deep within me, threatening to suffocate me in its ferociousness when I looked towards the stairs.

"Peggy, why don't you sleep down here with me? I could use the company."

Staring at the staircase, she shivered slightly before replying, "Yes, if you're sure you don't mind. I think I would like that."

"Then it's settled. Joey, we're going to have company tonight," I whispered, picking him up to give him a hug.

Thomas, who had been staring at us from across the room, swiftly got up from his chair. As he advanced towards us, his eyes seemed to darken with a forewarning look before he turned suddenly to disappear up the stairs.

Peggy shuddered slightly, her pink cheeks darkening. Cautiously she whispered, "I'm glad I'm sleeping down here."

CHAPTER THIRTY SEVEN

The following morning I waited anxiously by the phone for Jim to call. Peggy entered the room and sat eyeing me critically before speaking out. "Watching the phone isn't going to make it ring. You need to keep busy," she said with her hands on her hips.

"I know you're right," I said getting up to place my cup in the sink. As I rose, everything in my vision started to spin. I'm going to be sick," I said, making a mad dash for the door. There over the porch railing, into my rose bush, I upchucked my breakfast. Wiping my mouth with my apron I sank onto the swing, trying desperately to keep it still.

"Are you all right, dear?" Peggy said, poking her head around the door.

"I'm fine, really Peggy," I said noticing her skeptical look. "It's just nerves," I said, waving my hand in dismissal.

"Are you sure?" she asked, raising one eyebrow.

It couldn't be. Could it? I found myself trying to count backwards. The thought fleeing from my mind as the door opened hastily. Thomas strode out onto the porch, giving Peggy a withering look as he climbed into Charlie's old truck to leave.

"Not very friendly, I'd say," she said, watching the truck disappear from view. "Alright now, I want you to go and lie down. You're still looking a might peckish," she said, motioning towards the door.

Just nerves, I told myself, following Peggy's advice as I went towards my bedroom.

Peggy was a dear, taking over looking after Joey's every need.

"You're spoiling him," I told her with a slight smile, upon entering the kitchen.

"Oh, I'm sorry I didn't mean any harm, it's just that he's so easy to spoil," she said, her cheeks tinged with pink.

"Spoil away, no harm done. He loves the attention and I can't find it in myself to give it right now," I murmured, glancing out the window.

Placing her hand over mine, she gave it a little squeeze before announcing cheerfully, "He'll be back. I just have a feeling and I'm usually right, so don't you go giving up hope now."

"Thanks Peggy, you've been a dear to keep my spirits up like this."

"It's nothing dear. What are friends for?" she said with a glow in her rosy cheeks, clearly pleased she was being helpful.

Taking a chair facing the window, I sat watching through the glass. Looking up, I spied a lone bird loftily winging its way high in the sky, tossing and turning against the stiff breeze. The storm had abated leaving a dull gloomy day in its wake. Charlie had been missing for three days now. One of those days and nights had not been fit for man or beast to be out in. The piercing shrill of the telephone ringing had me grabbing it hastily. I listened anxiously while Jim on the other end quietly said hello.

"Beth is that you?" A faint voice whispered from the phone.

"Yes, I can hardly hear you," I screamed into the phone.

"The reception is down from the storm. I just called to tell you we are still looking and not to give up hope. I won't lie to you, but it doesn't look good. We found the boat broke up pretty bad from the rapids and most of the equipment. There isn't any trace of Charlie. I'll call you as soon as I know something. Have to go… signal fading."

"Jim wait, can I come down there? Jim? Jim, are you there?" My only answer was the steady hum emitting from the disconnected phone.

This time no one could comfort me. Starring in horror at the phone still clenched tightly in my hand, I dropped it hastily before running to my room. There I threw myself onto the bed, curling up into a ball, an icy cold feeling of dread ripping through my body, spreading itself to every nerve ending to leave me frozen in fear. Slowly the tears started to trickle from the corners of my eyes to form a damp puddle on my pillow. Charlie was gone. Slowly the sobs tore from my body, gaining in momentum while I rocked back and forth in anguish. I was vaguely aware of Peggy gently patting my shoulder before she left the room, closing the door quietly behind her, leaving me alone to deal with my misery.

The days seemed to all mesh together while I tried to go about my daily routine. My stomach had not settled down and I found myself upchucking at the most inopportune times. Peggy, always hovering near, would watch me, her foot tapping impatiently as I refused to see a doctor. Gradually the queasiness disappeared and Peggy focused on trying to keep my spirits up. She did her best to comfort me, telling me over and over not to give up hope. I found her words of encouragement were now failing, for I could see her hope had also slowly dwindled. Thomas avoided Peggy with a passion. Whenever she was not around, he would smile that Cheshire cat grin I had come to hate so much, watching my every move. At times I could hear him humming in an offbeat key, wandering from room to room. The work was almost completed now. There wasn't any reason for him to stay. I would tell him to leave.

It had been a week since Charlie had disappeared. On the morning of the eighth day, Jim's cruiser rolled into the yard. I watched him wearily get out of the car to slowly climb the steps leading onto the veranda. In my heart I knew what he had come to tell me. I slowly opened the door dreading to hear the words that would make Charlie lost to me forever.

Jim gently took me in his arms before murmuring the words that were about to change my life for ever.

"I'm so sorry, Beth. I wish I was bringing you better news, but I'm not."

I looked up to see the blue eyes that were so much like Charlie's, now brim with unshed tears. I had dreaded this moment. I knew in my heart it was bound to come as the days had multiplied without any word from Jim. Now standing before him I felt my knees slowly start to crumble. Nodding my head, I leaned against him for support while his arms tightened their hold in a protective grip. I had cried until I was dry and now all I could do was try to draw strength from the man that reminded me so much of Charlie. I knew I would need his strength for the days ahead.

Jim explained to me they had searched for miles but had found nothing to give them any indication that Charlie had made it out of the water. They had finally called in an underwater search team but had come up with nothing. The water was so cold and deep it made searching impossible. They had done their best but had finally conceded to defeat. Charlie was gone.

Jim stayed for the morning, quietly watching me to see if I would be alright. Satisfied, he announced he would have to go but would be back soon to check on us. "Is there anything I can do for you before I go?"

"Yes, there is one thing. Can you help me get rid of Thomas? I don't want him here. He gives me the creeps."

"I'll take care of that right now for you. Where is he?"

"He's in the barn. He spends most of his time there since Peggy came."

I watched from the window as Jim's lengthy strides took him to the barn door where he disappeared from view. It wasn't long before Thomas emerged. Jim followed close on his heels. Thomas's face was dark as thunder when flung the door open.

"I want my money before I go!" he snarled up close to my face. Grabbing the check book, I scribbled out a fair amount and handed it to him.

Snatching the check from my hand, his face darkened even more upon studying it. "Is this all you're going to give me for working my ass off all summer?" he raged, shaking the check in my face.

"I had to take off your room and board. What, did you think you were staying here for nothing?"

Thomas stepped towards me, his hands clenched into fists. "Stop right there, Thomas. Don't take one step further or you'll be sorry," Jim snapped, coming to stand between us. "I think you'd better leave. The lady is being fair. Get your belongings and I'll give you a lift to town. Right now!" He pointed towards the stairs as he waited for Thomas to leave.

Thomas glared at Jim, knowing that his luck had finally run out. Stuffing the check into his pocket, he turned to stomp up the stairs. In a few minutes he returned with a pillow case slung over his shoulder, his few meager belongings inside.

"You better not have taken anything that doesn't belong to you," Jim declared, eye-balling Thomas with a look of disgust.

"Huh!" Thomas mumbled. In two strides he stood before me, his face a few inches from mine. "I'll be back," he snarled.

"No you won't! You're finished here. Let's go," Jim said, grabbing him by the shoulder to swing him around before quickly propelling him towards the door.

"I'll call you in a couple of days, Beth. Hang in there, okay?" Jim said, pushing Thomas out the door.

Peggy came to put her arms around me. "I'm so sorry, Beth. Charlie was a good man, but I know you're strong. You and Joey will get along just fine."

Swallowing the lump that seemed to appear in my throat, I nodded slowly, mumbling my thanks. I was finished with crying. I had to move on without Charlie now. Somehow Joey and I would make it through this. I would have to rely on myself from now on. Joey needed me and I had promised I would always be there for him. So, squaring my shoulders I went to pick up my son, holding him tightly against me. I told him his father was gone it was just him and I now, while one tiny tear that had been overlooked escaped from the corner of my eye to run silently down my cheek. Peggy left that afternoon. There wasn't any more reason for her to stay. I reluctantly said goodbye. I would miss her chatter, but I needed time to be alone to just think and grieve in my own way.

The rest of that day I sat for hours just staring out the window, my mind spinning out of control while one memory after another resurfaced, adding to my pain. Charlie asking me to marry him, our honeymoon, and the wild flowers Charlie had shyly held out to me after our first fight. Charlie holding me close while I sobbed my heart out after we lost each precious baby. The memories swirled around in my head faster and faster until I wearily closed my eyes, too tired to think anymore. Rubbing my aching temples, I glanced up to find Joey watching me intently, a frown drawing his tiny eyebrows together. Joey, you are my salvation. Without you, I would be thinking of following Charlie into the water. You don't have to worry little one, I will always be here for you. Cradling him gently in my arms, I smoothed back the tiny cowlick as I slowly walked back to our room. We would get by. We had each other.

Chapter Thirty Eight

The next morning dawned clear and bright. Snow had fallen throughout the night, cloaking everything in a dazzling white. I watched despondently as a flock of tiny birds seeking warmth from the dark earth settled on a dark patch of the road were the snow had melted. The snow wouldn't last too long. Already the house eves dripped from the warmth of the sun. It wouldn't be long before Mother Nature would see fit to cover us with her winter cloak again. Higher in the mountains the snow would be building up already. The lake where Charlie had gone fishing would soon be frozen, the area around it as remote as a frozen wasteland. Down here the roads could sometimes become impassible for days. This was not the place for one who sought fun and adventure. Over the years I had come to love the solitude, but then, I had Charlie. Now I dreaded the thought of the impending long months of winter.

Coffee cup in hand, I stood gazing out the window, watching the steady drip, drip of water off the roof. The tiny little tracks of chickadees criss-crossing on the snows surface led my gaze to another's tracks leading up to the house. No bird or animal had made those huge prints in the fresh snow. Someone was here, possibly in the house at this very moment. Oh my god, Joey. Wrenching open the bed room door, I stared in horror at the form suspended over Joey's crib.

"Get away from him!"

Turning towards me, an insidious grin forming on his face, he said, "I told you I'd be back. Don't pretend you're not glad to see me."

"Give him to me!" I screamed, reaching out to take Joey from Thomas.

247 | **Rita** Van Damme

"Not so fast. I might drop him if you're not careful. A fall from this high just might kill him," he suggested, a sickening grin etched across his face.

"You can't mean that," I shuddered, taking a step forward, arms outstretched to claim my son.

"Back up or he goes down!" he snarled, holding Joey above his head.

"Please don't hurt him. He's just a little baby. Please?" I pleaded, taking another step forward.

Thomas, holding his hands suspended under Joey, instantly dropped him, only to catch him again after a few feet. Joey's whole body seemed to stiffen while he clutched frantically at thin air, his eyes widening in fear.

I stopped, frozen in horror.

"No! Please? I'll do whatever you want. Just don't hurt him," I pleaded, my eyes never leaving Joey's tiny face.

"Now that's more like it. You will do whatever I say or I will do exactly what I said. Now, don't you go getting any ideas about calling Jim or any of your other boyfriends, understand? Just remember, I got in here once and I can do it again. You'll have nobody but yourself to blame if you come in some time to find the brat's brains scrambled all over the floor. Even if you do somehow manage to complain to anyone, I know my way back here and when you least expect it—," he said, making a whooshing sound and then a splat. "You understand, heh!" he said with a shifty grin on his face.

"Alright, you made your point. Now give him to me."

"Not yet, I'm kind of hungry. How be we mossy on into the kitchen and you can make me some breakfast. Come on now, let's go before my hands get weak from lack of food," he said, pushing me towards the door. Simmering with rage, I turned to do what he demanded, all too aware of the feeble grasp he had on Joey.

"What do you want?" I asked, his finger prodding me in the back, herding me towards the kitchen.

"Don't play dumb with me. You know what I want," he hissed into my ear.

"I paid you before you left. Do you want more money? Just name it and then you can leave. No hard feelings, alright?" I suggested, trying desperately to barter with him.

"You think a few more measly dollars are going to pacify me? Make up for the way you treated me? Think again, bitch! Why should I settle for your charity? I can have it all. You need a man around here to keep you in line and guess what? I just appointed myself that man. Now shut up and make me some food, or do we have to go through this again? I'm getting rather weak from lack of food," he said with a sickening grin.

Joey seemed to sense something was wrong. He began to whimper, his small dark eyes trained intently upon me as if begging me to come and get him.

"Alright, I'll get your food but I want Joey when I'm done," I challenged, my chin held high looking him straight in the eye.

"We'll see. Still have a little bit of spunk, heh? I'll have to work on that. Although. A little bit of spunk can sometimes be useful. If you know what I mean," he said with a leer.

Ignoring him, I realized I would have to wait for an opportunity to get rid of him. My concern was for Joey. First I had to make sure he was safe. Joey continued to whimper with Thomas still holding him awkwardly in front of him. Hurrying, I slapped the scrambled eggs and toast down in front of him.

"Now give him to me," I demanded, my voice rising in agitation.

"Not until you say please—nicely," Thomas said, his eyes traveling up and down my body.

"Please?" I said jerkily, reaching out to take Joey.

"That's not nicely. I said nicely," he snarled, slapping the table with his one free hand.

Screwing up his face, his eyes searching frantically for me, Joey's whimpers now turned to a wail.

"Please," I murmured, giving him a fake smile.

"That's better. Alright, take the brat. He's getting too noisy for me anyways." I hurriedly reached out to take Joey from him only to have Thomas grab my arm and wrench it downwards. "Don't even think about trying to run. If you do, I'll come back here to finish what I started. You won't be able to hide from me forever. Remember, you have more at stake here than I do."

"I won't run, I promise," I said, staring him in the eye.

"I'm glad we understand each other. Alright, now do something to shut him up," he mumbled, pointing towards Joey.

"Shush sweetie, mommy has you now," I whispered against his tiny cheek, rocking him back and forth until his small body relaxed. Slowly, his wails reduced to a few sniffles. Thomas's shifty eyes followed my every move. Finally I turned my back to him. My eyes shutting out his image while my brain searched frantically for an avenue of escape.

Thomas continued to watch my every move, lest I try to escape. When I went to the bathroom he would stand beside Joey, a reminder of what he would do if I tried anything. The jangling of the telephone startled me. I reached out to grab it, only to find that he was faster. Grabbing my arm, he wrenched it behind my back, his foul breath fanning my face. His eyes smoldering with a warning, he nodded towards Joey.

"One slip up and you'll be planning two funerals instead of one. Remember my promise," he snarled twisting my arm until a shooting pain shot up it, making me gasp. I nodded quickly, anxious to be free from his deleterious hold. Pushing me towards the phone, he relinquished his grasp to stand behind me; his body leaning in close enough to hear all that was said. The relief at hearing Jim's voice was short lived. Grabbing my shoulder, he spun me around to face him. Then, pointing towards Joey, he effectively silenced me as he made a cutting motion across his throat.

"Hi Beth, how are you doing?"

"I'm fine," I lied while Thomas's hot breath slid down my neck, making me shudder.

"I said I would phone in a couple of days to see if you needed anything and finally found a few minutes to spare."

"When will you be coming out this way?" I asked, trying desperately to alert him that I was in trouble.

"I guess I could make it out tomorrow. Do you need help with something?"

Shaking his head at me, Thomas's grip on my shoulder intensified, making me cry out sharply.

"No, no, I'm fine. I don't need any help. I'd rather be alone. Don't bother coming all the way out here for nothing."

"Are you alright? You sound kinda strange."

"I said I was fine I just want to be alone. Is that so hard to understand?"

"Alright, I didn't mean to intrude. If you ever need someone to talk to, just remember I'm here."

"Yeah, yeah, okay, look I really have to go. Joey needs me," I said, looking in Joey's direction. I was all too aware of the fact that Joey did need me, desperately, for I was sure Thomas would have no qualms about keeping his promise.

"Sorry to have kept you. I guess we'll talk in a few days then, alright?"

"Yeh, alright, we'll talk in a few days. Bye, Jim."

I felt all hope dwindling away with the click of the receiver. The dial tone echoing in my ear signaled he had hung up. I could tell I had hurt Jim's feelings by the way I had excused him. My only hope was he had picked up on my unusual behaviour and would come here to check it out for himself.

"That's better. I know you didn't really want him out here to spoil things between us, now did you?" Thomas whispered into my ear, his foul breath fanning my cheek while his hand wandered down my back to cup my right buttock in a firm grip.

"Don't touch me!" I hissed, slapping his hand while I instantly jumped backwards out of his reach.

Thomas, as lithe as the snake he was, crossed the expanse separating us in a flash to reach out and grab a handful of hair from the back of my head. Dragging my face around to within inches of his, spit flecking my face, he ground out from between clenched teeth, "I'll touch you whenever I want and wherever I want. Got that?" he claimed, his one free hand darting out to grab my breast and give it a cruel twist. Gasping, I tried to twist away from his groping hand, only to have him wrench my hair downwards, bringing me to my knees. "I said, have you got that?" he screamed, wrenching my face up to meet his. My face contorted from the pain, I silently nodded my head, only to have him reach out with a booted heel to shove me backwards onto the floor. "That's better. We understand each other now, right?"

I nodded my head slowly, appearing to have accepted my position, while inside I seethed with rage. I would wait for a better opportunity and then he would feel my wrath, I vowed. Watching him through glinted eyes, I crawled to a sitting position before I slowly drew myself up to stand before him, my head bowed in submission. The hatred slowly infiltrated every inch of my being, making my body tremble with its power. For now I would wait.

Chapter Thirty Nine

Thomas continued watching my every move. At meal times I was to prepare him a full meal and was forced to sit and watch him eat. He had this image in his head that this was his home and I was at his beck and call. He had hidden all the knives from the kitchen drawer with the thought that I might use one on him. I was allowed to feed and change Joey but could not sit and cuddle him. He would take Joey and sit him in his chair beside him, a constant reminder that I was to follow his instructions. That night I took longer than usual giving Joey his bath, my mind exploring every avenue of escape. Thomas stood beside me, watching my every move, a strange glint in his eyes.

"You're good with your hands. I wouldn't mind if you gave me a bath like that," he said giving me a lecherous wink.

"I would have to be dead first!" I declared, looking at him with disgust.

"You're just like all the rest of them. Out there strutting your stuff when it suits you, but then playing the innocent little me act when it comes right down to it," he sneered.

I silently turned my back, willing him to go away.

"Don't turn your back to me, bitch! What do you think, you're better than me? You're going to find out what a real man is like before I'm done with you. Before long, you'll be begging me for it."

Oh my god, he intended to rape me. Placing Joey in his crib, I grabbed the only weapon I could find, a two inch long diaper pin. If he tried anything, I would go for his eyes with it. I carefully slid the pin into my pocket.

"What have you got, there?" he demanded, pointing to my pocket.

"Nothing, it's just a hankie," I said, pulling the corner of it from my pocket.

"That's all it better be," he said while sitting down on the edge of the bed. Giving me a wicked smile, he patted the bed, beckoning for me to come.

"No. I'm not tired yet," I said, trying to stall him.

"Who said anything about sleeping? Now get over here," he demanded, his eyes raking my body from top to bottom.

"No, please! Don't do this," I begged, both hands splayed palms up, backing away.

"Get over here right now or that brat is going to pay. In one lithe motion he scooped Joey up to hold him over his head, his legs splayed in a stance that showed he meant business.

"Alright, alright, I'll do what you say, just put Joey back in his crib," I pleaded, scurrying to perch anxiously on the edge of the bed.

"That's better. Now strip." His eyes held a strange light while he watched my face, noting the struggle taking place within.

"Please don't do this," I begged, my head bowed in submission. While tears squeezed silently from the corners of my eyes to slide down my face.

"Please, I'll do anything you say, just not that, please," I shook my head in protest, begging him to take pity on me and let me go.

Thomas never said a word. I could feel his hot breath on my cheek where I sat with my eyes shut, praying he would reconsider and leave me alone.

"If you think a few tears and pleases are going to get you out of this, think again. You need to be taught a lesson in how to treat your man and we might as well start now," he said, forcing me backwards onto the bed.

"No!" I screamed, slapping at his groping hands as he tried to pin me down. In a flash his huge hand snaked out to viciously slap me across the side of my face. My ears ringing, I sunk to a heap onto the bed, trembling in fear. Forcing myself to remain limp, I slid my hand into my pocket feeling for the pin.

"Come on baby, Papa has something for you," he whispered, climbing on top of me.

He was so intent on his attack that he never noticed my hand working the pin open. His face a few inches from mine, I raised my hand, swiftly bringing the pin downwards, stabbing towards his eyes. Oh my god, I missed. Horrified, I stared at the pin jutting out of his cheek. Howling in surprise, his hands scrabbled to find the object of his pain. Pulling the pin from his cheek, he stared at it for a second before flinging it aside. Then, like the snake that he was, he slid across the room to grab me before I had a chance to grab Joey and run.

"You filthy slut, I'll teach you a lesson you'll never forget," he screamed, grabbing me by the hair to slap my face back and forth with his free hand. Bringing his face close to mine, the spittle flying from his mouth, he uttered the words that would remain locked into my unconscious for the rest of my life. "Who shall it be, you or the brat?"

I numbly whispered, "Me," while my body shook with fear. This time there was no one to save me. Tying my hands behind my back, he took what no man has a right to take without permission. Closing my mind to him, I withdrew into a shell he could not penetrate. I don't know how long I lay in my vegetated state. The sound of Joey's whimpering seemed to resound in my brain, drawing me back from my impervious world. Fighting my way back to consciousness, I turned my head towards where Joey lay. Thomas was gone, leaving me naked on the bed, hands and feet bound.

I turned my head at the sound of someone approaching. Thomas was back again. He stood leaning against the door eating a sandwich while his eyes slid over my body. Popping the last of the sandwich into his mouth, he came towards the bed, wiping his filthy hands on my stomach. This time I regressed back into my shell, pushing the sight and sound of Thomas far from my mind, where I lay helplessly before him. Finished, he rolled over, giving me a look of disgust before he reached over to pinch my nipple. "Next time you better put a little effort into it. Now I can see why your old man had a fling with Rachael. You sure had to watch your back with that one, but at least she knew how to treat a man," he said, a slight grin lifting his dour face recalling some secret memory.

"Charlie never touched her! How dare you try and tarnish his memory with lies!" I spat out in fury.

"Boy, are you ever stupid. What do you think he was doing in the barn with her when he went to get that board?"

Was Thomas telling the truth, I wondered? I thought back to the image of Rachael slipping from the barn to be followed shortly by Charlie. Had I really been so naïve as to believe Charlie's excuses? Shaking my head to clear the negative thoughts, I hissed, "Charlie wasn't like that."

"Rachael could make herself mighty tempting and Charlie was no bloody saint. He was doing her for quite a while before her old man showed up. That sure spoiled her plans for taking your place. No wonder she figured she better get rid of her old man once and for all. She thought she would have clear sailing after that. Huh! The bitch even played me for a fool. She even got me to drive her to her old man's to stand guard while she hacked him to pieces. She said that she was just going to get some money he owed her; that she would give me half if I helped her. I called her on it but she said 'what did it matter who did it?' He had got what he deserved and now she was going to get what she deserved. We had a big fight about it one night. She said there wasn't any money, that she had paid me with her favours and we were finished. She was going after Charlie and no one was going to stand in her way. Were you really that dumb that you didn't see what was going on right under your nose?" he snorted in disbelieve.

I remembered the night I had stood on the stairs listening to the exact conversation Thomas was referring to. The flashback was so painful I gasped, acknowledging that what he said was the truth. I knew this deep in my heart but my brain refused to accept it. The seed of doubt had been planted, only to wither and die along with Charlie and Rachael.

"I have to look after Joey. Untie me," I demanded.

Thomas glanced to where Joey lay fussing. "The brat can wait."

"Please," I pleaded. "Just let me look after him, I won't try anything. Just let me go to him. You got what you wanted."

Thomas started to protest, but thinking better of it he loosened my bonds allowing me to be free. Rubbing my wrists, I slid from the bed. Grabbing my clothes, I hurried to dress lest he change his mind. Battling the fury threatening to engulf me, I picked up Joey, holding him close to my heart, soothing his fears. Trembling with rage, I silently vowed I would find a way to escape. If Thomas had to die in the process, so be it.

Thomas continued to watch me constantly. Thankfully he had eased up on Joey, allowing me to spend more time with him. Whenever he had to leave for extended periods he would tie me to a chair in the center of the room. Even though I was bound, I relished the time he was gone, savoring the feeling of not being constantly watched. He would go upstairs once a day at exactly two o'clock. I could hear him talking to himself up there. Sometimes he sounded so angry. Other times I could hear the low mumble of his voice as if he was conversing with someone amicably. He would always return with a curious light in his eyes and a sly grin plastered across his face to stand before me, his eyes boring into mine, before mumbling what he intended to do to me that night.

Five days had passed since Jim had come to tell me that Charlie would not be returning. I missed him terribly with each passing day. Gradually the loneliness turned to anger for leaving me. Finally the guilt slowly edged in until I hung my head with shame. It wasn't right to blame him for something that wasn't his fault. Thomas continued to torment me day and night. The nights were the worst. He would tie me to the bed every night, abusing me in any fashion he chose. If it wasn't for Joey, I would have tried to escape. Myself, I didn't care whether I lived or died, but Joey was helpless and I chose to live for him.

Jim had called two days ago, the hurt still evident in his voice. I had tried desperately to think of a way to alert him that something was wrong, but failed. I knew now that I was on my own. Thomas was becoming more relaxed around me and at times would even chatter away as if everything was normal.

"I'm getting kind of used to it here. It has a lot of advantages: pretty little woman at my beck and call and if she plays her cards right, I might even keep the brat. Teach him a few things. Yup, it's starting to feel more like home all the time," he said, putting his feet up on a chair.

"It's not your home. It's Charlie's name on the title, not yours," I snapped, giving him a look of disgust.

Thomas sat studying his hands a pensive look on his face. "Well, if it's not mine than you'll just have to sell it. I could use the cash just as well anyways," he casually remarked, looking up at me.

"If you think I'm going to sell everything and turn the cash over to you, you're crazier than a loon," I remarked flippantly.

Thomas' eyes narrowed before he silkily replied, "I guess your son means nothing to you then. I thought we were clear on that point already."

The rage bubbled inside me, threating to erupt while I starred with hatred into his face. Only the sound of Joey's whimpering evoked a response from me. Lowering my eyes I mumbled, "I'll do what you want." I knew it would only be a matter of time before he would slip up. Until then I would have to wait.

"Well now, it looks like we're starting to understand each other better. The first thing to go will be those bloody cows out there. I'll be dammed if I'm going to spend the winter going out to feed the useless things. I can think of a hell of a lot better ways to spend my time than playing nurse maid to a bunch of cows," he said with a leer in my direction.

From outside the sound of a car approaching could be heard. The thud of a slamming door had us both frozen, me in relief, Thomas in dread. Thomas swiftly crossed the expanse of the living room to scoop up Joey before demanding, "Get rid of whoever it is and don't do anything stupid. I'll be watching. Opening the door a crack, I was surprised to see Peggy standing there. A big smile plastered on her cherub face.

"Hi, I was worried about you and thought I'd drop by for a little chat," she gushed with a smile.

"Oh, you should have called first. I think I'm coming down with the flu. I wouldn't want you to catch it, maybe some other time," I suggested, trying to close the door.

"Nonsense dear, I've a very strong immune system. I never catch anything. Working all those years for a doctor has made me immune to just about everything," she said with a chuckle. "I know just the thing to help you get rid of that nasty bug. Come on, I'll have you feeling like your old self in no time," she declared, pushing the door open a crack further to squeeze her ample frame inside.

"Really Peggy, I don't want you to catch it. I'll be fine. Maybe you should go. I'll be fine," I repeated, holding the door open for her.

"Nonsense, I just wouldn't feel right leaving a friend sick when I could do something about it. No, I insist. I'll have you feeling as right as rain in no time at all. You do look awful peaked and I do believe you've lost some weight too. Not that you could afford to. Goodness girl, you're just skin over the bone. Not to worry, I'll cook up a dish that will help put some meat back on those bones and bring some color back into those pretty cheeks of yours. You just leave things to old Peggy," she maintained, shuffling towards the kitchen.

I quickly followed behind her towards the kitchen, all the while, protesting that I would be fine, only to find myself skidding into her abundant backside as she came to an abrupt halt.

"Oh, I didn't realize you had company," she stammered, a confused look forming on her face while she glanced hastily at me and then at Thomas who was holding Joey.

"I'm not company. Beth asked me to come back and stay on permanently. She said she needed a man around the place to help her with things," Thomas said with a sly grin.

Peggy's head swiveled as if on a stick while she briskly turned to stare into my face. "Really, is that right Beth? You called him?" she uttered in disbelieve.

I stared into Thomas' face, noting his eyes swivel downwards to encompass Joey. The warning was heeded. I gradually lowered my eyes to mumble, "Yes, I called him."

Peggy's eyes never left my face. "I'd like to talk to you alone, right now," she said, pushing me into the living room to stand before me, her hands resting on each ample hip.

"Alright, what's going on here? A week ago you couldn't stand to be around him. You had Jim throw him off your property and now he's your best friend."

"I needed the help," I replied weakly, starring at the floor.

Peggy stood there silently assessing me before she spoke. "I don't buy it. Something is going on here but I can't quite put my finger on it and if you won't tell me the truth. I'll have to ask that boor myself."

Whirling, she turned entering the kitchen to find Thomas and Joey gone. "Well, where did they go?" she said, only to turn around when Thomas answered.

"I'm right here, you nosey old piece of crap." Then, bringing his arm upward he sunk the knife he was holding into Peggy's abdomen, pulling it up with a sudden wrench. The sound of flesh ripping echoed in my brain as Peggy stared down at her insides spilling out on to the floor. Her lips puckered to form a silent o while she slid slowly to the floor. I stared into that cherub face, watching the light finally flicker and die in the brilliant blue eyes that had looked upon me so kindly a few seconds before. I was vaguely aware of someone screaming but could not associate it with the sound coming out of my mouth until Thomas slapped me.

"Shut up!" he screamed, shaking me furiously.

"Nosy old biddy, she should have left when she had the chance. Now I've got this mess to clean up," he motioned disgustedly towards Peggy. Grabbing me by the arms, he hauled me into the living room where he hurriedly tied me to the chair.

"Can't have you doing something stupid, now can we?" he said with a sick grin before turning to go back into the kitchen.

I could hear him huffing and puffing while he worked to dispose of Peggy's body. "Old bag, weighs a bloody ton," he muttered while the sound of the door opening and closing behind him could be heard, leaving me sitting in silence.

I sat on that chair shaking as if a cold wind had me in its grip, my mind whirling in disbelief. A low involuntary moan escaped my lips as I remembered Peggy's surprised face before she slid to the floor. The twinkling blue eyes, which had held so much life shinning from them, now snuffed out like a candle. Joey sat dozing in his chair a few feet from me. I was grateful he would never remember any of this. I ached to get up and use that same knife on Thomas. He would find out what it was like to evoke the hatred he had instilled in me. Thomas soon returned to stand proudly before me with Peggy's blood covering the front of his shirt. He seemed to take some perverse pleasure in watching me wince at the sight of it before I turned away.

"Little squeamish, are we?" he laughed before turning to disappear up the stairs, only to return a few minutes later, a clean shirt covering his wiry frame.

"You didn't have to kill her! She was harmless!" I screamed at him, my hands locked into tight fists while I stared helplessly at him. The hatred I felt for him oozed out of every pore in my body and was reflected on my face.

Thomas grabbed a chair and, straddling it backwards, slowly leaned forward his face a few inches from mine before letting out a huge sigh. "Beth, Beth, Beth," he said, shaking his head. "Here I thought we were making such progress. You know she had to go. She had too big of a mouth, always yammering away about this and that. She would have been running back to town to yap to your boyfriend cop that I was here. Getting him all worked up so he would come out here to check on you. We wouldn't want him coming out here to spoil our fun, now would we?" he asked, raising his eyebrows.

"You can't keep me tied up for ever."

"Well now, that's up to you. Depends on how much you care for the brat," he said, nodding his head towards Joey.

"Why are you doing this? If you need money, I'll sell off some of the cows. You can have it. Just let Joey and I go. No one will ever know you were here," I begged, my eyes bright with unshed tears.

Thomas, shaking his head, remarked dryly, "You don't get it, do you?" Letting out a huge sigh, he continued speaking, slowly enunciating each word, "I WANT IT ALL. Is that so hard to understand? I've been planning to take over here from the first time I laid eyes on you. Don't tell me you never guessed?"

"I'm married, remember?" I uttered, looking at the floor.

"You mean you were married. You're not anymore, sweetheart. I thought I'd have trouble getting rid of that over bearing piece of crap you called a husband, but then he up and made it easy for me. I really thought that bloody bull would get him when I opened the gate," he grinned, remembering. "I'll give him one thing though: he sure was fast on his feet," he chuckled, remembering the way Charlie had sprinted for the safety of the fence. "I like what I see here. It might take some time, but you'll come around to my way of thinking sooner or later. Now if you play your cards right and cooperate, we might be able to do away with the ropes.

Slowly, the tears trickled from my eyes while I hung my head in defeat.

Without warning, he leaned down to give me a quick peck on the corner of my mouth. "I'll be back shortly. I have to get rid of some garbage," he said with a wink. "While I'm out there I guess I'll round up those cows from the far pasture and bring them down here. I could use some extra cash right now."

The spot on my mouth felt dirty from where he had kissed it. I itched to rub away the stamp where his lips had been sealed on mine. Wiggling my fingers, I realized that in his haste he had not tied me as tightly as usual. Inch by inch, I twisted my hands, trying to widen the rope enough to let my hand slip free. The relief I felt as one hand slipped from its binding was so overwhelming I froze. My mind momentarily in a jumble, I wondered if maybe I should put it back on before he came back. How stupid, I thought. This was the chance I had been waiting for and now I was going to take full advantage of it. I worked feverishly to finish untying myself, all the while listening fearfully for Thomas' return. Tiptoeing to the window, I cautiously peeked out side searching for any sign of Thomas. Seeing none, I grabbed Joey, wrapping him in an old blanket. All the while my eyes searched for some form of weapon to defend myself with. Spinning around, my vision came to rest on Charlie's old baseball bat leaning indiscernible behind the logs piled by the fireplace. It would have to do, I thought, feeling the weight of it in my hands.

A scrapping sound outside on the deck had my hackles rise. I prepared to do battle. Thomas would not know I was free, so surprise would be my only element of defence. Standing behind the door, bat raised in anticipation I waited for it to open. The door opened slowly. From his peripheral vision, he caught sight of the raised bat in my hand. Whirling quickly he ducked as the bat slammed against the door frame over his head with a resounding crack. Lifting the bat to swing again, I heard him scream, "Beth, it's me, Charlie!"

Chapter Forty

My hands shaking, I slowly lowered the bat, starring in shock at the man standing before me. A reddish blond beard covered half of his face but no one could disguise those twinkling blue eyes peering out from beneath the shock of blond hair draped casually over his forehead. I felt as if I was witnessing a ghost suddenly come to life.

"Charlie? Is it really you? You're not dead, are you?" I asked, foolishly starring at the image before me.

"Not the last time I looked," he chuckled, coming to take me in his arms.

I clung to him, sobbing wildly, all the while raining kisses all over his face. "Oh my god Charlie, I thought you were dead. They told me you weren't coming back. How—, what happened? I can't believe it's really you," I babbled. "Please, don't tell me I'm dreaming," I said, reaching out to touch his face.

"You're not dreaming, sweetheart. It's really me. I'll tell you everything in a minute, although I would like to see Joey first," he said, glancing around the room.

Joey, upon hearing his name, suddenly wiggled under the blanket, giving a little grunt as if to say, "Here I am." Pulling back a corner of the blanket, Charlie was rewarded with Joey's bright smile as he wiggled to be picked up.

"There you are. Were you hiding on me?" Charlie asked, picking him up to rub noses with him. I smiled happily, watching father and son get reacquainted. The smile on my face quickly faded to be replaced with a look of horror when Charlie casually asked, "Where's Thomas?

"Beth, what's wrong?" he demanded, seeing the look of horror etched on my face.

"He murdered Peggy! He said he would kill Joey if I didn't do what he said. Charlie, he raped me!" I babbled, slowly sinking to my knees.

"What? What are you telling me?" Charlie demanded, starring into my stricken eyes.

"Oh god, Charlie, he could be coming back any minute. He went to get rid of Peggy but he could be back any second. We have to get out of here! He'll kill us all," I cried, grabbing the front of Charlie's shirt.

"He raped you and murdered Peggy?" I could see the shock registered on his face. He stood staring at me for a few seconds as if it hadn't registered in his mind, yet.

He grabbed my hand. Gingerly, he examined the fresh rope burns on my wrists. "How did you get free?"

"He didn't tie me as tight as usual and I got my hand out. "I found the bat and thought it was him coming back. We have to get out of here," I pleaded, tugging at his hand.

Charlie blanched upon realizing what I had just revealed to him. Standing before me, he hung his head, thinking. Taking me by the arms, he looked into my eyes to say, "He'll never touch you again. I'll see to that. I'm so sorry! I promise you he'll wish he had never been born. Now go and call Jim. Tell him what's going on and to get out here right away. Then take Joey and go and hide in the loft until Jim gets here. Do you understand?" he cried, shaking me by my shoulders before giving me a push towards the phone. Turning quickly, he crossed the room to open the door. Pausing, he turned back to say, "If things go bad, just make sure that you don't come out until Jim gets here." I gasped at the thought of what he implied. Hearing my gasp, he said, "Don't worry, I had to fight like hell to get back here. I won't lose you now." I could see Charlie trembling, his rage tenuously held in check. Thomas would now feel the extent of my rage through Charlie. Turning once more he slipped silently out the door.

★★★

Charlie's Rage

I could feel the rage building in every fiber of my being at the thought of Thomas molesting Beth. I had warned him before I left not to touch her and now he would have to pay for his indiscretion. From behind the barn the distinct sound of cattle bawling could be heard while Thomas separated the herd into pens. I cautiously slid around the corner of the barn, keeping low to the ground, advancing stealthily on an unsuspecting Thomas. He stood with his back to me trying to count the cattle milling in front of him. Arriving at a number that suited him, he sat down contentedly on an old pail. A smile plastered on his face, he sat deducing just how much money he would have coming in from the sale of my livestock.

Roscoe the bull was in a foul mood having been penned away from the cows. Back and forth his monstrous frame thundered, his hoofs spewing up a low cloud of dust that floated on the slight breeze. His low bawls blended with the noisy din of the apprehensive cattle that eyed Thomas warily. Sliding silently through the fence, I softly padded to the gate enclosing Roscoe's pen.

"Thomas," I softly called, lifting the first latch to release Roscoe from his pen. Thomas slowly turned to stare at me in confusion a befuddled expression replacing the smile he had previously worn.

"I told you not to touch Beth! Remember the promise I made to you before I left?"

"You're—dead," he stuttered, taking a step backwards.

"No, you are," I said, lifting the second latch to release Roscoe from his bondage.

Roscoe's two beady eyes focused on Thomas. Two thousand pounds of raging flesh thundered towards him like a freight train bent on destruction. A lone scream echoed throughout the air as Roscoe made contact with his target. The massive head tossed Thomas high into the air, time and time again, as lightly as if he had been a feather. Then, searching again for his prey, he lowered his head to finish what he had started, proceeding to grind Thomas into a bloody pulp, leaving him tossed on the ground like a used rag.

"I promised you I'd break every bone in your body if you touched my wife and I always keep my promise," I chuckled, sliding off the fence.

Whistling the tune Twinkle, Twinkle Little Star, I strolled towards the barn where Beth waited for me.

Beth was leery on coming out of the loft. She couldn't seem to bring herself to trust that Thomas was really gone and would not be around to abuse her any longer. Her living hell had come to an end. We sat on the porch swing, Joey tucked between us while she recounted the tale of degradation she had suffered at Thomas' hands. As the tears slowly trickled down her face, I found myself wishing that he had died a slower death. One that would have been more befitting to suit the crime he had committed.

While we waited for Jim, Beth phoned into dispatch, informing them that Thomas had been found dead in Roscoe's pen. Roscoe had saved the tax payers money, it seemed, as now there would be no trial to hold him accountable.

"Charlie, don't tell Jim about Thomas raping me. I don't want anyone to know," Beth said, eyes downcast as she plucked at a thread on her skirt.

"Why, you weren't to blame and you have to go to a doctor. You need to be checked out."

"No. There's no point in it now, he's dead. I don't want people pointing their finger at me and whispering behind my back, 'There goes that woman who claims she was raped.' No, Charlie, I just can't do it. I just want to forget about it," she said, her voice rising in agitation.

"But, Beth, you have to see a doctor."

Beth slowly raised her eyes to study my face. "Alright, I'll see a doctor, but I won't go to the hospital. There's no point in having them poking and prodding me to take samples. We both know it was Thomas and he's dead now. What more can we do to him? He has Peggy's death on his head to follow him to his grave. It won't help me to sit and recount all the details to a stranger. If you want me to see any doctor, it will have to be Lyle. That's all I'll agree to," she said adamantly.

"Alright," I finally conceded. "But promise me you'll talk to Lyle."

"I will," she said, eyes downcast.

The sound of the approaching police cruiser had us both standing at attention when it ground to a halt in front of us. Jim jumped from the cruiser, closing the ground between us to envelope me in a huge bear hug that lifted me clear of the ground.

"Man, I thought you were a goner. What happened? We combed that area for over a week and couldn't find hide or hair of you," Jim said, shaking his head in wonder.

"I'll tell you all about it in a bit, but for now we have a bigger problem. Beth says Thomas murdered Peggy," I recounted, looking at Beth for conformation.

★★★

BETH

Jim turned towards me, a pained expression on his face. Reaching out for my hand he drew me forward, enfolding me into the protection of his arms, before whispering, "I'm so sorry, Beth. I feel like such a fool. I should have known something was wrong when I talked to you that day on the phone. It wasn't like you to be so snippy. God, Peggy would still be alive if I wasn't so damn dense," he muttered, wiping a tear that had escaped from the corner of his eye.

"I called Lyle. He said he would be come right away. Its times like this that I wish I wasn't a cop. I hate the thought of telling Lyle about Peggy. He was very fond of her."

"We all were. She only came out here because she was worried about me," I sniffed, wiping my eyes with a trembling hand.

"What the hell was in Thomas' head to do this? He must have known it would just be a matter of time until he was caught."

"He said he planned to take over everything when he first got here. We were just pawns in his little game. I think he was just waiting, bidding his time for the first opportunity to get rid of Charlie," I said, picking up a sleepy Joey before going into the house.

I knew they had found Peggy's body when I spied the coroner's vehicle rolling in. Charlie later told me they had found Peggy's vehicle deep in the woods behind the barn, her body stuffed like garbage into the trunk.

Sitting beside the vehicle like a red beacon sat a can of gas Thomas had brought with the intention of going back later to burn the vehicle.

From the porch swing I watched Jim and Charlie slowly walk the distance towards the house, Jim's arm draped casually over Charlie's shoulder in comradeship. They would always be more than just cousins. Their friendship ran as deep as blood brothers. Jim had suffered terribly when Charlie had disappeared. Deep down I think he had blamed himself for the accident. Now he blamed himself for not protecting me in Charlie's absence. I knew it would be a long time before I was over the trauma Thomas had inflicted. I was stronger than anyone gave me credit. I would always carry the emotional scars, but I would not let it ruin the rest of my life, I vowed, glancing at Charlie. Silently we all strolled into the kitchen, each lost in our own thoughts.

Charlie, upon entering the kitchen, proceeded to make a pot of coffee, waving my offer of doing it aside. "I need to do something to make things seem normal again," he said with a wry grin. "Oh, man. Peanut butter. It feels like a million years since I had peanut butter," he said, spying the jar sitting on the counter.

Reaching over I brushed the curly softness of his beard through my fingers. "I almost didn't recognize you. You're lucky those blue eyes gave you away," I said, smiling. Leaning back in my chair, I surveyed his face. "I think you better lose the beard. I don't like it," I said with an apologetic shrug.

Jim reached out to cover my hand with his. "We will have to get your statement, but there's no hurry. You've been through enough for now. I'll call you in a few days and then we'll get it done. Turning towards Charlie he asked, "Now Charlie, I've been itching to know how you survived out there. How the hell did you get back here and why didn't you call me?"

Charlie looked soberly at Jim while he recounted what happened after their boat had capsized. "When the boat went over, I was sucked into the rapids. I knew enough not to fight against the current, so I let it carry me along, trying to keep my head above water as best as I could. I finally started to sink. I was so tired and cold; I didn't think I could keep going for much longer. Then I reached out and my fingers touched something. It was a log floating along beside me. I grabbed that log and hung on for dear life. It carried me to where the river divided. I went left and that's when I knew I was in big trouble. I could hear the falls before I even got there. I shot over those falls like a pea being squeezed out of its pod. How I hung onto the log, I'll never know. I kinda lost my senses after that. The next thing I knew I was floating in this shallow pool. I tried to stand but my leg had got torn up somehow. All I could do was crawl, but crawl I did. Solid ground never felt so good. I could have kissed it after that."

At this moment in Charlie's story, I placed my hands over my face and bawled like a baby. I knew deep down it wasn't just that Charlie had been hurt and nearly killed, my emotions had reached a peak and everything seemed to be spinning around me at once.

Charlie reached for me, holding me tightly against him, he whispered, "Sshh—, I'm back now, nothing more is going to happen to you. I will make sure of it, okay?"

My sobs reduced to hiccups, I smiled weakly up at him, encouraging him to continue.

"I knew I had to find some form of shelter or I'd die of hypothermia. That was one of those lessons of survival that stuck with me from school. I spotted an overhang up in the rocks, so I crawled up there and wedged myself under. I was surprised it was relatively warm in there. I pulled some of the rocks around the entrance to hem me in for the night. My leg wasn't broken, but it was twisted pretty badly. I laid there for two days before I finally realized I had to do something or I wasn't going to survive. I had my waterproof belt on with some matches, a pocket knife, and some fishing line and a few hooks inside. That belt saved my life. I found a branch for a crutch and managed to hobble down to the water's edge. Jim, I found the best fishing hole I've ever seen in my life. I can tell you one thing though, I don't think I'll be eating fish for a long while," he chuckled.

Jim seemed mesmerized by Charlie's story. Shaking his head in disbelief, he said, "We concentrated our search all along to the right of the divide. I never dreamed you'd gone over the falls. We did send a chopper to scour the river bank to the left, but it didn't see a thing. That's mighty rough country up that way. The only way in is on foot and even then you have to know what you're doing. Only the hardiest of guides travel that area."

"I was sleeping when I heard the chopper. I was just too damned late by the time I crawled out. All I could see was its tail going over the mountain. It took eight days for my leg to heal enough that I could put some weight on it. By then the snow was starting to drift in and I knew I had to get out of there fast. It took me five days to work my way off that mountain. I came to gorges that were sometimes a half a mile wide. Sometimes I was back tracking more than I was going ahead. I thought I was in heaven when I finally came to a road.I must have walked ten miles before an old truck came along. I thought I was seeing things at first. The driver was in his eighties and drove at a snail's pace. He said he was going right by our place and would let me off here. All I could think about was seeing Beth's face again. It's what kept me going when I felt like giving up; Beth and Joey," he said, the tears sliding down his face to disappear into his beard. "Then Beth takes after me with a baseball bat when I opened the door. It scared the living crap out of me. She only missed me by an inch."

"I—thought—you were Thomas—coming back," I stuttered, my cheeks turning red.

"I know. It's alright. I wish you had of brained the son of a bitch, though," Charlie snarled, his hands clenched into fists.

"Thank God it's over with," Jim sighed.

The promise I had made to Charlie the day he had left now resounded back into my brain. Turning to him I asked, "Why did you make me promise not to go upstairs? Thomas never listened to you. He slept up there every night. During the day he would go up there at exactly two o'clock and it sounded like he was talking to someone. Then he would come back down meaner than ever. His eyes looked weird. I felt like he was looking straight through me. Charlie, what's up there that you're afraid of?"

Charlie stared silently at Jim, a silent message communicating between them.

"Charlie? What is it?" I asked, this time my voice a little shriller than normal.

Charlie was saved from replying by the knock on the door. Jumping up hastily, he opened it to admit Lyle. Lyle's face registered disbelief and then shock when he found out his friend from so many years had been murdered so savagely. Fighting back his tears, he finally turned to Charlie. "I think I'd better examine you, Charlie. You're lucky to be alive."

Charlie waved his concern away with a shake of his hand. "I'm alright doc, just a tender leg, but it's almost good as new now. Beth's the one who needs your help."

Lyle put his arm around me, speaking softly, he ushered me towards the bedroom. "I'm sorry that this happened to you."

I nodded my head, the lump in my throat refusing to let me reply. In my heart I knew I would never fully recover from what Thomas had done to me, that I should seek counselling to deal with it, but I could not. I had seen too many doctors lately and now I had Joey to focus on. I would try to master it on my own.

★★★

CHARLIE—
CHAPTER FORTY ONE

"What the hell were you thinking, Charlie. How could you leave Beth alone with Thomas, knowing Max could control him the way he did with Vince? You told me everything was fine, that you had it all under control. You're damn lucky she wasn't killed. Sometimes I think you have sawdust up there for brains. Jeez—," Jim said, staring at me with a look of plain disgust.

"I know, I know, but I never thought he would try anything with Thomas. For God's sake, Max was my father! I know he got his hooks into Vince, but he was just a kid. You could have told him the moon was made of cheese and he would have believed you."

"What about you? You're not a kid and look what he did to you. What excuse do you have for yourself?" Jim asked, staring me in the eye while he waited for my answer.

"None. I really made a mess of things this year, didn't I?" I mumbled, not looking up to meet Jim's level gaze.

"You sure did and Beth had to pay for your stupid mistake. Last year was bad enough when you had to get rid of that drifter you hired. Did Beth ever notice the extra grave behind those bushes?"

"I don't think so. She never mentioned anything about it."

"I didn't think I'd be able to cover Rachael's and Amy's death for you," he said, scratching his chin while he eyed me steadily. "You're lucky that pervert can't speak that was hanging around the schoolyard. I made sure all evidence led back to him on Rachael's death. Amy's was easier. Yup, you got away lucky on that one," Jim said, nodding his head.

"I can remember covering for you too, or don't you remember that?" I asked, trying to show a bit of spirit.

"I hope you're not counting turns now. You only had yourself to blame for Rachael," Jim said, his tone a little miffed at me.

"I know. I never should have got involved with that greedy bitch. I had to get rid of her, Jim. She was threatening to tell Beth everything. I wasn't going to lose my wife over a romp in the hay with the likes of her. That one never bothered me as much as Amy. When I held her under the water, she never even struggled at all. I believe she wanted me to end it all for her. As long as I live I'll have nightmares about those big brown eyes staring sadly back up at me through the water. She wasn't going to give up Joey and it would have finished Beth if she took him away. I couldn't chance it. You understand, don't you Jim?"

"Yeh, Yeh, I know you had to do what you done, but you have a bigger problem here and you know it. Your old man's ghost in the attic is getting stronger. You can't stay here anymore. The old bugger is just plain evil."

"I know, but I can't leave. This is my home. I worked for years to keep things running. He's not going to scare me away."

"You better be damned careful. So far old Max stays upstairs for the most part, but that could change," he said, shaking his head.

"Don't worry. I'll make sure he never gets to Beth. At the first sign of anything going wrong, I promise I'll get Beth out of here damn fast."

"You'd bloody well better. That little lady has been through hell enough lately."

I slowly nodded my head, acknowledging the blame for what had happened. I had made a mistake and Beth paid for it in more ways than Jim knew. I would have to be more cautious in the future. I might even have to tell Beth everything.

"Well it worked out the same as last year, anyways," Jim said. "You didn't have to pay a dime for the help.

"Yup, I kinda figured I wouldn't have had to," I said with a slight grin.

Beth's spontaneous laughter surprised me as she rounded the door coming into the kitchen, her arm linked with Lyle's.

"Do you want to tell him or shall I?" she asked, smiling up at Lyle.

I think it would be better coming from you somehow," Lyle said with a smile.

Beth suddenly turned towards me to announce proudly, "I'm pregnant."

★★★

Nearly Seven Years later

I could hardly believe Lucas was six today. It seemed like only yesterday that Lyle had announced, "It's a boy, Beth." Lucas had adopted Charlie's looks. The fair hair and blue eyes that ran deep in his mother's side was now evident in Charlie's son. Joey still retained his mother and father's black hair and slight frame. I worried more about Joey than Lucas. His heart surgery had left him more susceptible to illness. Lucas was healthy, full of energy, and always on the go. He could tease his brother unmercifully until he had him crying. Joey on the other hand had the disposition of an angel. "There," I sighed, putting the last dab of chocolate frosting on Lucas' birthday cake. Grabbing my tea, I sat down to watch Charlie with the boys in the graveyard. He was teaching them how to weed around the graves. It was such a pretty picture, I thought, continuing to watch them. Lucas suddenly raised his small, sullen face to look up at the house, a smile forming on his lips. Raising his hand, he waved. Smiling, I lifted my hand to wave back until I realized he wasn't waving at me. The smile dying on my lips, I watched in horror as he slammed Joey's tiny kitten against the gravestone in front of him with a sickening thud and dropped it casually onto Joey's mother's grave.

Coming soon, the second part in this series.

A preview of...*The Boundaries of Evil*

THE BOUNDARIES OF

CHAPTER ONE

I lay on the floor, the shaft of betrayal stabbing deeper into my heart than the knife that was thrust between my ribs. Thoughts of Callie and Ben growing up without a father danced through my brain like a kaleidoscope. I closed my eyes. God, but the pain was becoming unbearable. Peering through the veil of darkness, I found another face edging closer and closer. I looked up to find a shaft of light penetrating the darkness, beckoning me to come forward, edging me on from the darkness that threatened to engulf me.

Like a moth drawn to a flame, I felt myself responding to a primitive urge as I edged closer and closer. The light seemed brighter now, while I watched a scene unfold before my eyes of two small boys with their father in a grave yard. The one child kneeling beside a grave with his father had hair the colour of black ink. The other child, as fair as the sun, stood holding a small black and white kitten. I recognized them! The fair child was my brother Luke. The dark child was me at the age of seven. My father, Charlie Sanders, was showing me how to clean the graves in the family grave yard beside our house. Lucas my brother stood to one side pouting. Father had just told him he was too young to help.

"But it's my birthday," he mumbled, his bottom lip hanging down to form a pout.

"You're still too young, Lucas. Joey is only the right age now, so go and sit down somewhere out of the way. We'll get done faster if I don't have to worry about you," my father said, giving him a tiny shove in the opposite direction. Even though Lucas was bigger than me, I was the eldest by eleven and a half months. One would never know we were

iii | **Rita** Van Damme

brothers by looking at us. Lucas was blond with blue eyes, like mama and papa, while my hair was dark and my eyes a dark chocolate brown. My father had never heard the words that spilled from Lucas' lips as he turned dejectedly away, but I had.

"I hate you. I wish you were both dead," he whispered. Turning towards the house, his eyes squinting from the sun's brightness, he held up his hand to give it a quick wave, a smile replacing the pout on his lips. A few minutes later, I heard the sound of a thud from the direction Lucas stood. Turning towards the sound, I saw Lucas standing before a grave calmly starring downwards, his lips twisted into a smile while he intently watched the grave in front of him.

I continued watching one scene after another unfold before my eyes. The journey my life had taken continuing to spin from one scene to another. The past now bound to the present.

"Lucas, I want you to come here right now!" my mother had screamed from where she stood shading her eyes from the hot noon sun.

My father looked up slightly confused at her tone. "What did you do now, boy?" he demanded, a frown furrowing his brow while he stared intently at Lucas.

Father always called him boy when he did something he shouldn't have. Lucas glared back at him. "I didn't do anything. Bow-bow fell and hit his head. I didn't make him dead. I swear papa," he cried, rubbing his feet in the dirt while making this omission.

"What do you mean he fell? Where is he?" Papa demanded, sweeping the grave yard with a curious look.

I could feel my tummy doing those tiny little flip flops mama called upsies whenever something bad happened. Right now the upsies felt really bad. My lip trembling, I sadly looked where I had seen Lucas standing holding Bow-bow. Bow-bow was my kitty. Papa had said so when he placed him into my hands not so long ago.

"What about me?" Lucas asked, looking at the other four spotted kittens nursing on their mother.

"You're too young to have a kitten yet. You wouldn't know how to look after it," my father said, taking the lid off the pail of water. Plucking the remaining kittens up, he dropped them one by one in a bucket of water. I held my hands over my ears as each kitten made a plop-ping sound, upon hitting the water. Then, placing the lid on the pail, he walked away, ending the discussion about whether my brother would have a kitten or not.

I slowly walked to stand before the grave with the word Amy written on it. There on the ground lay Bow-bow's still form, a trickle of blood slowly oozing from his ears and nose.

"I didn't do it," Lucas screamed, while his short little legs bolted for the safety of the house.

Papa had quickly scooped me up, holding me close to his sweat-dampened shirt. I wrapped my arms around his neck, burying my face in his collar while sobs shook my slight frame.

"Sshh little buddy, it will be okay," he said, wiping the tears from my face with his large calloused hand.

Mama, spying Lucas while he sped by, reached out to snatch his shirt tail, effectively bringing him to a sudden halt. Spinning him around, she grabbed him by the shoulders to shake him. "Why did you do that?" she demanded crossly.

"He—he—just—fell. I didn't mean to hurt him," Lucas stuttered between each shake, his eyes squeezed tightly shut.

"I saw you Lucas! Don't you dare tell fibs or Papa will have to use the belt," she warned, giving him a final shake.

At the mention of the belt, Lucas screwed up his face to howl. Tears suddenly streaming from his eyes, his body instantly went limp.

Mama took one look at his face before quickly scooping him up into her arms. Holding him close, she whispered, "Sshh—Lucas, we'll figure it all out. It will be alright."

Lucas clung desperately to her, burying his face against her neck, his sobs dwindling to the odd hiccup. Papa, holding me closely against him, strode determinedly up the path only to breathe a weary sigh upon spying Mama gently wiping Lucas' tears away. His eyes focused straight ahead, he strode by Mama towards the house without a sideways glance. Peeking over Papa's shoulder, I looked back to see a slight smile on Lucas' face while he looked towards the graveyard where Bow-bow lay, broken and discarded. Papa had taken me into the house where he set me down on his knee.

"I'm so sorry, Joey. Lucas didn't know he was doing something wrong. I know you loved your Bow-bow and I will make sure you get a new kitty," he said, smoothing my cowlick back.

"It won't be Bow-bow. I just want my Bow-bow back," I cried, hiding my face against his shirt.

"Oh Joey, I wish it was that simple. If it was I would give you a dozen Bow-bows, but I can't," my Papa sighed, wearily patting my back.

Mama quickly marched into the room, Lucas' hand firmly ensconced in hers. Abruptly she pulled him to a quick stop in front of Papa and me. "Alright Lucas, tell Joey what you told me outside," she urged, giving him a tiny shove in my direction.

"I'm sorry, Joey. I didn't know he would die. I was just playing with him. He jumped out of my hands and hit his head," Lucas said, slipping his arms around my neck to cling desperately to me.

"There, that's better. See Joey, Lucas didn't do it on purpose," Mama said, giving me a weak smile.

"I did," Lucas whispered into my ear so Mama and Papa couldn't hear while he clung tightly to my neck.

Jerking away from him, I looked into those brilliant blue eyes to see the warning lurking below them. I slowly lowered my eyes. If I uttered a word in protest, I knew Lucas would make me pay. I could still remember when Lucas left the gate open and the cattle had gotten out. He blamed me for it, but I had been helping Mama with the baking, so Mama knew Lucas was lying. Papa had used the belt on him. For that I lived in terror for the next three days while Lucas thought up ways to torment me. His favorite punishment was to hide around a corner with a pointed stick until I happened by. Then he would jump out, poking me constantly until I ran to Mama for protection. Sometimes he would dump water into my bed and tell mama I wet the bed. I never knew what he was going to do next, but I soon learned whenever he gave me that warning look I better keep my mouth shut or I would be sorry.

Papa stood up, his hands on his hips while he stared down at us. "Alright boys, go outside until lunch time. Lucas, you can help Joey dig a grave for his kitten beside the fence in the graveyard. Something like this better not ever happen again. Do you understand, boy?" he said, glaring at Lucas. Lucas quickly nodded his head before dashing out the door. I followed behind, afraid of what lay waiting beyond the door for me.

Papa had one day cut off the broken handle of a shovel. Handing it to me he had said, "Here Joey, it's just your size now."

Thrilled, I had run to Mama, proudly holding it up for her to see while I announced that it was mine. Now I wearily marched towards the graveyard with that same shovel in tow. Pushing open the gate, I searched for any sign of Lucas. Carefully I let my eyes rest upon each stone in turn, lest he be hidden behind one. Breathing a sigh of relief, I marched determinedly in the direction of where Bow-bow lay. It was easy to find the stone with the word 'Amy' written across it, for it stood slightly apart from the others. It was as if it didn't quite belong, but yet it did. Tracing the letters with my finger, I sounded out the word. I paid attention to the teacher when she showed us how each letter made a different sound. Now I was proud of the fact I could figure out most words by sounding them out. The teacher said I was a natural, whatever that means, but I think it's a good thing, the way she said it. I always felt a strange sadness whenever I gazed at the familiar stone now standing before me. I wonder who Amy was, I thought, feeling the same tug of sadness wash over me again. I asked Mama once, but she had only turned away mumbling, "It doesn't matter." I bet she was a fairy princess like in the book Mama was reading to us. She was probably killed by a fire-eating dragon while defending her family, I reasoned. Yes, that was it, I thought confidently, before picking Bow-bow's body up off the grave. His small body now felt cold and foreign at my touch. I slowly stumbled towards the fence, my eyes brimming with unshed tears. Why did Lucas do it? I vowed I would get even with him for this someday, while I pushed the shovel into the ground the way Papa had shown me. It didn't take long before I had a small hole dug the size of Bow-bow. Carefully I lowered him down before covering him with dirt. Mama said there was a God and we should say our prayers every night, to him to keep us safe, for he would punish all evil doers. Kneeling down beside Bow-bow's grave, I said a prayer to keep him safe. Then thinking about it, I asked God to punish Lucas for what he done.

Finished with my prayer, I glanced up to spy Lucas sitting on our Grandpa Max's grave, watching me with a curious smile on his face.

We sat warily watching each other for a few moments before Lucas jumped up to announce, "Come on, I'll show you what I found."

"What?" I questioned, suspiciously edging away from him.

"Come on, I won't do anything to you," he declared, seeing my hesitation while he motioned with his hand for me to follow him.

Reluctantly I got up to follow him around the tall hedge at the back of the grave yard, still keeping the distance between us intact.

"Look," he said, pointing towards the ground.

"I don't see anything," I said, starting to turn away.

"It's a pirate's grave," Lucas announced, brightly.

"How do you know that?" I asked, curiously. Turning back, I glanced down at the ground where a slight mound of earth resembling a grave stood poking up out of the tall grass surrounding it.

"Well, why else would he be buried here behind the trees instead of with the rest? He must have been a bad man to be put back here where you can't see the grave. Papa said there used to be pirates around here. I'll bet we found a pirate's grave," Lucas said proudly at figuring the puzzle out to his own satisfaction.

"How do you know it's a man? It could be a girl," I said, thoughtfully staring at the bare patch of earth with a few weeds poking out of it.

"Don't be stupid. Have you ever heard of girl pirates?" Lucas said, rolling his eyes at me with a look of disgust.

"I bet it's not even a grave." I said, staring again at it thoughtfully.

"It is too!" Lucas stated forcefully, marching away towards the hedge.

"How do you know? It might not be," I said, following behind Lucas, who promptly disappeared around the hedge.

"Because Grandpa told me," Lucas announced proudly before going to stand before our Grandfather Max's grave.

Printed in Canada